D0096764

$\mathcal{S}$heetal pressed her hands to her face, shutting everything out for the span of a couple of breaths. Then she rearranged her part to bury her pale roots, doused the light flickering at her core, and stepped out into the hallway, ready to play at being ordinary again. Just as normal and human as Radhikafoi and Dad and the whole world expected her to be.

Radhikafoi never talked about Sheetal's mother, as though silence could scrub the memory from Sheetal's heart and, more importantly, from her DNA. Her distasteful "condition." As though what her auntie refused to accept didn't exist.

But no matter how hard Sheetal tried to hide it, no matter how much Radhikafoi wanted to deny it, she would always be half a star.

Always.

WITHDRAWN

# STAR DAUGHTER

## SHVETA THAKRAR

HARPER TEEN

An Imprint of HarperCollinsPublishers

HarperTeen is an imprint of HarperCollins Publishers.

Star Daughter
Copyright © 2020 by Shveta Thakrar
All rights reserved. Printed in the United States of America.
No part of this book may be used or reproduced in any manner whatsoever without
written permission except in the case of brief quotations embodied in critical articles
and reviews. For information address HarperCollins Children's Books, a division of
HarperCollins Publishers, 195 Broadway, New York, NY 10007.
www.epicreads.com

Library of Congress Cataloging-in-Publication Data

Names: Thakrar, Shveta, author.
Title: Star daughter / Shveta Thakrar.
Description: First edition. | New York, NY : HarperTeen, [2020] | Summary:
    Sheetal Mistry, a rising high school junior who is half-star, half-human, must win
    a competition in the starry court to save her human father.
Identifiers: LCCN 2019040558 | ISBN 978-0-06-289463-2
Subjects: CYAC: East Indian Americans—Fiction. | Stars—Fiction. | Mythology,
    Indic—Fiction. | Contests—Fiction. | Courts and courtiers—Fiction.
Classification: LCC PZ7.1.T4472 St 2020 | DDC [Fic]—dc23
LC record available at https://lccn.loc.gov/2019040558

Typography by Corina Lupp
21 22 23 24 25   PC/LSCH   10 9 8 7 6 5 4 3 2 1
❖

First paperback edition, 2021

*For Aryasura, my (moonlight?) Lotus Prince*

# PART ONE

*We are all in the gutter, but some of us are looking at the stars.*

—OSCAR WILDE

*M*y mother is a star.

I am half—half of the earth, half of the heavens.

Cut me, and I might bleed silver. My skin is a rich brown, the exact shade of my human father's skin, but my hair is long and thick and frosted like the moon. In my chest burns a fiery core that beats in time with the music of the spheres, their song deep and layered with dreams.

My mother is a star, one of many bright jewels who sing praises in the skies, who view us from on high. She chose to come down and make a life on Earth, but it wasn't long before she yearned to go home. Nothing could truly hold her here—not my father's proposal of marriage, not my birth into the world, not even our nightly dances together in the yard after devouring the dinner my father had cooked, when we'd flee the sink full of dishes to spin and turn, washed in the light of her family above. Our family.

3

*She watches me now from her old throne, one more twinkle in the constellation Pushya, a figure as distant as the characters in the bedtime stories she once loved to tell me. In the evening, I see her clearly, laughing with her companions, radiant. Sometimes I catch rare glimpses of her during the day, when the sky is blue and everything is warm and golden, and it's almost like having her with me again. Some nights, while the world slumbers, I raise my head to the coal-dark heavens and dream I can even speak to her.*

*Yet I can't touch her anymore, can't go with her to the park, can't have her take me shopping or hug me or scold me or just be in the same room with me.*

*My mother is a star, so I can't do any of those things. Not while she's in the sky, and I'm down here.*

*It always felt like a betrayal, but there was something I didn't see, because I'd been looking at all the wrong parts, all the shadows between the stars.*

*I didn't yet know how to find our light.*

—FROM SHEETAL'S JOURNAL

1

$S$ ometimes keeping secrets was the hardest thing in the world.

Sheetal Mistry decided to make a break for it. Right past the mirrored walls that reflected one another until the swanky banquet hall expanded into infinity—a horribly overcrowded infinity made of noisy kids, successful aunties and uncles, and gossiping grandparents. Everyone watching, everyone talking and laughing.

She waded into the mob. All around her, gorgeous clothes shimmered in rich colors, ornate gold-and-gemstone jewelry glittered and gleamed, and a rainbow of syllables arced through the room. Without trying, she made out Gujarati, Hindi, Punjabi, Tamil, Telugu, and English—the heart of New Jersey's desi community, all under one huge roof.

Her cousin's birthday party should have been beautiful, like a glamorous scene from a faerie novel. Instead, it was all too loud, too much. Maybe she could hide in the corridor. Minal would just have to forgive her for vanishing.

She'd taken exactly two steps toward the exit when the Bragging Brigade, a group of the most annoying aunties and uncles ever, descended like hawks on their quarry. "Hi, Sheetal," said an engineer uncle who started every conversation with the exact same question. "How are your classes? Did you hear my Vaibhav got early admittance to Harvard?"

"And Bijal is a National Merit Scholar!" an oncologist auntie announced. "That will look so good on her college applications."

Sheetal faked a grin. "That's great." Summer vacation had just started, so she didn't have any classes, and anyway, this was all old news. Oh, why hadn't she kept running?

The other uncle smiled at her. "Your studies are going well? Still planning on a physics major like your papa?"

*Actually, clown college is looking better every day,* Sheetal almost shot back. She nodded inanely instead.

"What about your extracurriculars?" Oncologist Auntie cut in. "Now that you're a junior, have you thought about volunteering at the clinic like Bijal? You need to be well rounded these days."

"Sorry, Auntie, I was on my way to the bathroom," Sheetal mumbled. She could feel their judgment clinging to her as she slipped past, sticky as a spiderweb.

The kids they compared her to weren't any better than their show-off parents. Vaibhav and Bijal had everything Sheetal

6

didn't, and they knew it. Even now, they held court with their followers at the other end of the banquet hall, snubbing her every time she walked by. They'd written her off years ago after Radhikafoi had caught her in the pool at a community party and dragged her away in front of everyone—chlorine and her hair dye didn't mix, as her auntie had pointedly reminded her later—and she'd overheard them making fun of her more than once for being shy and boring.

Sheetal wasn't shy. She definitely wasn't boring. Of course, she could never show them the truth.

A soft, silvery melody pealed in her ears, stopping her where she stood. She shivered, the seductive tones caressing her spine and making her palms tingle. Her blood heated as something kindled at her core. If light had a voice, this would be it.

Starsong.

She already knew no one else could hear it, and not just because of the strident bass of the Bollywood hits pulsing through the restaurant like an erratic heartbeat. This was meant for her ears alone.

At each note, her skin prickled in recognition.

She forgot the party, forgot the annoying guests, forgot everything but a yearning to step outside and greet the late June night sky, to twirl under the endless open expanse of the stars. She would drink it all down in huge, thirsty gulps while their music washed over her and echoed within. . . .

Ring-clad brown fingers snapped in front of her face, followed by a crunchy samosa.

Just like that, the vision evaporated, and Sheetal was back in the banquet hall. Her mouth watered at the scent of the samosa, all spice and fried dough, but the rest of her still ached for the lost starsong.

"There you are." Minal looked amused beneath winged liner and blue-green eye shadow the same shade as her heavily beaded satin salwar kameez. "Your auntie just asked me if I'm signing up for that PSAT course with you. Does no one understand school let out two days ago?"

"I heard *it*." Sheetal reached for the numinous feeling, for the way her veins had lit up, but it was gone. "The *song*. You know." She gestured to the ceiling and the open doors at the back of the hall.

It took Minal a second, but then she frowned. "*That* song? Are you sure?"

"I don't know." Sheetal took the samosa and bit into it. "I mean, I think so."

"How long has it been?"

Trying to remember, Sheetal munched on the spicy potato-and-pea filling. "Good question. Not since last summer?" The sidereal melody had never been so *loud* before. If anything, she'd always had to focus to hear its strains.

It already felt unreal, like the wisps of dreams left behind upon waking.

She couldn't blame herself for imagining it, because honestly, who *wouldn't* want a distraction from Radhikafoi's family parties? As always, Dad's sister had invited everyone she

8

knew. Her neighbors. The stylist who threaded her eyebrows. Even the mailman, like he was ever going to show up. Family, of course, had no choice but to stay the whole time.

Sheetal wiped her oily fingers with a napkin. "Yeah, it probably wasn't anything."

"Admit it," Minal said lightly, "the only song you really care about is Dev's."

"Maybe." Sheetal laughed. Just thinking about Dev still made her all go mushy inside, like a toasted marshmallow.

"You're doing that dorky smile thing again," Minal said. She made a face. "How are you two not sick of each other yet?"

The bass-packed music abruptly shut off, and Radhikafoi's voice boomed from the speakers. A microphone squealed, making everyone jump. "And now for your listening pleasure, a live number from Edison's own Kishore Kumar, Dev Merai!"

Dev Merai, who was, for lack of a better word, really, really hot, with his longish hair and model's cheekbones. Dev Merai, who'd only moved from Toronto at the beginning of sophomore year but always had one girlfriend or another—until the Tuesday in March he'd offered Sheetal a cordial cherry and asked if she read any webcomics, because he'd just finished a really good one.

She knew people like Bijal and Vaibhav wondered what he saw in her. But as Dev winked at her from the stage, she couldn't care less.

He grinned at the crowd, then stepped close to the mike and launched into a Hindi song from a classic movie. It was a little unnerving how much he really did sound like Kishore Kumar, one of the old-time icons of Bollywood music. His voice was rich and melancholy, perfect for romantic lyrics about despondent poets and doomed lovers.

Sheetal closed her eyes and let herself slip into the song. Gods, his *voice*. It serenaded her, enfolding her until she started to melt like warm chocolate.

She fought to keep her expression neutral, in case Dad was watching—*Dikri, no boys until you're thirty-five!* Or, gods forbid, Radhikafoi—*Beta, I need to check his astrological chart and his family background and* . . .

Dev sailed into the refrain.

It felt like starlight. . . .

No, that was the astral melody trilling in her ears again, beckoning her toward other wishes, other worlds.

Sheetal's grin wilted. So much for having imagined it. The starsong was back.

It was hard keeping secrets when yours was much bigger than anyone else's, with their latest crush or the test they'd cheated on or the party they'd sneaked out to or the weed they'd furtively smoked in the park. When your secret was as vast as the constellation you couldn't help but stare at every night before you went to sleep.

Especially, Sheetal thought bitterly, her eyes open now as the distant strains of starsong grew louder, when that secret was you.

No one in the entire hall said a word, only listened to Dev, enrapt. Even Minal looked impressed. They were probably all pretending he was singing right to them, that his gaze sweeping the crowd saw something special in them everyone else had missed. His eyes were almost dark enough to be black, and if Sheetal hadn't been trying so hard to ignore the starsong, she might have thought silly things about falling into them. Maybe even about kisses and stealing some.

But the starry melody remained, an undeniable undertone, and her thumb smarted where she'd ripped at the cuticle.

She had to get outside. Had to find out what was going on.

Even before Dev's last note had died away, the party exploded into applause and cheers and calls for an encore. He shook his head and hopped off the stage, right into an adoring swarm of aunties and uncles.

Sheetal scanned the crowd. No sign of Radhikafoi or Dad. If she kept her head down, she might actually make it out of here without anyone stopping her.

Spice-laden aromas drifted toward them. "Oh, good, food time!" Minal said. "Come on."

"But—" Sheetal began, just a second too late. A bangle-covered arm had grabbed hers and was towing her toward the buffet, where waiters had finished uncapping the steaming dishes. Even Dev's admirers were abandoning him to get in line.

As Dev jogged up, Minal asked him, "So how much did you hate that? Having to sing on command like a trained parrot?"

He shrugged. "I'm used to it. You know how showing us off is basically the desi parent Olympics." His voice turned falsetto

11

with an Indian accent as he rolled his eyes, grinning at Sheetal. "'Oh, my son, he will be the next superstar!' Embarrassing, but what you are going to do?"

But Sheetal didn't know. No one had ever shown her off. And with the astral song competing with the buzz of a hundred overlapping conversations and the *thunk, thunk, thunk* of the Bollywood bass, not to mention the thudding of her own heart, she couldn't concentrate. The walls felt like they were getting smaller and smaller, or maybe it was her throat; the playful words she might have said got trapped there on the way up.

She widened her eyes in a way she hoped screamed for help. But Minal was too busy loading her plate with what had to be at least half the buffet to notice. Not knowing what else to do, Sheetal started filling her own plate.

"You really *are* good," Minal told Dev, carrying her mountain of food to a nearby table. She grinned wickedly. "I thought you were just boasting."

Sheetal sat down, too, staring at her meal of fluffy naan, vegetable biryani, aloo mattar, creamy dal makhani, and raita. She could still go chase down the starsong, but now, with Dev watching, all Radhikafoi's old prohibitions strapped her to her chair as securely as a seat belt. *Always blend into the background. Never let anyone suspect what you are.*

"You even have your own fan club," she teased instead.

Dev dropped down next to her, his smile crooked. Sheetal's stomach turned a series of cartwheels, and every part of her was incredibly aware of his knee pressing against hers. "Some fan club—I can't even compete with the food." He found her hand under the table, driving all other thoughts out of her head. "I bet they would have stayed if *you'd* gone up there."

"Yeah, right," she said, hoping he didn't notice how sweaty her palm was. She never should have told him she sang. "You, though—we should put you on one of those *so you think you can sing* shows where everybody sucks except for, like, five people, and even then, three of them are just okay."

Great. Now she was babbling.

"Okay, enough." Minal leaned forward on her elbows. "Save all that mutual admiration stuff for when I'm not around to barf everywhere. On to much more important things—like the great couch quest! Which, by the way, I'm going to win."

"You just love funding my comic habit, don't you?" asked Dev. "Out with it, Sheetal. What'd she say this time?" He shot Minal a sidelong glance. "I've got my eye on the new Kibuishi comic, you know."

"That's funny," said Minal, all glittering makeup and arch attitude, "since *you're* going to be buying it for *me*."

Normally Sheetal would be giggling with them. Some people collected stamps or dolls, even cars. Radhikafoi collected couches. Well, sort of. She'd buy one, decide she hated it after a few days, and return it. And then she'd buy a new one. It was so predictable, Dev and Minal had started laying bets on the reason why three months ago.

But Sheetal still heard the high, sweet melody in her ears, airy as an enchantment, beckoning, beckoning.

"Well?" Minal pressed. "It's too burgundy, isn't it? The last one was too blue, so it has to be."

Dev's phone buzzed, and he pulled away to type a reply, leaving Sheetal's knee cold. Lonely. And without something right here on Earth to hold on to. *Stupid phones.*

She poked him in the shoulder. "Don't tell me you want to forfeit."

He smiled an apology. "Sorry, my cousin wanted to know how the song went."

Minal struck her plate with a spoon, making it ring. "Can we try focusing, people? Preferably before I get old and gray?"

Sheetal took her time scooping up a bite of aloo mattar and chewing the peas and highlighter-yellow potatoes into paste. "The real question is, would my foi be flattered or horrified to learn she has such devoted followers? The kind that place bets on her?"

Minal and Dev turned identical glares her way.

"Quit stalling, Sheetu." Minal nudged her. "I want to get some rasmalai before everyone eats it all."

"Bad news, Minu," Sheetal said with mock regret. "Radhikafoi thought the color was fine. This week's impending return is because, and I quote, 'The leather gave me a headache with all its squeaking.' Guess you'll just have to enjoy your rasmalai with a nice dollop of disappointment."

Dev pumped his fist, then held out his hand for Minal's

money. She practically flung it into his palm. "I'll think of you while I read," he offered, grinning hugely.

The starry music sounded again, a command where before it had been an invitation. Dev's laugh fell away; Radhikafoi's warnings about staying off the radar faded. No matter how weird it looked, Sheetal had to answer. "Speaking of dessert," she blurted, "I should find Dad. I'll be back."

Dev nodded, obviously confused. Before Minal could say anything, Sheetal bolted.

Keeping close to the walls, she followed the insistent strains of song to the exit. What was happening? The music had come and gone over the years, but it had never demanded her attention like this, adamant as an unfed cat, and definitely not when she was in public.

"Sheetal!" a familiar voice called, one that made Sheetal freeze. "There you are, beta. I was just thanking your papa for bringing the cake." Radhikafoi hastened down the hallway, a category-three cyclone in a hot pink sari. "It looks—"

She broke off in midsentence, her eyes widening.

Before Sheetal could dodge, stubby fingers closed around her chin and yanked it down. She wanted to die. If Vaibhav or Bijal happened to be watching, they'd probably tell everyone at school she had lice.

Her auntie clucked her disapproval. "Dikri," she whispered in Gujarati, "your roots—" Without pausing, she switched to English, as if that would somehow keep anyone who might walk by from understanding. "Your roots are *showing*."

15

"What?" Sheetal wrenched away even as her pulse sped up. Not possible. She'd just dyed her roots. Radhikafoi was being paranoid. She had to be.

"This is no laughing matter!" Her auntie grabbed the dupatta from around Sheetal's neck and tried to put it on her head instead. "If someone were to see—"

Sheetal barely evaded her. "Radhikafoi, people are staring."

"Fine!" her auntie snapped, draping the dupatta back over Sheetal's shoulders. "But you need to get your *condition* under control as soon as you get home. We have Maneesh's engagement party this weekend!"

Sheetal nodded, two thoughts hammering through her mind. Had the dye really not taken? And had anyone else seen?

Oh, gods, had *Dev* seen?

He kept talking about wanting to hear her sing and writing a song for her. He was way too close to her secret as it was.

The secret that made her blood thrum in time with the heavens.

Maybe she *should* tie on the dupatta like a headscarf, even if it made her look like a village girl. If anyone saw—if they suspected . . .

This was why, as her auntie always reminded her, she couldn't let herself be noticed at school, why she could never give anyone a reason to look too closely, why she would always have to hide.

Even though part of her wanted to let it all show.

Another guest came up to Radhikafoi, and Sheetal seized

the chance to duck into the restroom across the hall. She met her panicked reflection in the mirror and stared. And stared some more.

It was impossible. She'd dyed her hair a deep, durable, normal black three nights ago. And yet tonight, right at her scalp, were the beginnings of roots.

Shimmering, sparkling, defiantly silver roots.

The fear she'd shoved down welled back up.

What was she going to do if the dye didn't work anymore? White hair was one thing; some people turned to bleach to get that look. But shimmering silver? Not so much. Nobody's hair glowed.

It was as if her hair was resisting being disguised.

The silver voices swept over Sheetal again, stilling her thoughts. Her heart leaped in response.

Like an invocation, the melody resounded within her, eerie and ethereal. Only a ceiling, at most a roof, separated her from her birthright. All she had to do was step outside, the music promised, and it would be hers. Her fingers grasped for phantom instruments, primed to dance over newly tuned strings.

Her voice bubbled up in her throat, so close to cresting over her lips.

Someone opened the restroom door. "Sheetal?" Minal called.

The sound of her name spoken over a flushing toilet, unwelcome as ice water, broke the spell, a brutal reminder of where Sheetal was and the roomful of people just outside. She clamped her mouth shut.

"You never came back," Minal pointed out. Her eyes narrowed. "It's the song again, isn't it?"

Instead of answering, Sheetal hugged her. "I'm fine. Thanks for checking on me."

The final chords of the silvery song lingered on her tongue like a layer of frost, and she rushed to swallow them. They would have to wait. As much as it hurt, *she* would have to wait.

She pressed her hands to her face, shutting everything out for the span of a couple of breaths. Then she rearranged her part to bury her pale roots, doused the light flickering at her core, and stepped out into the hallway, ready to play at being ordinary again. Just as normal and human as Radhikafoi and Dad and the whole world expected her to be.

Radhikafoi never talked about her sister-in-law, as though silence could scrub the memory from Sheetal's heart and, more importantly, from her DNA. Her distasteful "condition." As though what her auntie refused to accept didn't exist.

But no matter how hard Sheetal tried to hide it, no matter how much Radhikafoi wanted to deny it, she would always be half a star.

Always.

An hour after fighting off Radhikafoi and faking her way through the rest of the party, Sheetal lay back on the cool grass behind her house. Alone at last—just her, an industrial-size bag of cheese puffs, a rolled-up hoodie for a pillow, a reading light, and a library book.

She turned the page and realized she hadn't absorbed a single word of the previous chapter.

Oh, who was she kidding? If she wanted to read, she'd be nestled in her bed under a pile of blankets, not in the backyard sneaking glimpses of the stars over the top of her book.

Her inner fire hadn't ignited like this since before her mother left. She'd thought she was safe—until tonight, when she'd almost started singing in a public restroom. A restroom!

She shuddered and plowed into the cheese puffs. If Minal hadn't found her in time . . . If Dev had heard her . . .

And her hair! Her own hair had betrayed her.

Why?

Overhead, the stars glittered in their usual patterns. Constellations, asterisms, clusters. The lunar mansions, where the moon's twenty-seven wives lived. Sheetal traced the faint lines of her relatives' faces, the flow of their glimmering tresses. As a kid, she'd known all their voices, strung together like pearls in a cosmic necklace. The memory flickered within her, a silver-toned, subtle language that had little to do with human speech.

Twinkling among them, of course, was Charumati. In Sheetal's eyes, her mother burned more brilliantly than the others in the blue-black heavens, almost too vibrant, too visible.

Sheetal stuffed her face with more cheese puffs and chewed really hard.

If you lopped it off at just the right place, her parents' romance could be a fairy tale: Charumati, eager for adventure, had abandoned her place in her nakshatra, her royal house, and descended to Earth because she'd thought human lives looked glamorous and exciting. And who had she met there but astrophysicist Dad, who'd made a career out of studying the stars?

He liked to say it was love at first conversation, a love made of inspiration and dreams and enchantment.

In the fairy tale, they met, they married, they had Sheetal, Dad solved a huge problem in his field, and the three of them lived happily ever after.

But life wasn't a fairy tale, and unfortunately for Charumati, the time when humans believed in magic had passed. Except for a few handfuls of dreamers here and there, mortals had built themselves a new fantasy, a boring one where they already knew everything worth knowing—all empirical evidence and explicitly defined labels. Anything else was foolish superstition and couldn't possibly exist. There wasn't room for her mother in a world like that, and so she went home to the starry court.

Leaving Sheetal with nothing but these occasional scraps of melody that both soothed and starved her.

*Superstition? Tell that to my hair,* she thought, Radhikafoi's aghast face looming in her mind. She gingerly probed the top of her head with orange-dusted fingers. A strand came loose in her hand, its tip gleaming bright as frost.

*How* was it silver again? Why was any of this happening? Why tonight?

Her chest pulled as taut as a harp's strings. She gulped down a breath and trained her eyes on the celestial canopy above her, picking out the various nakshatras. *Ashvini. Svati. Vishakha. Satabhishak. Pushya.*

As if she'd invoked them, the stars began crooning down their ragas in voices as glossy and polished as a favorite dream. Their essence suffused the sky in light and song. Until she'd first tried to share them with Minal when they were six, Sheetal hadn't realized that only she and Dad could see the faces in her nakshatra, let alone hear their music. No one else.

The balmy night sky draped dark folds over her like a jewel-studded shawl. She tried to fight its spell, to fight its song, even as the spark at her core flared in acknowledgment.

"Listen," the stars murmured. "Listen."

She slowly relaxed, her muscles loosening. The part of her that had never stopped waiting for her mother to return *wanted* to listen. It had never stopped longing for Charumati's gentle touch on her head, had never stopped dreaming of her mother's warm hugs, of her sparkling stories and her shimmering smile. *I miss you, Mom.*

As Sheetal sank into the starry song, sipping it like silver wine, it spread through her body, illuminating her veins, the secret chambers of her heart. It felt like reaching into lore and legend and yet-untapped reservoirs of dreams. She was close to understanding, so close. . . .

Her hands tingled.

"Nice night," Dad remarked, jolting her out of her reverie. He'd changed out of his kurta pajama into chinos and a T-shirt. "Saying hi to your mom?"

Sheetal leaped up, her breath coming in gasps. She must not have heard the sliding door.

Normally she loved having Dad around. But right now his easy presence felt jarring, a false note that sent hairline fractures through the delicate spun glass of her link to her constellation— to her mother. The astral melody receded from her grasp.

Without the silvery chimes to keep it at bay, her suspicion came flooding back. *Why?* she wondered again, feeling the carpet of grass under her bare feet. Why were the stars calling to her? What did they want?

One corner of Dad's mouth turned up. "Or maybe you're

thinking about somebody else?" He started humming a familiar tune, but deliberately off-key.

Sheetal froze. "Oh, my gods, Dad! *Stop!*"

Dad mangled a few more lines. "What, you don't think I sound like Kishore Kumar?"

Her face burned as hot as the new-lit flame inside her. "Can we, I don't know, *not* talk about this?"

"But I love this song. Don't you?" He hummed it again, exaggerating the notes.

"Dad!" If only she could sink into the lawn and disappear the way her appalled eyebrows must have vanished into her hair. "What. Are. You. Doing. Please stop."

Still keeping a straight face, Dad helped himself to a cheese puff. "Don't tell me I need to invite the Merai clan over for Scrabble night just to keep an eye on you."

Sheetal wished she could zip her hoodie up over her face. "Radhikafoi told you, didn't she." Not that there was really anything *to* tell. It wasn't like she and Dev had been making out in public.

And ew, she did *not* want to be thinking of making out with anyone while Dad stood two feet away.

Dad chuckled. "No, but you just told me yourself."

Here came the no-boys, no-dating lecture. But Sheetal knew how to throw him off. As a kid, she would ask Dad what he saw when he watched the heavens, and he always said the same thing: *Your mummy.*

Tonight, still overwhelmed by the sudden appearance of

the starsong, she whispered, "Aren't you tired of missing her? Mom, I mean?"

"I hear her, dikri," Dad said simply. "I'll never be tired of that."

"How, though?" Sheetal stared at him. "She's gone."

"I hear her," Dad repeated. "I hear her singing. It's as beautiful as the day we met."

"I don't understand." He'd never told her that before. Her chest tightened in confusion and hurt. Did he hear Charumati more often than Sheetal did?

Dad looked up at the sky, and his gaze went soft. There it was, the murky gray sorrow they'd both gotten so good at keeping from anyone else. "You're going to be seventeen soon. Growing up."

"In four days." Sheetal didn't know what else to say. Maybe it didn't matter how much Dad could hear her mother. It didn't make her not being there any better.

"Chakli," Dad said, pulling Sheetal to him. "My little chakli. You know I love you, right?" She buried her head in his chest. He smelled like shaving cream and security.

For a minute, she let herself forget that she wasn't his little sparrow anymore, let herself forget all her questions, all her doubts. She just let herself be in the past, when everything was the way it was supposed to be. Summer days wading into the ocean at Point Pleasant with Dad, but only up to her waist so her hair stayed clear of the salty surf, while her mother knelt on the shore to chat with the seagulls.

Or Friday nights ordering pizza and playing Trivial Pursuit, which Charumati somehow always won. She'd reject the pizza as too greasy, but she couldn't get enough of human trivia and politics, to the point that Dad took to calling her an undercover spy for the stars.

Of course, all that had screeched to a halt when she left. Though seven-year-old Sheetal had pleaded for Dad to keep playing with her, he'd stashed the game away in a closet and given her biographies instead.

They were mostly about physicists. But it wasn't like science could teach her how to be half a star.

Or how to keep her stupid silver roots from glowing like a beacon for the entire banquet hall to see. Ugh—she *so* didn't want to tell Dad about that, but if she didn't, Radhikafoi definitely would.

Sheetal stepped back from the hug. "Dad, my hair. The dye—I don't know what happened."

"Say what?" he asked, his voice calm. His *just collecting data* scientist voice.

The story poured out of her. Something like alarm flitted over Dad's face, but when she looked closer, he was only frowning. "Just try another box. It was probably a bad batch."

"Yeah, probably," Sheetal said. Too bad her tingling palms didn't agree.

Dad had glanced up again to where clouds were rolling in, concealing the stars from his sight, and melancholy spread over his face. After Charumati left, well-meaning aunties and uncles had tried to set him up with other women, insisting Sheetal needed a mother and he needed a wife. He'd politely but steadfastly refused every single potential match. Sheetal knew there would never be anyone for him but her mother.

"Dad—" she began, wanting to reach out but not sure how.

"Almost seventeen. You're still too young for boys," he said sternly, cutting her off. "Don't think I forgot."

Sheetal's sympathy dried right up. Gods, he really had no clue. Half the desi kids she knew dated, even if they did it behind their parents' backs.

But that wasn't the point. Something bizarre and kind of scary was happening to her, and here Dad had gotten hung up on making sure she didn't date. "It's not like Dev saw. No one did!"

Dad shook his head, still staring up into the night. "No, Sheetal. You're my daughter, and it's my job to keep you safe. No boys at least until you finish high school, understood? I want you to promise me."

It was so unfair. Why wasn't he listening? "Dad!"

Iron entered his words, a warning not to push him any further. "I mean it."

Sheetal managed not to sigh out loud. "Fine."

Her heart twisted. Even if he was being totally unreasonable, she hated lying to him.

Dad rubbed his forehead. "Good."

It wasn't good at all, and Sheetal really didn't like how he could be okay with all this. With Charumati abandoning them to fend for themselves. With Sheetal having to hide. She gesticulated wildly at the glittering firmament with its landscape of stars and shades of blue and black, and anger erupted from her like lava. "You can't wait for her anymore, Dad. You know that, right?"

The second the words were out of her mouth, she wanted to snatch them back.

When Dad spoke, it was clipped. He rolled up the bag of cheese puffs. "Bedtime. For both of us."

Crap. Why had she said that? It wasn't as if she meant it. Feeling like a jerk, she chased after him into the shadowed house.

Dad didn't say anything else until they'd reached her room. "Don't forget to brush your teeth." He pressed a quick kiss to her forehead, then disappeared down the hall.

Alone, Sheetal crumbled. The stars blinked through her bedroom window, but their song had gone quiet. She wanted to know what she should do, why her roots were showing, why her own music swelled so urgently against her rib cage, a chorus of shining pewter notes chiming for release.

But Dad couldn't answer those questions. Only the stars could.

Tossing under her sheets after four movies in a row had all failed to grab her, Sheetal knew the night was toast. Even after she'd put down her tablet, she left the light on. She couldn't stop thinking of how the starsong had sucked her right in, how close she'd come to . . . something.

Worse, the hole in her heart she'd so carefully cemented over ten years ago was cracking open again.

She tore at the skin by her thumbnail until a drop of blood appeared. *I'm not afraid,* she told herself, trying hard to believe it. *I'm not.*

Her gaze wandered over the familiar things in her room: the baby dragon plushie; the desk weighed down with scented candles and clippings of gourmet recipes she'd never make; the turquoise shelves crammed with novels, biographies from Dad, comics from Dev, collages, Post-its scribbled with inspirational quotes, and framed pictures of her with Minal, with Dad, even with Radhikafoi, Deepakfua, and her bratty cousins; the glow-in-the-dark stars Minal had stuck on the ceiling as a joke.

*Think about those things,* she ordered herself. *Count sheep. Whatever.* She even tried replaying Dev's song from the party in her mind like a lullaby. But the astral melody only chimed alongside it in her thoughts, its gossamer strains a perfect score to his lyrics. Her palms tingled, and the flame at her core shot up.

*And there goes sleeping.*

She reached over and dug her phone out from under a half-read biography about the mathematician Srinivasa Ramanujan. A couple of taps, and Minal's recording appeared, showing a grinning Dev onstage. As his voice floated from the phone's speaker, Sheetal's insides went all bubbly. He was seriously good—good enough to go pro if he wanted. And, okay, it didn't hurt that he was seriously nice to look at, either.

28

She texted him, even though he had to be asleep. *My dad's onto us.* 🙀 *Run for your life!*

*Us.* They were an us. Sheetal still couldn't really believe it. The memory of him singing to her from the stage would never get old, especially not that wink. Or that knowing smile.

He'd asked her to sing for him. Her mouth grew dry. He'd asked her to sing *with* him. She never could, of course, but what a delicious daydream. . . .

Her lips were already shaping words, and her fingers ached with the urge to touch the starry music, to conduct it through string and song. The need burned, demanding she feed it. As the pressure built, it felt like she might just go up in silver flames and take the whole house with her.

Sheetal padded back downstairs, past the wall where Charumati's pictures still hung, and threw aside a floor-length hanging tapestry to reveal a bronze door pull in the shape of a serenely smiling naga. Her mother's secret room.

Charumati had decorated it to feel like the vast library of the stars, which supposedly contained every story or piece of lore anyone could possibly want, all organized by color and song. It was her sanctuary on Earth, packed with all her old treasures, all her private dreams. The fragrance of wild roses and jasmine wafted out, as if she still waited inside.

But it was Sheetal's room now. Taking a deep breath, she opened the door and stepped through.

She glanced past the rich fabrics and fairy lights lining the

29

walls and the LED cherry blossom tree, past the gilt volumes of folktales and magical texts from around the world, until she spotted the two things she'd come for. *The harp,* she debated, *or the dilruba?* Both called to her from their corners, and both rang out brightly, their tones round and full, when Sheetal tested their strings.

Dad had bought the instruments after Sheetal woke night after night singing songs no human knew, when it became clear the music in her blood wasn't going away just because Mom had.

Sheetal's throat constricted. How many hours had she hidden here, strumming through her grief, her pain, her isolation—all as bulky and cold as sodden blankets? How many hours begging the night sky to give her mother back?

At least until the day her tears ran dry, the day she'd finally admitted Charumati was gone for good. She'd tried to put it all away. To turn her back on the secret room.

She couldn't do it, though. Here and there—between homework and sleepovers, dish duty and trips to the aquarium—when that missing part of her got to be too much, she'd sneak in here and explode with all the things she couldn't say. Couldn't be.

More embers kindled in Sheetal, silver and hot. Why did she always have to hide?

She picked up her journal, a lined hardback book with an embossed peacock cover, whose pages she'd filled with all the stories her mother used to tell her. Where she'd written out her own pain when it got too big to swallow. But none of that would help tonight.

Why couldn't she show the world what she could do the same way Dev or Minal or anyone else got to?

*The harp*, she decided, trading the journal for her tuning key.

Finally, seated on the silk-sheathed daybed, the harp's carved wooden frame resting against her shoulder and thigh, she started to play.

The air tasted sharp and crisp, sweet with moonlight. Another breath, and music flowed out, tunneling through her fingers, rushing into the strings. It didn't matter that she hadn't played in months; her fingers always knew just where to go. She plucked and damped, flipping levers up and down, up and down, melodies swirling through her. Octaves and open fifths, D-sevenths and delicate trills all reverberated through the room and glided out the window, borne aloft on intangible wings.

The music wound itself into her heart, unlocking its passageways, searing away her defenses. It stung, but she refused to stop. She didn't want to. It felt like miracles, mercury, mysteries—all soaring higher and higher, swallowing everything but her.

She played through the crystalline haze, faster and faster, the strings cutting grooves into her skin. Each new memory was a note, each note a wealth of sound and light. Cooling wonder blossomed from the pain, from her body, until the room was tinted silver.

Her voice, too, rippled forth, first halting, tripping over

itself, then finding its rhythm. It dissolved the lump in her throat into words, dissolved her doubts into chords. She played, and she sang.

Sheetal hated how the stars, the sky, owned this part of her. How every time she played or sang, their own melody entwined with hers, underlying it, flavoring it. But she could never hate the music, this power that let her express all the things blazing within.

There was something she hadn't figured out how to say, about Charumati, about Dad, about herself. There was a story she had to tell, one no one else could.

Someday soon, Sheetal swore, playing even faster, she would keep it from shape-shifting long enough to pin it down.

# 3

The late-morning sunlight, which had made a furnace of her bed, now batted at Sheetal like a kitten's paw, poking and pestering until she forced her eyes open. Her fingers hurt, the pads sore.

Yawning, she stretched and blinked in the unforgiving sunshine. A splash of black caught her eye. Weird. She twisted to see it better.

Something was wrong with her bed. *Ink?*

She rubbed her bleary eyes and checked again.

No, not ink.

Her pillowcase looked like a crime scene, if the victim were a can of shoe polish. Black gore splattered everywhere.

This was two-day-old dye, dye that had soaked into her hair and dried, but now stained her pillow, her sheets. Even though there was no way it could be.

Just like her roots couldn't have been silver last night—but were.

*No one can ever know what you are.*

Sheetal wobbled into the bathroom and looked right at the mirror. Her stomach clenched.

Every dark, inky drop of the dye was gone, from her roots down to her hip-length, blunt-cut ends. Unlike the diamond flower in her nose, which only glittered when it caught the light, the thick, tangled waves spilling down her back gleamed and dazzled all by themselves. She might have her dad's skin with its tendency toward blemishes, but this was one hundred percent her mother's hair.

And it was shining bright for the whole world to see. Alien. Inhuman. Not of this earth. Just like the hair that had once had to be disguised by an expensive wig because it refused to accept dye. The hair that had flashed and flowed when Charumati had cast off the wig and returned to the heavens.

Like mother, like daughter.

Except Sheetal was still here.

Minal held up a lock of Sheetal's shimmering hair, turning it so silver light scattered across the blue tile of the bathtub, then looked regretfully at her own dye-spattered, plastic-gloved hands. "Are you sure we have to do this? It's so gorgeous."

Perched precariously on the side of the tub, Sheetal moaned. Her head hurt. The ratty old towel around her shoulders made her neck itch. Everything smelled—all sharp, corrosive chemicals that burned her nose every time she went through this ritual. No one wanted to skip it more than she did. "Can we please just finish? I'm so tired."

She didn't add that it had to work. It had to.

"Sure," Minal said, reaching for the bowl of raven dye she'd just mixed. "Even though it's a crime to cover up fairy-tale hair. You're making me commit a crime, you know. I hope you're happy."

Sheetal gave Minal her best side-eye.

"Hey, hold still, unless you want a black ear." Minal started working in the dye. "I never really saw you like this before, you know. It was always dyed." She came around to study Sheetal from the side. "Not going to lie; if my hair looked like this, I'd never cover it up."

Sheetal had never really seen herself like this before, either. She *did* look pretty. Her mouth turned up in a tiny smile. Dev would love it.

Her smile collapsed in on itself. Except he'd never see it. No one would.

"So," Minal said, going back to the bowl. "Last night in the bathroom. Care to explain what that was about?"

Busted. Sheetal focused on the butterfly-patterned shower curtain. She should have known Minal wouldn't let her off the hook.

"You looked like you were about to fly away. What's going on?"

Longing as deep as the sky—longing to hear the astral

35

melody again, to understand it—lit Sheetal's cells. "They're . . . I don't know. The starsong. It did something to me."

Minal's brush paused its careful painting. "What does that mean?"

Sheetal shook her head. "I don't know."

"Did what, though?" Minal pressed. "That sounds ominous."

All the things Sheetal wasn't saying flashed through her mind, one silver spark at a time. Like how the sidereal music had woken something in her bones, and she'd almost completely lost control and given herself up to it. Like how, desperate to reach it again, she'd gone into her secret room and played her harp until it felt like her fingers would fall off.

How in daylight the starsong was thankfully dormant, but every part of her was freaking out.

Just the thought of trying to explain made her want to take a nap right there in the bathtub. "No, nothing like that," she said quickly. "It— I had to play a lot last night. Like, my calluses are going to have calluses."

"Do you think it had something to do with your hair?"

"Maybe." Sheetal winced. "Radhikafoi's going to kill me if she finds out about it."

"So don't tell her." Minal put the brush aside and sat down next to Sheetal. "You know, sometimes I think your foi looks at you like one of her clients. Like, she couldn't save them from getting hurt, but she can still save you."

Sheetal scoffed. "From what, having a life?" Radhikafoi

36

helped battered women escape terrible situations, but as her auntie knew, Sheetal's home with Dad couldn't be safer.

"No, I mean she probably feels like she has to make up for your mom leaving."

"Yeah, well, I never asked her to," Sheetal pointed out. "Why can't I have *your* family? You guys all get along."

"Have you *met* my siblings? Just this morning, Yogesh was whining about how unfair it is I get to have a car, but he doesn't— uh, because he's thirteen?—and Soni knocked my dad's coffee all over his shirt. The one he'd just had dry-cleaned." Minal snorted. "Ordinary. That's us. But look at *you*, star princess out of some fairy tale. You're magic."

"I guess," Sheetal said. She definitely didn't feel like a star princess. She felt like a weirdo, and weren't fairy-tale heroines supposed to be free of zits and tangles and general awkwardness? Without even trying, Minal had better skin than she did. No split ends from nonstop dye jobs, either.

"Besides," Minal asked, wistful, "do you really want to be ordinary? Ordinary's boring. I always wanted magic, and you actually have it."

*You don't get it,* Sheetal thought. *Magic isolates you. You're this misfit who doesn't belong anywhere, and you want to make it all go away, but at the same time, you crave it, and you can't help craving it. You're just stuck.*

Minal stood and picked up the bowl again. "Think about it. My mom yells up the stairs or texts me to check on me. Yours sends you starlight."

Her mom. Oh, man. Sheetal hadn't let herself even dance around the question of whether Charumati in particular wanted to tell her something. "Can we not talk about this anymore?"

"Okay. But if you ever decide you want to say hi to her in person," Minal added, her tone cheeky, "don't even dream of leaving me behind."

At least that was something Sheetal could answer. She lifted her head enough for Minal to see her watery smile. "Never."

"You better not." Minal changed the subject to her latest work in progress, a mixed-media circus cart made from a cigar box and sea glass, and resumed kneading the dye into Sheetal's hair.

She'd basically finished when Sheetal's phone dinged with a message from Dev. *Just got your text. I'm not big into running. Maybe a leisurely jog for our lives.*

*I heard that's really bad for your knees,* she texted back. "Ow!" Minal was folding her hair into the plastic cap with a little too much enthusiasm.

"Sorry," said Minal, not sounding at all sorry. "It's supposed to be tight. Read the directions if you don't believe me."

"Show me where it says you're supposed to cut off my circulation!"

Sheetal's phone dinged again. *Then we'll just stroll. Mosey right along.*

*What if we wander? You can't go wrong with a good wander.*

*Wandering could work. Just no shambling—unless you're a zombie,* Dev went on. *Anyway, I had this dream last night. I was eating cookies, and you were guarding me with this seriously kickass sword. It shot lasers whenever anyone got too close.*

Sheetal felt like she'd broken into two people, one overlaying the other. The ordinary human girl who flirted with her boyfriend, and the bizarre alien girl hiding in the skin of that ordinary girl, frantically pretending everything was fine. Her skin wasn't big enough for both of them.

But all she typed was, *Excuse me??? As a knight, I can do better than guarding Cookie Monster. All he does is eat cookies! Tell your subconscious I want a promotion.*

*Excuse ME,* Dev replied, *but you should be honored to have such an important job. Clearly all those people wanted to steal my cookies. Who's Cookie Monster without any cookies, huh? HUH?* 🍪🍪🍪

Sheetal hesitated. What she really wanted to say, just as breezily, was, *Hey, so guess what? I'm half star, and my hair's going rogue, and the sky's singing to me, and I don't know what to do. Wanna get tacos?*

She settled for, *I guess I can do my part to prevent that existential crisis.* ⚔️ 🛡

*All hail Sir Sheetal, champion of Cookie Monsters everywhere.*

One side of her mouth lifted in spite of itself. *Omnomnom.*

*So are you going to ask what I did today?*

*Maybe. I'm still deciding.*

*You know you want to.* 😜

*Do I?* Sheetal made him wait a couple of minutes before typing, *Fine, what'd you do today?*

*I finished my song! The whole thing. It took me all night, but it was like I finally broke through this wall, you know?*

*I can't wait to hear it,* Sheetal replied, and now she really was smiling.

*So come over. No one's here but me.*

An electric thrill ran through her, mixed with guilt. She hadn't gone to Dev's house once in the three months they'd been together. Dad would never be okay with it.

But he didn't have to know, and besides, she really, really didn't want to obsess about star stuff anymore.

Minal broke into her thoughts. "The moment of truth. Time to wash it out."

*Okay,* Sheetal typed. *See you soon.*

She got up and put her phone by the sink. "Minu, what if it doesn't work?"

"It will." Minal gave her a quick hug. "Even if I kind of wish it wouldn't." With that, she left Sheetal to the shower.

Even after everything, as Sheetal climbed under the hot jets, she kind of wished it wouldn't, too.

Minal's car idled against the curb in front of Dev's white colonial house, engine rumbling. All Sheetal had to do was open the door and get out.

All she had to do . . .

Her butt stayed planted in the passenger seat like it had been glued down. "Check again," she begged for the fifth time.

"Good news," Minal said, glancing up from her phone. "Your hair's still black as a politician's heart. Same as it was five minutes ago."

The dye had set for real. Sheetal should be overjoyed. Instead, it felt like she was teetering on a seesaw between relieved and regretful. "That's pretty black, all right. No roots, even?"

"Nope." Minal gestured with her chin toward the house. "Going in?"

*Relieved,* Sheetal decided, testing a strand of her undeniably ebony hair. It was lank, dry, and coarse from being dyed twice in one week, and she really did need to take scissors to those scratchy little branches of split ends. But at least they were black scratchy little branches.

So what was she waiting for? "Maybe?"

Minal reached past her to point out the window. "See that rectangular thing there? Between the pillars? It's called a *front door*. I know it's a whole ten steps from here, but you can't get lost, I promise."

Sheetal pressed her crimson-stained lips together. Maybe it was stupid, but her palms were sweaty and prickling, and an entire ensemble of butterflies was performing a ballet in her belly.

She *had* remembered to put on deodorant, hadn't she? And brush her teeth? Oh, gods, what if she was breaking out—

"Just think, Sheetu," Minal said, deadpan, "if you don't get out of my car, starting tomorrow, you'll spend the rest of the summer stuck in that test prep class, cramming vocab lists under your auntie's watchful eye and wishing you'd actually gone inside instead of just staring at his house when you had the chance."

Sheetal sat up ramrod straight at that. She smoothed out the lace-draped aquamarine waterfall skirt Minal had lent her, then reached for her messenger bag.

Smiling, Minal pressed the unlock button. "Go find that boy you like."

Sheetal swung her legs back and forth on a stool at the island in the middle of Dev's kitchen, playing tag with the sunshine splashing through the windows while he tinkered with the oven. It was the first week of summer vacation, and she was at Dev's house. *Dev's house.* Just the two of them.

They'd never been alone like this during the school year. A wild sense of possibility bloomed inside her, making her feel bold and shy at the same time.

She inhaled the aroma of vanilla and butter and sugar wandering over from where he stood. "That smells *amazing.*"

"Yup." He straightened and turned around, a baking sheet in his hands. "Now you just need a sword."

Cookies. He'd actually baked her cookies. Sheetal caught her mouth stretching into that dorky smile she always got around him.

He must have showered right before she came over, because the last of his dark hair was still drying into waves. Sheetal tried to focus on it while he transferred the cookies to a rack, on the blue band T-shirt that fit him so well, but her gaze kept straying to his mouth, and she found herself wondering what it would taste like after a cookie.

Dev made a *ta-da* gesture toward the cooling cookies, so clearly pleased with himself that she commandeered the whole rack. "If you're nice," she offered magnanimously, "I might let you have one. Maybe."

His eyebrows came together in mock outrage. "I baked them!"

43

"And I stole them." Balancing the rack in one hand, Sheetal searched the island drawers until she located a butter knife. "Look, it's my sword!"

Dev nabbed a cookie anyway. "Figures you'd be a dark knight."

Sheetal brandished the knife at him, then put the rack back down and reached for a cookie herself.

Her teeth crunched into what should have been gooey and warm chocolate-chip bliss, and she tried not to wince. He'd left the baking sheet in the oven too long. But who cared? He'd baked her cookies!

"Not bad, right?" Dev took a bite of his. "Huh, I thought they'd be softer."

"Not bad at all," Sheetal agreed, and she wasn't even lying.

They pushed their stools together until their sides were touching. Dev broke a cookie in two, ate one half, and fed her the other.

He didn't even wait for her to finish chewing to lean in for a kiss. Just a brush of lips before he sat back on his stool and grinned. A dimple appeared near the corner of his mouth. "Oh, right; each cookie costs one kiss. By my calculations, you've already had one and a half."

"I do like to pay my debts," Sheetal said, and leaned in for her own kiss. "There. Now *you* owe *me* half a cookie."

"Actually, accounting for inflation, you just earned one-fourth of a cookie." Dev grinned evilly, but when she protested, he gave her the other half.

While she ate, Dev produced a DVD still in its shrink

wrap: *Furious Fungus 5: Shiitake Strikes Back.* The cover looked like someone had colorized angry mushroom clip art and then run the results through a terrible photo filter. "Hey, so we could either watch this thing I found on clearance, *or* . . ."

Sheetal stared for a minute, trying to figure out why anyone would pay even the ninety-nine cents listed on the price sticker. "I'm guessing you really want me to pick option B?"

Dev glanced at her, face serious, then at his feet. "Or, you know, we could go up to my room."

His room. Her heart started pounding, and her skin prickled with nerves. Even the silver flame at her core kindled.

"That's where I write them," he hurried to add. "My songs, I mean."

"Okay." Just saying the word set off the butterfly ballet in Sheetal's stomach. She surreptitiously wiped her palms on her skirt. "If it means not watching whatever that was."

"Good." He smirked. "I didn't actually want to watch it, either."

Leaving her bag on the kitchen table, Sheetal followed him up the gleaming hardwood stairs. All she could think about was how close he was and what might happen next.

At the door to his room, his easy stride faltered. "Guess I should have cleaned up a bit. It's normally not this bad."

He wasn't kidding. Books, crumpled pieces of paper, and graphic novels lay all over the beige carpet. Clothes were heaped in front of the closet, half hiding a Batman poster. He hadn't made his bed, but at least the sheets looked clean.

Dev quickly started dumping things in the closet. When Sheetal bent down to help, she saw one of the balled-up pages was covered with scratched-out words. A draft of the new song?

"I wasn't kidding," he said, watching her with his dark, beautiful eyes. "This is pretty much all I've been doing, writing songs. You just make me want to write so many."

Sheetal turned into one big cheesy grin on the inside, but she tried to sound skeptical. "That's a bit much even for you."

Dev shrugged. "It's the truth." He chucked a bunch of laundry into a hamper and slammed the closet door. "There."

Sheetal's pulse stuttered. Here they were in his room, with the blinds drawn, and he was lighting a candle. Should she sit on the bed? Or stay on the floor and pretend she wasn't sneaking peeks at the song?

Struggling not to feel completely awkward, she looked around for something to do and noticed the pictures on the orange walls. *Whew!*

She let go of the rejected draft and walked over to the nearest wall. The photos told a story: Dev with his family; Dev with his friends; Dev with a curly-haired older boy. She stopped at a shot of Dev trapped in the older boy's headlock, both of them wearing green soccer jerseys and huge grins. "Who's this?"

Dev ran a hand through his hair and frowned slightly. "My cousin Jeet." He flopped onto the bed, propping himself up against the pillows, and motioned for Sheetal to join him.

A quiver ran through her. Never mind the pictures. She had her answer about where to sit.

Her belly heating, she climbed up beside Dev, half thrilled, half terrified. Suddenly his arms were around her, his face so near hers she could feel his eyelashes when he blinked.

"Caught you, pretty girl," he teased. "Now what?"

She met his gaze head-on. "Maybe I wanted to get caught," she said coyly. Part of her couldn't believe she'd just said that. But right now, here with him in his bed, she felt dangerous. Unbound.

For once, Dev seemed at a loss for words. "Oh, yeah?" he asked at last, his voice lower. His eyes, velvet-dark and hungry in the candlelight, searched her face until everything beyond them faded. She really could fall into them now, she thought, giddy, an electric flood of energy setting her every nerve sparking.

She shivered.

"You look cold," Dev said, pulling a blanket over them. "Better?"

Sheetal refrained from pointing out that it was eighty-four degrees in June. Instead, she leaned into his chest.

This close to the heat of him, her skin tingled. Her heart thrummed chords that matched the ones his heart drummed out. Something brilliant shone inside her, and she couldn't tell whether it was her flame or what happened when you were just a girl who liked a boy.

Just a girl who wanted Dev to take all of her in, to really get her. And for his mouth to find hers.

Between kisses, she wanted him to tell her his private dreams and wishes. In return, she wanted to divulge all the things she'd kept in confidence for so long, air out all the truths moldering in the chambers of her too-full heart.

His arms felt so right around her. Strong, solid.

She was already breaking about thirty rules by being here, and he'd never believe her anyway, so what if she gave him a hint?

"When I was a kid, I used to sing all the time. With my mom," she murmured, her fingertips learning the line of his jaw. "We'd go outside and look at the sky, and she'd tell me stories, and we'd dance and sing all these songs. Maybe it's stupid, but I thought . . . I thought we'd always do that."

Dev squeezed her hand. "That's hard. I'm sorry." His mouth was close to her ear, and his breath tickled.

"She's the one who taught me to sing. Under the stars." *The song of the stars.* "I—I miss her sometimes, you know?"

Dev nodded. "What if you sing one of those songs? Just for me. No one else has to know."

"What?" Sheetal said too fast, the tapping in her heart turning to painful thuds of a sledgehammer. "I thought *you* were going to sing for *me*."

"I'd rather hear you. But—"

"I'm not a performer like you." The brilliance flared inside her again, and now it merged with the notes of the sidereal melody. She'd never sung for anyone but Minal and Dad. She certainly couldn't sing for Dev. One note, and he'd know she wasn't fully mortal; with the starsong chiming in her chest, she was sure of it.

Before Dev could argue, she took his face in her hands and kissed him.

She'd only meant to distract him, to turn him away from what she couldn't share after all, but his lips were so warm and soft, and the way they parted against hers made her forget, too. He did taste sweet as he drew her to him, though nothing like a cookie. His fingers ran over her back, wove through her hair.

Here in the dark, the starry song she'd refused to sing aloud surged through her in a gale of thundering bass notes and shimmering ornaments. It rang in her blood, in her lips where they touched Dev's, in the furious beating of her heart. Right now, as long as it didn't try to take over, she couldn't care less what it did.

For the duration of that kiss, and the one after, and all the ones after that, she was just a girl who liked a boy who liked her back.

She could stay like this forever.

They finally broke apart, cheeks flushed, lips swollen. "Wow," said Dev. "You should sneak over to my house more often."

"Yeah," Sheetal agreed, trying to catch her breath. "Wow." She hadn't known it would be like *that*.

Dev lay back against the pillows, his hair rumpled. *She'd* done that. She nestled against his chest, enjoying its rise and fall like the sea.

Just a normal girl and her boyfriend.

They stayed like that for a while, the shadows cast by the

candlelight dancing over them. Eventually Sheetal asked, "If you could have anything, anything at all, what would you want?"

Dev took a minute to think, and she breathed in his boy smell, a bit of shampoo and a bit of whatever it was that made him Dev. "A tiny elephant to ride on my shoulder would be cool," he said. "That—and not having to care about what anyone else thinks I should do. 'Dev's going to be a hotshot lawyer!' 'Dev's going to be a famous singer!' How about 'Dev just wants to be left alone'?"

Maybe he'd meant the words to come out sardonic, even mocking, but they only sounded frustrated. Sheetal knew how that felt, even if his situation was the mirror opposite of hers.

Dev played with a lock of her hair. He sounded light-years away. "What do *you* want?"

Sheetal started to answer. Then she realized she couldn't. Not really.

What did she want? Adventures. Cupcakes and kulfi. To be star bright and mortal dark and make her own choices, too. To not be bound by other people's expectations.

More than anything, to be *seen*.

If only she could just tell him.

But she'd taken so long to consider, his eyes had slipped shut. She remembered he'd stayed up all night working on his mysterious song. "You're so comfortable," he mumbled.

Sheetal kissed his cheek, then moved so her ear was pressed to his chest. *Thump, thump, thump*, beat his heart, a metronome keeping perfect time. It was steady, but slowing as he drifted into sleep. She snuggled deeper into his arms, wanting to be carried off like that, too.

Listening to his pulse, she realized she was humming. With the memory of last night's music glinting silver in her mind, it felt good. Besides, he was out cold, so it wasn't like he could hear her.

Her own eyes closed.

And the spark at her core ignited. The sidereal melody flared to life, its strains streaming from her throat like glowing garlands, each woven from shining threads of starlight.

The threads came together to form a web around Dev and her. A corner of her mind wondered what the hell was going on, but the starsong soothed it into silence. She was only dreaming.

In a dream, at least, Sheetal could have what she wanted.

So she followed the melody and let her heart reach out for Dev's.

She could see the rhythmic throb of the blood that brought life-giving oxygen to Dev's cells, could sense the buried river of his recollections and dreams. Her own blood turned to music. Silver fire slipped through her veins as she hummed, flowing from her heart into Dev's like a bridge between them.

Images began to form along the bridge, first vague as unspun cotton, then finer, more detailed, the more she sang, a sketch gaining depth and dimension. Then she saw six-year-old Dev among the rest of his family, their plastic plates laden with party food: buttery pulao, its white grains fluffy and flecked with carrots and peas; puri, fried to golden perfection; lightly fried bhajia, spicy and stuffed with potato and onion. Dev chatted happily with the other kids. *Even at that age*, Sheetal thought, *he was a charmer.*

An old man started speaking, and everyone else fell quiet. One of the kids standing with Dev, a curly-haired boy about nine or ten, looked excited, as if he'd heard this story before. "Once there was a star . . ."

The scene changed, taking Sheetal and her song with it.

Stars walked quietly among mortals, their long manes sparkling and their dark eyes agleam as they sloughed off inspiration like snowflakes. In their wake, sleeping mortal passions soon transformed into art: painters rendered masterpieces accented with gold leaf and gems, dancers refined their subtlest gestures into movements worthy of apsaras, musicians spun notes into complex compositions to be handed down for generations, and storytellers penned reams of epic verse that effortlessly blended the mundane with the mythical.

The stars never advertised their presence to the world. They merely wandered in and out of lives as they were needed, kindling and then fueling the flames of creativity.

Most artists soon forgot their astral muses as their work devoured them—if they saw the stars at all. They spent their days as if in a dream where the only truth was their work, until that work was done. Royal chefs concocted recipes; architects constructed enameled monuments to love; jewelers fashioned pieces so intricate they looked like dreams made metal. The world gleamed brighter for it all.

But occasionally an artist turned their head long enough to become infatuated with their star, making of that fixation its own kind of art, a delightful drama of yearning.

And occasionally a star would forget their place and respond to that hunger, with glances leading to caresses and secret trysts, until silver fire ignited between muse and artist.

Yet with time, these mortals began to wither, consumed from the inside out.

They ceased to eat, to bathe, to sleep, even to work. Their faces grew skeletal, their hair lank before it fell out, and they lay in shadow chanting their lover's name until the last trace of air left their bodies.

The stars burned their very essence away.

Rumors began to spread, both on Earth and in the heavens. The sidereal court convened and punished those stars who had dallied with humans, removing any children of these unions until they were old enough to purge their mortal blood. "Mortals cannot bear such prolonged exposure to our inspiration and our light," came the verdict, delivered by an imposing older couple on their twin thrones, "and to join with them in this way is an abomination."

Not long after, a star who in human years might have been twenty or twenty-one and whose beauty was as luminous as her light sought out her mortal lover. As they embraced, her long silver tresses fell around them in a shimmering canopy. Though they had only recently begun their affair, she had to end it, she explained. Her expression entreated him to understand. "If I leave now, you might still be safe."

The man, youthful and dressed in a kurta pajama stained with rich pigments, caught her by the wrist. "You can't leave. What do I have without you?"

"Do not be foolish," chastised the star. She gestured to his paintings. "You have your family and your friends and your art. I have given you inspiration, nothing more."

"Look at you," he said. "You're magic. Where am I going to find that again?"

The star touched his cheek. "We still have tonight. Let us make the most of it."

They nestled together all that night, the man whispering stories to the star. She had dampened her radiance, so they were lit only by the oil lamps scattered around the windows.

"Do you truly have to go?" the man asked as day began to break.

"Yes," said the star through her tears. "Lord Surya's chariot will soon drive across the sky."

He gripped her hand. "I'm not ready to say goodbye."

"Nor am I, but so it must be. I have given you all I can— all my light, all my love. If the court knew I was here right now . . ." Yet she held him tight.

He considered, then nodded. "One more night. Just one more. Surely you can spare that?"

The star conveyed her agreement in little kisses. Then she stood, extinguished the oil lamps, and disappeared into the dawn.

When she reappeared after sunset, her glow driving away the gloom in the man's small house, the man took her into his arms. "Won't you reconsider?"

The star smiled into his hair. "For your sake, I cannot." She looked over his shoulder at the red cloth covering a large object in the center of the room. "A new piece in progress?"

"In a manner of speaking." He stepped back to offer her a small package. "For you."

The star opened it to find a mangalsutra, the gold-and-black necklace a bride wore once wed. "How lovely! But I cannot accept it."

"Why not?" asked the man. "Don't you want to be with me?"

Sorrow infused her words. "If only I could."

"You're everything to me. My life has color now." The man pressed each word into her throat with a kiss.

"Your life has always had color. How else would you make art?"

"Not like the colors I see now." He unclasped the mangalsutra. "Won't you stay?"

The star's voice quavered. "I cannot. You know I cannot."

Dropping the necklace, the man reached for the red cloth. He thrust it aside to expose a giant cage with iron bars. The star had no time to speak before he shoved her through the open door and slid the latch into place.

She blazed with shock. "What are you doing?" she cried, grappling with the thin bars. "What sort of game is this?"

The man smiled, but it was a mournful thing. "Don't you understand?" he asked desperately. "I can't let you leave. My paintings will turn to ash. *I* will turn to ash."

The star was silent for a minute, and her luster dimmed. "You planned this, did you not? That is why you asked me to return today."

"I can't let you go," he repeated. "But you'll see. Now they can't take you back, and we can be together."

"Release me," she said. "You know this is wrong. I would never choose it."

"I can't," he told her a third time, his voice like stone.

Days passed, and the star clung to the back of the cage, weeping. She refused any food or drink the man offered and shied away when he reached through the bars. "You're here for your own good," he asserted. "Can't you see how your court only tries to control you? Regardless of what they claim, you haven't hurt me."

The star turned her face from him.

More time passed, and the man attempted to paint. First the brush was wrong. Then the paint wouldn't mix properly. When he couldn't get the undercoating right, he tossed the canvas away in disgust. "Help me," he urged, but the star remained curled up in a ball, her back to him. "I thought you valued my art. Or was that another lie?"

The star paid him no heed.

Over the next few weeks, the man tried and tried to paint, yet nothing came forth. "What have you done to me, you stupid woman?"

The star remained withdrawn, only glaring at him through her tangles. Her eyes were bloodshot and swollen, and tearstains marred her face. The corona limning her frame seemed a faint mockery of what it had been.

One morning, after another failed attempt to create, the man approached the cage and unlocked the door. "Enough," he said. "Come here." The star cowered. "We're meant to be together. You're meant to inspire me. Why are you doing this?"

When she didn't answer, the man brutally pried her from the cage. "If you won't be with me, at least you will inspire me."

The star stared at her bare feet, now caked in grime. The man jerked her chin up so she had to meet his wrathful eyes. "Speak!" She swiped at him with her nails, but that only enraged him further. He beat her with a wooden broom handle. "Why won't you talk to me?"

The star fought back, scratching and slapping and even scorching the man. Yet in the end, he was well rested and nourished and she was not, and so she capitulated beneath the broom's onslaught, folding into herself and shielding her face with her arms.

At last the man stopped. Blood, silver and viscous as mercury, coated the handle of the broom.

The star spat at him, but the man stood entranced by the blood. "What manner of light runs through your veins?" He scraped every drop into a clay dish.

"This," he told the star, herding her back into the cage, "must be the source of your power. I'll let you go once it's mine. I just want my art back."

Then, disregarding the burns on his wrist, he dipped his brush in the blood and waited for the outpouring of inspiration.

When nothing happened, he swore. "Why isn't this *working*?"

He hurled the dish at the wall, where it splintered. A sliver of red-brown clay rebounded and punctured the side of his thumb. Cursing, he ripped it out.

The lips of the cut grazed the silvery blood on the shard, and the man drew in a loud breath when the cut not only closed but vanished altogether. The burns on his wrist, too, were gone, the skin whole as if they had never been.

"So your blood *does* have power," he said, his mouth contorting into a slow plague of a smile. "Just not the kind I thought." The star made no reply, but it was too late. He knew.

The man left without another word, abandoning the whimpering star in her cage. When he returned, he carried a clinking satchel. "You stole my vision from me," he hissed, "and now I must find another way to make a living. There are many who would pay for what your blood can do."

"No," she begged. "Just let me return home. I will say nothing of this to anyone; you have my word. Only let me go."

58

"Hardly," said the man. He emptied his satchel of its glass vials. "I gave you so many chances to return my vision to me. You wasted them all."

"How could I return what I never stole?" the star objected. "Your vision is still in you, as it has always been. All I did was wake it."

The man laughed. A glittering blade appeared in his palm. "I have a different vision now."

And, ignoring the star's pleas for mercy, her screams of pain, he began to bleed her with small, careful strokes of his knife.

Sheetal screamed, and the web of song tattered all around her.

When she came back to herself, she lay on the floor of Dev's room, right in the pile of rejected compositions. *What* was *that?*

Her heart thundered so hard she thought she might faint.

The scenes with the star and that horrible man—her lover?—had been so clear, like a movie. The thought of being able to walk freely among humans, back when they still believed in magic, blew Sheetal's heart wide open with hope. Total freedom, even acceptance. Her whole body hungered for it.

But superimposed over all of that was the bloody knife.

Her hands tingled and tingled, aching like the pins and needles that came from sitting in one position too long. No, like lines of fire running just beneath her skin. She tried massaging her palms, but that only made them hurt more.

Above her, still in bed, Dev rubbed his eyes. "I had the

weirdest dream. This is why I don't nap." He blinked blearily at her. "What're you doing down there?"

"I . . . I don't know. I had a nightmare."

"You, too? I guess we're both allergic to naps. Are you okay?"

Sheetal shifted so she could hide her hands under the bed. "I'm fine. What was your dream about?"

Dev rolled his shoulders before switching on the bedside lamp. The sudden light made Sheetal squint. "My cousin and me at some family picnic."

"That doesn't seem so bad," she said. "Unless, I don't know, you don't like eating outside."

"Well, it got weird after that. My grandfather started telling us a story." Dev frowned. "Huh—I haven't thought of that day in years."

Cousin, family picnic, grandpa telling a story. The question slipped out before Sheetal could catch it. "Wait, was the kid with the curly hair Jeet? Like in the picture?"

His frown deepened. "What?"

"And the story," she rushed on, "the one your grandpa told about the . . ."

Her tongue lurched to a halt. Even with all the momentum behind it, she couldn't bring herself to say *stars*.

*You must never let anyone know what you are.*

Her brain caught up with her mouth two seconds too late, and Sheetal blushed hard. What was she doing? Dreams were creepy sometimes, but that was no reason to make him think *she* was, too. "Never mind."

"What about the story?" Dev asked slowly. He wasn't quite meeting her eyes.

She tried for casual. "I think we both dreamed about your family. Isn't that funny?"

"What exactly did you see?" Dev's tone was cautious, as if taking care not to spook a feral animal he'd found on the street.

That decided her. She didn't need to be gentled, thanks very much. Besides, it wasn't like he'd even believe her. "A man and a star woman."

"A star woman," Dev echoed.

And then, because she clearly didn't know when to stop, Sheetal added in a spooky voice, "And a *knife*."

Dev stared at a poster on the wall, nothing relaxed or easy about him now.

Anxiety flickered deep at her core, kindling her flame. Why wasn't he teasing her back? "Dream logic, right?"

Dev took his time replying. "What happened with the knife?"

Well, Sheetal had already stuck both feet in her mouth as far as they would go, so maybe she should just tell him the rest, and then they could make fun of her over-the-top subconscious together. "The man trapped the star in a cage and then *cut* her. For her blood. Isn't that awful?"

"He cut her," Dev repeated, still looking at the poster. "You saw that."

"Yeah," she whispered, creasing and uncreasing the nearest discarded song draft. Okay, that had been a terrible idea. Now he just thought she was into violence or something. "You know what? Forget it. Who knows why anyone dreams anything?"

Dev ran a hand through his messy hair. "Jeet was right," he muttered. "I don't believe it."

That wasn't the reaction she'd expected. "Right about what?"

He faced her again, his expression oddly clinical. "Damn. You really did, didn't you. You saw my dream."

Sheetal felt like she was moving underwater. Everything was blurred and unreal. "What?"

She vaguely remembered singing to him as he'd slept, remembered the way her flame had sparked and taken her over as she'd reached for his heart with her own. But that had been part of the dream itself, hadn't it?

Or was she still dreaming right now?

When Dev spoke, he sounded awed. "You saw my grand-dad's story."

Sheetal's palms tingled even more. Now *he* was scaring *her*. She sat on her hands, hoping they'd go numb. "I don't understand."

"I'm the one who's sorry," he said, shaking his head. "I should have told you I knew."

Sheetal had to go over his words three times before she could parse them. "Told me you knew what?"

Shoving more pages out of the way, Dev joined her on the floor. His apprehensive glance skated past hers. "I've never talked to anyone outside my family about this."

"Okay . . . ," she said as patiently as she could.

"So. This is the moment where I make my grand confession," he said, but the attempt to lighten the mood fell flat. "Argh, this is— Let me put it this way. It's not . . . it's not just a story. It's a memory. My memory."

Sheetal looked down to see she'd been ripping at her cuticle. She'd never heard of being able to see other people's memories or dreams or anything like that. "I don't get it."

Dev blew out a breath. "It all really happened. A long time ago."

The ground felt like it was tilting, uncovering new vistas she'd never imagined. What was he saying, that stars really used to walk among humans like it was no big deal? And that there had been other half-stars?

A suspicion buzzed at the back of her mind like a mosquito she couldn't reach to swat: And wouldn't *that* mean he knew stars like her were real?

"Ha, ha," she said, though she couldn't be less amused if she tried. "So funny."

"I know how it sounds, but I swear I'm not making it up," Dev went on. "That guy in the story, the artist? He was my great-great-great-great-whatever-grandfather."

The artist in the story had pulled a knife on the star. Had imprisoned and bled her. Sheetal backed away, her heart contracting with horror and sadness. "Your great-great-whatever-grandfather tortured a star?!"

Charumati's vague warning to stay hidden echoed in

her ears, resonant in a way it had never been. *Where there is magic, there will always be hunger to possess it. You must hide what you are.*

Dev ran a hand over his face. "Well, this is going great." He started to reach for her, then stopped himself. "Listen, I'm so sorry. You have to know that."

Her head whirling, Sheetal slumped against the bed. She scarcely felt the metal frame biting into her shoulder blades.

She still had to be dreaming, she thought desperately. None of this made any sense. Forcing the horrific vision aside, she asked, "But why aren't you surprised I could see your dream?"

After all, if *she* hadn't known she could do that, there was no way he should be taking it so well. Right?

Dev looked confused. "Uh, because you're a star?"

The mosquito buzzing cut off. It was just Sheetal and the cosmos, holding a collective breath for her reply.

*"What?"* She laugh-snorted. Normally she would have been mortified, but that was before she'd woken up in Bizarro World. "Wait, you're serious? You really think *I'm* a star?"

It sounded pathetic even to her, a last-ditch effort to throw him off the trail.

"Look," Dev said, brushing at the back of his neck, "I'm sorry I didn't tell you I knew, but what are you playing at? I don't get it."

"What are *you* playing at, saying I'm a star?"

His gaze flicked to the pictures on the wall. "My family's always known about stars, but it's more like a superstition at this point." He shrugged. "You know, like saying you're related to Cleopatra. I didn't even really believe it until I met you."

*Because you're a star.*

Dev kept talking, describing how his forefather had gone on to become the first star hunter, but it fell on her ears like white noise.

He knew what she was. He'd known the entire time, and he'd let her think he didn't.

How had they gone from cookies to this? If only she could rewind the past hour. Her nail dug deeper into the wound on her thumb, making it scream.

"And then you inspired me, and it wasn't just a story anymore. . . ."

Sheetal's head jerked up. Her hands were on fire, the pain dialed up to ten. "What are you talking about? I didn't do anything."

The ghost of the starsong chimed as if in contradiction.

Dev was studying her like he wasn't sure if she was kidding or not. She stared at him, arms crossed, willing him to explain. "You do know I'm not your manic pixie dream girl or whatever?"

Understanding crossed his face, making his eyes crinkle. He even laughed. "No one told you stars are muses? How do you think I finished my song? You inspired me. Like, with your light."

Outrage and incredulity boiled at Sheetal's core, sending her flame roaring high. Her whole body grew hot with shame until she was sure she'd singe the carpet and all the false starts that littered it. This human boy she'd met three months ago knew more about her than she did, knew more about her magic. More than her own family had ever bothered to tell her.

The world had dissolved under her feet, leaving her unmoored.

She glared at the ceiling, wishing she could pierce it with her gaze. Wishing she could pierce the stars so they hurt like she did.

Her mind was a tornado of doubt and wrath and dread. She seized onto one thought at random, gripping it close like a life preserver, and rounded on Dev. "Oh, gods, were you going to bleed me, too, for your songs?"

He shook his head hard. "No way! How can you even think that?"

"But you knew I'm a star, and you let me inspire you, and . . ."

The clutter on the floor, which had been cute before, felt oppressive now. All those versions of his song, inspired by her. Just like his ur-grandfather and his poor star muse.

If Dev hadn't just been using her, her heart raged, why hadn't he been honest in the first place?

"I didn't *let* you inspire me!" Dev protested. "You just did it. It's what you do."

What she did? Sheetal couldn't move. What was happening to her? First her hair, now this ability to see into people's dreams . . . and inspire them without even trying.

Fear made her shout. "You knew what I was and pretended you didn't!"

"What did you want me to say, Sheetal?" Dev yelled back. He'd crushed the hem of his T-shirt in both fists. "My family hated stars? My great-whatever-grandfather tried to kill one? Because yeah, it's true, he did. But here's the thing: nobody except Jeet even believes you exist anymore—"

"Dev. Stop," she cried. "Even if they don't believe it, why would your family want to remember a story like that? That man would've wanted me *dead*. He would've wanted my mom dead. What would Jeet say if you told him you'd found me?"

Dev looked as miserable as she felt. "He's actually the one who told me where to find you. He wanted me to get to know you, but—"

"He what?" Sheetal's knees trembled. What was she supposed to do with all of this? With the silver flame crackling violently at her core?

She scrutinized him, this beautiful boy she'd kissed and confided her silliest thoughts to, who made her alternately laugh and swoon, whom she'd thought she might love. She traced the planes of his face, the arch of his lips, the mischievous, dark eyes that never failed to make her melt—until now.

You didn't lie to the people you cared about. You definitely didn't pretend to like them.

Her cheeks burned. She was a fool.

Dev reached for her again. "I should've told you I knew sooner. I wanted to—"

"My mom warned me about people like you." The words fought their way free of Sheetal's mouth, ready to scald everyone and everything to cinders. "I can't believe you knew all this, and you didn't say a word. How am I supposed to trust you?"

He bowed his head. "Will you please just listen—"

"I have to go." She needed to get away from this house owned by people whose relatives had—had—and who might still . . . She couldn't even think it, it was so huge and awful.

All of this was so huge and awful.

Sheetal sprinted down to the kitchen for her bag, skirting the island so she wouldn't glimpse the leftover cookies. The thought of them just made her want to throw up or cry or both.

In a daze, she went outside and texted Minal. The first rays of the setting sun spilled down, a sweet-tart torrent of mango juice that meant Dad would be home from work soon—and the sidereal song would be back in full force.

Naturally Minal didn't answer, and of course Sheetal didn't have any cash for a taxi or even a bus. And it was too far to walk. Of course.

She figured she might as well do the one thing guaranteed to make this crap day even worse.

Sheetal called Radhikafoi to come get her.

An hour later, huddled on the burgundy leather sofa in Radhikafoi's Pine-Sol–scented living room, Sheetal watched her cousins jab buttons on their video-game controllers while her auntie and Dad talked in low voices. This latest model would be gone within a day or two; Radhikafoi had just cooed to Dad about a gold-and-green Victorian settee in a local antique store. It wouldn't match any of her contemporary décor mixed with Indian folk art, but since when did that matter?

Since when did anything matter?

Dev's claim that she'd inspired him set her even more on edge. She tugged on a piece of fringe lining a throw pillow, almost unraveling it. How could that be true?

Sheetal's messenger bag sat at her feet. Now it dinged with a text message. Her eyes dry and scratchy, her nerves sparking like live wires, she reached in and pulled out her phone.

*I never wanted you to inspire me. I want to write songs about you, not because of you.*

"Who was that?" Radhikafoi called from the kitchen. "Is it that boy?"

"It's no one." Even as Sheetal lied, she sent back a string of flame emojis followed by plenty of knives and skulls. It felt awesome.

But not for long. Smoldering underneath was the hurt, the broken heart emojis she typed and then deleted before pushing her phone away. It wasn't just that he'd lied, as much as that rankled. But by not telling her the truth, he'd cheated her. She could have had one more person who shared her secret, someone she could've been herself with while hiding from the rest of the world.

Her throat stung. She wouldn't have had to be so alone.

"Chhokri," said Dad from his recliner, calling her "girl" in the angry tone he almost never took with her, "what did I tell you about boys?"

Radhikafoi bustled into the room, set down three cups of masala chaa on the coffee table, shooed out Akshay and Kumar, and commenced hovering.

"Well," continued Dad, "I'm waiting. What did I say?"

Sheetal stared at the teacups, at the wisps of spiced steam dancing up from them. "You said no boys until I'm older." Which was so unfair; when had she ever given Dad a reason to worry about her with Dev?

She glared at her phone. Though apparently he'd been right to worry about Dev.

The starsong, which had been chiming nonstop since the sun set, rang out fully, and Sheetal's palms tingled with the force of it. She couldn't sit still, her feet digging into the sofa cushion and her fingers tearing at the skin around her thumbnail. What good was being half star if she couldn't burn the feelings out of her chest?

"Chhokri," Dad said again, sipping his tea, "I've been lenient with you, and you went behind my back. What does that tell me? That I should start listening to your foi and keeping you home?"

"When we were children, we would never have dreamed of disobeying our parents," Radhikafoi interjected. "Even today, if my mother came in and told me to sit down, I would sit down without thinking."

"We're not in India," Sheetal said, knowing she was out of

line and not caring. At least she didn't add, *Where Dad told me you two got in trouble all the time.*

"Aray vaah! Listen to this girl, so much smarter and grown up than us," her auntie mocked. "So in America, you talk back and misbehave?"

"Didi." Dad raised his hand. "Let me handle it."

"I'm only saying, Tashan's mummy told me she is busy working through the PSAT practice test book while Sheetal wants to waste her summer running around with boys!"

*You're not my mom,* Sheetal thought. *It's not your business what I do!* Sweat dribbled down her back and pooled under her arms. Gods, she hated this stupid leather sofa and the way it clung to her skin. "Can we *please* turn on the AC? It's burning up in here!"

Radhikafoi gave her an odd look. "It *is* on. Beti, you don't look well. I'll get you some water." She scampered into the kitchen, then returned with a metal cup of cold water.

Sheetal gulped the water, enjoying the cup's chill on her prickling palms, as Dad explained the need to be respectful and trust one's parents. "We don't say these things just to say them. My job is to keep you out of trouble."

"Really, Dad?" she interrupted finally, unable to take it anymore. Her heart blistered with resentment. "We're talking about trust? That's funny."

Dad exchanged a worried glance with Radhikafoi. "What do you mean?"

Once the words started to flow, Sheetal couldn't hold them

back. "Did you know? About stars inspiring humans? I mean, of course you knew. You were married to Mom."

Dad's shoulders drooped like she'd struck the wind out of him. He opened his mouth and closed it again.

Radhikafoi, of course, had no problem answering, but whatever she said blended into an insipid hum as Sheetal focused on Dad.

She hated seeing him so despondent, but she also hated that he'd thought it was okay to hide this from her. Enough with secrets. Keeping them hadn't helped anybody. "I know stars are muses, Dad. I saw it."

With a sigh, Dad moved to sit by her on the couch. "Tell me what happened. Did you inspire Dev?"

"So you did know." It still felt like a blow to the stomach. She choked back the sudden rush of tears in her throat. "Why didn't you tell me?"

Dad patted her knee. "I wanted to protect you, dikri."

"We both did," added Radhikafoi. "For your own good."

The humming worsened into a whine. Sheetal's brain was vaporizing. Her core was liquefying. Radhikafoi, always interfering. Always presuming to know what was best for everyone else.

For a second, all Sheetal saw was silver.

"From what?" she demanded. "Didn't *Mom* inspire *you*?"

Dad stilled. "Once. The Nobel Prize."

When Sheetal was five, Dad and his team of researchers had won the prize for a theoretical discovery that addressed the problem of radiation exposure during space travel. The award was a sensational first milestone in what should have been a long and illustrious career.

But it hadn't been. Making that discovery was the last time Dad had ever stood out, to the point that his colleagues called it a cosmic fluke.

How had Sheetal not known? How had she not realized?

Her phone dinged. Another message from Dev. *I was going to tell you, I swear. Eventually.*

"Does he know?" Dad asked urgently.

"That I inspired him? What I am? All of the above." Sheetal left out the part about Dev's ancestor attacking hers. Radhikafoi didn't deserve the satisfaction. "*You* should have told me, Dad."

Trying to ignore the sweat beading over her entire body, she leaned back against the couch and closed her eyes. The whine in her head grew louder, one question repeating itself: Why would Dad have kept this from her?

Radhikafoi came over and felt Sheetal's forehead. "You're burning up!" To Dad, she said, "First her roots, now this. It's happening."

Sheetal jerked away. "It's not a big deal. Honestly."

Ding. *I threw away the song. I'm sorry. Just talk to me?*

"I wanted to spare you this." Dad's mouth turned down, and he sighed again. "I'm sorry, dikri. I thought if we just kept you safe . . ."

She grabbed the now-lukewarm chaa he'd abandoned and gulped it down. She was so hot, so thirsty. Someone had switched out her heart for a live coal, and she felt incandescent. She felt like starlight and fire and fury all mixed into one. All she could do was burn.

Ding. *Sheetal?* 😵💔

"If we don't look out for you, beti," asked Radhikafoi, "who will?" She turned to Dad. "Bhai, we have to give it to her. It's time."

The astral melody brushed past Sheetal's ears, her heart, soft as rays of starlight.

All the words began to smear together—Dad's, Radhikafoi's, Dev's. The red of the sofa and the yellow of the lamplight swirled before Sheetal's eyes until all she could see was the spark that had flared within her. She stared, transfixed. It appeared in her left palm, then in her right, and then . . .

*No*, thought Sheetal. *No.*

The flame in her rose up.

Sheetal had only glowed once before in her life, and that was when she'd danced with her mother in the shadow-cloaked field behind their house, their constellation—their family—singing above them. It had been so natural to unleash the radiance inside her, simple and automatic as the beat of her breath. She was half a star, after all.

The flame rose higher still.

Yet after a night of nursing her fears, Charumati had warned Sheetal about people who would hurt her, had warned Radhikafoi, and Sheetal had had no choice but to push it all down. Until now.

Her phone rang, and she jumped, knocking it to the floor.

Dad grasped her wrist. "Sheetal."

Her hands, one wrist securely in Dad's grip, sparkled.

It was the silver fire at her core, eager to be free—and for the space of a second, it was.

The brush of eyelash meeting eyelash.

And it should have been all right—would have been all right—except Dad didn't let go. In that same instant, the silver flame limned him, searing.

Gasping, brown face gray, Dad dropped her wrist and clutched his chest. Before Sheetal could say a word, before she could do a thing, he collapsed.

6

Someone at the ICU finally waved Sheetal through, and someone else escorted her to the door of Dad's private room. All she could see was an army of ugly machines surrounding an adjustable gurney. Screens, wires, electric arms . . . Where was Dad?

There, lost in the metal-frame hospital bed. He'd been dressed in a sad little paper gown. Wires and tubes protruded from what seemed to be every part of him, chaining him to hulking devices with their monitors and pitiless beeping.

*Go home,* Sheetal told herself even as she approached the bed, where Radhikafoi stood talking to the attending physician, a black woman with a light blue surgical mask hanging around her neck and a matching scrub cap. *You don't want to see this.*

"Your brother has suffered a severe cardiac arrest," the doctor explained. "We've stabilized him, but there's been loss of tissue. How much, we're not yet sure. We're going to continue monitoring him."

Radhikafoi mouthed a prayer to the wallet-sized picture of Gayatri Ma she always kept in her purse. Its saturated turquoise and lotus pink made the rest of the room look washed out in comparison.

Sheetal fought against the urge to get lost in those colors until she shut down. *Severe cardiac arrest. Loss of tissue,* her mind chanted. Because of her.

The doctor noticed Sheetal and softened her tone. "I need to warn you that it might be hard to see your father like this. He's on a respirator, and there are a lot of wires and equipment. It can be frightening if you're not used to it."

"It's all right if you change your mind," Radhikafoi said in Gujarati.

"I need to see him," Sheetal stated in English, so the doctor would hear, too.

The doctor nodded. "We'll need to keep this visit brief, to allow him to rest," she said as she left. "Just five minutes."

Sheetal skimmed Dad's sleeping face. The mild pitting at his temple held her fast. It was the enduring stamp of childhood chickenpox. *Run,* her heart cried. She could pretend she'd never seen the scar, pretend she didn't know this withered man.

The doctor was wrong. It wasn't the machines that scared her. It was this.

Beep. Beep. Beep.

*Dad.* Sheetal closed her eyes, then fumbled for his hand. It was warm, his pulse thready. This strong, careful hand had taught her how to hold a pencil, then how to use that pencil to add and subtract and play with imaginary numbers. It had patted her head when she'd done well and tweaked her nose when she hadn't. Even more than the scar, this hand told her the doctors hadn't made a mistake.

She sucked in air until it hurt. Her lips trembled as she squeezed his unresponsive hand. She wouldn't cry. She wouldn't.

Helplessness ate at her stomach. If she hadn't gone to see Dev, Dad wouldn't have gotten so stressed, and they wouldn't have fought, and she wouldn't have burned him.

She had put Dad in this bed. She was responsible.

Beep. Beep. Beep.

She looked down at the wound on her thumb, barely scabbed over. Something glimmered within her—her own blood. A memory surfaced, one she'd locked away with everything else.

Years ago, Sheetal had crashed her bike and scraped her knees. She'd sobbed as Charumati later dabbed the skin with rubbing alcohol but had forgotten to cry when her normally garnet blood then turned the color of stardust. Her mother had offered a shaky smile. "Stay calm, and it will go back to the way it was," she'd murmured, blowing on the abrasions, and it had. "Let us keep this our little secret, shall we?"

No matter how many times Sheetal had gotten injured after that, she'd never seen the silver again.

79

Beep. Beep. Beep. The annoying machine shocked her back to the present. Radhikafoi now stood on the opposite side of the bed, clutching Dad's other hand. What an awful room this was, with its sand-pale walls and sick, antiseptic smell. A room to die in.

"It doesn't look good, dikra," her auntie murmured. Her purplish lipstick had worn away, leaving only a ring around the edges of her mouth. It made her look old. "Internal hemorrhaging. They've stopped the bleeding, but they can't repair the tissue that's already dead."

Something hot and consuming engulfed Sheetal. "Who said that? Who said it doesn't 'look good'?"

Radhikafoi fished a paper napkin out of her purse. "The doctor. She didn't want to say it in front of you, but she doesn't think he'll wake up."

"What does *she* know?"

Radhikafoi didn't respond, only dabbed at her eyes, and that made Sheetal even angrier.

Her *dad* was in that bed. Her dad, who called her his little sparrow and played Scrabble with her and had surprised her with her very first book on astronomy. That still, silent body lying there now, the body she couldn't look at—how could that be him?

Her auntie always had something to say. Why wasn't she offering solutions now?

Sheetal held her breath, hoping. Hating herself for needing Radhikafoi to take charge.

More than anything, for needing Radhikafoi to say it was nobody's fault.

When her auntie stayed quiet, Sheetal paced around the room, skirting the bed. She couldn't look down. She couldn't quit being mad. Without her ire, she'd be small and squishy, a snail without a shell.

Snails without shells got stepped on and smashed into the pavement.

"I don't want this, either," Radhikafoi said, but that was it.

Sheetal clawed through her memories, hunting for something, anything her mother might have said or done. A clue.

One of the monitors tracing Dad's vital signs lit up, and she automatically glanced toward it. She found herself gazing right at Dad, at the sallowness of his skin, and felt like someone had body-slammed her.

There had to be something. There just had to.

Her frenzied thoughts chased one another by the tail, circling around a particular vision. Silver . . . the drop of blood . . . that star . . .

Sheetal fast-forwarded to the end of Dev's dream, even though it made her gag. That man, that monster, had lit up with avarice when he'd—what? She froze that frame and zoomed in. There it was—his smirk, his fully mended hand. The moment when he'd realized the star's blood had done it, and that she could still be useful to him, after all.

Sheetal's own palms prickled in sympathy. Then—she jammed her fist against her mouth—then he'd cut the star.

He'd meant to bleed her. Again and again. So he could sell it. Again and again.

Because, like a magic potion, the star's blood could heal.

Sheetal gulped down huge lungfuls of chemical-tasting hospital air. She was half a star. A star's blood flowed in her veins. *What if?*

She had to try.

Pushing Dev and his horrible ancestor out of her head, pushing aside Radhikafoi and her judgment, Sheetal ripped away the scab on her thumb.

A single red droplet welled up.

Still watching Dad's face, she shoved down the collar of his hospital gown. Then, pretending to hug him, she pressed her torn cuticle to the skin over his heart. His pulse beat weakly beneath his ribs, but at least it was there.

"I'm sorry," she whispered against his chest.

*Please*, she begged the blood, the gods, that long-ago star. *Be enough. Help him.*

The smear of blood flashed pewter like mercury, becoming light, a beautiful, soothing, starry light. She stared at it, waiting for Dad's pulse to gain strength, praying he would open his eyes. *Please. Please, please, please.*

It fizzled out, fading back to scarlet.

A nurse rapped on the doorframe. "Time's up," she said firmly.

Now Sheetal did cry—ugly, snotty, racking sobs. She'd failed. At the sight of the red smudge, the guilt she'd kept at bay stormed over her, leaden, devastating. She barely felt Radhikafoi's hand on her back, guiding her out.

She was going to lose Dad, and it was all her fault.

Sheetal had barely gotten out of the car before Minal hopped up from Radhikafoi's front stoop and pounced, nearly knocking her over and setting off the motion light in the process. "Sheetal texted me," she explained. "I'm so sorry, Auntie."

A solitary point of warmth glimmered amidst the cold and sorrow in Sheetal's chest. She hugged Minal back as tight as she could.

"Thank you, beti. Come in. Just be quiet; the boys are sleeping." Radhikafoi unlocked the door and hurried them inside to the great room, where she turned on a standing lamp before heading upstairs.

"All right," said Minal, sprawling over the leather sofa. It squeaked in protest. "Lay it on me. How's your dad? How're *you*?"

Sheetal sat down, too, trying not to think of how, just hours earlier, she'd been here with Dad. "He's—not great."

She recounted the afternoon at Dev's, coming home to burn Dad, and her botched attempt to heal him. Like a ticking clock, the astral melody framed the moment in chimes and trills.

As if she didn't know how little time Dad had.

She stared at the familiar cloth painting of Krishna dancing with all his gopis. Her blood had come so close. Almost close enough. But almost wouldn't heal anyone.

"Ouch," Minal said. "I'd say that definitely qualifies as the day from hell." She paused, then added, "You know none of this is your fault, right?"

Sheetal wouldn't look at her. Of course it was.

Her phone dinged. She glanced at the screen, then buried the phone under a cushion. "Why can't he take a hint?"

Minal held out her hand. "Give me that." Sheetal did, and Minal scrolled back through the messages. "Listen, I really need to talk to you."

Sheetal tilted her head. "We *are* talking?"

"That's what *Dev* said, you dork: 'Listen, I really need to talk to you.'"

"Well, too bad for him." Sheetal had meant that to be sarcastic, but it just sounded sad. "He had his chance."

When Minal didn't immediately agree, Sheetal narrowed her eyes. "What?"

"It was crap of him not to tell you what was going on sooner, for sure, but how do you bring up something like that? 'Hey, so I hear you're a star?'" Minal shrugged. "I'm just saying it might be worth hearing him out."

Sheetal didn't want to be reasonable, not when she couldn't forget the red smudge on Dad's chest, couldn't help fearing he was gone for good. She wanted to be *mad*. "I don't care. He should have told me."

Radhikafoi charged back in then, armed with an envelope. "I knew this day would come," she announced, cutting off whatever Minal might have said, "and I prayed every night it would be years from now. Decades. But your naseeb says otherwise, and I cannot hold you here. Take this."

"What is it?" Sheetal asked. She wasn't sure what to make of that little speech.

When Radhikafoi met Sheetal's stare, there was pain in her face. She looked weary. "A letter from your mummy. About you."

Radhikafoi's words seemed to echo through a long, winding tunnel, barely finding Sheetal before breaking apart. And when they did, they didn't fit together. A letter from Charumati? About her?

It took Sheetal three short steps to reach her auntie and claim the envelope. The paper's velvety texture felt like the spell that held her in its sway when she played her music, when she gazed up at the stars. It felt like something immense and wondrous, like the night sky itself. "Where did you get this, Radhikafoi?"

"Your mummy—who else? She never forgot you, beta. She left you here to keep you safe."

Just one day ago, Sheetal had been so sure she knew the people in her life. Now she had to wonder if they'd all turned into strangers.

She grasped for the anger that had sustained her all evening, but all she found was emptiness. "You had my mother's letter," she whispered. "All this time."

"Yes."

"Why didn't you tell me?"

85

"What do you think I'm doing now?" Radhikafoi asked with her usual impatience. "It's in Gujarati. I'll read it to you."

Sheetal shook her head. She couldn't let her foi read her mother's message to her. "Minal can do it."

Minal watched her with concern. "Are you sure?"

Part of Sheetal—her raw, lonely heart—couldn't wait to devour her mother's words. The rest of her, the bones that had always acted as armor to shield that susceptible heart, wanted to shred the letter before it could possibly hurt her.

*She left you here to keep you safe.*

Sheetal sat back down next to Minal. "I'm sure."

The envelope and single slip of paper within were a light purple the color of lilacs, with a blue-green peacock feather motif in the corner of each. Charumati's neat Gujarati script lined the page in silver ink bright enough to be starlight. As Minal read the words aloud, Sheetal imagined she could feel her mother's pen pressing the syllables into the paper.

*Dear Radhikaben,*

*You and I might have had our differences, but trust me when I say you can no more marvel at the stars than we do at mortal men and women. Indeed, you have always been a source of wonder and fascination to me, in your rigidness and love of order and your distrust of all things outside your control. Surely you will be the first to applaud my decision to return to Svargalok. This world of mortals is no place for me, where your kind would stone me merely for shining or hunt me for my blood. How merrily, how callously, you prey on one another like predators in the lanternless dark.*

*So I take my leave but beseech you as one mother to another to turn your vigilance to your niece, my daughter. My heart grows heavy with regret at parting from her sweet smile, yet my court is no haven for her at present. Still, the time will come when she must ascend, when she will hear our call, and as I have told Gautam, you will know when to give her this missive and bring her to the harp sisters. They will show her the way. Until then, I trust you to teach my Sheetal all the ways of being human and, above all, to guard her well.*

*And Radhikaben, do be gentle with Gautam, for despite your valiant efforts, he has yet some of the dreamer in him. As do you.*

*Fondly,*
*Charumati*

Sheetal's eyes stung. Her mother *hadn't* just abandoned her and never looked back.

She used to dream about this moment, pray for it, and now that it was here, she didn't know what to feel. Hollow, maybe. Like she wanted to go to bed for a million years.

Just like Dev, Radhikafoi had kept the truth from her. All this time, she'd let Sheetal think Charumati didn't care.

87

And Dad had gone along with it.

An abyss yawned behind her ribs, the exact shape of her blood as it silvered before returning to a worthless red. Her palms tingled furiously, and the sidereal song pulled hard at her skin, her core, almost like strong arms trying to carry her away.

But something began to emerge from her despair. *When she must ascend, when she will hear our call.*

The starry melody. No wonder it had ramped up like that. It was summoning her to the sky. Maybe this had to do with her birthday—she *was* about to turn seventeen.

She took the letter back from Minal and stared at the graceful handwriting until the tingling dissipated. Then she addressed her auntie. "Harp sisters? What harp sisters?"

"Your mummy told me about a Night Market where people . . . people like *her* sold things." Distaste seeped from Radhikafoi's words. "Magical things. I never would have believed it if I hadn't seen your mummy do . . . what she did. Not even these could have convinced me."

She deposited something in Sheetal's lap.

Miniature clouds. Two of them. Or to be more accurate, miniature clouds with barrettes attached to them. Sheetal prodded one, and it promptly turned dark gray, like its brethren in the sky. A minuscule lightning bolt forked through it, followed by a rumble of thunder the strength of a kitten's purr.

Stunned, Sheetal almost threw it down. The cloud calmed, now fluffy and white. Playing innocent.

Sentient cloud barrettes. A letter from her long-absent mother. A call to ascend. Every time she thought she was getting her footing back, the ground shifted again.

"Your mummy gave those to me not long before she left." Radhikafoi sounded anything but pleased. "A waste of money. Where was I supposed to wear them? The bank? To get my oil changed?"

Sheetal kept her eyes on the painting of Krishna, even as her fingers edged back toward the barrettes. Magic. In her lap. And her auntie had hidden that, too. "You really didn't like her, did you?"

"We didn't have much in common, if that's what you mean." Radhikafoi paused. "But she made your papa happy, and I know she loved you."

Minal, who'd been studying the barrettes like a magpie, now snatched them up and clipped them into her hair. Indignant, they exploded with seed pearl–sized lightning.

"When your mummy gave me those *things*," Radhikafoi said, "she asked me to show you her letter and take you to the Night Market where she bought them. We were to look for a pair of sisters who played the harp."

"And you decided for me that I couldn't go?" Sheetal's voice climbed higher. "You didn't think you should even tell me that kind of market existed?"

"Sheetal," Radhikafoi said, her own voice devoid of emotion, "my first husband abandoned me and stole my dowry."

Sheetal went still. Her auntie had mentioned her first

husband exactly once before, and that was just to say how much better off she was without him.

"I had to fight to get to this country," Radhikafoi went on, "only to find the same ugly things happened to women here. You tell me—what good have fairy tales ever done any of us? As long as my family is safe, and I can be of some use in the world, I'm happy."

It made Sheetal itchy to think of her forceful auntie being discarded like garbage. "You never told me that, about being abandoned."

"There was no need to. The point is, dikri, we were doing all right. I was protecting you."

"Until I nearly killed Dad."

Silence. Even Minal's barrettes stopped thundering.

As Sheetal watched her auntie, waiting for the inevitable comeback, a thought popped into her head. Her mother's letter had mentioned blood—being hunted for it.

Being a half-star wasn't enough. Her blood wasn't enough. But Charumati's would be.

The rightness of the idea warmed Sheetal beat by beat, in time with the sidereal song. There was still a chance to fix things. "You have to take me to this Night Market right now." Then she uttered the words she'd never dared even think. "I need to find my mom."

To her astonishment, Radhikafoi merely nodded. "Why else did I give you the letter?"

The flame at Sheetal's core leaped high as if she were already on her way to the skies, as if this had already been decided long ago. It was scary how relieved she felt. Her mother, her family, was calling her to them.

But they'd also just thrown her away all this time, like it didn't matter what she thought. What she needed. That was enough to make her at least try to resist. "Wait, it's an enchanted market, right? Maybe we can find a healing potion, and I won't even need to go."

"That may be, and I certainly hope so, but you still need to learn how to control your . . . gifts." Radhikafoi's pinched expression made clear she thought said gifts really should have come with a return receipt. "I can't teach you that."

"So what are we waiting for?" Minal looked expectantly at Sheetal, the clouds in her hair now a dove gray.

"Not we," Sheetal corrected. "Just me. If it wasn't safe for my mom down here, who says it's any better for you up there?"

"I can take care of myself." Minal sounded insulted. "Besides, you promised not to take off without me, remember?"

Sheetal hesitated. She really, really didn't want to do this by herself. "I don't know. I wouldn't even go if it wasn't for Dad."

Yikes, that scathing quirk of Minal's eyebrow could shame whole armies into submission. "You wouldn't, huh? You'd just keep pretending there wasn't a magical Night Market *in our town*? Or that you're not dying to see your mom's court for yourself?"

She definitely had Sheetal there. "Okay, what about your parents? You can't just disappear, and I'm going to guess phones don't work up in the heavens."

Minal smiled smugly and rested her head on Sheetal's shoulder. "Radhika Auntie will tell them I'm at your house, comforting you." She grew solemn. "I'm not going to let you do this alone, so deal with it. Plus, you know, *magic*."

The hole in Sheetal's heart shrank a little. Even if everything and everyone else was falling to pieces, she still had her best friend.

She laid her own head on top of Minal's, careful to avoid the mercurial barrettes. "Fine, you can come. Twist my arm off, jeez."

Radhikafoi eyed them with open doubt. "And just how will Minal go with you?"

"I fold up small," Minal said, right as Sheetal said, "She'll fit in my bag."

Radhikafoi clicked her tongue, but whether it was in exasperation or just plain defeat, Sheetal couldn't say. "You'd better pack your things, then."

7

Radhikafoi turned the car right onto Oak Tree Road, and Little India came into view. A golden mist had replaced the mortal stores and restaurants, a gauzy mantle behind which a carnival of stalls glittered, beguiling against the darkness.

The Night Market. It had been here all along. How many times had they come to Little India as a family to go shopping for desi groceries and clothes or for a vegetarian thali or chaat at their favorite spots? And no one had ever thought to inform Sheetal that there was magic for sale, too?

They'd been arguing the whole drive about exactly that. "There was no need for you to know," Radhikafoi reiterated.

From the back seat, Minal poked Sheetal hard in the shoulder, but she ignored the signal to shut up. "No need?"

"You and your questions!" Radhikafoi sucked her teeth. "Let's just do what we came here to do." Her face was impassive, even disapproving, but her hands shook as she parked on the vacant street.

As soon as the engine turned off, Sheetal stomped out of the car. She felt as limp and wrung-out as an old dish towel, and what she wanted more than anything was a hot bath and spiced drinking chocolate and, oh, to wake up from the nightmare that she'd put her own father in a hospital bed. Did the Market sell *that*?

Radhikafoi quickly caught up, Minal beside her. "These people are not trustworthy. Stay close to me."

As they drew near, the Market shimmered into solidity. An arch in the shape of a peacock's fan appeared before the entrance. Its feathers were composed of segments of glass in teal, green, cobalt, and violet, all of which glowed from within. Forgetting her exhaustion, Sheetal drank in the light, letting it slide down her throat and into her bloodstream, but froze when the peacock lowered its house-sized head to study her with living eyes. It let out a catlike cry.

Radhikafoi tensed as if to run, her own eyes wide as a cartoon character's. "Beta, get back! Both of you!"

Sheetal didn't. Meeting the peacock's disturbing stare straight on, she said, "We're here for the Night Market."

"It's not going to eat us, right?" Minal whispered.

"If it does, it was nice knowing you," Sheetal whispered back. It felt nice to joke for a minute, when everything else was awful and unpredictable. To know she didn't have to do this alone.

She did hope it wouldn't eat them, though.

The peacock blinked once, twice, then opened its beak

until the entire archway shone through it. Just beyond, figures moved, tinkling laughter merged with baritone chuckles, and out wafted scents so fine they could only have come from the heavenly realm.

*Dad*, Sheetal told him, praying he could hear it somehow, *this is for you.*

Then she linked arms with Minal, and they stepped into the peacock's mouth. Behind them, Radhikafoi made a choking noise.

Before Sheetal knew it, she stood inside the Market, its sinuous allure slinking into her bones and her blood. Music swirled invitingly through her as she gazed at the glimmering horizon. Her thoughts bloomed with wonder, all jewel tones and reinvigorating hope.

If there was a way to save Dad, it would be here.

All around them, intricately decorated stalls overflowed with impossible goods, and the patrons who browsed them were just as odd. A family of kinnaras, their equine heads fusing seamlessly with their human lower bodies, examined a carved copper lantern encrusted with gems in colors Sheetal had never seen before. Nearby, an apsara who might have been sculpted from marble, she was so enticing, haggled over a selection of black-and-silver bottles shaped like birds in flight. "But I want green," she said, her perfect mouth set in a pout.

"I'm sorry," said the stall owner, a young man who could have himself been the hero in a Bollywood love story, "but all I have in stock is what you see here."

Sheetal stood rooted to the mosaic-tiled floor, trying really hard not to ogle. By accident or ardent wish, she'd stumbled into a mythic wonderland. It was all so strange, so seductive, that if this had been any other day, she would have been raring to see it all, taste it all, to unearth rusty keys to hidden cabinets of curiosities and gulp down steaming purple potions that would send her on adventures in imaginary realms.

"Sheetal!" snapped Radhikafoi. "Minal!" She gripped Sheetal's arm hard enough to bruise. "I've been trying to get you to listen for ten minutes. Come now."

Ten minutes? It had felt like thirty seconds. Sheetal fought to loosen herself from the Night Market's glamour. How could she have forgotten Dad?

Minal, too, looked dazed. "This place . . . I could lose myself here. We need to be careful."

"Ah, yes," said a sly voice far too close to Sheetal's ear. "A young girl brimming over with want. Stewing in it like vegetables in dal. Want goes so well with rice, wouldn't you say?" A wrinkled brown finger beckoned. Sheetal stared down its length to find an old woman in a maroon-and-gold sari. "Come to my stall, child, and see if we can't find something to plug up that hole in your heart."

"*My* heart's not the one that needs help," Sheetal said.

"Everyone's heart seeks something." The vendor scurried back behind the counter of her stall. "A cream, a charm, a confirmation."

Radhikafoi sniffed but waved Sheetal forward.

She shared a cautious glance with Minal, then took in the tent before them. It might have been an illustration in a storybook: fireflies floated from the roof on delicate chains, illuminating the assortment of wares in lavender, powder blue, and hot pink light.

They were pretty spectacular wares, to be sure: Diamond-eyed onyx spiders that perched in customers' hair, weaving elaborate cobweb headdresses while whispering arcane secrets in the arachnid tongue. Bouquets of silver poppies, garlands of copper jasmine blossoms, long-stemmed rainbow roses. Bottles of serenity and stillness, bottles of chaos and creation. Gems containing freshly harvested dreams.

"How about a potion to help my dad's heart?" Sheetal asked.

"Some hearts," said the vendor, as if she hadn't heard, "seek their reflection in the form of a lover's rapt gaze." She thrust a silver hand mirror at Sheetal, ordinary but for a single brown eye where the glass should have been. As if someone were peering through the frame—and winking.

Sheetal nudged the mirror away. That was *not* how she wanted Dev to see her. Not that she cared what he thought anymore. "No, thanks. If you don't have a potion, can you at least tell me if you've seen anyone who plays the harp?"

The vendor cackled. "I have a better question. Tell me, do you know the secret at the center of a rotting mushroom?"

"This is foolishness," Radhikafoi told them. "Come, dikriyo."

In another stall, Minal asked after the harp sisters while twirling a golden apple on its dew-damp branch. In a third,

Sheetal picked up, then put down, decanters of black beetle-wing wine and unguents for forming a peridot carapace of one's skin. Wonder steeped in her like starlight.

"I want it. All of it," Minal murmured, her voice heavy with longing. "Promise we'll come back?"

Sheetal loved this place, all the glorious things, all the ghastly things. She could spend the rest of the night spellbound. But they hadn't found either the harp sisters or anything to help Dad, never mind a way for Minal to get to Svargalok. "We will. After."

Then, across the way, in a stall so impenetrably dark the night paled next to it, she saw a jar full of marbles, each an entire world. Infinite worlds like infinite stories—the old yearning tugged, heartsore, in her chest. A pull toward something else, something she had no name for.

The flame at her core kindled. Here, it whispered, she could be seen, fully and freely.

She picked up the jar of marble worlds.

"Ah," said the vendor, a vetala cloaked all in black with a hooded yellow stare every bit as shrewd as the spiders'. "You pursue it even now, do you not? Your place in all things? A place to belong?"

Sheetal felt coated in invisible slime. Had this creature, a spirit that had possessed a corpse to get around, just read her mind? "I'm looking for the harp sisters. Do you know where I can find them?"

"Find yourself first, little child caught between. Always

floating, always seeking," the vetala said. His smile grew sharper. "Did I mention that with practice, you can visit each of the worlds in the jar?"

For a sliver of an instant, Sheetal let herself imagine slipping away to another world, one where she might find answers scattered like coins from a change purse. Or better, an alternate timeline in which Charumati had stayed, Dad was fine, stars walked freely among humans again, and Dev had no ugly family history. A place where Sheetal could just relax. That sounded like the true heavenly realm.

She was so tempted, it hurt.

"My price is so small, a pittance. Merely a piece of you. I know—how about a prized memory?"

An image broke through her thoughts, Charumati's warm lips brushing five-year-old Sheetal's forehead the day Dad unscrewed the training wheels from her bike and gave it a first push into independence. *I can do it, Mommy,* she'd insisted, nervous but trying not to show it. *Take them off!*

The memory strained to uproot itself and sail toward the vetala's open flask. Sheetal shoved it, and the jar, back down. "No!"

Dev's grin shone in her mind, followed by Dad's disappointed ire. Too bad today hardly counted as a prized memory. She'd give *that* up in a heartbeat.

"A year of your life, then," offered the vetala, leaning over the counter. "You would never miss it."

Minal inserted herself between them. "Nope. Not ever."

"Why are mortals always so certain their life is worth living?" the vetala groused, though his smile remained wide and eerie. "Even the most wretched among you clings desperately to the same miserable existence you pray to be rescued from."

"Dikra!" Radhikafoi cautioned.

"A simple thing, really," said the vetala to Sheetal. "A single strand of your hair would do. But free of that unseemly pigment." He tittered. "Who do you believe you are fooling, child?"

It would be so easy just to pluck a strand in exchange for the chance to escape. To have the *more* she'd always craved.

But the Dad in that other world didn't need her. The one in this world did. "Another time, maybe."

"Buy now, or buy never," the vetala warned. His disconcerting eyes vanished into the mass of folds created by his gleeful grin. "For what you see here today may well be gone tomorrow."

"Buy nothing now!" barked Radhikafoi, glaring at him. "We're here to help your papa, dikra, nothing else."

"He speaks true, my neighbor does!" called the merchant in a nearby stall, a middle-aged woman with the voice of a flute. "The Market fluctuates with each breath, and none can know who will remain from night to night. So come close and let me dress you! I have such exquisite fabrics on offer, all cut in the latest styles. Cloth-of-sky! Velvet spun from amethyst! If you can dream it, you can wear it, as I like to say."

"Amethyst velvet? Just take my money." Minal led Sheetal toward the adjacent stall.

A spectrum of opulent textiles greeted them there. Each bolt was more luscious than the last: shining crimson spider silk, pure flame tatting with gracefully smoking edges, blue-green organza obtained from cresting ocean waves. Sheetal ran covetous fingers over the delicate sea-foam trim. She remembered seeing her mother wearing clothes like this once or twice when Dad took her out to New York City.

The apsara Sheetal had seen earlier entered the shop and began to riffle through the bolts. A stylized golden crown sat atop her long black hair, and jewels dripped like afterthoughts from her ears, throat, and wrists. She draped a length of cloth-of-sky against her shapely frame and considered her reflection in a full-body looking glass. The luxuriant cerulean fabric shot through with cumulus clouds reminded Sheetal of her auntie's temperamental barrettes. A heavenly nymph, wrapped in the heavens themselves.

"You should absolutely buy that," Sheetal blurted. "It was made for you."

"It is nice, is it not?" the apsara murmured. Her words flowed like running water, too smooth to sound human. "But I rather fancy this taffeta." One slim, tapered hand drifted from a swatch of deep pink lotus-petal fabric to a bolt of purple velvet. "Or perhaps a richer color."

Sheetal fought the urge to snatch it away. *She* wanted that cloth, wanted it to slip through her fingers like liquid. She could already feel it on her skin, supple and decadent. Dev wouldn't know what hit him.

Irritated, she threw that last thought right into the mental trash can.

Her mouth curving in amusement, the apsara released the velvet. "For you, then, star's daughter, though I would have thought you to prefer all the shades of the night." She resumed sorting through the bolts. "Then again, it is a wonder you and those around you survived long enough for you to care about such things, half-mortal that you are."

Sheetal ignored the apsara's rudeness. "Is there someone here who sells healing potions for a star's burn?"

"Poor child," cooed the apsara, pausing to drape a shawl of sunshine about her shoulders. "Is your own blood not enough?"

"Do you know or not?"

The apsara twirled. "I know many things." She danced away, taking any hope of a straight answer with her.

Sheetal left the apsara to her shopping, then accompanied Radhikafoi and Minal past a kiosk serving ice cream and kulfi in wacky flavors like churel fangs and Lord Kama's love spells. A customer wrestled with a cone of smoky gray soft serve that towered over him. "Bhoot's breath," he said cheerfully. "You should try it."

The repulsive breath of a ghost? Sheetal exchanged a grossed-out glance with Minal, who exclaimed, "Why? Why would you do that to ice cream?"

"Shreemati! Shreemati!" called a rakshasa with a lion's head, racing over. Radhikafoi hopped backward, but he either didn't notice or didn't care. "I have been looking everywhere for you!"

"Rakshasa," Radhikafoi whispered. "Get away from me, monster!"

With a grunt, the rakshasa switched forms, becoming a green-skinned man with long, half-moon-shaped fangs protruding from his mouth. Sheetal was sure her auntie would faint when he tried for what he obviously considered an ingratiating smile and laid his clawed hand on her shoulder. "Shreemati, it is said you are a connoisseuse of quality couches? Then you *must* come with me. In my shop, we have settees, divans, daybeds, sofas! Anything you can dream of, in colors and styles you cannot begin to imagine. For the right price, anything—*anything*—can be had!"

Radhikafoi twisted away. "Don't touch me!"

"Couches shaped like turtles," he continued, undaunted. "Couches *made* of turtles! Couches shaped like teeth, like roses, even one like the golden thrones Lord Indra and Lady Indrani sit on in their kingdom of Svargalok." His voice dropped to a stage whisper. "I have reason to believe the piece in question originally belonged to Lord Indra himself. It would be perfect for a discerning lady such as you."

Sheetal had to tell Dev about this. He would die laughing.

No. She caught herself. Why couldn't she get him out of her head?

The rakshasa had snagged Radhikafoi, not her arm but her will. Radhikafoi, who had done her best to shield Sheetal and

Minal from the glamour of the Market, who hadn't let herself pick up even a single trinket or talisman, hesitated. "I—I can't," she stammered. "My brother—"

At the same time, harp strings sounded from afar—insubstantial, airy as cotton candy, each chime a key to a hidden door—and the luminescence in Sheetal's blood intensified, shining out from her skin.

The harp sisters. They were playing the sidereal melody, or at least a version of it, and it reached deep within her, sparking the flame at her core until the part of her she'd spent the last ten years bricking off, the part that was all star, flared to life, impatient to ascend.

Somewhere inside, Sheetal had known it couldn't be as simple as just finding a potion, that her auntie was right and she would have to travel to Svargalok and confront Charumati.

"That way!" she cried, pointing. "Come on!"

But Radhikafoi hadn't looked away from the rakshasa, and the silvery notes were fading, lost amid the chatter of the Market and the rakshasa's expert salesmanship.

"You go, Sheetu," said Minal. "I'll stay with her. You keep looking for the harp sisters, and don't let anyone trick you. Meet back at the entrance?"

Sheetal barely nodded before heading farther into the bustling Night Market.

Bold dyes glistered at her, delectable aromas teased her nose, and laughter meshed with the lilting of hidden instruments, always just skirting the edge of hearing. Here the bowing of a sarangi, there the strumming of a sitar. The strains of song, high and melancholy, were enough to make her heart burn flame-bright.

And just beneath them, the transcendent sound of the harp, soft as the breeze that bore it.

The rows of stalls were arranged in interconnecting spirals, and Sheetal dashed right in, catching glimpses as she ran. One stand was entirely peacock-themed, selling peacock feather crowns, peacock feather saris, miniature peacocks that leaped into the air, even pairs of peacock wings that allowed the wearer to fly. Only as high as peacocks could fly, of course, which wasn't that impressive, but still.

Another displayed fruits she had never seen before, all strangely shaped and colored. The vendor held up a slice of something blue and faceted that made her think of tropical oceans. The whole fruit looked like an uncut geode.

Sheetal, though, kept running, following the music, only pausing when a scattered rainbow of powders glowed an invitation from within a white kiosk. They ranged from the earthy palette of ground cumin and black mustard seed to the brilliant colors thrown at Holi: magenta, beryl, goldenrod, sunset orange, claret, royal blue, grape jelly. Sheetal ate them up with her eyes and imagined the hues swirling through her, casting mysterious incantations.

The purveyor, sensing weakness, swore all the spices were edible—even the dusts of gold, silver, and copper. "Won't you tarry awhile and avail yourself of all I have to offer?"

Sheetal's taste buds hungered for the untried flavors. Crafty as these people might be, they were *her* people, with the magic that Radhikafoi had denied her all these years. Dad, too.

They should have told her. It was her right to know.

*Dad...*

She reluctantly shook her head at the spice seller and ran even faster. Above, the twenty-seven nakshatras stretched across the sky. Sheetal visually sifted through them one handful of stars at a time, hunting for hers. There it was—with her mother blazing at its center.

Something burst open in Sheetal then. Fireworks sparked in her vision, leaving behind orange and green spots. Like at Radhikafoi's house, her hands sparkled, but this time, she let it be.

It was the call again, the one her mother had mentioned in her letter. The starsong.

The sooner Sheetal found what she was looking for, the sooner she could appease her core's need to rise. Resisting was like trying not to breathe. It felt like someone had squashed her forehead in a vise.

How had she ever thought she could ignore this?

Sheetal massaged her temples. When her sight cleared, the stalls stood at a remove, and silver vines curled over the ground, each laden with plump glass pumpkins in a kaleidoscope of colors. In the middle of the pumpkin patch sat a pair of long-haired women with harps.

The women wore kajal around their eyes and crimson bindis

106

on their foreheads, but were otherwise bare to the night. Sky-clad. "Who is this strange, searching young child? Her heart beats so silver, so wild."

The harp sisters! Sheetal could have hugged them. "Charumati said to find you when I was ready to go to her."

"I am Amrita," one sister said, her long black tresses draping over her like creepers. Her smile was kind.

"I am Vanita," said the other, equally long white locks veiling her body. The voracious moue of her mouth sent a tremor through Sheetal.

"Our songs are the same, but one sister heals the listener," said Amrita.

"And the other sister steals the listener!" cried Vanita.

"Uh, great. Listen," said Sheetal, her excitement waning, "my mom sent me—"

Exchanging an impenetrable look, the two spoke in unison. "Who is who, you wonder? That you must ask the wiliest of ladies herself, our maiden Chance—or simply listen well. We sing the answer you seek but once."

As if on cue, they began to play pedal harps carved from blue-white ice and strung with honeysuckle.

The song both jarred and charmed Sheetal, its notes twisting together in a struggle for dominance. Her stomach roiled in protest, then calmed, then roiled once more. She'd never had her own instrument turned against her before, and she didn't like it.

"There is the milk of cobra fangs, tinctures of nightshade

and rue," chanted Vanita, plucking at the strands of honey-suckle. Its sweet, heady nectar lulled Sheetal like a drug.

"There is lead-laced vermilion, and black swan's adrenaline, too," added Amrita.

Sheetal's head grew woozy. She had to get away. Yet part of her wanted to grab her own harp and join these devious sisters, be the third in a pair of two, the gray that separated black and white, the balance between them.

*But Dad.*

"Stop it!" she cried, her words meaningless against the shining music. "My mom told me to talk to you when I was ready to find her."

Amrita giggled. "They will have you sing for art and for power." The strings trilled beneath her fingers.

"But who will sit in the silver tower?" Vanita sang out. Now she was the one with the kind smile.

"Surely that is just an old wives' tale." Amrita's malicious stare grated on Sheetal, but she couldn't move, couldn't even look away. "For wherever might a star's blood be for sale?"

"Just a single drop," said Vanita. She lifted her hand to reveal a fiendishly sharp thorn. "A simple prick, a simple pop."

Amrita threw back her head, and Sheetal glimpsed mercy and mayhem in her eyes. "Just a drop, just a drop! Plop, plop, plop!"

Together the sisters howled, "And what of you, little star, little star? Is your blood still as thick and dark as hot, sticky tar?"

"Surely you know only star's blood heals . . ."

". . . All star-inflicted burns and weals!"

The harp sisters smiled. "Stellification," said Amrita.

"Catasterization," said Vanita.

"The process of becoming a star," they said together.

Sheetal shook free of her paralysis. "Please, just listen. I need you to tell me how to get to the sky." If they rhymed more nonsense after this, she'd leave and find her own way.

Amazingly, Vanita produced a carved silver box. "You need only have asked."

Somehow Sheetal kept her eyes from rolling right out of her head.

With a snap of her wrist, Amrita opened the lid to reveal a wad of translucent white silk. Sheetal squinted at it. A handkerchief?

But as she watched, the silk expanded. One petal after another unfurled until the object had blossomed into a pale, gently illuminated lotus. Sheetal's guilt, her grief, subsided beneath its tranquil light, and she could even smile again.

The lotus was made of moonbeams, subtle and silvery white. In it, she heard the song of the stars, felt the summons of the sky. Her blood fizzed, frothy as champagne bubbles. She longed for the comfort of the lotus; she hungered for it.

No wonder her mother hadn't trusted Radhikafoi with this. She never would have handed it over, not when she knew Sheetal could just leave whenever she wanted.

"Perhaps *I* will journey to the heavens," Amrita mused, stroking the flower.

"He loves me." Vanita reached for a petal. "He loves me not."

*Oh, no, you don't,* thought Sheetal, and sprang. Maybe they were just playing, but she wasn't taking any chances.

Then she was holding the moonlight lotus, pressing it to her cheek. It was smooth, sleek as sugar glaze, and the rest of the Night Market dissolved before its rich radiance. The sheen on her skin was cool water on a parched tongue, soothing the ache of not being enough. Of failing.

The lotus shone softly, its lambent petals pledging she would soon fly.

Sheetal peeked at the harp sisters, with their keen, cutting smiles. What had Charumati given them for helping her?

But it didn't matter. Sheetal had the lotus now, her way up, and with its silver glow pooling over her, nothing else mattered.

Amrita and Vanita spoke as one. "This is our counsel: if you would rise, if you would take to the skies, you must hold this near and have no fear."

"That's it?" Sheetal asked, not hiding her skepticism. "It's *that* easy?"

In response, the sisters reached for their harps and launched into an eerie tune that made her think of the story of the Pied Piper. The moonlight lotus clutched to her heart, she turned away. *Time to get out of here.*

"Go and soar now, little sister," Amrita and Vanita called after her. "And do take care not to blister."

## 8

Just outside the Night Market, as the giant peacock watched over them, Minal showed Sheetal her purchase. She'd found a stall wreathed in all manner of wings from dragonfly to condor, and had successfully haggled with the owner, a garudi with the body of a muscular human woman, metallic golden skin, a white face, an eagle's beak, and feathery red wings looped back over themselves so they fit in the stall. In exchange for the two cloud barrettes, Minal had received a thumbnail-sized corked glass bottle filled with a fragrance that would allow her to walk on actual clouds.

"Don't worry; Auntie specified that I had to get inside Svargalok and back to Edison in one piece, unhindered, safe, and at a consistent speed I determined, and that I'd always be the one in control from start to finish." Minal grinned. "Old bird wasn't too happy about that, but Auntie wouldn't take no for an answer."

"Of course I didn't. And what did you find out, dikri?" Radhikafoi prompted. "Those sisters must have had something useful for you, no?"

Sheetal produced the moonlight lotus from her messenger bag, shocking her auntie into silence, and started toward the nearby church parking lot. She still couldn't believe Radhikafoi had kept the letter from her. "Too much to get into right now."

Soon Minal and she stood in the shadows, ready to depart. Radhikafoi had pressed vermilion and a grain of raw rice to each of their foreheads in blessing, presented them both with Tupperware packages of carefully wrapped homemade food, and now waited by the lamppost to see them off.

Above, the moon had taken up lodging in the lunar mansion of his newest astral lover, where he shone down with extra ardor, a silvery lamp lighting the way for Sheetal. The world was hers, just as it had been when she was small and dancing with her mother.

With nothing to keep it at bay, the astral song tugged unrelentingly at her. *Silver in your bones,* it whispered. *Silver in your blood. Come to us.*

Sheetal rolled her shoulders, stretching out the kinks. It felt so good to stop fighting, to finally accept the invitation. Now she could just be.

She sensed the nakshatras in the sky above, their song a knell in her ears. Her blood rushed through her in reply, hot and hungry, setting her spinning.

Even knowing Minal and Radhikafoi were watching, she

couldn't stop. She was like smoke, like flame, like dreams that whirled eternally through the deep jet-black expanse of space. The world around her had been cast in silver and shadow and gone so still. Not a single car drove past.

*Come,* urged the stars. *Come home.*

Sheetal danced, her hands reaching up to the heavens. If only Dev could see her like this.

In that moment of distraction, her body went awkward, flesh instead of light, the thrall broken.

He'd betrayed her. Why did she keep thinking about him?

Everything had happened so fast, she realized, she hadn't really been able to think. Not two days ago, she'd been hiding, playing at being ordinary, and now, after breaking up with her boyfriend and almost killing her dad, she was on her way to the starry court via an intoxicating, mind-muddling Market.

It was too much.

She had no clue what was waiting for her in Svargalok, no sense of what her starry family might be like, and the whole day had left her drained. What if while she was getting a drop of her mother's blood, Dad . . . died?

Sheetal cradled the lotus against her chest. *Tell me what to do.*

The flower radiated soothing silver-white light, reminding her to breathe. Dad needed her. This choice, this plan, would have to be the right one.

Under the balm of the blossom, she relaxed, the slow pulse of her blood turning to a soft drumming that became words. First a mantra to Ganesh Bhagavan for the removal of obstacles, then an invocation to Durga Mata for courage. She wanted to be strong like a tigress and brave like a hawk, ready to swoop down and take out her enemies. She wanted to face her mother and save her father.

The stars' song stoked the fires at Sheetal's core, making her hands tingle and her hair blaze beneath its prison of black dye. *Up*, her blood cried, as the dye dissolved like sugar in water. *Up.*

She shoved her earthly concerns from her mind: Dev, Dad, Radhikafoi, school, the kids at the mandir. All that existed was the sky.

The lotus expanded, becoming a halo around her before dispersing in a cascade of glittering sparks, a miniature meteor shower that sank beneath her skin to merge with the flame inside.

With a single breath, she began to soar.

This feeling—*This, yes, this*—she knew it. She'd always known it.

Sheetal glanced down and saw the concrete swiftly receding beneath her feet and Radhikafoi calling out to them to be careful. Her fire, her own fire, was bearing her aloft, erasing every problem that had ever bothered her on the ground. Ecstasy spread through her, a murmured spell that sang in her like the silver notes of the stars themselves.

Meanwhile, Minal had uncorked her bottle of cloud perfume and dabbed it on her wrists. She hung suspended in the air, as graceful as if she *had* bought the pair of dragonfly wings she'd mentioned. Leaping forward, she landed on the nearest cloud, then the next, and the next, as though they were no more than rungs on a ladder.

"This is awesome!" She held out her arms to either side. "We're flying, can you believe it? And your hair, it's silver again!"

So many things swirled inside Sheetal as she ascended into the sky, dreams and wonder and delight. She was going to the heavenly realm, where her mother lived. Where their family lived.

The flame at her center a celestial compass, she rose higher and higher into the night. Kohl-dark and limitless, a sheath of black velvet studded with sparkling diamonds, it was familiar in a way she felt in her bones, in her skin. Her flame flickered, then flared in recognition.

Before her, the infinite dark beckoned. She answered.

Next to her, step by step, Minal climbed the cloud staircase.

Together they would find the starry court—and Charumati.

# PART TWO

*Stars got tangled in her hair whenever she played in the sky.*

—LAINI TAYLOR

"*O*nce, a very long time ago, a naga maiden from the subterranean world journeyed to the heavenly realm. She had decided she would dance among the deities," my mother told me, her tone deep and rich with metaphor. It was a storyteller's voice. She didn't need to be quiet; everyone was sleeping at this late hour. The two of us stood there in the shadowed field, reigning queen and princess of the whole hushed world. It belonged to us, only to us.

I twirled through the slumbering daisies and dandelions, pretending they were characters in the story. The stars laughed overhead, blazing bright against the velvet cape of the night. I could hear their whispers, and the full moon winked at me.

"She dined with the gods," my mother continued, weaving herself a crown of daisies, "and they showered her with divine blossoms in a rainbow of colors. The apsaras found her so fetching that they danced with her as one of their own. The gandharvas played their finest music so she might always be in motion. The kinnaras requested her *every story of earthly existence. Even the stars prevailed on her never to leave, for it pleased them greatly to shine down upon her face. It seemed as though the nagini had found her true place, her home.*

*"Countless years passed in this way, marked only by festivities and feasts. But time is the trickster that changes all things, and the novelty of the dancing nagini grew as thin and worn as an old sari."* My mother curved her hands like a cup, and a length of luminous fabric formed there, fraying as I watched. Her face glowed in its radiance. She tore the fabric in two and tossed the pieces into the night, where they floated like fireflies before dissipating.

*"The gods did not ask for our maiden as they once had, instead seeking out new pastimes. The apsaras left her out of their performances, and the kinnaras no longer requested tale after tale. Soon the maiden danced alone. Even the myriad stars, constant though she had thought them, had turned their lantern light elsewhere. Only a smattering remained by her side, but their presence failed to soothe the maiden's lonely heart, which ached for her jeweled cavern by the blue-green sea, for the family she had not seen in many cycles."*

*"But why was she sad?"* I interrupted. I hated this part of the story. *"She should have lots of adventures! That's what I would do."*

My mother looked at me for a long time. *"It is a hardship to be away from those you love, Sheetal."*

I thought about this. *"Oh."*

My mother bent to stroke a dandelion bud. At her touch, it bloomed like an evening primrose. *"Abandoned and isolated, the maiden took her leave of the skies. Upon her departure, those few stars who loved her still dropped one by one into her hair and became* entangled there. Ever after, deep beneath the earth where she roamed with her family and friends, the maiden wore the cosmos like a glowing crown.

"Only when she finally passed into the next life did the stars come loose. In their grief, they strewed themselves throughout the caverns to illuminate the deceased maiden's footsteps, so she would always be remembered. But a new generation came, and then another, and yet another, until the maiden and the stars, too, were forgotten in the subterranean darkness. Their light scattered, their hearts stilled, and they slowly transformed to stone." My mother adjusted her daisy crown. "And that, my daughter, is how diamonds came to be."

"Again, Mommy!" I cried, bouncing up and down. "Again! Tell me again."

She swept me up into her arms, her eyes burning from within. I nestled into the mass of silver waves that hung to her knees—the thick, silky mane that rebuffed all dye, gleaming against the smooth brown of her skin. "Tomorrow," she said, carrying me into the house. "Tonight, little ones should sleep soundly, knowing their aunts and uncles and grandparents and cousins are watching over them."

Though I wriggled hard in protest, she put me to bed and turned out the light. I could still see the moon peeking through the curtains until she drew them closed. Without his round face to encourage me, I started to yawn.

Then she left my room. I heard the front door open. My eyes were falling shut, but I knew where she was going. Back outside to talk to the sky, the way she did every night.

The next morning, I begged for the story again, but my father only held up the serving bowl of egg salad he'd just made. "We're late for the cookout. The neighbors wanted us to help set up, remember?"

The conspiratorial smile on my mother's face clouded over. "Must we? You know I have nothing to say to them. Nor they to me."

"Oh, please, Mommy, please!" I said, hopping from foot to foot. "Mr. Sanchez always makes the best ice cream!"

She looked from my father to me, and I sensed her resolution wavering. She was like a peacock among pigeons at these events—in our world—and we all knew it, but she could never tell us no.

"I know they're not the most exciting crowd," my father said, "but we did say we'd go. What if we just put in an appearance? An hour, tops. What do you say, Charu jaan? For the best ice cream?"

"Only an hour," my mother agreed, "during which I will pretend to understand school administration and home equity." She knelt before me with a smile. "And then I will tell you the story of diamonds, and we will make moon mandalas and pick flowers and sing." She stood and took the bowl from my father's grasp. "And later you and I will cook a proper meal. What is this 'egg salad' business?"

"Deal," my father said. "Sheetal, go put on your shoes."

I hurried to the hall closet and found my sandals. When I looked back, my parents were embracing, her face tilted up to meet his.

She didn't love mortals, I knew, but she loved us. She stayed for us, in a place where she had no friends, no allies. No one she could confide in.

And she always would.

—FROM SHEETAL'S JOURNAL

122

Sheetal floated among the stars, one of them. Her nakshatra, her constellation Pushya, beckoned, its song vibrant in her blood, in the beat of her heart. She was so close, she could fall into it as easily as a puzzle piece sliding into place. All she had to do was get there. She beamed, her whole body glowing. It felt so natural, so right. It was as though she had never been anywhere else.

How beautiful the sky was, out here where it was always night, beautiful enough to make her ache. Shades from midnight blue to squid-ink black, an entire continuum of darkness. She'd expected to be frightened, or at the very least flustered. The universe was a gargantuan, humbling place, and she'd never even been away from Earth. Yet now, as she rose and rose, Sheetal felt herself enlarging, transforming, illuminating.

Her arms lifted and spread, mirroring her legs until she made a pentagram. Music like silver chimes and veena strings swept through her, turning to light that scattered out from the five points of her body.

The darkness was beautiful because of her presence within it.

It was funny, the way things changed. How people could be shocked by something, a bit of information that didn't fit what they knew of the world, and then expand and grow around it, into it, until it became part of them, just another piece in an overarching narrative.

She'd known she was half star, of course. She'd always known that. But she hadn't known what it *meant*.

Sheetal was expanding, widening, as the magic sparked through her. She could feel it molding her internal landscape, rearranging it into something new. Silver in her bones, silver in her blood—she was truly becoming a star.

But it wasn't time yet. There was something—no, someone—she had to remember. Someone who was calling her name. Someone who needed her.

Dad? Radhikafoi? Minal?

*Minal.* Minal was calling her name.

The starshine ebbed below Sheetal's skin as she glanced over to where Minal waited on a fleecy white cloud, tiny against the enormity of night. "Look!"

There, just out of shouting distance, hovered a golden palace. It was mammoth in scope, so large and surrounded by ample tracts of grassy loam that it was really more of an island.

Ornate crenellations topped the seemingly never-ending walls, probably designed so the demigods could retaliate when the demons assaulted them.

Svargalok. Sheetal stared, awestruck.

"Come on," she called back. Raising her arms once more, she soared toward the palace.

At last they reached the entrance, a far grander and more elegant thing than Sheetal could have envisioned, all curves and marble inlays. Minal hopped from her cloud onto the loam. "Okay," she said, all business. "What's the plan? How're we getting in?"

"I don't know," Sheetal admitted. She stared at the palace gates, a few minutes' walk from where they stood. "I hadn't really thought that far. Find my mom and get her to help us, I guess."

Minal looked doubtful. "We can't just waltz on in. My grandma told me humans aren't allowed here unless we die a heroic death out on the battlefield. Then an apsara brings us, and we get to be spoiled before our next life." Her smile was all mischief. "I could rock a sword no problem, but it'd be harder to pull off the dead part."

"Well, you *were* a pretty convincing zombie that one Halloween." Sheetal squared her shoulders. "Maybe I'll go full-on Radhikafoi. 'Don't you know who I am?'"

Minal snickered. "They don't stand a chance."

They approached the gates arm in arm, where two

mustached guards in golden turbans and red uniforms waited, hands resting on the long swords in decorative scabbards at their waists.

"What is your business here, mortals?" the guard on the left asked, shooting their clothes dubious looks. "You do not appear to be dead."

Sheetal kept from commenting on his razor-sharp powers of observation. Even though she really wanted to. Instead, she put her palms together in greeting. "I am Sheetal, daughter to Charumati of the Pushya nakshatra."

"Daughter of Charumati!" said the guard on the right, returning Sheetal's greeting. His voice turned chiding. "You are late. The welcome ceremony has already begun."

*Welcome ceremony?* Her mother had a lot of explaining to do.

"A half-mortal star?" The guard on the left gripped the hilt of his sword. "I was unaware Princess Charumati had a daughter, let alone one with mortal blood."

Sheetal let haughtiness bleed into her voice and through her skin as silver fire. "You deign to question a daughter of the sidereal houses?"

The guard on the right hushed his partner. "He means no offense, Lady Sheetal."

Still channeling her auntie, Sheetal gave the guards her best poker face. "I should hope not."

"Pray indulge me, daughter of the House of Pushya," said the guard on the right, "but as you come unescorted, I must ask you three questions to verify your identity. Pardon the impertinence, but protocol must be observed. You understand."

Sheetal started sweating. She was supposed to have an escort? Like, another star? And what if she didn't know the answers?

The guard on the left turned to Minal, his lips pursed in distaste. "As for you, mortal child, you must be the lady's companion?"

"Indeed. My lady's flame could rival a supernova. Her heart is all star," Minal intoned, oozing obsequiousness like syrup. "I am not worthy of being the dirt on the soles of her golden chappals, let alone her blessed maidservant, but my lady requested I accompany her on this journey, and far be it from this mere mortal to question her will."

"Your companion seems very . . . pliable?" the guard on the left asked Sheetal doubtfully.

She tried not to laugh. Nothing to do but run with it. "Yes, she's perfect. So eager to please."

"Aha." He sniffed. "In that case."

"Shall we begin, daughter of Charumati?" asked the guard on the right.

Her laughter cut off. "Certainly," she said, praying she sounded arrogant and not afraid.

"First, what offering did the elephant who sought divine rescue from his enemy make to Lord Vishnu?"

"Oh, that's easy." That was one of her favorite Hindu stories growing up. Gajendra, leader of a herd of elephants, neared a lake where he fell prey to a crocodile's jaws. They stood locked in that stalemate for a thousand years, the crocodile patiently waiting for Gajendra to give in and become dinner, and Gajendra fighting to free his leg from the crocodile's powerful grasp. "A lotus from the lake where he was trapped."

The tension in her shoulders gave way. If the questions were all this simple, she'd be fine.

The guard's expression remained inscrutable. "Correct. Second question: After Damayanti was abandoned by Nala in the forest, with whom did she seek shelter?"

Sheetal knew this, too. When she was little, Dad had given her a comic version of *Nala and Damayanti*. She'd eaten it up.

But she hadn't read it in so long, the minor details had fled her memory. *Think,* she told herself. *Think!*

Her palms tingled. Why wouldn't her exhausted brain come up with the name?

When a minute had passed, Minal said, "My lady, you are drifting. These poor sentries await your reply." Under her breath, she whispered, "Chedi. The Princess of Chedi."

Her gaze never leaving the guards, Sheetal gave them the answer.

"Correct," admitted the guard on the left. He sounded irritated.

Two questions down, one to go. Sheetal yawned. She couldn't help it; it had been such a long couple of days, and she was so tired. She tried to stifle the yawn, but the guard on the left had already seen.

Now he smirked openly. "Third and final question: When the nagini left the heavens, what did she take with her beneath the earth?"

They'd been toying with her. Anyone conversant with the old myths could have answered the first two questions. But only a star could ever know this. It was pretty clear the guard on the left—and maybe the other one, too—didn't think Sheetal did.

The whole charade made her furious. Her mother was waiting inside.

"Some trouble, madam?" the guard on the right inquired mildly. "Surely not."

The guard on the left had drawn his sword and was inspecting the line of its blade. "A true star's daughter would know the answer."

A true star's daughter. One who wasn't mortal, he meant.

The flame trembled within her. It would be so easy to just let it loose on the guards. Every second they kept her out here was another second she wasn't helping Dad.

Minal laid a steadying hand on her shoulder. "My lady, you know the answer."

And Sheetal did. After all, she'd written it down herself in her journal, the same journal now tucked into her messenger bag along with some toiletries, Radhikafoi's snacks, and a picture of Dad.

"The stars," she told the guards, her words bold and precise as the silver light dancing up her arms. "A few stars went down with her. We say they became the first diamonds, because they lit the way, but really, they were just the first to mix with humans."

"Correct," the guards said in unison, their expressions melting into grudging respect.

The one on the left sheathed his sword. "Come, then. Your mortal companion, too."

10

The guard led Sheetal and Minal into a long corridor lined with carved marble pillars. No human building Sheetal had ever seen—not the Taj Mahal, not the Palace of Versailles—could hope to rival that intricate mosaic ceiling, its enamel-and-gold inlay telling stories that moved, unfolding in time with her footsteps. It was enormous, eternal. It made her feel small and dizzy.

When she sneaked a peek beside her, Minal was taking it all in with wondering eyes.

They emerged into an area that was open to the sky, a spacious courtyard full of beautiful people dressed in sumptuous clothes that might have come straight from the Night Market. Some of the faces looked like they were glowing, but it was hard to tell in the light from the hanging lanterns.

"You are likely to encounter your mother here," the guard said abruptly, then merged into the crowd.

"Thanks so much," Minal called after him. "You've been *ever* so helpful."

Across the chamber, two jeweled thrones rested on a dais. Her blood thrumming, Sheetal took in their owners. There sat Indra, warrior king of the demigods and the heavenly realm, bringer of thunder and rain, wielder of the thunderbolt. On his left lounged his queen, Indrani, the goddess who presided over wrath and jealousy but paradoxically also over their banishment.

Sheetal stood just feet away from the gods. The gods! Her knees quaked with deference, with dread. *My mom* lives *here,* she marveled, hurrying Minal into an alcove where they could try to get their bearings. *Right alongside the gods.*

What did she know about being noble, let alone divine? Even that guard hadn't believed she belonged here.

It didn't matter, she told herself, annoyed that any part of her cared. All she had to do was find Charumati. Then she could put all this behind her and go back home.

Minal nudged her. "Wow. Sheetu, how is this even happening?"

"I don't know," she said honestly.

Svargalok was massive, an entire other realm. The adrenaline she'd been riding high on flagged, and all the bruises on her heart resumed throbbing in concert. She needed sleep. She needed time to process all of this.

Time she didn't have, not if she wanted to save Dad.

The sound of a sitar rang out, followed by a tanpura, and

132

onstage, a troupe of apsaras in vivid green saris swept into motion. Their performance was breathtaking, full of involved movements and flirtatious glances, and the gandharvas' music swift and complex, but Sheetal barely noticed. She was too busy searching the room for a familiar face.

The crowd around her was distracted, too, yakking away. Minal, though, was riveted, taking pictures until the dance had finished.

"Wow," she repeated, fanning herself. "So pretty!" With a grin, she added, "I'd take one of them as a reward for my loyal service. Any one. I'm not picky. They like hanging out with humans, right?"

Despite herself, Sheetal laughed. "I'll see what I can do, my dear maidservant."

"Thank you, ladies, for that superb recital!" a herald cried out. "Such a marvelous opening piece to a competition we have not seen in many an eon. It is a fitting tribute to the reign of the Esteemed Patriarch of House Dhanishta." He waited for the applause to die down before continuing. "And now, let us recognize the competing nakshatras and their mortal representatives. Welcome to House Magha and its champion, Priyanka Chauhan!"

Houses Dhanishta and Magha. Those were nakshatras. And they were competing?

Foreboding coiled in Sheetal's stomach like a cobra. It couldn't be, could it? This wasn't why she'd been summoned?

*Surely you heard the call.*

"Hey, didn't that guard say something about a welcome ceremony?" Minal whispered. "Guess this is it."

No, Sheetal was just overreacting. And who could blame her after the day she'd had? As unobtrusively as she could, she peeked out from the alcove again.

The first thing she saw was a spiky-haired human girl a couple of years older than her, one who dangled a Rajasthani-style marionette and made it dance. Then, looking past the girl, Sheetal glimpsed stars. Lots and lots of stars both on- and off-stage, all chattering excitedly. All gorgeous and glowing, like figures out of a fairy tale.

Something tugged in her chest. Her people.

That meant her mom was probably somewhere in this room, too. Her palms grew tingly.

"Priyanka is single-handedly reviving the art of Kathputli puppetry in her community," one of the older stars of House Magha proclaimed. "She has mastered the craft of creating the traditional marionettes and performing with them, earning herself a number of prestigious prizes, and we are confident she will shine brightly as our champion."

So this was some kind of talent competition. Envy surged through Sheetal. Must be nice to show off a talent instead of hiding it.

Studying the groups by the stage, she realized she could pick out various nakshatras by the constellation embroidery on their clothes. House Krittika, House Ashvini, House Magha, House Revati . . .

Where was Charumati?

Minal tapped at her phone. "No service, like I thought." She snapped a few more pictures and showed them to Sheetal. "I was trying to get Indra and Indrani, but all I can catch is light."

"Everyone would think you Photoshopped them, anyway."

The band of stars cleared the stage to a round of applause, and another group swiftly took its place. "Welcome to House Krittika and its champion Leela Swaminathan!"

Leela looked like a typical desi grandmother: short, plump, and wrinkled, her white bun matching her plain white cotton sari. She beamed, evidently at home here. Definitely more at home than Sheetal felt. As Leela raised a paintbrush for all to see, one of the elder stars spoke.

"Our champion found her way to the easel late in life, but her work with the dark feminine has already set the Mumbaikar art scene alight. It is said she paints not with pigment but with emotion. House Krittika could not be more delighted to have Leela representing us."

It was a good thing *Sheetal* wasn't competing. It wasn't like she had anything to recommend her. No juries awarding her prizes, no fans clamoring for her next album. No one even knew who she was.

Maybe if she hadn't had to hide, she thought, still combing the crowd for her mother, she would have had all this, too.

"Welcome to House Ashvini and its champion Sachin Khanna!" The stars of the Ashvini nakshatra formed a tight, possessive loop around a middle-aged man who lifted a stone statue above his head.

"Sachin is a sculptor of—"

But Sheetal missed the rest, because the starsong rang through her so forcefully, she let out an "oof" and doubled over. *Come to us. It is time.*

"Are you okay?" Minal whispered, kneeling beside her.

Nails digging into her palms, Sheetal staggered forward. The astral melody was almost hauling her toward the stage.

"House Pushya," said the herald, "if you are unable to produce a champion at this time, you must withdraw from the competition."

Champion. Her. The light in Sheetal's heart couldn't touch the shadow spreading there. Her family really had brought her here to compete for them.

She was going to be sick. They couldn't just spring this on her with no warning, no training, nothing. She'd thought they wanted her by their side for her, not for this.

"No champion, and yet still in the running?" someone questioned. "Oh, that is true hubris. Call the delay what it is: desperation."

"House Pushya must withdraw!" someone else shouted.

"Ah, but she *is* here," a familiar voice corrected, silencing the titters. "Our champion."

Sheetal's breath hitched. Another group had claimed the stage, wrapped in black-and-silver silks embroidered with the constellation she knew as well as her own name.

136

Right in the middle of that group stood a woman with the indescribably lovely face that had never dulled in Sheetal's memory. Charumati.

Her mother.

Sheetal had thought she was ready for this.

All the grief and anger and utter yearning of the past ten years raced toward her, an avalanche, until she thought she might suffocate beneath it. She wobbled, gasping, trapped between sprinting to the stage and retreating from it. For an instant, she even forgot Dad.

The stars of House Pushya began to sing. The entire hall hushed. The song was the silver of starlight, of wind chimes and ringing bells and stories braided with skeins of myths and dreams and wishes. It called to the blood in Sheetal's veins, stoking the fire at her core, making her ache for the strings of her harp and her dilruba.

The song *was* the stuff that ran in her veins, the liquid flame that could heal. It needed to be free. She needed to free it.

Bright, pure notes soared from her throat to join the harmony, and radiance spilled from her skin and out of the alcove where she stood.

She stepped into the open and sang to Charumati, just a handful of notes, just enough. *I'm here.*

"Sheetu!" hissed Minal, right on her heels. "What are you doing?"

The courtiers around them skewered Sheetal with their

stares. "The missing champion has surfaced!" exclaimed the herald. "Can it be true?"

Charumati, too, looked directly at her. Their eyes met, dark brown echoing silvery brown, and relief gleamed there. Though her mother's song didn't falter, its tone deepened. It became a ballad of recognition, of connection, and the surrounding stars' voices shifted to accommodate it. *You came.*

Sheetal felt how the chorus wove its song, how it entwined filaments of light into a living net that enclosed the sky. She was part of that cosmic flow, part of a great glittering web. In that moment, even Dad and Dev seemed long ago and far away. All she knew was the gaze tangled with hers, and the way her heart had grown whole at last.

Charumati beckoned her to the stage.

"Half-creature," a voice jeered, its owner hidden in the throng. "Mortal half-thing. Go home!"

Minal whipped around. "Who said that?"

Sheetal's mind screamed at her to pay attention, to hear how the entire hall was whispering, to stop and *think* about this. The slur, the strange circumstances, all of it.

But the song was stronger, overpowering everything else. She was home, it warbled, and she'd found her mother once more.

Following the call of the music, Sheetal glided through the audience, up the stairs, and onto the stage, where the shining ring of stars waited.

"Welcome to House Pushya," the herald cried, "and its champion Sheetal Mistry!"

11

So here they were, together for the first time in ten years—just Sheetal and the mother who'd left her behind.

They wordlessly faced each other on a pair of royal blue mirrorwork-embroidered divans in Charumati's apartments, while Minal pretended to doze on an ornately carved bench. Her mother had brought them here right after Sheetal's introduction, leading them offstage through a rear exit to bypass all the prying eyes.

Charumati wore a translucent black sari dotted with tiny diamonds, and her dangling chandelier earrings and necklace were wrought from silver. In her long, shimmering hair perched a circlet of silver stars outlined in obsidian, and her delicate, ring-covered hands were folded in her lap.

"I was afraid your foi might not give you the message," her mother said, slicing through the silence. "I am so very glad she did."

She looked different than Sheetal remembered, far less human, much more a being of light, if light were made flesh. Except for her silvery aura, she could have been an apsara or even a goddess. Not anyone's mom.

This close to her, Sheetal didn't know what to do with her own hands. Her skin didn't fit right, as if it had grown too small. Her legs jiggled like overcooked spaghetti. She felt every bit of her human half, grimy and gawky and in desperate need of a nap. "She wasn't going to. But then you forced her with the starsong."

*Like you forced me.*

She brushed the scabbed-over cuticle on her thumb. Nope, she would never forget how it felt to be manipulated like that, right into being her constellation's champion.

Her mother's smile faded. "You came, and that is what counts."

Sheetal jiggled her leg harder. "I'm not going to be in that competition," she blurted. "Whatever it is."

There went her plan. All the clever things she would do, all the persuasive words she'd say when this moment came, had slipped out the back door of her brain, leaving her numb.

Her mother sighed. "Oh, dikri. If only it were that simple." Even her sorrow was captivating, a sculptor's finest expression of tragedy.

Sheetal didn't belong here. "It *is* that simple."

Charumati studied her. "You are so beautiful. Just like your father."

Sheetal's hands flickered with pewter fire. On Earth, she was cute enough, even pretty. Here, though, among these people who had no idea what it was like to wake up with a monster zit or to have to cut off an inch of split ends at a time, she felt less than plain.

Unbidden, her imagination called up Dev, the hint of mischief in his eyes when he grinned. *He'd* thought she was beautiful. She felt sick, remembering the shivery feel of his lips on hers. Remembering how she'd trusted him.

It didn't matter, though. Only Dad did.

Her mother leaned forward. "I watched you every night," she said, tears like dewdrops on her long lashes. "I listened to your music and waited for the day you would come to me. I never forgot you."

There they were, the words Sheetal had *ached* to hear. But she wasn't sure she cared.

"It is a fair thing to wonder why I left, as I know you must. Our house struggles: the court hierarchy is unstable, as is our position in it, and your nani and nana needed me by their side." Affection sweetened Charumati's bell-like voice. "We have always kept a place for you. Do you know how long your nani and nana have waited to meet their grandchild? How long I have waited to show you my childhood home and everything that will be yours?"

Nani and Nana. The grandparents Sheetal had never met, in the family home she'd never visited.

From the moment she'd seen the letter, this had been a

quest, a business transaction, even: make it to Svargalok, find her mother, get the drop of blood, and go home. Now the flood-gates in her heart opened wide.

All the holidays she'd missed, all the hugs, all the stories and sleepovers. A whole chunk of her childhood, just ripped away.

It was too much. She began to shake, her exhausted body giving out.

"I'm not going to be in your competition," she said more slowly, fighting to stay upright on her cushion.

*Dad.* The name cut through her stupor like a beam from a lighthouse, and she clung to it. Dad needed her, not her grand-parents.

Definitely not her mom.

Sheetal took a deep breath to steel herself. "I need your help. That's why I came here."

Her mother tucked a lock of Sheetal's hair behind her ear. When she spoke, her voice was soft. "Whatever help I may give is yours, my daughter."

Sheetal worked to keep her own voice calm. "It's Dad. His heart. He's dying."

Charumati frowned, delicate eyebrows coming down over a luminescent gaze, and clasped Sheetal's fiery hands in her cool ones. "So soon? He should have many years yet, by mortal time."

The inferno was rising now, roaring from inside Sheetal. She was so tired. So very, very tired.

*Say it,* she told herself. *"I burned him." That's all you have to do. Three words.*

But with her mother watching expectantly, Sheetal couldn't do it. The shame sat sour on her tongue, and she couldn't—she wouldn't—spit it out.

"He needs your blood," she said instead. Somehow, her mother's hands still on hers, she doused the flame at her core—and with it, the last of the energy that had sustained her these past two days and through the trip into the heavens. Her vision blurring, she slid down to the marble floor.

An instant later, Charumati knelt at her side. Minal ran over, followed by Charumati's ladies-in-waiting. "Let us remove her to the guest chambers," Sheetal heard her mother say. "She must rest."

"And get her some water," Minal added. "She's probably dehydrated." Other voices murmured agreement, and one asked about the competition.

"That can wait," Charumati said. "Hand me that glass."

Sheetal's eyes had slipped shut, and her lips felt like weights. Still, she took a few sips from the cup her mother held to her mouth before muttering, "You have to help him, Mom."

Message delivered, she leaned back against her mother's familiar warmth, inhaling the fragrance of jasmine and night breezes, and passed out.

When Sheetal opened her eyes, she lay in a bed of cloud framed by black crystal posts draped in a cumulus canopy. The richly

143

decorated room around her bore the thinnest of diamond ceilings, through which the sun—Lord Surya—shone down, washing everything with the first dawning rivulets of pink and gold.

She'd been twisting and tossing her way through dreams. Dreams of Dev feeding her cookies and Dad's physics lectures and the days when Charumati still lived among them that turned into dreams of Sheetal's flame leaping higher than the house and burning them all alive.

This, though, was a much better dream. An A-plus dream. *Good job*, she told her brain, then snuggled up in fetal position beneath the cirrus cloud coverlet, ready to find out exactly how comfy imaginary beds could be.

"Oh, good, you're awake." Minal tugged on her arm, rudely cutting into her research. She was wearing a beautiful silver satin dressing gown that gleamed in the morning light. "Time to get up."

Sheetal stared muzzily at her. "Excuse me, I'm not done sleeping? Get your own dream."

"That's a shame," Minal said, not budging, "because your family's waiting for us."

Sheetal buried her face in the pillow. "Tell Radhikafoi . . . not . . . hungry," she mumbled.

"Sheetu, do you even remember last night? Your mom, the competition?"

The competition. It hit Sheetal all at once, and she almost smacked her skull against the ebony headboard trying to sit up. She was in Svargalok, where her mother lived. And all the other stars, some who had made it clear they couldn't stand her, and others who thought she was going to fight House Pushya's battles for them. "We have to save Dad! Right now."

"Whoa," said Minal. "Slow down there." A private smile flitted over her face. "You were so out of it, we had to carry you in here last night."

"Where's 'here'?" Sheetal demanded. How could she have fallen asleep? Dad needed her. "What'd my mom say?"

"The guest quarters for all the champions. All I know is, your family wants to have breakfast with us, and Padmini's going to be back any second to dress us. I already washed so you could sleep longer." Minal tapped the headboard. "You owe me."

Sheetal tried to keep up. Breakfast with her family. Being dressed. "Who's Padmini?"

"Your grandma's lady-in-waiting."

"She must be cute for you to be so chipper in the morning."

"Funny." Minal waited a second, then asked, "How do you feel?"

"Dry." Sheetal's mouth was as desiccated as her fingers had been the time she'd helped Minal with a mosaic project, and it tasted just as foul as the grout had smelled.

Minal poured her a glass of water muddled with what looked like blue rose petals from a crystal pitcher on the bedside table. Next to the pitcher glinted two room keys embossed with the Pushya nakshatra and a small blue basket of silver and black candies, like in a luxury hotel.

145

Sheetal tested the water. It had the same sweet floral notes she'd tasted last night.

She drank more than she actually wanted, taking forever to swallow each sip. Maybe if she kept drinking, she'd float away. She wouldn't have to think about how she'd let Charumati take care of her as if she were still the naïve little girl who was so sure her mother would always be there.

The water left her replenished and even energized, like it had magic electrolytes. It even calmed her fear. Charumati still cared about Dad. She'd give Sheetal the blood, and Sheetal would just have to explain to Nani and Nana that this whole competition thing was a big mix-up.

Minal poked her in the shoulder. "That's it?"

Sheetal returned the poke. "What else would there be?"

Minal pressed her lips together the way she always did when she was contemplating something. "I wasn't going to say anything," she began. "I can't even imagine what this must be like for you. But I think maybe you need to hear that as cool as Magic Land is, it's okay to be mad at your mom. Or to not even know what you're feeling. I mean, you just had how much stuff dumped on you in less than twenty-four hours? Huge, life-changing things?"

"I'm not mad," Sheetal protested automatically. The shame of last night festered like a bruise on her heart, and she cringed away from it.

"Your mom *left* you. Whether or not she had a good reason for it, she left you. And no one told you why, and now it's up to you to save your dad and deal with this competition stuff. Seriously, I'd be freaking out if I were you."

Sheetal didn't know what she felt, and that was the problem. Feeling things hadn't been part of the plan. What she *did* know was that she didn't want to talk about it. "I'm fine. Let's just worry about the blood."

Minal let out a gigantic sigh. "You're the most stubborn person I know. Also, you sound like a vampire."

Sheetal bared her teeth in a fake snarl.

"Sheetu!"

But the image of Dad lying helpless in the hospital bed chased her grin away. How long could he survive without the blood?

"Okay, okay, I'm up," she said, kicking her legs over the side of the bed. "Where's the bathroom?"

## 12

Scraps of sun-burnished blue sky peeked between the pillars lining the corridor as Sheetal's grandmother's personal attendant, Padmini, led Sheetal and Minal from the champions' quarters to the Pushya nakshatra's wing of the palace.

Where Nani and Nana waited. Or as Padmini called them, the Esteemed Matriarch and Patriarch.

Once Sheetal had dried off from her bath, it had taken Padmini all of ten minutes to fit her with a choli, dress her in a blue-and-silver sari, plait jasmine blossoms into her hair, stick a diamond bindi to her forehead, and cleverly cover up the pimple sprouting on her chin—because of course there was one.

And yet Padmini had needed five whole minutes to fuss over the end of Minal's expertly folded sari, pleating and repleating it and smoothing it over her shoulder before steering Sheetal out the door to meet her fate. Apparently Minal wasn't the only one with a crush.

Padmini took it upon herself to play tour guide, too, rattling off names and histories as they passed marble statue after marble statue. Minal ate it right up, offering so many opinions and smiles that Sheetal very nearly offered her a spoon. *"I love a good sculpture"?*

At least one of them fit in here.

While they bantered, she hung back, staring up at the torans hanging from either side of the ceiling, black stitched with silver constellations like shining coats-of-arms. The sidereal melody danced through her, high notes and chords of anticipation, invitation—even sadness as she thought of Dad.

The Pushya nakshatra's toran flashed past. Sheetal stopped to study it. Her constellation.

Nani and Nana had only ever been characters in a story to her. She'd wished for them the same way she'd wished for Dad's parents when other kids built gingerbread houses and sand rangoli with their grandparents at holidays or got spoiled with souvenirs at Disney World. But except for a visit to India when she was little and sporadic video calls, she didn't really know Baa and Baapuji, either. The thing was, she'd gotten over it. She'd grown up.

And now she was supposed to waste time making small talk with strangers when she could be rushing back to Dad?

It was a relief when Padmini ushered Minal and her through a large scalloped archway straight into a chamber that could have been designed for midnight masquerade feasts, the kind where you might never know who else you dined with.

Jeweled silver oil lamps dangled overhead at different heights, tossing rainbows over the ink-black walls and floor. Shimmering blue curtains lined the picture windows, which alternated with silver-framed paintings of figures from Hindu myths. In the middle of the room, an oversize crystal table had been set with steaming thalis and black linen napkins.

And there were people. So many people, all flawlessly gorgeous and impeccably dressed. All with hair like hers. All turning in their chairs as one, their various conversations going still.

*Wait.* Sheetal had been nervous enough when she thought it was just going to be Charumati and Nani and Nana. How was she supposed to say anything real to them with all these strangers listening?

Minal looked just as taken aback. Padmini must not have bothered to let her know, either.

Gazes swooped over them, evaluating. They varied from shocked to intrigued to faintly put off. But most of the stars watched with interest, silver light skimming over their brown skin and smoldering in their dark eyes.

Who cared what these people thought? After today, Sheetal would never have to see them again. Ignoring her sweating palms, she raised her head higher.

"Are you excited for the competition? I certainly am," said a male star about her age. It took her a second to figure out he was addressing the female star next to him. That competition again. She turned away.

And caught sight of a stately old woman holding court at the head of the table. She wore a starry circlet over her white-streaked bun, and though her face was wrinkled, Sheetal could see she shared Charumati's large eyes. Her delicate chin. Nani.

To her right sat an elderly man with broad shoulders, a regal bearing, and a matching starry diadem. Nana.

The starry melody whispered in Sheetal's ears, ethereal as lace and replete with a yearning so pure it made her throat hurt.

Padmini moved between Sheetal and Minal. "Esteemed Matriarch, Esteemed Patriarch, Princess Charumati, permit me to present to you the Lady Sheetal and her mortal companion."

Charumati, Nani, and Nana rose and joined their palms before their faces. "Aav, beti, aav. Be welcome."

Sheetal's grandparents. Nani and Nana. Her grandmother's music rang out as surely as if Nani had opened her mouth to sing; it linked them more soundly than any bloodline.

It *was* their bloodline, Sheetal realized. It was the beat of her grandmother's heart. Of her grandfather's. Of her mother's.

Of hers. Her own pulse rose and fell in time with the notes.

"Go to them," Minal murmured.

Sheetal strode past the rows of watching faces to her grandmother. "Nani."

Nani grasped Sheetal's hands. Her skin was soft and thin as tissue, in contrast to the firm set of her mouth. She looked like an empress. "Dikri, my granddaughter, my dear one. You've come home to me."

*My dear one.* The flame at Sheetal's core kindled. The words sank into a fissure in her heart she hadn't known existed, sealing it. *You've come home.*

This was so unfair. She'd long ago accepted Dad and Radhikafoi and Deepakfua were her family. All her family. Not this hall full of people with starlit eyes and astronomical expectations.

When Nani released her, Nana spoke. "Be welcome among us, beti. May you burn bold in the deepest night."

Charumati silently touched Sheetal's forehead. Sheetal's shoulders dropped, then tensed right back up. She couldn't ask for the blood in front of all these people.

"And who is your companion?" Nani asked as Minal came up alongside Sheetal.

Sheetal cautiously returned her grandmother's smile. "My best friend, Minal."

"From Earth," Minal added helpfully, putting her palms together before her bowed head. "Namashkaar, Esteemed Matriarch. My mummy-papa send their pranaam."

"Such gracious manners! But please be at ease among us, children. We are your nakshatra." Nani put a hand on Sheetal's shoulder and turned her to face the table. "Bolo. At long last, our daughter is returned to us. House Pushya, I present to you now your own Sheetal, daughter of our daughter Charumati! Welcome her to our fold with open arms."

The room chimed with greetings, some probably more sincere than others. Sheetal kept her face as blandly polite as

152

she could, even as her insides shrank in on themselves. She wasn't hungry at all. She wouldn't be until she knew Dad was okay.

Nana indicated the two empty seats on Charumati's right. "Minal, do not be shy. Be seated, both of you, and eat. I trust our astral fare will be palatable to your mortal tongue?"

"I'm sure it's delicious," Minal said, helping herself to the farther of the two chairs. In full view of the entire table, she scooped up something red-violet and sparkling from one of the small bowls in her thali. "Thank you for having me."

Echoes of the starsong, the music of the spheres, drifted from around the table, each strand uniquely pitched, all weaving together into a web. Weaving around Sheetal, through her. She felt the curiosity thrumming in each note: Where had this long-lost granddaughter been, and why?

She almost laughed. *Why, indeed.*

Nani waggled her head from side to side in that particular desi dance that could mean *yes* or *no* or even *maybe.* "No thanks necessary. Eat, beti, eat." At that signal, everyone else reached for their food, too.

Sheetal finally sat down, sandwiched between Minal and Charumati. She scanned the thali before her. Oh, thank the gods; there were a few things she recognized, like spicy dal, jeera rice, and vegetables. Her nervous stomach could probably handle that. "It smells good."

"Eat, beti," Nani urged. "You will need your energy for the training."

Training? Sheetal exchanged a baffled look with Minal.

"We had the gulaab jamun made especially for you," Nana said. "Your mother told us how much you loved it as a child."

Sheetal actually preferred milk-soaked rasmalai these days, but she took a bite of one of the golden-brown fried dough balls in syrup. Instead of the traditional rose water, the syrup tasted of a flower she couldn't place. It looked right but wasn't.

Kind of like her.

"So quiet, child," Nana teased. "Talk to us. Speak of your life."

Sheetal hesitated. What was she supposed to say?

"You are quite ordinary of aspect for a star's child, are you not?" a woman with a long, gleaming plait asked across the table, studying her. "It is an odd thing to see."

"Indeed! I am confounded anew by the bluntness of mortal features. How much like ours, and yet how unlike," a man said.

Others chimed in with their agreement, as if Sheetal were on display at a zoo. She bristled. Was this how they would have treated Dad?

Charumati delicately cleared her throat, and the woman dropped her gaze. But Sheetal was sure it didn't stop the others from thinking it: Her human blood. Her human friend. So very strange.

She pushed her plate away and opened her mouth to tell them exactly where things stood. She would *not* be ashamed of Dad or Minal. Not now, not ever.

Charumati pressed Sheetal's hand as if to stay her protest.

"Is this how we speak to guests?" Nani asked quietly, her restrained tone belying the steel beneath it. "To those of our line?"

"But is she not plain?" the woman protested.

Nana silenced her with a glower.

Even Sheetal could feel the disquiet altering the starry melody. The shift was slight, a deepening of notes, yet enough to raise goose bumps along her arms.

She froze. Did that mean they could sense *her* feelings, too?

Nani surveyed the table, letting the heft of her stare rest on each of the stars. "I realize it has been some time since we invited mortal guests to our realm, but that is no excuse for speaking in this way."

Heads lowered, and no one seemed foolish enough to protest.

"Think on it," Nana said, his face grave. "How will we look to the court if we cannot even maintain solidarity among ourselves? If we decry one who would represent us all, our champion?"

*Represent us all?* This competition thing had officially gone too far. "Uh, Nani?" Sheetal began.

But everyone was looking at Charumati, who'd stood. Her enchanting eyes gleamed with all the warmth Sheetal had been starving for, making Sheetal go soft, even fuzzy, inside. "Our blood flows in my daughter's veins. She is our hope, our future. Treat her—and her friend—as such."

"I meant no harm," said the woman with the long braid, sounding repentant, "truly. Pardon my misstep, Lady Sheetal."

Still watching her mother, Sheetal forgot she needed to answer. An expectant hush hung in the air.

Minal was the one who replied. "It's okay. I'd be curious, too."

"It's fine," Sheetal echoed, a half step too late, wanting the whole weird conversation behind her. She wasn't anybody's symbol or anybody's hope. "But I need to say something."

She braced herself, then peeked up at her mother, whose gaze harnessed her own.

The scales within Sheetal tipped, weighted with worry, with recognition, and with joy. *Mom. My mom. Dancing in the daisy field. Telling me fairy tales.*

As if the sidereal song were a sea of starlight, the tide crashed over her, and for a second, a minute—an hour?—it was all she knew. When she glanced around again, everyone had resumed eating. Charumati sat beside her once more, humming. It felt wonderful and alien at the same time.

And scary. What was that?

The beautiful sensation vaporized into fury. Had her mother just used the starsong on her?

"I have waited so long to teach you of our house, our history," Nani said, beaming. "Your place in our line. And now here you are, where you belong. There is so much to do."

Sheetal's hands tingled; her skin prickled. She shoved back her chair and got up. Screw politeness. Screw family ties. None of that would save Dad.

156

"What is the matter, child?" Nana asked. "Be calm, for you are safe here."

Every eye in the room bored into Sheetal, and the star-song soared to a crescendo. She plunged forward anyway. "I'm sorry, but you crossed some wires somewhere. I can't be your champion."

The stars' glow flared hotter as they gasped. Giving Charumati a meaningful look, Sheetal added, loud enough that no one could miss it, "I'm just here to get—"

Minal caught her eye. *Don't,* she mouthed.

Sheetal had been about to say "blood," but at that, she changed course. "—help for my dad. You know, on Earth."

She'd been prepared for anger, for argument, but Nani only raised her hand for silence. "Vacate this chamber," she commanded. "All of you but my daughter and granddaughter. And speak of this to no one, or you will answer to me."

After the others had left the long table, she asked, "Minal, how would you appreciate a tour of the palace while we speak as a family? Padmini will escort you."

Minal hesitated, but Sheetal caught her eager expression. "Go," she made herself say. "I've got this."

All she could do now was pray that was true.

In their sitting room, Nani and Nana watched Sheetal with complicated expressions. Pride shifted among other things she couldn't name but wasn't sure she liked.

"Sit, dikri," Nani said, gesturing to an indigo divan next to a wide ebony bookcase. "I realize how bizarre this must all seem to you. We have much ground to cover, starting with a bit of family history."

The crater in Sheetal's chest spread. The guard had said they'd been expecting her, and the astral melody had as good as sucked her into the sky, it had been so strong. Compelling her to ascend.

What was it her mom had written in that letter to Radhikafoi? *The time will come when she must ascend, when she will hear our call. . . .*

She stayed standing near the doorway. "I'm kind of in a hurry. You know—the reason I came here?"

Nana smiled. "We understand. Please hear us out."

"Sit, Sheetal," Charumati said gently. "I have not forgotten what you asked."

Sheetal sat. At least they hadn't said no. "Five minutes."

"When our house led the court of the stars," Nani began, "we and we alone governed how the nakshatras would interact with mortals."

"We serve as muses to them," Nana interjected. "Then and now."

Nani smiled at him. "Indeed." To Sheetal, she said, "We cut off free passage between the realms in the wake of the star hunters. It was simply too risky for our kind."

Star hunters. Dev's family. Sheetal shuddered.

"Over time mortals forgot who we were and that we existed

outside stories, stories that in time were also lost to memory." Nani's smile darkened. "Yet nothing lasts. The Dhanishta nakshatra later took ascendancy, soon reintroducing ideas of a sort better left alone and reopening the gateway, exposing us once more to mortal whim and violence."

"Mortals do not know how to control themselves," Charumati said. "It is our responsibility to correct for that."

The look Nani gave Charumati was less than flattering. "We will discuss that later, Daughter."

"That's interesting and all, but what does it have to do with me?" Sheetal asked. Every minute they talked was another minute Dad could die.

"How do you think I made it down to meet your papa?" Charumati answered. "Few of our kind were interested in walking among mortals any longer, yet I had always desired to know more."

"Yes, and what a foolish decision!" Nani snapped. Nana stroked her arm, and the annoyance melted from her face. "But now we have a chance to restore order, beti. *You* are that chance, Sheetal."

"I still don't understand, though." Sheetal was trying to be patient, but they kept talking around the question. "How am I involved?"

Charumati patted her hand. "The court holds a competition to determine the successor when either the Esteemed Matriarch or Patriarch of the ruling house ages into the final stage of existence, the supernova, or, less commonly, when they

159

choose to step down. To compete, each interested house must present a champion—a mortal artist it then inspires."

"From the sky we come, and to the sky we return—the great Void that is Mother Kali," Nani intoned. "Yet before that, there is much to be done. With the Esteemed Patriarch of House Dhanishta taking his leave and you as our champion, we will reclaim our old position and resume that work."

"But I didn't sign up for this." They thought they could send for Sheetal out of the blue, and she'd jump to do their bidding? "And I'm not an artist."

"Then what is your music?" Nana asked. "That is the mortal part of you."

"We *are* music," Nani put in. "You, however, are a musician. We have witnessed that."

What did that even mean? Sheetal thought she was good, even awesome, at music in the way mortals were, but with the astral melody always "helping," she'd never gotten the chance to find out for sure. She hunched into herself. It was one thing to be in her secret room and know the sky outside was watching and another to hear it in person from the family she'd only just met.

"No," she said. "I'm here for Dad." It felt like she'd said the same thing a hundred times, and no one was listening. "Mom—Charumati—knows. Ask her."

"She spoke with us last night," Nana said. "Gautam will have the blood. Indeed, we shall deliver it to him."

*Really?* It seemed too easy, but Sheetal wasn't going to

question her good luck. "That's so great! Thank you." She hopped up. "I'll take it right now. Why wait?"

Something unsaid passed between Charumati and her parents. "Anything for our own granddaughter," Nani said slowly, "but it is not as simple as all that."

Sheetal stared at her. "What are you trying to say?"

Nani smiled. "It seems we are both in difficult situations and can be of mutual assistance."

The trap, so glittering and hypnotic at first, was closing around Sheetal. She could almost feel its jaws snapping shut.

She walked to the bookshelf, keeping her back to Nani and Charumati so they couldn't see how mad she was. And so they couldn't mesmerize her with their unearthly beauty into doing what they wanted. "What do you need from me, exactly?"

Charumati replied this time. "We will inspire you, and you will play your music for the panel of judges in the competition."

"We stand behind you, dikri," Nana said, his voice kind. "Always."

"How do I even qualify?" Sheetal hoped she sounded indifferent. "I mean, I'm half star."

"Ah, but you are half mortal, too." Charumati's satisfaction was unmistakable. "An advantage no other house can claim."

"And when *is* this competition?" Running her finger over the silver-gilded spines in front of her, Sheetal fell right into one of her oldest daydreams. She'd sit onstage in an elegant silk dress, her harp leaning against her shoulder, and smile out at her adoring audience before launching into a beloved folk song, her voice soaring like a kite. Her name would be everywhere from the marquee to the program to her cheering fans' lips. "It's got to be at least a few weeks from now, right? I'd have to go home first and help Dad. . . ."

"Two days from today. The anniversary of your birth," said Nani.

Sheetal spun around. "Two days?! I don't even know what I'm doing!" At the very least, she'd have to pick a song and rehearse in front of other people.

"We will have our first lesson anon," Nani continued smoothly. "It would have been ideal if you had arrived when the call for the champions first went out, but never fear; I have drawn up a rigorous schedule to make the best of what time remains to us."

*Calm down,* Sheetal ordered herself. This had to be a prank. Weird star humor. "What—what about Dad? You said you would take the blood to him. He'll die if you don't!"

"Win the competition for our house, and anything you wish for will be yours," said Nani, unmoved. "Including a drop of blood from my own veins."

Wow. Sheetal almost laughed. All she had to do to save Dad was win a contest she hadn't even known about twenty-four hours ago. When she'd never played in front of strangers in her entire life, and the very thought made her stomach shrivel. No pressure.

But her hands tingled. She'd be inspired, the way she'd

162

apparently inspired Dev. He'd smashed through his creative block like demolishing a dam.

The memory kindled something at her core. Fire like mercury flame traced over her skin, glittering against the onyx of the sitting room, threatening to engulf her. What had she actually done to inspire him? She didn't know that any more than she knew how to untangle her music from the starsong. . . .

*Silver in the bones,* the astral melody seemed to sing then, *silver in the blood.* It gushed through her, a current of starlight and suggestion sweeping her along, and all she could do was try not to go under.

Sheetal was minuscule, a pathetic puppet for forces so immeasurable she couldn't begin to understand them. They would devour her. They already were.

"Where is Gautam?" Nana asked, coming closer. "Can you describe his condition?"

"I don't know. He had a heart attack. I—I tried giving him a drop of my blood, but it didn't work," she babbled. "I thought— I don't know what I thought."

She didn't realize she was tearing at the cuticle on her thumb until she looked down. Blood welled up—the blood that wasn't enough. That would never be enough.

Nani traipsed over and looked Sheetal in the eye, searching. "Tell me, child. What brought on this sudden case of cardiac distress?"

Sheetal tried to blink, but Nani held her gaze like she'd nailed it there. She cocked her head as if listening. A few seconds later, she nodded. "I suspected as much. You know not how to wield your flame. We must remedy that straightaway."

Nani had read her mind! Sheetal wanted to crawl out of her own skin in mortification. She *had* to learn how to shield herself.

"Beti, in good conscience, how could we send you home when you might burn yourself up? Or others?" Charumati sounded genuinely concerned. "We must teach you mastery of your abilities, for they will only grow stronger with each day that passes."

"Do not worry for your papa," Nana said. "Your blood may not be pure, but it is enough to tether him to the mortal world until you return. But your nani is right; we must train you for your own safety."

Sheetal flailed. "Mom?"

Her mother nodded. "Heed the song. It will always tell you what is true."

That was something, at least.

Sheetal breathed in as deeply as she could, then allowed herself to fall into the astral melody. Strands of starlight connected her to the other stars in the sky, and her earthly concerns dissipated like stardust over vast swaths of night. It assured her Dad would be safe for now.

With a flutter of soft, silvery notes, she melted back into the moment, back into Nani's study where her mother and grandparents waited for her answer.

"You swear you'll give me the blood if I win?" she asked.

164

Nani raised cupped hands filled with silver flame. "I vow it on the light that is our bloodline," she pronounced. "If House Pushya wins, the blood is yours."

They had Sheetal cornered. If she wanted to save Dad, she had no choice.

"First lesson," she chirped, all false enthusiasm. "I can't wait."

# 13

Nani paused in the doorway to her study, her starry circlet gleaming like a guiding light. "Did you have enough to eat, beti? Are you still hungry?" She sounded so attentive, so considerate, the perfect grandmother.

"No," Sheetal said, still reeling. To save Dad, she didn't just have to compete in whatever this was. She had to *win*. In two days, no less. How in the world—how in the universe—was she supposed to do that?

She'd glanced over the detailed training schedule Nani's secretary had inscribed on thick blue parchment—voice and instrument rehearsals, tours of the court, etiquette schooling— but it only made her want to hide out somewhere safe, like her bedroom at home, and scream until her throat was raw and this all made sense. How had Dad's fate come to depend on *her*?

Dad would tell her to observe and take notes, that this was

a problem, and problems had solutions. She clung to that like a rope to keep from slipping off the cliff of despair. "No, thanks. I'm full."

Nani clapped, one smart clap, and just like that she was the tall, dignified monarch again. "Good, then let us begin. We have a full day of instruction and training planned."

For the next hour, Nani led Sheetal on a tour of their nakshatra's wing of the palace, detailing who lived in which suite. Sheetal made a mental map as they went along. Each star's standing in the house hierarchy determined the number of rooms they had, with Nani and Nana at the top, of course.

The palace proper, Nani explained, was laid out like a many-petaled flower composed of smaller flowers, each flower devoted to a different group of beings and joined by a covered bridge to the gods' courtyard at the center.

One of those smaller flowers housed the twenty-seven nakshatras, each in its own wing. It was all so lovely, with enamel and silver and ebony everywhere she looked, that Sheetal couldn't get over the feeling she'd landed in one of Charumati's leather-bound volumes from the secret room at home. There was the multitude of lushly adorned spaces, many of which had no ceiling but the sky. There were the so-beautiful-it-hurt-to-look-at people in their clothes made of silk and stardust. There was the orchard of skyberry and blue mango trees, its arresting aroma permeating the air.

As they passed through the residential section of the Pushya wing, Nani pointed out the various suites of rooms and named their residents. She even took Sheetal inside her own impressive apartments. "You are always welcome here, dikri. Do not be shy."

Charumati's set of rooms was on the left. "I will leave that to your mother to show you."

"Wait, what about that one?" Sheetal asked. Nani had skipped over the suite to the right of the one she shared with Nana.

"It is unoccupied," Nani said shortly, "and has been for some time." Her nostrils flared. "If I had been able to arrange it, you would be lodging here, not in the guest quarters with the other champions. A daughter of our line should be with us."

"It's fine, honestly," Sheetal said. Even that champion's dorm room had been prettier than any place she'd ever stayed in on Earth.

Like a bewitching film score, the astral melody played in the background of her thoughts, urging her toward fantastical dreams. Her bones knew this place. They wanted to sink into it and forget everything else. Sheetal shook it off. *Disloyal, two-timing bones.*

Nani gestured to the end of the hallway carved with statuary of flowers, gods, and stars from the past. Pewter sconces shaped like garudas and winged nagas washed the walls with flickers of starlight. "If you wish to visit a friend in another house, you simply cross the edge of the court and enter the appropriate passageway. I am certain you will make many friends and be paying many visits."

"Twenty-seven passageways for twenty-seven nakshatras," Sheetal guessed, ignoring the question of friends.

"Indeed. And our house is—was—the highest in the court."

"But if there're only twenty-seven nakshatras, what about all the other stars in the universe?"

Nani nodded slightly, as if Sheetal had just confirmed a private theory. "Your mother did not teach you much about our ways, did she?"

Maybe it was because of Nani's obvious irritation, but Sheetal's first reaction was to defend Charumati. She pushed back against it. What had her mother done to deserve her loyalty? Not stick around, that was for sure. "Some. I know stories."

"Yet do you know *us*?"

What was Sheetal supposed to say? Of course she didn't. Until last week, she hadn't even known her mother ever planned on seeing her up close again.

"You might have been raised as a mortal," Nani said firmly, her uncanny eyes kindling, "but here you are one of us, and it is time you learn."

They walked on. *One of us*. What did that mean? What did Sheetal want that to mean?

*Nothing*, she reminded herself. Dad was the only reason she was here at all.

Making a clicking sound of disapproval, Nani closed the distance between them and gripped Sheetal's hand. "Stop that."

Her thumb stung. She'd been tearing at her cuticle again.

"You must never treat yourself like that," admonished Nani. "Self-flagellation is a foolish habit, a mortal habit. You must behave as the precious being you are."

*Well, yeah,* Sheetal thought. *Of course you think I'm precious. Without me, you have no champion.*

"I realize this is a great deal to take in at once, but it is vital you learn as much as possible in the time we have. When I called to you," Nani said, releasing her, "we had already waited too long."

She smoothed a nonexistent stray strand back into her bun. "As I was saying, the nakshatras. Without question, there are many stars in the heavens, but it is as with your mortal courts: a few royal houses govern the masses, and to preserve order, one house rules over the rest."

Silver radiance haloed Nani's form. In that moment, Sheetal glimpsed both aspects of her grandmother: the old woman who stood before her and the blazing star. Her power was obvious, a tangible thing. Here was someone who had ruled entire courts, who had sung before Lord Indra and had his ear.

"There is a good deal of responsibility that comes with our position. It is our duty to light the way for others, to burn brightly in the darkness. We are the children of possibility, and we wake that possibility in those who witness our flame. That flame," Nani declared, standing taller and yet more brilliant, "is in you, mortal blood or no."

"Or maybe that mortal blood is inside me, flame or no," Sheetal muttered, but so softly Nani didn't catch it. "I have questions," she said more loudly.

Nani waggled her head. "Then ask as we walk."

In rapid succession, Sheetal learned that stars didn't need to sleep but instead had an aspect that spun in the sky each night; that there was indeed a place stars watched humans, called the Hall of Mirrors—a place she intended to check out as soon as possible—and that the stars had devised a method for inspiring mortals from afar.

Nani led her through a long colonnade. "Speaking of that, I suspect you will enjoy this next part."

They emerged onto a balcony that bordered a round, dark room, its ceiling and floor both open to the night sky. Crystal jars as high as Sheetal's hip lined the balcony, their contents casting a slight silver glow through the space.

"This room is off-limits to our mortal visitors," her grandmother said, "as I am certain you can understand. Every night, we empty jars of stardust into the heavens. These are the bits of us that fall through the clouds and enter mortal imaginations, what you call inspiration." She frowned. "It is not as powerful as when we walked the earth, but the risk of face-to-face contact is too great."

"Why?" Sheetal asked, expecting Nani to bring up Dev's ancestors, but Nani only motioned to the jars before them.

"Pick one up," she said. "It matters not which." Sheetal picked up the nearest jar. To her surprise, it weighed almost nothing. "Now turn it over the balcony."

"But—"

"Go on," Nani said.

A soft hum stirred the air, rousing Sheetal's skin, and she sucked in a breath when she realized it was coming from Nani. Her grandmother was singing.

The contents of the jars responded with a high, sweet counterpoint that felt like yearning in its purest form. Melancholy, longing, an ache for something more. The ache Sheetal had always known like an old injury that had never quite healed.

Humans needed this like flint to the tinder of their imagination. Inspiration. And *she* needed to give it to them.

Leaning over the railing, Sheetal raised her arms as high as she could and upended the jar. A million tiny stars streamed out, silver bright and scintillating. Their music might have been the haunting, elusive pitch of a bansuri, a bamboo flute. Instead of falling straight down, they swished across the room, swirling around Sheetal and Nani and wreathing them in lambent warmth before dancing down through the open floor toward the mortal world, bearing with them the prospect of hope, of dreams, of magic.

"It feels good, yes?" asked Nani, watching her expectantly. "Right, perhaps?"

It did feel right, like someone had turned on a string of fairy lights inside her. Sheetal's heart thrummed with her own song, harmonizing with Nani's notes in her own internal soprano. It was the astral song, the song that connected her to their shared nakshatra. The tingle spread from her hands to the rest of her body, waiting.

"There," said Nani, smiling. "Your first lesson."

Sheetal reflexively reached for invisible strings. If only she had her harp or her dilruba right now.

"As you know," Nani continued, "you will reach majority on your birthday. I have begun preparations for a lavish ball in your honor to precede the competition."

*A ball!* Sheetal did a little shimmy at the idea of being celebrated for once, on display in a way her auntie had never allowed. She could imagine the sparkles, the enchantment, the outfits.

The ball would be silver and crystal and wrapped in night, a revel out of a fairy tale.

Right then, Earth felt a universe away.

Sheetal gave herself a shake. She wasn't here for balls or daydreams. It would be so very easy to get smitten by the fantasy Nani was crafting. So very, very easy to pretend it was more than what it was. And Nani knew that. "Tell me again how Dad's going to be okay until I get back?"

"Certainly. Your blood possesses enough of our healing ability to hold him in a temporary stasis. He will, in effect, sleep until he is woken."

"In three days," Sheetal stressed. "Counting today." Somehow thinking of it like that made it seem a tiny bit less impossible.

"In three days, counting today. I vowed it, did I not?"

Sheetal relaxed just enough that she could imagine actually pulling this off. "Can we can talk more about the competition?"

"Of course. What do you wish to know?"

173

"Like, what's in it for the other champions? Somehow I don't see them doing this out of the goodness of their hearts."

Nani rewarded her with a gratified smile. "I have been waiting for you to ask. Let us continue." As they headed back toward the center of the starry court, she said, "Four nakshatras other than ours have—what is your mortal idiom? Declared a desire to compete?"

"Thrown their hats into the ring?" Sheetal suggested. She'd been filing away all the engraved doors and brilliant portraits they'd passed, all the carved marble pillars, all the statues, until she couldn't take in another thing. It was like wandering for hours in a museum or on a movie set, except nothing was behind glass, and none of the people they ran into were actors.

And no museum on Earth, not even the strangest ones, had magic.

"Yes, precisely. Four other nakshatras have thrown their hats into the ring and provided you four challengers to contend with." Nani swatted at the air, as if batting away a particularly irksome fly. "Each was selected for their artistic potential after having been located and observed through the Hall of Mirrors."

So Sheetal was up against four different people, who'd all been chosen for being the best at whatever they did, and who'd probably been preparing for weeks now. Wonderful.

She thought back to the competing nakshatras lined up by the stage. Charumati had led her away before the final champion had been welcomed. "House Revati. Who's its champion?"

Nani's mouth curled with displeasure. "A story crafter or some such."

A pair of stars approached, nodding at Nani before returning to their own conversation.

"But never mind that," she went on. "Perhaps it would interest you to learn that not everyone accepts our offer. That is rare, however; by the time we approach a prospective candidate, we have thoroughly assessed both their level of skill and degree of ambition."

Had they been watching *Sheetal* like that, gauging her strengths and weaknesses? Or did they just assume she'd be the best because she was half star? "But you still haven't told me why they would bother. The champions, I mean."

Nani frowned. "Few mortals can resist the lure of such a potential prize: instant recognition and universal acclaim in the annals of human history, from the moment they return home until the end of time. Like a fire that never ceases to burn and shines its light over all that comes after."

Sheetal gawked at her. "Wait, so they're like Shakespeare? Or the Taj Mahal?"

"Indeed," said Nani. "What artist does not wish to be remembered? To know their work speaks to others across eras and cultures?"

"But—but how do you reach out to them at all?" Sheetal asked, thinking of how entranced Minal had been with everything since they got here, and how *she* probably would be, too, if it weren't for Dad. "And how do you keep them from breaking in half when they get here? This stuff is *huge!*"

Nani stopped before a pair of silver doors embossed with all the twenty-seven nakshatras. "Each house sends a representative to speak to its selected candidate. A trace of magic is necessary to allay any culture shock, as you noted; and to keep them further grounded, each candidate is permitted one mortal companion of their choosing." She smiled. "That one you brought, she appears quite attentive to your needs. You have chosen well."

That, at least, explained how the guards had reacted to Minal at the palace gates. "But what happens to the people who don't win?"

"Then that same magic later removes all memories of their encounter with us from their minds. We are not in the business of being cruel."

*And so they can't talk about you,* Sheetal added, remembering how Charumati had once warned her to hide.

But if people like the star hunters still existed, was that such a bad idea? She didn't know.

Nani pointed to the double doors, each with an antiqued silver pull in the shape of a four-pointed star. "This is our common room, a space where stars of any nakshatra may gather freely. Behind it, you will find the guest quarters. Soon we must hurry to your rehearsal, but would you first care to step inside for a beverage? It is important to show your face, so that none believe you afraid."

Sheetal balked. Show her face? *Afraid?* The insult from the welcome ceremony came back to her then. *Mortal half-thing.*

Nani touched her shoulder, and her concern was sincere, crisp and bright in the song around them. "Hear me, dikri. The choice is yours to make. If you wish to move straight into the rehearsal, we will do that instead. My inclination is simply to offer you all possible advantages."

Maybe it was stupid of her, since the starsong would only reflect the emotions Nani wanted it to, but Sheetal warmed at feeling her worry, anyway. Besides, she didn't have anything to hide from the other stars. "We can go in," she said, returning Nani's smile. "A drink sounds good."

They entered the common room, a pentagonal chamber lined by huge scalloped windows, lit by perforated star-shaped lanterns and more of the sconces Sheetal had seen in the corridor, and festooned with rich blue-and-silver draperies and ebony furniture with matching upholstery. Stars stood in small clusters of three and four, all casting her suspicious glances as she passed by.

Sheetal hadn't expected celestial gatherings to feel so much like parties on Earth, everyone in their little cliques—and her on the fringes. Where were *her* stars? Where were Minal and Padmini?

She missed Earth. She really missed Dad. "After my rehearsal," she told Nani, "I want to see the Hall of Mirrors."

"I am certain we can find an opportunity at some point." Nani led her to the marble fountain at the center of the room, where a handmaiden dipped silver cups into the flowing sky-hued liquid. "First, however, let us focus. There is so little time to prepare you."

*Whose fault is that?* Sheetal thought.

The handmaiden inclined her head. "Skyberry cordial, pressed from our own orchards. Would you like a taste?" Sheetal nodded, and the handmaiden offered her a cup.

It was like drinking the cloud-streaked sunsets she'd dubbed "cotton candy sky" as a kid. Sweet and refreshing, with a hint of tartness. "Nani, how well did you know my dad?"

Nani hadn't heard her. Her mouth thinned as stars bearing the House Revati insignia came into view, along with a human man with curly hair who looked to be around nineteen or twenty. "Those upstarts think to offend us, that we might simply hand over rulership to them. As if they could cow us so!"

"What do you mean?" The man looked vaguely familiar, maybe, but that was all. Not what Sheetal would call threatening.

Two people hurried toward them, blocking him from sight. "The other competing houses have called a convocation and wish you to join them at your earliest convenience, Esteemed Matriarch," the taller of the two visitors crooned. "Hello again, star's daughter."

It was the apsara from the Night Market, swathed in a sari of the pink lotus-petal taffeta she'd considered in the fabric stall. A starry page, who looked about ten years old, accompanied her.

"You got it after all," Sheetal said. "The taffeta."

The apsara struck a runway-model pose. "It suits me quite well, I must say."

"It does," Sheetal agreed. "We met on Earth," she told Nani, whose forehead creased.

"Esteemed Matriarch," the page said when Nani didn't move to follow him, "the convocation awaits."

Nani considered him for a full thirty seconds, then nodded. "Tell them Jagdeesh and I shall receive them in our study in twenty minutes."

"And the Esteemed Patriarch? Shall I seek him out?"

"No need," Nani said. "I will send him word via the song."

The page put his palms together in acknowledgment, then scampered off.

"My apologies, beti," Nani said to Sheetal. "I am disinclined to leave you here, yet it cannot be helped. Can you find your way back to my apartments when you finish making your rounds here?"

Sheetal couldn't think of anything she wanted less than to fumble through this crowd of strange faces alone, but she tried to sound like she didn't care. "I'll be fine."

Nani leaned close and whispered, "You are of the House of Pushya. Our song rings in your bones. Our light is your light. Let no one tell you otherwise."

"How perfectly scrumptious!" the apsara cooed as Nani strode away. "It has been so frightfully *dreary* around here. But now that you mortals are appearing . . ."

179

"Right. How long has it been since any humans visited?" Sheetal asked. The more she talked, the more she could put off going over and introducing herself to House Revati's champion.

"Oh, perhaps half a millennium? Who can keep track?" The apsara launched into what would have been juicy court gossip if Sheetal hadn't been too floored to enjoy it.

The most recent competition had been *five hundred years* ago? And she was somehow expected to win this one on zero knowledge or experience?

*You can do this,* she reminded herself, nursing her cup and nodding every so often at the apsara's prattle. *You're awesome.*

Too bad she didn't believe a word of it.

And there, approaching like a mirage, was a different familiar mortal guy. A guy who in fact looked just like her boyfriend.

Okay, now she was hallucinating. Wasn't she?

Even in jeans and a T-shirt, Dev Merai was as beautiful as the stars.

# 14

Sheetal literally did a double take, her heart somersaulting in her chest. Unless Dev had a doppelgänger, it was him.

Why would he be here? His ancestor had kept the woman he'd claimed to love in a cage after she'd tried to leave and had abused her when she didn't do what he wanted. And he'd bled her for profit on top of that.

Sheetal wanted to call out to Dev. But she couldn't stop staring long enough to catch her breath.

The stars pressed in around him, apparently not grasping the concept of personal space. They pelted questions, scarcely letting him answer one before the next arrived on its heels. "Do you drive a car?" someone asked. "What is it like?"

A second star pushed the first one aside. "No, tell us if you have ever been in a movie. Is it true you leave part of yourself behind in the camera?"

Dev glanced uncertainly from one star to the other as he tried and failed to put some distance between them. "Uh—"

"Hey, hey, give him some space," said the curly-haired human man behind him, who had to be House Revati's champion. He waved the stars back. "I get that you're curious and all, but don't smother the guy."

Sheetal kept her eyes trained on Dev's profile, hoping he could feel her gaze boring into his skull. Hoping it hurt.

If it did, he didn't react, so she marched right over, ignoring the astounded expressions around her, and tapped him on the shoulder.

He raised his head, and now she couldn't deny it was Dev, from the dark eyes that drank her in to the familiar mouth she was ashamed to have kissed. A lot. Her mind helpfully wandered back to yesterday afternoon, in his bed, and she flushed.

"Your hair," he breathed. "Wow."

"Why are you here?" she demanded, hating how part of her was glad to see him, to hear him admiring her shimmering starlight tresses. What was wrong with her?

"Nice to see you, too," Dev said, like he'd just casually run into her between classes at school.

She grabbed his wrist, and a shock passed between them, making her shiver. "We need to talk."

He jerked free. "Oh, so *now* you want to talk?"

The curly-haired man had to pick that exact moment to join the conversation. "Hi," he said, sticking his hand out for her to shake. "So you're the famous Sheetal. You ran off before I could say hi at the welcome ceremony."

"Bhai," Dev mumbled, dropping his gaze.

*Bhai.* Sheetal realized where she knew this guy from. The pictures on Dev's wall. Jeet. The flame at her core sparked, ready to burn things. "Is someone going to tell me what's going on?"

"Maybe we should go outside," Jeet suggested lightly, and with the stars of House Revati—and that apsara—goggling at them, Sheetal couldn't argue. She deposited her half-full cup on a nearby table and nodded.

"Excuse us a minute," Jeet told his entourage, and it parted just enough to let the three of them pass.

They hurried through the double doors and into the corridor, where Sheetal turned her glare on Dev. "What are you *doing* here?"

Jeet smiled agreeably. "I know things got out of hand, but it wasn't his fault."

"Out of hand? You sent him to spy on me!" With her stupid lips still tingling, it was easier to look at him than Dev.

Jeet held up his hands. "You're right. That was out of line, and I own it. I never should have asked him to do that."

When Sheetal didn't say anything, he went on. "Think I'm a jerk all you want, but don't blame him. He really let me have it after he met you, and I backed off."

He shifted to stand directly in front of her, and for a second, it looked like his skin had a weird silver-pale cast. But then she realized he was just reflecting her own furious flame. So was the entire hallway. "What are you trying to say? Yes, you did spy on me, but it's okay because you stopped?"

"No. I'm trying to apologize." Jeet and Dev didn't look alike at all, but that self-deprecating expression was one hundred percent Dev. "And doing a bang-up job of it, huh? Listen, I'm sorry."

Against her will, Sheetal thawed a smidge. She nodded stiffly. She hadn't expected an apology, but she wasn't ready to forgive him, either. Or Dev, for that matter.

"Well, I'll leave you two to catch up, but seriously, Dev was trying to do the right thing. I just want you to know that." Jeet nodded at her and disappeared back into the common room.

Now that they were alone, Sheetal didn't know where to look. Every bit of her was all too aware of how close Dev was, how all she'd have to do to touch him was take that last step. Finally she settled on a patch of wall just behind his ear. "You didn't answer my question. Why are you here?"

Dev crossed his arms. "I thought you didn't want to hear anything I had to say."

"Are you serious?" Sheetal couldn't believe him.

"I'm here to provide moral support. The trusty sidekick, or mortal companion, as they call it here."

"I guess I shouldn't be surprised," she said. "What I can't get is why anyone would want a star torturer's whatever-grandkid as their champion."

She was so mad, but something treacherous deep inside

her wanted to forget everything and just kiss him. That made her even madder. She leaned against the wall, trying to look bored.

"How long are you going to hold that against me, anyway?" Dev asked the mosaic ceiling. "It's not like I even had anything to do with it. Jeet didn't, either."

"No, but—but," Sheetal stammered. "But you knew what I was, and you pretended you didn't!"

Gods, why did she feel like crying? He was just a stupid boy.

*Just the stupid boy who knew I was a star and spied on me.*

Dev stuck his hands in his pockets. "Look, none of us believed in that whole family legend thing, all right? But then someone from the Revati nakshatra showed up and asked him to be their champion."

*They should have picked you.* She quashed the thought, horrified at herself. "How did they hear about him?"

"His fiction is starting to take off. You know, the kind of stuff in the *New Yorker*? Literary fiction?"

"Your cousin writes for the *New Yorker*?" Sheetal couldn't help being impressed. "You never told me that."

"No, but he wants to. Anyway, the desi community out there is buzzing about him, especially after he won a Flying Start grant last fall." Dev smiled proudly. "Growing up, he didn't always have it easy like I did, you know? But he always supported my music no matter what anyone else said. He's earned this shot."

"But he's a star hunter. A *star hunter*." Sheetal stared at him,

185

waiting for that to sink in. "How is anyone here remotely okay with that?"

He threw her an annoyed glance. "Don't you think you're overreacting just a little? You might as well call *me* a star hunter, then. It's been, like, fifteen generations since that happened. Most of my family doesn't even believe you exist."

Overreacting? Sheetal could have screamed. "So why do they keep telling that awful story?"

"I told you. It's bizarre, something to make them stand out, like when people say they're descended from Jack the Ripper. Does that make every single person who shares DNA with him a serial killer?"

Put like that, it sounded really stupid. Her cheeks heated. "Whatever. Did you ever even like me?"

She'd meant to hurt him, but he only looked mystified and a tad vulnerable. "Of course I do. Why are you asking that?"

"But your cousin made you talk to me. You said so." Sheetal didn't know why she was pushing this. What was she hoping for, anyway?

"Look, everyone here knows your mom had a kid on Earth. I guess that's kind of a big deal? And the star from Revati told—"

"Told Jeet, and he asked you to spy on me," Sheetal finished for him. Her throat stung, and she found herself tearing at a hangnail. "So what'd you report? Was I useful? Is he all set to win the competition now, what with his insider info on stars and our weak spots?"

"It wasn't like that!" Dev protested, moving closer. "I didn't tell him anything."

"Only because I didn't know anything for you to tell." Sheetal shook her head. She kind of believed him; that was the worst part.

"Sheetal, listen—" His voice cracked, then broke off as a band of stars headed their way. The stars nodded at Dev but frowned at her. She made herself smile brightly in return.

"Save it, Dev," she said the second they'd left. "Just admit you tried to use me."

"Well, we both did things. I mean, you ran off without letting me explain!"

Sheetal laughed. "'We both did things.'" Like kissing. Rivers of silver flame gusted up her arms and to her face. What if *that* had happened while they were making out? "You're kidding, right?"

Eyes wide, he shrank back. "You didn't exactly tell me you were a star, either."

She was glad to have scared him, she told herself, even as the flames died away. She was. "Seriously? We were together for *three months*."

"So? Would six months have been better?" Dev looked skeptical. "A year? Ten years? Were you ever going to tell me?"

"Oh, no," Sheetal said. How was he putting this on her? "This is not my fault. Don't even try that."

"I'm just trying to say you had your reasons, and so did I."

She couldn't handle how calm he sounded. "Reasons? Really?"

He took a step toward her, his smile hopeful as he reached out a hand. "Look, I miss you. Can't we just go back to how it was before?"

*Yes*, a pathetic part of her whispered. It urged her to tell him she missed him, too. She buried that part as deep as she could, where no one would ever know. Because she couldn't say yes.

"Go back to how it was?" she retorted instead. "You mean, when you were using me to write your songs? Or how about go back to when I burned my dad because of you? Back then?"

Let Dev hurt the way he'd hurt her.

His hand dropped to his side. "Because of *me*?"

"Yeah," she said. "I was so upset when I got home yesterday that I couldn't control it. If you hadn't lied to me . . ."

Dev's warm gaze went opaque. "You're right; I should've told you sooner I knew what you are, okay? I'd be mad, too." Sheetal opened her mouth, but he kept going. "But don't tell me I made you burn your dad. *You* did that."

The fire in Sheetal died, a match blown out. She slid down the wall. He was right. She'd done it. Only she had done it.

Dev yanked open the doors, then wheeled around. "And just so you know, I was supposed to come here the night of the party, when Jeet did. But I didn't because I wanted to spend more time with you. And then because I didn't want to just take off after we had that fight." He shook his head. "I don't know why I bothered."

Cringing inwardly, Sheetal shot back, "But you're still supporting him?"

He nodded. "I am."

"Even though you know I'm his rival or whatever?"

Dev didn't nod again, but he didn't need to.

There was no limit to how many times a heart could break in a row. "I guess we know where things stand, then," Sheetal murmured, as much to herself as to him.

"Yeah," said Dev. "I guess so." He vanished inside, letting the heavy doors bang shut behind him.

From her hiding spot behind a cabinet in Nani's and Nana's study, Sheetal listened to the convocation argue about her. A group of stars wearing diadems like her grandparents' sat around the formal table, ignoring the silver crystal cups in front of them to glare at her family.

A middle-aged star from House Magha finished railing against the injustice of a half-star champion, but instead of replying, Nana only took a leisurely pull at his drink. None of the delegates missed the slight. The sidereal song darkened with their hostility, and starlight bright enough to dazzle even Sheetal's eyes overwhelmed the space.

Nani, however, merely smiled. Beside her, Charumati held a tightly rolled scroll with rounded silver dowels. In their place, Sheetal would have been sweating bullets and buckets and anything else she could, but her mother and grandmother just looked serene, graceful and glowing, as composed as if they were sipping tea in a garden. A little vexed at being bothered, maybe, but that was it.

"If protocol is not meant to be observed," the star from House Magha asked, "why bother with a competition at all? What prevents my house from simply claiming the ruling seats right now?"

"If it is that simple," a younger female star added, "I deem it so: the court belongs to the Ashvini nakshatra!"

A star about Nani's age from House Krittika lifted his cup just to set it back down with a clatter. "You may grasp for power as much as you wish, Eshana. That is your right. Nevertheless, it does not extend to flouting the regulations."

"We adhered to the bylaws and selected purely mortal champions," the star from House Ashvini called. "Why is the Pushya nakshatra not bound by the same?"

"A fair question," Nani said coolly, every bit the sovereign. "Please permit me to pose a question of my own. Where in the bylaws does it say a champion must have solely mortal blood?" She signaled to Charumati, who untied her scroll and let one end of the parchment unspool.

Charumati ran a long finger down the text. "'Qualifications for eligibility: each prospective nakshatra must name a mortal champion. The champion must then be trained and prepared to compete.' Odd—I see no stipulations beyond that."

The star from House Magha glowered. "Let me see that." When Charumati offered him the scroll, he snatched it from her.

"It is about the spirit of the law, Eshanaben," the star from House Krittika said, waggling his head. "Not the letter."

Nani folded her arms. "No one is preventing any of you from seeking out a mortal champion with naga blood or apsara blood. Do so now, with my blessing. I merely chose to select a mortal champion from within my family."

"Then the bylaws must be rewritten for specificity," the star from House Ashvini declared.

"By all means," Charumati said. "In time for the next competition."

Sheetal almost laughed out loud. It was kind of fun to watch Nani and Charumati manipulate someone else.

When Nana shook his head in warning, she realized she'd stepped out too far past the cabinet and made herself visible. Her heart shrieking like an alarm, she skidded backward.

But he wasn't the only one who'd noticed. While the other representatives of the competing nakshatras all continued griping and protesting, a woman about Charumati's age pointed to Sheetal. "And there she is, the source of contention herself. Loud and untaught, a liability to the nakshatra she represents."

Sheetal's pulse drummed even harder with a horrifying thought. Oh, gods, had these stars heard her feelings about Dev? The anger, the longing, all on display for strangers—she wanted to crawl out of her skin. She was half a star, so why couldn't she just dissolve into pure light and escape through the wall?

Not knowing what else to do, she schooled her face into a placid expression and waved.

The star who had called attention to Sheetal smirked. She had a pearl-smooth complexion and large, knowing eyes, and her silver locks were threaded through with black diamonds. She had to be from House Revati, but unlike the others, she didn't have a circlet. "Oh, everyone knows how dearly you care for the sanctity of rules, Charumati," she purred. "After all, were you not the one who flouted your own house's ban on consorting with mortals?"

Sheetal wondered just what had gone down between this person and her mother to make her so vindictive. Had they been friends? Rivals? No love lost there, for sure.

"And now you have enlisted your half-mortal daughter to help you regain the court," the star from House Revati accused, her mirth dwindling. "You will never change, will you, Charumati? Everything is about you and your convenience."

Sheetal glanced at Nana. His gentle face had gone hard-edged, but he stayed quiet.

"They are consistent that way," the star from House Magha agreed. "Eshana and Charumati both. And now their house thinks it will take over speaking for the rest of us again."

"With a half-mortal brat as your mouthpiece, no less!" The star from House Revati sounded disgusted, but the gleam in her eyes betrayed just how much she was enjoying this. "Have you no shame, any of you?"

"Come, Rati," Charumati said, retrieving the scroll and rolling it up. Though her voice was cool, her ire rang out in the astral melody, all crescendi and bass. "I am well aware of what you think of me, but there is no reason to bring my daughter into it."

Rati smiled, a slow and sharp smile. "Ah, but *you* brought her into it, as your champion. I am merely commenting on the injustice of the situation."

"Enough," Nani said, her silver-brown eyes sparking. "I will not hear another word against my kin."

The star from House Ashvini grimaced. "Please, Rati, hold your insults. Our goal is not to inflame House Pushya."

"The truth is now considered an insult?" Rati sipped her drink. "Such an interesting era we live in."

"Surely you see the fault in this, Jagdeeshbhai?" the star from House Krittika asked. "The strife this propagates between our houses—will you not put an end to it?"

Nana lay his hand on Sheetal's shoulder. "Esteemed colleagues, I fully concur that animosity among the nakshatras brings harm to all. For that very reason, as we have ascertained no bylaws are in breach at this time, I suggest we table this discussion and allow the competition, rather than any one of us and our biases, to decide the outcome."

The other delegates exchanged disgruntled looks. "As you are not in breach of the bylaws," the star from House Magha said slowly, as if the words caused him pain, "I have no choice but to acquiesce." He rose to leave. "Know, however, that I *will* see the regulations redrafted, House Pushya."

"Please do," said Nani amiably. "Specificity can only be to the good of all."

There was still so much Sheetal didn't know, but one thing she did: she wasn't going to let a bunch of incensed stars or anyone else interfere with her mission. Dad needed her.

"Thank you, everyone," she said, "for this opportunity to air your concerns. I look forward to seeing you again at the competition."

"Now, if you will excuse us"—Charumati flashed Rati a smile as sweet as jalebi—"our champion's training awaits."

Rati bowed slightly as she moved toward the door. As she passed Sheetal, she whispered, "I am certain we will meet again, mortal girl, and soon."

# 15

"Shall we go?" Charumati asked Sheetal. "Your voice rehearsal awaits, and our time is running short."

Sheetal definitely didn't need the reminder. The competition was in less than two days, and they'd already burned through the morning. She could almost hear the timer counting down in her ear. "Lead the way."

But forty minutes into their rehearsal slot, she was ready to hightail it out of the central court. First she'd wasted twenty minutes racking her brain for songs she might sing and play her own accompaniment to, complicated ones she knew well enough to pull off without weeks of practice, but it was like someone had scrubbed her memory clean.

She'd finally decided on two possible candidates, an Irish folk ballad and a classical Hindu bhajan, when Charumati announced they'd be doing warm-up drills. "Let us begin with the lip trill."

"*You* don't have to do this when you sing," Sheetal muttered. She'd always avoided this particular exercise; there was no way not to feel stupid when burbling "brbrbr" like a kid blowing raspberries. Did Dev do this?

"I am not half mortal," Charumati said simply. "You are."

Sheetal sullenly pushed through the trill until she was sure her lips were going to vibrate right off. *For Dad,* she reminded herself.

"Good!" Charumati applauded. She faced Sheetal and pressed down on her collarbone, forcing her shoulders back. "But you must strive for proper posture. Now hum for me."

While her mother held her shoulders in place, Sheetal hummed, trying to relax her vocal cords. She'd learned warm-up technique from online tutorials, but it was completely different to have someone standing right there, critiquing her.

Then Charumati led her up and down a set of scales, making Sheetal go through them over and over. It seemed like an eternity before her mother was satisfied and stepped back. "I believe we are ready to try singing."

Finally! Sheetal inhaled all the way down to her diaphragm. She thought about how terrific it felt to sing, how natural. How she'd always wanted to be seen, and how now was her chance. She opened her mouth.

And remembered how exposed she'd been at breakfast, all her feelings on display for the entire court. The first notes of the ballad spilled from her throat, and they were shrill. Off-key. A satire of herself.

Even Charumati startled, her smooth brow furrowing.

Sheetal hummed, then tried again. This time, she heard Dev asking her to sing with him and the whole disaster that followed. Her throat closed. This was hopeless. She was going to fail Dad.

"Again," Charumati directed. "The song is in you."

Sheetal made the mistake of glancing up at the imaginary audience in its rows and rows of seats, at the stage where the Esteemed Matriarchs and Patriarchs—two rulers for each nakshatra, as Nani had told her—would preside over everyone, and she choked. Her voice quavered. It shattered like glass.

Where was the talent she'd always been so impatient to show off now?

"Perhaps we should have reserved our slot for tomorrow's rehearsal instead," Charumati observed at last, sounding doggedly cheerful. "A more intimate setting may be more conducive to your comfort."

*Or how about not being in this competition at all?* Sheetal thought. Everyone was acting like she'd always been here. Like she'd grown up with this part of her family and shared all their values and goals.

How could she? She didn't even really know what their values and goals were. She didn't even know her mom.

Five hundred years. They needed her to be a mortal, but they expected her to be a star.

She pictured herself faltering, stumbling on the wrong note, forgetting the lyrics, and flubbing the whole competition.

All while Dev witnessed each and every gaffe. House Pushya might as well hand out popcorn.

This was ridiculous. She knew how to sing better than anything else. Lifting her hands and sticking out her chest, she tried for a single long C.

The note came out as a squawk.

Just in time for the company of stars gliding into the court, led by a spiky-haired human girl carrying two Kathputli marionettes in a sling pouch. Priyanka.

Putting her hands on her hips, Priyanka sized Sheetal up. When she tilted her head, the purple streaks in her black hair gleamed. "Well, look who it is. The star girl who thinks she can just swan on in all late and have fancy meals with her family like she's better than the rest of us *humans*."

"Your marionettes are really something," Sheetal replied. She refused to take the bait. Plus, she did get it. In Priyanka's shoes, she'd be furious, too.

But she wasn't here for glory. She was here for Dad.

The stars frowned at Priyanka, then at Sheetal. "You need not befriend the other champions."

"Oh, don't worry; I don't need to be friends with anyone who sings like a duck. Some champion." Priyanka rolled her eyes. Her ruby nose ring sparkled in the silvery light of the stars flanking her like sentries. "I guess that's what nepotism gets you—a talentless hack."

She shot the accusation like an arrow at Charumati, who

watched with narrowed eyes but said nothing. A few of the other stars tittered.

Sheetal's resolve to be pleasant disintegrated.

"I'd just go home now if I were you," Priyanka said. "Save yourself the embarrassment of letting the whole court watch me beat you." She quacked, a depressingly accurate imitation of Sheetal's tragic attempt at a high C.

Now even those stars who hadn't laughed smirked behind their hands.

Burning with shame, Sheetal shoved past Priyanka. Her starlight tresses hung in her face, taunting her. *Half-star. Half-thing. One hundred percent hack.*

Her music was the one thing she'd always been sure of, and the first time an outsider heard it, she'd made a fool of herself.

How was she going to do this? All she wanted was to walk away. At home, at least she knew the rules.

Charumati overtook her at the exit. "There will always be those who speak in darts and spears. You must not allow yourself to be pierced by their ill will."

"Please," said Sheetal, trying to sound like she didn't care, "just let me go see Dad."

So this is the legendary Hall of Mirrors, Sheetal thought. It looked kind of like a fun house on Earth. The black-crystal walls were alight with mirrors of all different sizes and shapes, each framed in a dark blue satin studded with star-shaped gemstones. Except the hall was far too elegant to be a fun house, more like a palace made all of glittering ice.

Minal and Padmini, who'd found her on the way here, wandered through the room, checking out their reflections. "These mirrors really capture my good side," Minal decided, "if I do say so myself, and I do."

"Do not grow too attached to your own splendor," Charumati teased her. "We cannot tarry." She smiled at Sheetal. "A few minutes should suffice for our purposes."

It would have to. But Sheetal hung back, watching a trio of stars gathered around a mirror and commenting on a wedding reception. Now that she was here, she was afraid.

The stars giggled at something she'd missed, and Padmini herded Minal closer to the mirror for a better view. "This should be good," she murmured.

In the mirror, the bride, jubilant in a vivid blue gharara kameez and gold jewelry, stood with the groom, who wore an ivory sherwani and a cream-and-gold turban. Around them, dancing guests played dandiya raas, their cloth-wrapped sticks striking one another and then retreating. The bride, ignoring the hesitant groom's claim that he didn't dance, handed him a pair of dandiya. "Your wife says you have to," she said. Finally he laughed and followed her into the circle, where he managed to keep the beat.

"It is like your mortal television," Charumati explained. "A never-ending serial of delights. It is how I found your father, Sheetal."

Minal might be charmed by all this—and by Padmini—and Charumati might be used to it, but right now, Sheetal just wanted something ugly and plastic. All this beauty was overwhelming in its richness, like eating three bowls of chocolate mousse in one sitting.

Like Dad had done that one winter when she'd dared him. He'd claimed he couldn't even look at chocolate for months after, though that didn't stop him from sneaking bites of the brownies she baked. Sheetal missed him so fiercely, she couldn't breathe.

Charumati had been there, too. So had Minal.

"Do you remember," Sheetal whispered, ducking away from the mirror-gazing stars, "that New Year's Eve when we made chocolate mousse and went out to watch the fireworks, and after, Minal was our emcee, and I sang while you and Dad danced in the snow?"

They'd been, what, seven? Dad had dipped Charumati and done an exaggerated tango until both Sheetal and Minal were in stitches on the icy grass. At Minal's urging, Sheetal had sung wilder and wilder songs, until she finished with a slow one. Dad had pulled Charumati to him, swaying to the melody, and they'd gazed into each other's eyes as if no one else existed, then and always.

"Of course I do." Charumati's eyes shone like twin moons. "That is one of my most treasured of our memories together. Minal suggested such entertaining songs."

"That was so fun," Minal said. She stepped away from

Padmini and the mirror to stand by Sheetal, who glimmered happily. "I kept trying to find a song that would stump you, but you were all in."

"You were always such a wonderful singer, my dikri," her mother said. "So full of joy."

Sheetal started to thank her until she noticed the trio of stars had abandoned their mirror and were shamelessly eavesdropping. "How do I do this?" she asked instead.

Charumati gestured to the nearest wall. "Gaze into a mirror and think of your papa. Any one will do."

"Look," Minal said, staring at an oval one, "there's my mom!"

Padmini hurried over to see. "I have always been curious about mortals. What is that box? Some sort of storage compartment?"

Minal laughed. "I guess you wouldn't need washing machines here, would you? Well, our clothes get gross from being worn, and thanks to modern technology, we don't have to kneel by the river to scrub them clean anymore."

"Fascinating! So this 'washing machine' cleans your clothing for you? But without hands?"

"If you think *that's* great," said Minal, her elbow brushing Padmini's, "wait till I tell you about dishwashers."

Padmini nodded, but she was gazing at Minal, not the mirror. "Do tell."

If it had just been them, Sheetal could have gotten started, but the strangers were still staring. She looked pointedly at her mother, who nodded and whispered something in Padmini's ear.

Sheetal closed her eyes and inhaled until she'd shut everything out. When she looked again, the hall was empty except for Minal and Charumati.

She could deal with that. She picked a relatively private rectangular mirror and faced it. *Dad,* she thought, frantic, hot as silver fire. *Show me Dad.*

The mirror responded, her convulsing chin and overbright eyes resolving into a picture of a hospital room.

There he was, in that poisoned-apple coma, the briar patch of machines all around his bed, their thorn-needles in his arm. He'd turned ashen under the fluorescent lights, a doll, a mannequin, all emotion washed away.

Sheetal bit back a rush of grief. Dev's words haunted her. *She'd* done that. If she'd just listened to Dad and never gone to Dev's house that day . . . *I'm so sorry, Daddy.*

If he heard her, she couldn't know. She watched him, humming refrains from songs he loved.

At least, at least, at least, she told herself, thinking of Nana's promise, he didn't look any worse.

Radhikafoi appeared in the frame. She rubbed her tired eyes before sitting down next to the bed. "It's almost Sheetal's birthday, Deepak. What if she doesn't come back to us?"

Deepakfua pulled up a chair beside her. "Why wouldn't she? We're her family."

Radhikafoi made a dismissive click with her tongue. "She should be home with us. Whatever happens to Gautam, we should be together."

Sheetal's chest squeezed. For once, she agreed with her auntie.

"She was always going to go," Deepakfua said. "I know you want to protect her, but you can't shield her from who she is."

"I can't protect anyone," Radhikafoi said, and her laugh was bitter as the karela she loved to cook.

Deepakfua put his arm around her. "You need to trust her. She's a smart girl."

Radhikafoi sighed. "Of course she is. But a girl still needs her mother. I should never have let Charumati leave without her."

"Radhika jaan, the weight of the world cannot sit on your shoulders. Let people make their own mistakes." Deepakfua's expression turned wry. "They're going to do that anyway."

"But this shouldn't be her responsibility! She's just a child." Radhikafoi took Dad's hand. "What are we going to do if she fails—"

Sheetal couldn't stand to watch anymore. She pressed her knuckles to her eyes. The starry melody resounded in her ears, her heart.

Her auntie was right. Winning had seemed a tiny bit possible when Nani had spun her that fantasy, embellishing it with grand stories and even grander speeches, but who was Sheetal kidding? She was going to fall flat on her face and blow her one chance to help Dad.

When she looked again, all she saw was her own reflection gazing out of thousands of mirrors, accusing. Her eyes burned, but she wouldn't cry. Not here.

She turned to find Charumati and Minal standing behind her. They'd obviously seen the whole vision. Charumati's mouth had crimped into an odd cross between a smile and a frown.

It was petty, but Sheetal hoped her mother did feel bad. She'd *left* them. And now Dad might die, and Sheetal was stuck in this competition she'd never asked for because of it.

A girl needed her mother. Sheetal never would have burned anyone if Charumati had stuck around to teach her how to control her fire. Her mother had watched her all that time and let her struggle. Did she not care?

Minal rested her chin on Sheetal's shoulder. "Don't listen to Auntie, Sheetu. She's just scared. You can do this."

"Yeah, well, so am I," Sheetal said. She pretended she didn't notice Charumati's silence.

## 16

When Sheetal emerged from the Hall of Mirrors, Padmini stood waiting in the corridor, as lovely as any of the statues surrounding her. The illusion shattered when she flipped one page, then the next, in the historical romance novel she was tearing through, her mouth rounded with fascination.

Only one person could have given her that book, and Sheetal signaled for that person to distract Charumati. Once Minal and her mother had started chatting a few feet away, Sheetal nudged Padmini, making her start in surprise. "Come with me?"

Padmini *had* to help her. Sheetal couldn't do this. Even Radhikafoi didn't believe in her. This whole competition was a joke, and if she didn't get out of here in time, Dad would be the punch line.

"Certainly, Charumati. I apologize for my inattention, but I must confess I find myself unable to set this tome down for even a moment!" Padmini sneaked a wistful glance at the book before marking her place with her finger.

"I'm not Charumati?" Sheetal pointed out, not sure how to feel about that.

Padmini studied her more closely, visibly perplexed, then laughed. "Oh, my apologies, Sheetal. With your hair about your face like that, I mistook you for your mother."

Sheetal flicked her starry hair over her shoulders and out of the way before urging Padmini farther down the hall. "Look," she said, hoping her desperation didn't sound as gross as it felt, "I don't know how much you heard about all of this, but my dad needs me. If you'd just give me a drop of your blood, I could go heal him right now."

Padmini's smile, though striking, was less open and more practiced than it had been with Minal. Now it disappeared completely. Before she lowered her gaze, Sheetal glimpsed a mix of alarm and pity there. "I am sorry, Sheetal, truly, but I am afraid this is a request I cannot grant."

"But *why*?" Sheetal pressed. "It's just a drop." Padmini didn't answer. "I'll pay you, if that's what you're worried about. Want more romance novels? I'll get them from Earth. Just help me. Please."

She didn't even care that she was begging.

Padmini sighed softly. "It is not that."

"Then what?" Sheetal glanced over her shoulder. Any minute now, Charumati would catch up to her. She couldn't risk her mother overhearing them.

"I cannot." Padmini raised her head, and her silver-brown eyes had cleared. Whatever she felt was bound up tightly, far from the strains of starsong. "Please do not ask me again."

Feeling like a bully, Sheetal advanced on her. "Why not, though? Tell me, or I'll go to her myself."

When Padmini spoke, it was between gritted teeth. "The Esteemed Matriarch forbade it the night you arrived."

Blood roared in Sheetal's ears. "She did what? I don't believe you."

"Our song tells us so," Padmini said. "Feel it for yourself."

Sheetal let the starsong wrap around her, searching for the threads that led back to Nani. When she thought of taking Padmini's blood, a *no* boomed in her chest. No star in their nakshatra was to shed the blood of any other star for any reason. The mere idea of disobeying made her feel ill.

She flung herself out of the song before it could entrap her any further.

"You see?" Padmini looked sad. "You must heed the decree of the Esteemed Matriarch and Patriarch. They know things we cannot."

She paused, then asked in a brighter tone, "Now that that is settled, would you care for some lunch?"

Sheetal was shaking. How could her own grandmother do this to her? How could her mother let Nani do it?

It was a safeguard, of course. They didn't trust her. And they were right not to, not that she'd tell them that.

She mumbled something to Padmini about eating in her room and fled. Her hands weren't just tingling, they were on fire. Twinkling. Sparkling. Flashing.

Not again. No, no, no.

Trapped. She was trapped. The walls were getting smaller, or she was fading, or . . .

Through the haze of terror, she realized what was happening. *Panic attack.*

The champions' quarters weren't far from the common room, but they might as well have been a universe apart. It felt like she ran into every single star in her constellation on the way, and some just had to stop to ask her questions or wish her well. A couple even tried to give her advice from previous challengers. All of it evanesced into background noise.

Somehow, even though darkness had infiltrated her chest, even though she was sure her mind was cracking in half, Sheetal managed to smile. To hold herself tightly tucked in so she didn't spill out everywhere. She didn't know what she actually said to all those people—they blurred into one big smear of starlight—but the astral music chimed merrily, a million bright bells, so it must have been okay.

An eon later, she toppled over the threshold to her room and closed the door behind her. Then she sagged onto the newly made-up cloud mattress. The determination that had sustained her since she'd left home ruptured, leaving her empty.

*They trapped me. All of them. I'm burning.*

209

She twisted her weird, dangerous hands behind her back. There, no more twinkling. If she couldn't see it, it didn't exist, right?

But that didn't keep the fire from spreading through her. Or the fear as her radiance stained everything a blinding silver. She was going to go up in flames. Turn to ash.

*What am I going to do? What am I going to do? What . . .*

Her breaths came faster and faster, shorter and shorter, choking her until she couldn't breathe at all.

She was going to immolate herself and disappear, too, just like Dad. . . .

The door swung open. "Sheetal?"

Then Minal was there, tucking the cloud coverlet around Sheetal. "She's hyperventilating!"

Padmini stood behind her, wetting a cloth with water from the pitcher someone must have topped off.

Who took care of all that? Sheetal wondered distantly. She'd have to find out.

Minal spread the damp cloth over her forehead. "Count to ten for me, Sheetu. You can do that."

*I can do that,* she parroted. It hurt to hold her breath, but she somehow stopped hyperventilating long enough to count to ten. Then she inhaled rose-scented air and did it again. The whole time, she thought of Dad, of Minal. Even of Dev.

"You're okay," Minal soothed, handing her a glass of water. "You're okay."

It was just a wisp of hope, like smoke, but Sheetal latched

onto it, sipping the water. *I'm okay.* Then she started counting the beats in the starry melody, letting it flow in and out of her.

She repeated the numbers slowly, purposefully, like a chant. They marched through her mind, soldiers corralling her errant thoughts and bringing them to heel. Slowly, her breath calmed and began to deepen, and her flushed skin cooled. The hazy room grew distinct around her, bold and full of color.

She *was* okay. "Thanks."

Minal hugged her, then sat back. "Just glad I could help."

"How'd you know I was here, anyway?"

Minal hooked a thumb at Padmini, then at a tray of food sitting on the bedside table. "She told me you wanted to eat here. So we got you some food."

"Thanks," Sheetal said. When Padmini didn't leave, she added, "But I need to talk to you. Alone."

Padmini stepped back. "I will leave you to speak in peace." She offered Minal a shy smile, adding, "Find me outside when you are finished."

The second the door had closed, Sheetal laid her head on Minal's shoulder and told her everything, from Nani's bargain to seeing Dev to Padmini's refusal to help with the blood.

Minal was quiet for a minute. "She answers to your grandparents. What do you want her to do?"

Sheetal jerked upright. "Whose side are you on?"

"Yours, obviously." But Minal lit up like she was the star in the room. "Did you know she loves fashion? She actually designs your grandma's clothes! Can you imagine the *fabrics*?"

"So?" Sheetal shrugged. Who cared about that? It was so unfair that Minal got to come along and experience nothing but magic and beauty while Sheetal only got the pressure of not failing. "If she won't help me, I'm stuck here in this competition!"

"I'm not sure that's such a bad thing."

Sheetal stared at her. "Huh?"

"Listen, I've been thinking. It sucks that you got roped into this, no doubt. But maybe, instead of trying to run away from it, own it. Fight back." Minal fanned her arm out to take in the whole room. "This is yours, you know. And your dad is safe for now. We saw him."

Nothing Minal was saying made any sense. "Why are you trying to make me do this?"

Minal got up to examine the little silver statue of Hanuman on the dresser. "I've heard you sing. I know you can win this competition. But it can't just be for your dad. It has to be for *you*. You've never gotten to claim this part of who you are. You've never—sorry, I have to say it—gotten to shine."

"But I don't care about eternal glory or whatever!" Sheetal protested.

Except, she thought, that last night in Charumati's secret room, wouldn't she have given anything to claim that part of herself? She'd been so sick of hiding. Of letting everyone underestimate her.

"I'm not talking about that," Minal said. "I'm saying you deserve to have your turn in the spotlight. Show them what you can do. You're a princess of a royal house, Sheetal! Own it."

Sheetal groaned. "Even if I wanted to, I choked! Who says that won't happen again?"

"It's called stage fright, and it happens to everybody." Minal's glare could have set fire to the bed, clouds and all. "You can't let that stop you. The more we know about what we're working with here, the better your chances of winning."

Sheetal felt even worse. Some friend she was, jealous that Minal got to have all the fun, and here Minal was looking out for her like she always did.

Minal plunked the lunch tray down in front of her. "Anyway, you might want to eat. They say it's good for you."

"Okay, Mom." Sheetal rolled her eyes, but it did feel nice to be looked after, and anyway, she'd only picked at her breakfast. On top of that, her panic attack had left her ravenous. She could eat two giant trays' worth of food. No, three. She dug in.

Once the contents of the tray were safely packed away in her stomach, she started rolling Minal's advice over in her head, poking at it. Dad was safe; Nani had sworn on it. And whatever Nani's agenda, even she probably couldn't swear a sham oath on their flame.

For the first time, Sheetal really looked at the room and all its elegant furnishings. At her couture-quality clothes and jewelry. At the silver serving tray that held the remnants of her hastily scarfed meal. At her best friend, so sparkly and in her element. She'd been so busy rushing to find a way to save Dad that she hadn't stopped to appreciate any of it.

She was still afraid, still so scared for Dad, and the guilt of burning him would always be branded on her heart. But, the spark at her core insisted, she *could* sing. She *could* play. So what if Priyanka had overheard her botched rehearsal?

Only the competition counted.

Besides, something deep inside her whispered, making her palms tingle deliciously, it was a chance to finally be seen. "So what'd Padmini and you talk about while I was gone, any-way?"

"Mostly just fabric patterns and how proud you're going to do your house." Minal frowned. "Oh, right—there's some kind of fancy library we definitely have to go see. It's in your schedule."

That got Sheetal on her feet. "Fancy library?" How could she have forgotten that was here?

"Yeah, it's ordered by color or something? I didn't really get it."

Gears whirred in her mind. "Okay, fine, you're right. I should do this my way. Let's go to the library. What better place to figure out what it means to be a star than with books?"

Minal didn't budge. "What about your schedule? Don't you have something now?"

Sheetal opened her schedule booklet, which Padmini must have tucked beneath the lunch tray. Next up was her session on the history of the competition, followed by hands-on stellar instruction with Nani and Nana in their suite of apartments. Like Minal had said, she'd be going to the library, but not until tomorrow, when she had a class on court etiquette.

But so far this hadn't been about Sheetal at all, only about what she could do for everyone else. What Dad needed from her. What her nakshatra needed from her.

What about what *she* needed?

"Just a quick trip," she said. "I'm sure Padmini can fill me in on the competition's history later."

Faint lines appeared between Minal's brows. "Why not wait? It's only one day."

Sheetal searched for the words to explain. "You want me to make this mine." She wandered over to the window and stared at the vastness of the sky, all that blue, a brilliant pane of leaded glass that went on forever. "To own it. But you *know* your family's history. Your heritage. I have no clue about mine. Like, I don't know, what do we do for starry holidays?" She laughed. "Do we even *have* holidays?"

"I get that," Minal said quietly.

"Honestly," Sheetal said, turning back around, "who says Nani or my mom is actually going to tell me the truth, not just what they want me to think? What if . . . what if this is my only chance to learn about the court? About my family? I have to take it."

"Awesome." Minal smiled. "Do what you need to do."

Sheetal's stomach rumbled again. That panic attack must have seriously sapped her. She nibbled some of the chevdo Radhikafoi had packed before stuffing the Ziploc into her messenger bag. "Let's go sing some ragas."

The library was in the heart of the palace, not too far from the central court and their own quarters.

Sheetal stepped through the doors, and she instantly knew why Charumati had wanted to re-create the feel of this place. With its moon-phase sconces and horoscope-patterned ceiling, rich carpets, and wealth of scrolls and silver gilt-edged tomes on the stacks and stacks of scallop-framed ebony shelves that practically extended into infinity, the library felt just as magical as the Night Market.

But even better, here she could look for answers.

Sheetal took a second to gaze around her. So many books! So many books, and so much possibility.

A few stars sat at the long mosaicked tables, engrossed in their reading, and she even spotted two of the other champions, Leela and Sachin, cozy in brocade-covered armchairs. And there was that rude star from the convocation, Rati, brazenly checking out Sachin's hoard of reading material.

"Oh, wow," said Minal. "I wonder if they have sequels that haven't even been written yet." She wandered toward the stacks. "Coming?"

Figuring it couldn't hurt to be friendly, Sheetal waved as she walked past the tables. Leela glanced up long enough to smile before going back to the scroll she'd been jotting notes on. Rati looked right through her, which was fine by Sheetal. Sachin, though, bounded over. "I'm Sachin. Nice to finally meet you, Sheetal."

Except for the filmy green-and-peach scarf knotted around

his neck and multiple pinna piercings, he looked like he could be one of Dad's colleagues at the lab. Sheetal instinctively wanted to call him "Uncle," but of course she refrained. "Nice to meet you, too. I hear you sculpt?"

Sachin chuckled. "My work is more than mere sculpture. Having studied under some of the finest masters alive in both India and Germany, I like to imagine it papers over the gulf between East and West. My fiancé—also my manager—can talk for hours about the implicit critique and paradoxical embrace of the precolonial era as expressed by way of the Enlightenment and neoclassicism."

Sheetal guessed he was one of those people who thought picking random terms out of the dictionary made them sound smart. She peeked over at the books piled carelessly on his table. Two lay open, showing pictures of classical statuary and more modern art installations cobbled together from DayGlo paint, barbed wire, and driftwood. "I can't wait to see it," she lied. "I'm sure it's great."

"Oh, you will," Sachin said. "We're all friends here. Just because we're in competition doesn't mean we can't get to know each other, right? I've always believed in promoting camaraderie in the workplace. Keeps things fun."

He was saying the right things, but they didn't ring true. More like he wanted her to know how insignificant she was, pitted against the genius of his word salad. "I guess not," she said. "Well, gotta go. My friend's waiting!"

Without looking back, she hurried behind the tables and

217

into the stacks. If the other champions were that pretentious and full of themselves, it was going to be a long couple of days.

Minal had vanished, so Sheetal wandered through the rows of books alone. In contrast to the usual silvers and blacks and blues, there were salmon pinks, sunny yellows, mango oranges, twilight purples, dark indigos, and deepest blue-blacks, all grouped by color, just like Charumati had said.

She grinned. The colors represented dawn and midday and afternoon and evening and night, all standing for ragas, songs that corresponded to the time of day. She'd been studying those since she started playing the dilruba.

Charumati had told her all subjects fell under one of those ragas, and you sang for whatever it was you wanted to read about. The problem was, Sheetal didn't know which raga to sing. Where did history go?

She plucked a nearby tome off the shelf. It had an orange cover and silver Devanagari script. Sanskrit, but she could somehow understand it: *wild strawberries*. Which was pretty wild in and of itself. She went down a different row and reached for another book. Yellow, and more Sanskrit. She scanned the surrounding spines. All yellow, and nothing close to what she needed.

But Leela and Sachin had found what they needed. There had to be a system. She just needed to crack it.

Sheetal unrolled a scroll far enough to see that it was elaborately illustrated. She'd seen versions of this Mughal painting before: Radha and Krishna leaning together in a swing as Krishna played his bamboo flute.

Had a star inspired this one? Did they inspire all art ever?

A few feet away, someone hummed a recurring melody. Whoever it was had a remarkable voice, high and haunting like wind through a cave.

She rolled the scroll back up and followed the music. The song plucked at her heart, turning it into a veena. As she reached the end of the row, her own tongue readied itself to sing.

"A morning raga," she muttered.

Her voice must have grown too loud, because the stars in her line of sight glanced up. Recognition spread over their faces, and whispers spread through the air. The humming stopped, too.

Trying to tune out the stares, Sheetal waited until the humming resumed. Then she followed it to the next row of stacks, where a boy she vaguely recognized from breakfast perused a shelf lined with pink spines and pink-tied scrolls.

His hum ended as she reached the edge of his stack, and she watched as he extracted a volume from the shelf and thumbed through it.

Now that she was paying attention, Sheetal noticed other voices singing, too, as their owners moved through the stacks. A star appeared in her row, and the book she was looking for began to glow in time with her song like starlight glittering on frost.

It was the oddest and loveliest take on the Dewey decimal system Sheetal could imagine. She hummed a little, too, as the star took the book from its shelf.

And now that she knew how to access the library, she

wanted more. More of all of it. She pulled down another book without reading the title. She was going to find out everything about the history of the competition and the court and win—

"Psst!" The boy near her nodded to the book in her hand. "Have you come to join our class?"

Sheetal put it down on a mirror-worked blue stepstool. "Class?"

"Indeed, champion," the boy said. "The art of waking mortal hearts." He indicated the tables of younger stars just beyond the stacks. "Normally my sister would stop in, too, but she is presently attending to your companion."

"You're Padmini's brother?" He did resemble her, come to think of it, though he looked about twelve to her eighteen.

"Indeed." The boy treated her to a smile as warm as a solar flare. "I am called Kaushal. It is a fine thing to make your acquaintance."

"Okay, Kaushal, explain something to me. I'm kind of in a hurry. How do you know what books are filed under? Like, if I'm looking for dilrubas and harps through time or whatever."

Kaushal burst into laughter, ignoring the other patrons' calls for him to be silent. "You ask an archivist, of course!"

"Huh?" Sheetal hadn't noticed anything like a reference desk, let alone a person.

But Kaushal showed her the open book on the tall, round stand at the end of the aisle. Its pages were clear, like a mirror that reflected nothing. "History of dilrubas," he told it. The book shimmered and turned the gray-purple of a midsummer gloaming. Its pages emitted a sprinkle of notes—an evening raga.

No. *This* was the loveliest take on library coding she'd ever seen.

"Any text that falls under the category of evening raga can be located in a section with purple books," Kaushal added, and Sheetal glanced around. There were purple books just one shelf over.

"*You* should be an archivist," she told Kaushal, making him beam bright.

"I will help you find your books," he offered, but as they turned the corner, curiosity overtook the sidereal melody, and a handful of younger stars from the class crowded in around them. Just like the ones back in the common room, they teemed with questions: Would she show them her phone? Had she ever been on television? How could mortals eat dead animals? Was it true mortals thought magic a fiction? Were they truly so foolish?

"Wait, wait," said Kaushal, holding up his hands. "Let her sit down first!"

The students unwillingly made room for Sheetal to pass, the brilliant light of their interest chasing her all the way to their table.

Three more sat there pretending to be lost in their studies, but they weren't fooling anyone. Sheetal bit back her amusement. "How about this?" she suggested. "You want to learn about mortals, and I want to learn about you. So tell me about this 'art of waking mortal hearts.' Does that mean inspiring them, or . . . ?"

As if Kaushal had been waiting for the chance to play teacher, he launched into a lecture. "Mortals are meant to create. They do so all the time, solving problems and bringing visions to life. Some of that is inherent, and some of that is due to us."

By now, everyone had put their books and scrolls down. "Do not aid her!" a star cried. "She belongs to the Pushya nakshatra."

"Yes, and that is my house," said Kaushal. "Why would I not aid my champion?"

The star who'd objected shut her book, as did three others near her. "She is not our champion, and we will not help."

"You may be a fine singer, but you will never best our Leela," the youngest bragged before following his friends to another table.

"Uh, thanks?" Sheetal said.

"Never mind them," Kaushal said. "Ask your questions."

"Yes, do!" a girl about Sheetal's age urged, bouncing on her toes. "I am called Beena. Let me aid you, dear champion!"

Sheetal couldn't resist her enthusiasm. "Sure. How does inspiration work?"

"You have seen the jars of stardust?" Beena asked. Sheetal nodded. "It is the distillation of our light. It renders mortal hearts fertile, so the ideas that grace them might take root to sprout and blossom."

"That's all inspiration is?" Sheetal recalled Dev's dream. "But—"

"Only from a distance," Kaushal said. "In person, our work

222

is strongest. We open to our inner flame and guide it into a mortal." He mimed pushing something toward Beena, who lit up on the spot.

Sheetal glanced at her own palms, remembering how they'd tingled, remembering that she'd somehow inspired Dev—and how she'd burned Dad. "Does it, I don't know, feel weird when you do it?"

Kaushal seemed at a loss. Finally he said, "It feels like inspiring. How else should it feel?"

"Enough boring talk," Beena declared. "Tell us about your world. Is it as we see from up here? Mortals change so swiftly, in an instant."

Sheetal supposed they did. How quickly she'd let Dev get close to her. How quickly he'd destroyed it. "Don't you?"

"No, of course not. Stars are timeless." Beena grinned. "What *do* they teach mortals down there?"

"As much as they teach stars up here, I'd guess." Sheetal's neck grew warm as flame danced inside her again. Why were they acting like she was on the tourism board for Earth? She needed to get back to the books and sing one free.

Beena moved to touch her face. "You look so very mortal, yet your hair is as silver as ours."

"It is because she is a half-thing!" one of the other stars muttered. Everyone's eyes widened.

Kaushal blazed so harshly their entire table turned red with radiant heat. "Do not *ever* use that word. Have you forgotten what *I*—?"

At the same time, Sheetal twisted up and out of her seat. "You want to know about Earth? Well, here's your crash course: Not everyone eats meat. It rains sometimes, and it snows, too, when it's not all drought. We have oceans full of seashells and jellyfish and sometimes even hypodermic needles if you live in the right part of New Jersey. When we're not busy trying to blow each other up with nuclear weapons, we're destroying our environment with pollution and chemicals. Some people believe in things other people are afraid to. We can't stand being alone, but we still look for ways to separate ourselves. Kind of like crowing about who's pure star and who's not. Oh, we get sick and old and die."

Her hands smoldered as silver as Kaushal had, and mouth dry, she couldn't help thinking yet again how she really, really needed to learn to hide what she was feeling better. The whole court had probably heard that.

Now the stars gawked outright. "No wonder mortals need our inspiration," Beena said.

The star who'd thought he was being so clever hung his head now. His eyes had glazed over with tears, and he refused to look at anyone.

Sheetal's anger cooled as fast as it had come. He was just a kid spouting what he'd been told. "I'll let you get back to your class."

Kaushal waggled his head. "Come. I will help you find what you need."

"Don't you have to study?"

"We do not study," Beena said. "We train. We learn by soaking up the stories of those who have gone before us."

"Yes, just as everyone dabbles in dance and singing and painting." Kaushal guided Sheetal back to the archivist. "Once we understand the soul of mortal arts, we can then inspire them. But we each have our specialty, and yours, we hear, is music. If you are our champion, I am certain you play like the gandharvas themselves."

As soon as they were out of earshot, he faced her. "Do not take Urjit's foolishness to heart. He has always been too clever for his own good. There are many among us who could not be happier to see you here."

He sounded worried. But the slur hadn't scared Sheetal off. She wasn't ashamed of what she was. That would mean being ashamed of Dad. "Don't worry, I'm not going anywhere."

Kaushal's smile returned, warm with relief. "I am pleased to hear that."

Sheetal told the archivist what she wanted next—books on the history of the competition—but her mind was chewing on something else. That slur had really upset Kaushal. "What did you mean, had they forgotten?" Her eyes narrowed. "Forgotten what you were?"

He examined the archivist, then glanced up. "Yes."

"Are you—no, *were* you like me?"

Kaushal just looked at her. He wasn't bothering to hide his feelings, she realized, and more than anything, she sensed loneliness. An old desire to be understood.

225

It was like he'd held up a mirror to her own heart, this star from her nakshatra. Her own loneliness brightened into acknowledgment. She felt absurdly grateful, enough that she wanted to hug him.

Except . . .

Except if she hadn't blown off her schedule and come here, she might never have known. No one—not Nani and Nana, not Padmini, not even Charumati—had thought she could use a friend who got what she was going through?

"But you're a full star now?" Sheetal asked finally, calming herself. She might not get another chance to talk to him once Nani found out she'd skipped her lesson.

A thread of fear wove through Kaushal's emotions, and then they were gone, back behind the impenetrable wall of his neutral expression. "If you have found what you needed, I should return to my class."

"Yeah, probably." She grabbed the chevdo from her bag and tossed it to him. He'd taken a risk letting her know she wasn't alone, and the least she could do was offer him a taste of the life he'd left behind. "Some mortal food to say thanks for your help."

Now Kaushal shone openly. "My favorite."

On a whim, Sheetal added, "Share it with Urjit." It was always easier to open kids' minds, after all.

"I will," Kaushal promised.

# 17

Sheetal used the archivist to look up another subject, half-stars, and located a single title. Then, her arms heaped high with reference books, she staked out a quiet table in a remote corner of the library. By the enormous clock on the wall, she had an hour left before her next lesson, enough to at least start skimming.

Some authors wrote more favorably of her grandparents' reign than others, but all agreed that in their day, Nani and Nana had ruled the court with iron fists. Not only had they closed the gates between the worlds after a violent incident on Earth, but they'd cultivated the attitude that only children took an interest in mortals beyond the duty of inspiring them. At one point, they'd even convinced the court to seal off the Hall of Mirrors. But so many stars had protested the loss of their mortal soap operas, they'd had to backtrack. Eventually Nani's and Nana's popularity had waned enough that they'd basically had to abdicate their offices, and House Dhanishta had won the ensuing competition.

Wow, her grandparents really, really didn't like humans. It made Sheetal sad and angry—what did they think of her? Especially since, unlike Kaushal, she wasn't about to give up her human heritage.

It was a gross thing to think, but maybe they would try to separate the realms again if she won.

With a shudder, she scoured the texts for any details about the incident that had set them off. Had it involved Dev's ancestor? But except for that vague mention, the books were silent, as if the woman in the dream-memory had never existed. So who was she?

Still pondering that, Sheetal dove into the book about half-stars. Like she'd witnessed in the dream, up until about a thousand years ago, stars had walked among mortals, inspiring them. All the time, even. Occasionally the already-close muse-artist relationship grew intimate in more ways than one, so it was no shocker that babies often followed. They always took after their celestial parent—the starlight hair, the inner flame, the ability to inspire—but their human heritage meant their blood couldn't heal.

All stuff Sheetal had known, but seeing it written out like this, reading that there had been other half-stars, made her feel like she was part of something. It meant she wasn't an anomaly, an accidental one-off, and that for the first time she fit somewhere. It almost didn't matter that Dad was lying in a hospital bed or that Dev was here to support her rival. She felt like she could breathe again.

Thirsty for more, she read on.

The mortal world was a hard place for half-star children. They were lost, full of longing; and without guidance, their powers often blew up, harming themselves or others. Sheetal hurt just reading that.

Worse, in the age of the star hunters, word spread of the healing nature of stellar blood, making stars targets for eager buyers and the curious alike. A pair of hunters seeking to hone the process discovered that ingesting the blood even heightened mortals' receptivity to inspiration, creating yet more demand for it. Those stars who survived had all eventually ascended to the starry court for good. And then of course the gates had been closed, so there were no more half-stars.

Until her.

Sheetal scrunched up her nose at the book. She paged through to the end, hunting in vain for stories of half-stars who'd gotten their powers under control and stayed on Earth.

Well, fine. She'd be the first.

There weren't any mentions of Charumati leaving Svargalok, either. Only a footnote that, under House Dhanishta's rule, the gates had been reopened.

No wonder Nani was determined to regain control of the court.

Sheetal gathered up her books and was about to go search for Minal in the stacks when Rati appeared at her elbow.

Glorious, with glossy hair that cascaded down her back and a sultry smile, Rati might have been an actress on Earth. Her lively, kajal-lined eyes sparkled, hinting at a cosmos of tantalizing beauty and clandestine pleasures. "It seems we have gotten off to an unnecessarily rocky start. May I sit?"

"What do you want?" Sheetal asked, wary.

"A moment of your time, mortal girl." Though Sheetal hadn't said she could, Rati sat down across from her. "I have a proposition for you."

Sheetal made a show of opening the top book in the pile and running her eyes over the text. "Not interested."

Rati only laughed. "As I said, I would like us to begin afresh. Am I correct in assuming your mother has told you nothing of me?"

"Just say what you're here to say. I'm busy."

Rati nodded. "You wish me to speak plainly? Gladly; it will save us both time." She leaned forward, her ring-laden hands folded on the table. "I know you have come for a drop of blood for your ailing father. I also know your house has forbidden anyone from giving it to you."

So much for Nani's command to keep quiet about Sheetal's request for help. "Even if it's true," Sheetal asked, turning the page, "why do you care?"

"Did I not say I had a proposition for you?" Rati waited until Sheetal looked up from the book they both knew she wasn't actually reading. "You know you do not belong here. That is hardly a secret."

"My family thinks I do," Sheetal pointed out.

"Do they?" But Rati brushed aside her own question. "That is not important. Understand that I am trying to spare you pain. Come, girl, you do not truly wish to step on that stage and degrade yourself before the entire court. You have no training, no drive to be here. And why would you? Your life, your true life, beckons below."

"Why do you care?"

Rati leaned even closer, until her mysterious eyes dominated Sheetal's field of vision. "No one need ever know you cannot do this."

*Hack.* Priyanka's sneer echoed in Sheetal's head, and she had to fight the impulse to pick at her thumb again. She stuffed her hands in her lap. "I'm not a hack."

"And I am not the one you would need to persuade of that." Rati reached over and shut the book. "Sheetal, no one in your nakshatra may aid you in this, but I can. I will give you the blood you seek."

Sheetal's ears had to have tricked her. No way had Rati actually said that. "Excuse me?"

"I will give you the blood. You see, *I* am not forbidden from aiding you." Rati surveyed her lacquered fingernails, a triumphant smile playing over her lips. "All I ask as recompense is that you withdraw from the competition."

Sheetal gripped the sides of her chair. Whatever she'd expected Rati to say, it wasn't this.

Rati didn't give her a chance to recover. "Take it and return home to heal your father. You need not spearhead your family's attempted comeback."

"I . . . I can't." Sheetal's tongue tangled in her mouth as her entire body lightened with hope.

She could go home now. She didn't have to wait for Nani to help save Dad. She didn't have to worry Nani might shut the door between the two halves of her life.

She didn't have to win.

All she had to do was say yes.

"Of course you can. Call it my natal day gift to you," Rati murmured.

"Why would I believe you, though? What's to keep you from just disappearing once you get what you want?"

Rati gestured to the stack of books. "I have been observing you. You wish to know if you can trust your nakshatra. I am here to tell you you cannot. If for only that reason, you may believe I honor my promises."

Observing her? Like, through the Hall of Mirrors? Revulsion snaked down Sheetal's spine, and she wondered again at Rati's lack of a starry circlet. "I don't even know who you are."

"I will say this." Rati's smile melted into icy resentment. "I know well what it means to be left behind. To have your choices taken forcibly from you. I would not see that happen to another."

She sat back and spread her arms wide, blatantly courting the curious gazes around them. "Are you truly so keen to be a pawn?"

"Why aren't you worried about anyone seeing you talking

to me?" Sheetal countered. "What's to stop me from going to my mom right now and telling her about this?"

She waited for Rati to backpedal. To beg her not to.

Instead, Rati's eyes gleamed. "With all haste," she said. "Indeed, nothing would please me more."

She pushed away from the table and tossed her length of hair over one shoulder, making its jeweled clips dance like grains of black sand in a silver sea. "Do not dally with your answer. I may well think better of it and retract my offer."

Sheetal and Padmini stood inside Nani's and Nana's apartments, silent as Nani fumed. Nani had called to Padmini through the sidereal song, and Padmini had immediately arrived to fetch Sheetal from the library, where she'd been searching in vain for Minal.

"How could you treat your lessons so cavalierly, beti?" Nani paced before them, a booklet like the one she'd given Sheetal clasped behind her back. "We have so little time to prepare you, and every part of the schedule I arranged has its purpose. Such irresponsible behavior will not be tolerated."

She whirled on Padmini. "And you! I entrusted you with the care and preparation of my granddaughter."

Padmini's lip trembled. "I allowed myself to become distracted, Esteemed Matriarch, and for that you have my sincerest apologies. I will not do so again." She joined her palms before her distraught face.

Sheetal's thoughts were bubbling over with Rati's proposal

and Kaushal's status as a former half-star. How much angrier would Nani get if she mentioned either of those things?

But she'd already put her training too far behind schedule to risk another argument.

"No," Nani asserted. "You will not." She inclined her head, dismissing Padmini.

"Come," Nana said gently. "What is done is done. Let us not squander what time we yet have."

He led Sheetal and Nani onto the balcony. Even though it was only early evening, the night sky spread out before them, an eternity peppered with sparkling silver diamonds.

"You have noticed the song that flows through us, yes, Sheetal?" Nani didn't wait for her to answer. "It both stems from and binds us. We are a constellation, a galaxy, a cosmos, all connected. As a star, you are made to illuminate the darkness, to inspire, but as a mortal, you are made to be inspired."

"During the competition," Nana added, "each champion will be inspired by a member of their nakshatra, and they will then have an hour in which to produce or perform a work of art as they feel so moved."

Sheetal was pretty sure she might burst with impatience. There were questions she should be asking her grandparents, like how an hour could be long enough to make a sculpture from scratch, and how it actually felt to be inspired. Like if they really did plan to close the gates again and trap her in one place.

But all she could think was that a drop of blood was waiting—if she could trust its source.

Nani watched her intently. "I can feel your misgiving from here. What troubles you, beti?"

"I'm just nervous," Sheetal lied. "So I'm going to be inspired?"

Nani arched an eyebrow but accepted it. "Indeed."

"Then why do I need to bother rehearsing?"

"To prepare you for the stage." Nana's wrinkled face shone. "To keep your voice and muscles limber for your moment of victory."

Sheetal couldn't meet his eyes. He had way more faith in her than she did. They all did; their whole house was betting everything on her. What if Priyanka and Rati were right, and she would only make a fool of herself up there?

A tender smile illuminated Nani's face and sent starlight streaming over her body. "This puts me in mind of teaching your mother when she was a child. She was an apt pupil, yet so restive and so swift to lose interest."

"You taught my mom, too?" Suddenly the obligatory lesson took on a completely different tone, one of tradition being handed down. A flower added to a lengthy garland.

One of family.

*No.* Even thinking the word hurt, like she was parched and still refusing to drink the glass of clean, sweet water that sat within reach. But she couldn't let herself forget that Nani had forbidden their nakshatra from helping Dad. *I already have my family.*

It would be so easy to take Rati's offer and run. To heal Dad right now. What would he want her to do?

"Naturally," Nana replied. "Who better to teach her the ways of inspiration than her own mother?"

"She was a willful slip of a girl, always stealing mangoes from the orchard and eating them on the balcony with her friends." Nani giggled, a light, girlish sound Sheetal would never have expected from her. "Always sneaking into the Hall of Mirrors. Do you recall, Jagdeesh, how proud she was of her craftiness? As if we failed to notice!"

Sheetal couldn't help her grin. She'd never thought of Charumati as a little girl before.

"I would find her in the library, reading stories, and bring her back to her lessons," Nana said. "Oh, how she would plant her feet and protest that she had learned more than enough and deserved to get her circlet early!"

Nani laughed again. "She always longed for more, precisely as my sister did."

Sheetal sat up straighter. She had a great-aunt? That would explain the vacant suite of rooms by Nani's. "Your sister? Where's she now?"

Nani's laughter broke off, and her next words were clipped. "She left the court."

"Oh." Sheetal looked away, out into the unfathomable expanse of black. It drew her, tugging on the part of her that, like her mother, had always longed for more.

And she'd finally started to find it. Not only was this her house, her nakshatra, but she had a great-aunt she'd never known about, one who didn't even live here. Maybe Sheetal could go look for her after all this was done.

"Perhaps," Nana suggested, "as we have spoken of inspiration, we should now demonstrate."

*All I ask is that you withdraw.* Just yesterday, it would have been an easy choice. Take the blood and run. Save Dad.

But now, Sheetal wasn't so sure.

"Yes," she blurted. "Show me. I need to know what it feels like." What was this thing people were willing to kill for? The thing she had unknowingly done to Dev?

She needed to understand her inspiration. She especially needed to be able to control it.

"A fine idea," Nani said. Her light was still dimmed, her profile in shadow. She stepped back into the living room and beckoned for Sheetal to take a seat on one of the divans. "Let us begin."

Sheetal had just gotten comfortable when starlight shot through her. It wasn't a thing she saw so much as sensed: a river of silvery radiance sweeping in, opening channels in her spirit she had never known were there. Opening portals to wonder, to creation.

It was like a canvas had been installed inside her heart, only she was also the artist who would paint it. All possibility, all potential, existed in her, and now she had to create.

Music unfolded like a flower at her core, a moonlight lotus made of melody, and her lips parted in preparation. The stars in the firmament sparkled and grew larger, merging into a glowing canopy until they were all she could see. She could already hear, could already feel, the tendrils of song that yearned to spill forth, a series of pure, perfect notes.

But then the inspiration was gone, leaving her blank. Dark.

She stared at Nani, then Nana, desperate to anchor herself. She had done *that* to Dev? No wonder he'd stayed up all night drafting songs. If she didn't sing now, she would explode.

Nana had put his hand on Nani's arm. "You see the power of the stars. *Your* power," he began.

Nani cut in to say this had only been a taste, because they wanted to save the full effect for the competition itself, and Sheetal nodded. But the nitty-gritty of her grandmother's explanation zoomed right over her head.

Her palms tingled as her star half flared awake, obscuring the dazed human half. Pouring out jars of stardust had nothing on this. Here was true inspiration, true purpose.

Flame licked her fingertips. She couldn't stop thinking of how close Dev's ancestor and that star had gotten. How close she and Dev had gotten. The starry part of her wanted to inspire him like that again and again and again, while the human part, smothered as it was, said nothing.

"Do not let that pesky mortal boy continue to distract you," Nani chastened her. "Your destiny is far greater than the blink of his entire mortal existence."

A sick sensation brewed in Sheetal's chest. Had Nani just read everything she'd been feeling? Gods, had Nani seen them

238

making out? Had Nana? Her most private moments, out on display for the world?

She wanted to scream.

"Don't worry," she snapped. "There's no chance of that."

"Good." A satisfied smile crossed Nani's proud face.

Good? Sheetal glanced up sharply. What was that supposed to mean?

"Perhaps," Nana hastened to say, catching her expression, "we should break for dinner. The poor child needs nourishment and a chance to rest."

"Certainly," Nani agreed, turning away. "We will resume instruction early tomorrow morning."

# 18

One step into the champions' dining hall, and Sheetal was regretting her decision to have dinner here. It had seemed so smart when she'd persuaded Nani not to risk alienating the other houses too much. The more Sheetal came off like any other champion, she'd said, the better. It was true, even if she'd really just wanted to get away from her grandparents and be around other humans, who couldn't read her feelings. And remember she still counted as one of them.

Sort of.

She flinched. What exactly had happened back there in Nani's and Nana's apartments?

Savory aromas enveloped her, their promise of tasty things a reminder that, no matter what else might be happening, she still needed to eat. She rubbed her forehead and hurried to find their source.

The way Nani had derided it, Sheetal had pictured the

cafeteria at school, all white cinder blocks and buzzing fluorescent lights that burned out half the time or, when they worked,
turned everyone a delicate shade of about-to-vomit green.

Yeah, not quite.

The dining hall was decorated in the palatial style, with all
twenty-seven nakshatras emblazoned on the walls, shimmering peacock feathers in iridescent vases, a heaping snack bar
made of crystal, and a large fountain that flowed liberally with
skyberry cordial. Servers in uniform zipped back and forth, taking orders and delivering entrées to the champions and their
companions, who were seated on the mirror-worked cushions
dotting the gleaming onyx floor.

According to Nana, the space was big enough to comfort-
ably fit up to twenty-four people. But they'd all still pushed
their cushions into a rough circle in the center.

A circle with no place for Sheetal.

Her eyes were searching for the exit before she realized it.
Where was Minal, anyway? It was stupid, but Sheetal couldn't
help feeling abandoned.

Dev, though, was right here, so hot in that black-and-silver
sherwani, laughing with Jeet. In fact, everyone was deep in conversation but her. Just one big, happy family.

She remembered how her heart, her lips, had sought his.
She heard him ask shyly if she wanted to go upstairs and listen
to his song.

The song she had inspired. The silver flame at her core
flickered.

*Fine*, she thought, irritated at him, annoyed at herself, and plunked down on one of the cushions nearest to the exit. Her whole body was hyperaware of Dev's presence a few feet away, pulling at her like a magnet, but she made herself ignore it.

As she tried to catch a server's eye, a familiar voice called, "Look who deigned to eat with us mere mortals!" Then, unmistakably, Priyanka quacked.

Sheetal wanted to die. Someone must have traded her heart for a hummingbird's, the way its beats blurred together in her chest. Could stars turn invisible? Better yet, could she morph into a black hole and swallow Priyanka in one bite?

"Hey, give it a rest," Jeet said, sounding annoyed. "Why were you listening in on her practice session, anyway?"

That was decent of him, Sheetal conceded. Dev had been right. You couldn't help your ancestry.

She should know.

As if he'd heard her thoughts, Dev's gaze found hers, softening with that hopeful glint, and the corners of her mouth started to lift. But then his face closed off again, and he turned away. She actually felt cold, like the embers at her center had died out.

Sheetal couldn't deny the pang in her chest or how her hands—her lips—longed for the warmth of Dev's, how much she missed his dorky jokes and the way his playful expression went distant when he was thinking. *Oh, Dev.*

Sachin glanced at her. "Jeet's right. Surely we're above mocking our rivals?"

Leela waved. "Sheetal! Come sit with us. You can't eat alone."

Sheetal hesitated.

"Yes," Sachin said, "pull that pillow over here." The pale blond man next to him scooched over to make space. That had to be his manager, the one who apparently liked to babble as much as Sachin did.

Priyanka scoffed. "Brilliant. Sleepover in my room! Let's build a bonfire and make s'mores! That's why we're all here, right, to be besties?"

Until then, Sheetal hadn't noticed Priyanka was the only other champion without a companion. Probably too self-centered to bother with one. Or maybe no one in her life wanted to come. With her attitude, who could blame them?

Sheetal forced a grin, like there was no place she'd rather be, and wedged her cushion in between Leela's and Sachin's. "Hi."

It felt so weird, like they were all friends hanging out, instead of rivals. Like some of them didn't deeply begrudge her claiming a spot among them. She made sure to meet every single pair of eyes, even Priyanka's scorn-filled ones.

Well, almost every pair. Dev stubbornly stared at his plate.

Sheetal felt the brush-off like a blow, and her grin turned brittle. How could the entire dining hall not feel the tension between them? It hung dense and stifling as smog.

*Look at me,* she thought, mentally retracing the curve of his cheek beneath her fingers. *I'm sorry.*

Jeet sipped his drink, watching them both. *He* hadn't missed the tension, in any case.

"So what brings you all here?" she tried, and immediately wanted to wire her jaw shut. The prize, obviously. Why couldn't she be more like her mom or Minal and not keep embarrassing herself?

Priyanka made zero effort to curb her snort, and Dev's mouth twitched. The others pretended not to hear.

"Sheetal," Leela said kindly, gesturing to the woman next to her, "this is my niece Kirti. She runs an organization in India that helps promote female artists. It's because of her that I picked up my paintbrush again after my husband died."

"Guilty as charged!" Kirti smiled. "One look at her old paintings and I knew I couldn't let her throw away all that passion, not when she has so much to say about women and power and patriarchy."

"I may be eighty-one," Leela said, returning the smile, "but I'm just getting started. Why shouldn't people know who I am?" Before she'd even finished speaking, Sachin was introducing his companion. "My darling Jürgen was actually the one who pushed me to do this. He said it would be a waste for my talent to go uncelebrated."

Sheetal bit down hard on the inside of her lip to keep from replying.

"The art world needs to be shaken up," Jürgen announced. "It's time it really *examines* its obsession with postmodern overtones and self-congratulation in the transgression of boundaries by majority voices. It is *imperative* we find innovative new ways to incorporate the current cross-cultural bleeding together of underrepresented voices and its impact on our narrative vision for the future."

*Words,* Sheetal thought. *So many words.* She was pretty sure those were actual sentences, even, which blew her mind, seeing as how they didn't mean anything.

"Plus you're dying for that vacation house on the Amalfi Coast," Sachin teased. "Don't forget that part." With Jürgen at his side, he seemed calmer, less moody than he'd been in the library. He darted a glance at Jeet, then back at Jürgen, who tapped him on the nose.

Sheetal relaxed back onto her cushion. Maybe she could actually survive this.

"My turn," said Jeet, resting his arm on his knee just as a server approached Sheetal with a thali full of food.

"But I didn't even order yet," she protested.

The server set the plate before her. "No need—your house left instructions as to your diet. You are to have particularly caloric meals to provide you with extra fuel for your training as a star."

Suddenly the food didn't look so great. Nani had done what? And she'd let Sheetal find out in front of the other champions?

Priyanka was smirking, like she'd been proven right yet again. "Just one of us, huh?" she mocked. "What would you know about struggle, with your perfect little star family?"

"That's not how it—" Jeet cut himself off. "Never mind."

Sheetal stared at him. What did he think he knew about her family? What did any of them?

"You were going to tell us something," Dev prompted. He kept avoiding Sheetal's gaze. She felt herself getting mad, the flame at her core kindling. Why was he being like this?

"That's right." Jeet's voice deepened. "I'm a writer. I want people to read my stories and carry them around in their heads. I want to change how they see the world. There's literally nothing I wouldn't do to have what I want. Nothing."

The intensity with which he said that made everyone grow quiet. Even Dev seemed caught off guard.

Jeet must have noticed the shift in mood, because he laughed and elbowed Dev. "Unlike my cousin here and his music, I take my writing seriously."

Dev shot him a dirty look. "Dude, calm down. This isn't reality TV. You don't have to throw me under the bus to prove yourself." They stared at each other, and Sheetal held her breath, nervous.

Finally Jeet nodded. "You're right. I got carried away. Sorry, bhai." He held out his fist for Dev to bump.

Dev did. "It happens."

"What about you, Sheetal?" Kirti asked.

"Yeah," Priyanka goaded, "what *about* you?"

Sheetal realized she'd finished half her thali without really tasting it. "Uh—"

Priyanka's lip curled. "'Vacation house.' You know why *I'm* here? My family in India has made Kathputli puppets for generations. They were known for it. But no one has time for old things anymore, and my grandfather had to sell his land and the studio where he made the puppets to keep us afloat. But I promised him I was going to bring back his legacy, and I am." Scowling at Sheetal, she jumped to her feet. "No cheating star is going to stop me."

She pivoted on her heel and flounced out.

No one said much of anything after that.

# 19

Sheetal knew she should've been asleep an hour ago, but she couldn't relax, not with Priyanka banging away in the next suite. What was she *doing* in there?

It was a riddle for the ages how Minal, who'd gone to bed while Sheetal was still at dinner, could sleep through that. *Who needs company?* she thought, hurt. She hadn't even gotten to tell Minal about being inspired. Or—her breath caught—to ask if she'd ever inspired any of Minal's art projects. It was possible, wasn't it?

Priyanka's parting words jabbed at her again, digging in like fishhooks. But Sheetal couldn't worry about other people trying to help their families. Even if she knew exactly what that felt like.

Her pulse ticked relentlessly. Two days left. Two days until her birthday. Two days until she had to win this competition for her own family.

In the other neighboring suite, Sachin and Jürgen started flirting. Loudly. Sheetal's eyes widened to what had to be shojo manga proportions. She didn't know any German beyond *ich liebe dich* and *Rotweinkuchen*, but like with the Sanskrit in the library, she understood every suggestive syllable just fine, and besides, talking wasn't the only thing they were doing.

Someone really needed to tell the stars about soundproofing. What was the German word for *awkward*?

"Some of us need to sleep!" she called, knocking hard on both walls, but the noises didn't stop.

Sighing in defeat, Sheetal mashed her face against the pillow. The anger that had been driving her yielded to something softer, sadder. With her guard down, Dev's indifference at dinner, the way he wouldn't even look at her, came right back, and Sheetal's stomach soured, as sick as if it had just happened.

Gods, she missed him so much it hurt. It wasn't fair. She was burning, literally burning, to ask what he thought about all this. To hear him laugh at how seriously everyone else was taking the competition and sneak her a chocolate-covered cherry like he sometimes did at school. To ask him exactly what he'd felt when she'd inspired him.

Pain crushed her heart with a claw-tipped fist. Was he even thinking about her?

She didn't want to be mad at him anymore. She didn't even want to be mad at Nani. She just wanted everyone to quit deciding things for her. Why was that so much to ask?

The dam holding everything back since she'd run out

249

of Dev's house, since she'd hurt Dad, burst, and she cried a reservoir's worth of tears into the cool, soft pillow. *Be this. Don't be that. Do this. Don't do that.* She'd tried. She'd tried so hard. And she'd still put Dad in the hospital.

Was there no place for her the way she was, star *and* mortal? Just Sheetal?

If so, no one was telling.

It wasn't fair. None of it was. She cried, shoulders shaking, until the pillow was waterlogged, until her eyes stung and her nose leaked, until she couldn't cry anymore.

Instead of being exhausted enough to pass out, she lay like a lump on the bed, alternating thoughts of Dad and Rati's offer whooshing through her head. *Fan-freakin'-tastic.*

A few feet over, Minal turned and murmured something, probably dreaming of starry ladies-in-waiting with jasmine blossoms in their hair.

Sheetal thought about waking her up but decided against it. What could Minal do? She knew who she was. She didn't have to worry about silver hair spitting out dye or silver fire shooting up randomly from tingling palms.

*She* knew where she belonged, and right then, Sheetal really resented her for it.

Instead, she got up and moved to the window. She stared at the great dark sky that arced over everything like an infinite ocean, taking in the uncountable coruscating stars, and wished as hard as she could. Her palms pressed against the glass, she

wished and wished, fiery desires that left her lips as soft song—
a call to the sidereal melody.

She swam in the night's glittering waves, feeling them
flow in and out of her with each breath, nourishing her. It
felt so good to sing for herself, with no one listening, no one
judging.

As she watched, beyond the window, the faces of the stars
became clear. Most were from outside the royal court, the com-
moners, if such a thing could be said of stars, but the court was
present, too. Sheetal picked out Nani, Nana, Charumati, Padmini, Kaushal, and even Rati.

She pored over their features, all glorious, all serene. She
took in the way they flared against the heavens, both person
and ball of flame.

If she reached out, she could almost touch them. . . .

Their song came to her gradually, silence ripening into
something more. She could be among them, could ascend to
her rightful place in the constellation. In the sky. In the cosmos,
where everything was born of the play of shine and shadow, fire
and frost.

Here, there was no pain, no disappointment. No estranged
boyfriends, no dying dads. No self-doubt.

*Join us.*

In that moment of dream and dance, Sheetal wanted nothing more.

She lifted a hand to the heavens. Someone, she wasn't sure

who, reached out in return, and once their fingers met, Sheetal stepped through a door dark as night. Her mortal eyes fluttered shut, and when she opened them again, she was the sky.

No, that was wrong. She *wore* the sky, had wrapped it about her like shadow-stained silk. She danced with it, within it, spinning softly, so softly, a sway here, a slow turn there. She whirled and floated, twirled and dipped, changed places with partners, and changed again.

She breathed her family, sang their story. Their flesh was her flesh, their skin her skin.

Here, there was no question of being liked, only of belonging.

The light, the song, laced itself through her, knitting her to the nakshatra. With luminescent eyes, she saw the spirits of the stars passing over the sky, blazing across millennia. She saw the beginning and the end, and she swirled past everything in between.

Stars were born; stars died. A sun blinked out; a black hole loomed. Below, in the mortal realm, a queen conquered; a fool felled a king. An artist painted; an assassin slew. How fast, how brief, these mortal lives. A twinkle of a star's lifespan.

Yet they smoldered with a fire all their own, these humans. They raged with passion and creativity, nurtured by the dust of the stars, the glistening marrow of silver bones.

Humans needed stars, Sheetal thought as she watched her mother in orbit, and stars needed humans. They were all part of the great drama, the slow and continuous spiral of creation and destruction, and they all played their roles.

And always, always did the brilliant stars burn bold in the deepest night.

When at last the ring of hands released hers, she found herself resting by the window in her palace bedroom.

It was still nighttime, and the stars still turned slowly above, just as Nani had mentioned on their tour of the palace. But Sheetal felt wrong. This wasn't her body, this frail, fleshly creature. She was a giant thing jammed into a tiny cage.

Already the impression of the—what? Event? Ritual? Whatever the word, already she'd lost it, the memory shrinking, flattening to fit into the borders of her mortal mind. Already her throat had gone raw with thirst, and her sweat-encrusted body cried out for a shower and a change of clothes. She needed to sleep.

She didn't want to do any of that. She wanted to expand back out, to be that enormous celestial aspect made only of light and song that spun in eternity without judgment or human emotion—or split ends.

Sheetal raked through her shimmering tangles with clumsy hands. Whoever heard of a star with bad hair days? She'd just trimmed the ends herself, and here they were scissoring apart again.

*What if you went full star?* a voice in her head suggested, small and shrill compared to the song of the sky. *You could look like Charumati.*

She recoiled. It wasn't about the hair. It was about the steadiness, the sense of concord on that cosmic level. Up there, they were all part of the slow and sensuous dance.

Up there, everything made sense.

Rati's face appeared in her mind, and Sheetal knew she would never say yes to her offer, not if it meant leaving all this behind.

But she wasn't giving up being human, either. She would find a way to have it all.

Her hands tingled, and she let them grow warm without fear.

## 20

The stained glass windows in Sheetal's grandparents' sitting room were a wash of constellations and moonlight lotuses in a palette of peacock blue, silver, and black. Their light splashed onto carved ebony furniture, a fine writing desk, and pewter shelves lined with scrolls and blue-and-silver blossoms. It should have been a welcoming place, especially after the dining hall last night.

Not this morning, though. Sheetal, her neck stiff and aching from sleeping awkwardly on the windowsill, did her best to appear even halfway alert. Somehow, after a quick bath that did nothing for her knotted muscles, followed by the usual dressing routine Padmini had refused to cut short, she'd lugged herself here. That had to count as a miracle, right?

*For Dad*, she thought. Nothing else could have gotten her out the door.

Her head throbbed horribly, her skin sparked with acutely

offended nerve endings, and her whole body felt wrung dry, as if she hadn't just gulped down two large glasses of blue mango juice. Her lungs, which she'd expanded until they hurt during yesterday's rehearsal, complained with each breath. Listening to Charumati and Nani argue about instruments while Nani's advisors tried to get a word in, too, drove freshly sharpened spikes through her skull. Kids at school talked about post-party hangovers; if her stomach weren't growling for food, she would've called this one.

Servers finally brought in a spread of dishes, and Sheetal homed in on the buttery sweetness of the warm sheero placed before her. Fat and sugar and the rich flavor of cardamom— eating the ghee-drenched semolina felt like collapsing into a hug.

But the sheero turned bitter almost as soon as it melted on her tongue. She only had one full day of training and rehearsal left. One—and she felt like she'd been run over by a whole fleet of trucks. How was she supposed to do this?

And with the court laughing at her the entire time.

She was done being laid bare, a specimen sliced open and prodded with pins on an examination table. She definitely didn't need Nani or anyone else reading her feelings and judging her. Or possibly catching her debating with herself whether to bail on the competition.

Nana smiled and folded her hand over a warm piece of puran poli. "You look tired, dikri. How are you feeling?"

Looking into his gentle face, she figured it was worth

a shot. "Nana, there's got to be some way for me to hide my thoughts so I'm not broadcasting them to the whole court. Will you teach me?"

"Veiling yourself from the astral melody is a vital skill," he said. "Eat for your strength, and then we will commence."

Sheetal wolfed down both that piece of sweet stuffed flatbread and the second one Nana offered her. Then, following his directions, she closed her eyes and *felt* the sidereal melody, a sea of silver notes that went on and on and on. Her emotions were minute threads in its boundless tapestry, all different shades from pewter to frost, and she could pull on each one, directing it in or out of the song as she wanted.

The argument between her mother and grandmother faded, and so did the advisors' persistent attempts to change the subject.

"It is simply a matter of weaving and unweaving," Nana encouraged her.

Sheetal located the thread of her bad mood and plucked it from the starsong. A simple tug, and it drifted away into the background. Around her, the starry melody livened subtly. She was just as irritated as before, and her head still felt like someone had dropped an anvil on it, but at least now, if she'd done it right, none of that showed.

Nana considered her. She waited, worrying a tooth with her tongue. Had it worked?

He smiled. "Well done. I sense only hope."

Her mood perked up right away, and she smiled back.

Success! That had been a lot easier than she'd expected—obviously she deserved a second bowl of sheero and a third glass of blue mango juice.

"So we will have the ice harp delivered," Nani declared, and Sheetal snapped to attention. "Nitin, have it brought to Charumati's practice chamber."

"Of course, Esteemed Matriarch," Nani's secretary said with a bow of his head.

Sheetal rapped her knuckles on the table. "Excuse me, but can I maybe have a say in what I play? You know, since I'm the one who'll be playing it?"

Everyone looked at her as though they were shocked to see her sitting there.

"Well, you play the harp and the dilruba," Nani asked, "do you not?"

"Yeah," Sheetal said, "but I haven't even picked a song yet."

Nani's expression shuttered. "Would you please leave us," she commanded her advisors.

Their faces ranged from hassled to fretful. "Are you certain?" one asked. "There is more we have not yet addressed, such as the upcoming skyberry harvest."

"I appreciate your concerns, but I am certain. We will speak later." Nani treated them to a weary but implacable smile, and one by one, they filed out.

She plucked a crystal rose from a vase on the table and ran her fingers over the faceted petals. "You are newly brought here, beti, so permit me to explain. We do not encourage mingling with mortals, and that includes indulging their customs. Here we defer to our elders and their best judgment."

"Understand," Nana put in, "it is our intention to ease the path for your success among us."

"I appreciate that," Sheetal said sweetly. Time to dust off an old trick for dealing with Radhikafoi—acting humble. Too bad she almost always got too worked up to remember to do it. "It's clear you put a lot of thought and planning into all of this, which I really appreciate, because I wouldn't have any idea where to start. But if it's okay, I'd really like to be the one to choose my instrument. I do feel I know my music best."

The lines on Nani's forehead grew starker. Unlike Radhikafoi, she didn't appear at all flattered. "I suppose you do, at that," she allowed. "Which song would you play, then—the ballad?"

"The bhajan." After Priyanka's *quacks like a duck* routine, Sheetal wasn't sure she'd ever be able to sing that ballad again.

And something about Nani choosing the harp made her want to do the opposite.

"You will need a dilruba, then," Charumati said. There was a quiet note of triumph in her words, as if Sheetal had scored her another point in whatever tug-of-war was going on between Nani and her.

"Yes," Sheetal said, keeping her voice neutral. "Can I see the options?"

Nana laughed and patted her hand. "That you will have to entrust to us! I am certain you will not be displeased with the results."

Trust them? Yeah, right. Sparks flared at her core, and her hands started to tingle. How was she supposed to trust anything they did, now that she knew they'd once closed the gates between the worlds?

"Actually," she said, "I have a question."

Nana waggled his head. "Ask."

Sheetal pressed her hands flat on the schedule to still their shaking. "You said something about not mingling with mortals. What exactly do you mean by that?"

Her throat closed as something sizzled under her palms. She lifted them from the cover to see scorch marks. Scorch marks in the shape of two hands.

Everything was skyrocketing out of control. It was like burning Dad all over again.

Nani, Nana, and Charumati exchanged troubled looks. Nani recovered first, her eyes darkening. "I told you she should have returned to us sooner. How will she ever take her place among us if she burns herself up first? She should have learned how to wield her flame long ago!"

*Take my place?* Sheetal eyed her own palm like it was a strange thing someone had grafted onto her wrist. Her throat refused to unclench, and the fire hissed through her, furious, famished.

Charumati circled the table and squeezed Sheetal's hands as if to pacify them. "She is *my* daughter. I will help her. Leave her be."

When Nani spoke again, her voice was a quiet thunderbolt. "You think what you did affected only you, beti? You were to be my successor, we were to retake the court together, and you threw it all away for a mortal!"

Charumati's light licked the air like tongues of flame. "And I will never make amends to your liking, no matter that I left my life on Earth—left my husband, my *daughter*—in order to return and aid our house."

"*I'm* a mortal," Sheetal muttered, remembering what she'd read about how Nani had sealed off the Hall of Mirrors. "Did Mom throw away her time on me, too?"

After she'd shared in the connection of the cosmic dance, after she'd felt the entire universe unified, she couldn't bear to hear her grandmother say it. But she needed to know the truth.

Nani's furrowed brow softened into an affectionate smile. "What sort of query is that, dikri?" Starshine blazed fiercely from her. "You are our Sheetal, and you always will be."

The astral melody vibrated with tension Charumati wasn't even bothering to hide. And with her own, too, Sheetal realized. Nani's answer was beautiful, but it hadn't actually told her what she wanted to know.

Before she could think how to reword the question, Nani returned the flower to the vase. "While we are on the topic, it is important to understand that there are boundaries and values we must adhere to." She cut her eyes to Charumati. "Traditions exist to preserve our integrity."

Charumati's mouth twisted into a parody of a smile. "Mother, perhaps we should change the subject?"

"What *you* did, Daughter," Nani emphasized, each syllable as sharp and cold as icicles, "brought dishonor down on all our heads. Breaking the taboo, endangering our future if I had not contrived a way to turn it to our advantage . . ."

"It is hardly a taboo any longer!"

"You are the princess of a royal house. You cannot simply follow your whims—"

"Stop," Nana ordered. The kindly glint in his gaze had been replaced by iron. "No more of this, either of you. We have our beautiful, healthy child now, and that is where this dispute ends. She needs our guidance. Let us leave the past where it belongs."

He pushed a saucer of sweets toward Sheetal. "Be at ease, beti. All families have misunderstandings on occasion. Cast these angry words from your thoughts and look forward."

But Sheetal could only look at her hands, the same hands she'd finally accepted just hours before, and wonder who they would hurt next.

Somehow Sheetal made it to her lesson on etiquette. She nabbed a seat next to Kaushal at the far end of the library table and unrolled a scroll, ready to take diligent notes. Unfortunately, the instructor, a middle-aged star who looked like he'd be at home in a mortal professor's tweed jacket and bow tie, killed that plan, droning on and on about manners and propriety in excruciating detail—glowing the whole while.

She mimicked falling asleep and snoring to Kaushal, who barely hid his grin. It didn't take her long to boil the instructor's rambling down to three basic things: One, she needed to channel Minal and sweet-talk everyone. A lot. Two, she had to couch any complaints in tactful terms. Three, she must hide her true feelings in the astral melody, except when sharing positive ones. If someone displayed negative emotions, you could be sure you'd really rubbed them the wrong way, and they wanted you to know it.

Like during the convocation yesterday morning.

Sheetal fidgeted in her chair. It was great and all to learn the proper number of times to refuse a gift before giving in— five—but how did that help her right now, when she could be practicing her dilruba? The finer points of when and how to compliment someone's outfit wouldn't impress the court. Only her music would. Not to mention she still had to figure out how not to set everything on fire.

Every minute she wasted here was a minute she wasn't doing either of those.

*Two days.* Her palms tingled, and she gripped her pen harder, determined to stay calm. Well, two days if she didn't blow everything up first.

Kaushal nudged her under the table. Startled, she glanced

up from her scroll, where she'd been doodling pictures of her dilruba. "Your boredom is showing," he whispered. "Bright as a mortal neon sign."

Sure enough, the instructor had stopped talking and was frowning at her. "It seems you have yet to master a key aspect of fundamental court etiquette, which leads me to question your proficiency in the rest."

The other students tittered, and Sheetal flushed. But she found the strand of her impatience in the sidereal melody and plucked it out. "Better?"

The instructor waggled his head in approval and went back to the lecture.

Class finally ended, and Sheetal was off like a rocket. But then Kaushal and Urjit stepped in her path.

"That mortal food," Urjit asked, "what was it called? Chevdo?" Sheetal nodded. "I appreciate your sharing it with me."

"And what else?" Kaushal prompted.

Urjit made an annoyed sound. "I apologize for my discourteous remark yesterday."

Sheetal had forgotten all about that. "Don't give it another thought."

She tried to swerve around them, but Urjit asked, abashed, "Might there be any more?"

"No, but I might still have some other snacks. I'll look." Sheetal pretended not to notice the way Urjit's face lit up at that, beaming silvery warmth all around him, until he caught himself and snuffed it out. "Anyway, I have to go. I've got my next lesson."

Kaushal walked her to the exit. "He truly enjoyed that chevdo, as did I. It reminded me of my childhood."

"I'm glad," Sheetal mumbled, mentally going over her schedule for the rest of the afternoon. "Hey, how much do you know about the star hunters?"

"Very little. Why do you ask?"

She shrugged. "No reason."

"Listen, you should know that it also took me some time to gain a handle on my powers. It is a difficult process for those of us who began like this. However, with time, it becomes exponentially simpler." Kaushal gestured to himself. "All of it does."

But Sheetal didn't need his sympathy. She just wanted to go. "I'm not staying," she pointed out, "so it doesn't matter."

"Ah," he said, visibly deflating. "I suppose not, then."

# 21

"I thought we would rehearse in here today," Charumati said, unlocking her suite of rooms. Her enigmatic smile shone as bright as the starlight tresses that tumbled down her back.

Confused, Sheetal followed her mother inside. She had to grin at the hues that fell outside the sidereal color scheme of silver, black, and blue. They were small things—subtle accents like a scarlet cushion, a green fairy-tale compendium, a purple candy dish—just enough to show Charumati hadn't forgotten her time on Earth.

"Hey, I made this for you!" Sheetal recalled, picking up the candy dish. She'd sculpted it in second-grade art class and then carved two interlocking horseshoes on the side before glazing the whole thing in a pretty aubergine.

Something in her chest softened. She'd thought Dad had accidentally thrown it out.

"I have always prized it." Charumati's lips brushed Sheetal's cheek. "Come. Your practice dilruba waits within."

They passed through one more set of doors at the back of Charumati's apartments, and what she saw there made Sheetal forget everything else.

Moonlight lotuses bloomed from the pond's crystalline waters, frosting the air a familiar silvery white. Like with so many of the rooms Sheetal had seen in the palace, the night sky served as a ceiling, making the water sparkle as if it were studded with diamonds.

"You have a *pond*?" Sheetal whistled.

"Every nakshatra has its own crop of moonlight lotuses." Charumati beamed with pride. "It is what mortals might refer to as 'waterfront property.'"

Peace rolled over Sheetal as she knelt by the pond, soothing as the whisper of the dark water against the shore. She felt the tension draining from her muscles, felt her heartbeat slowing in time with the astral melody. Her mouth curled into a dreamy smile.

Charumati beckoned to her from beneath a trellis overgrown with twinkling blue, black, and silver rosebuds, not far from the water's edge. A moonlight lotus blossom glowed from behind her ear, highlighting the plain wooden dilruba at her side. She looked every inch the shining queen among her flowers, preparing to be serenaded.

*My mother, the fairy tale*, thought Sheetal, and maybe it was

267

the moonlight lotuses, or maybe she was tired, but she couldn't muster up the anger she'd felt just that morning.

Inhaling the flowers' heavenly fragrance, she tackled her warm-up exercises, even the stupid lip trill, as earnestly as she could. She leaned the dilruba against her thigh, and Charumati pushed her shoulders back. "No slouching," she chided.

Sheetal brought the bow to the strings and called the bhajan to mind. It was a gorgeous devotional song composed in the sixteenth century by the mystic poetess Mirabai to celebrate her love for Lord Krishna, but as Sheetal silently tasted the lyrics and tried the accompaniment, she knew it wasn't right.

If she was going to win this competition—if she was going to save Dad—she couldn't choose any old song. She needed to draw on her own anguish, her own confusion, to sing a song that would make the listener feel.

And she knew just the right song, the song Dad had played on a loop after Charumati had left. The song her mother had sung to him when she'd said goodbye. Sheetal wasn't supposed to be there—Charumati had already put her to bed for the last time—but she'd slipped out and sneaked over to their bedroom, where she'd gone for comfort so often. Her mother had left the door ajar.

Sheetal hadn't totally understood that Charumati was leaving them, not until she heard her sing the old Lata Mangeshkar film song "Tu Jahan Jahan Chalega." Sheetal had watched enough older Bollywood movies with her parents to understand Hindi and even a dash of Urdu, so when her mother, radiant in the gloom, had pressed her cheek to Dad's and crooned how, whatever direction he turned, her shadow would always be with him, how he should not mourn her, how her tears would always be there to stop his, she caught it all.

Even as Charumati had sung those words, she'd wept. "Watch over our Sheetal," she'd whispered, kissing away Dad's tears.

Sheetal had fled to her room before she could hear Dad's reply. Mommy couldn't be leaving. No. It was a bad dream. She'd burrowed under the covers and counted the floating shapes on the insides of her eyelids until she finally fell asleep.

When she woke up the next morning, it was just the two of them in the big house. Just her and Dad.

"You can't keep a star from the sky, chakli," he'd tried to explain, his reddened eyes ringed by bruises. Sheetal had refused to believe him. No one had made her mother leave, but her mother had done it anyway.

Sometimes she wondered if the song had been a curse. Dad had said it was Charumati's music that had brought the two of them together, after all—her music and a slow dance in an empty parking lot.

"Ready, dikri?" Charumati asked now.

All the old sorrow, the crushing abandonment, the unbearable loss, threatened to submerge Sheetal, to drown her, moonlight lotuses notwithstanding. She surrendered to it, letting it carry her into the song. Her bow swept along the dilruba's strings, evoking a sound like melancholy, like grief. Like a

269

sundering. The pain poured out of her in gorgeous poetry, a lover begging her beloved not to give up on life simply because they must part.

Sheetal remembered every bit of Dad's silence, of her own loneliness. Of her self-doubt—what had she done wrong? She remembered how still and empty their house felt without its heart, as if no one who lived there would ever breathe again.

*"My shadow,"* she sang, the lyrics wringing out everything she'd worked so hard to suppress, *"my shadow."*

The final notes of the dilruba trailed off, and Sheetal opened her eyes. She hadn't even realized she'd closed them. She was panting, sweating. She let go of the bow and took a huge breath.

Charumati had pressed her slender hands to her heart. She watched Sheetal with wide, desolate eyes. "That song."

Sheetal leaned back against the trellis, studying this woman who was at once so familiar and also a stranger, the ethereal star princess of wonder tales, sylphlike and made of magic. Her mother's fey expression didn't match the crack in her voice when she'd uttered the word *song*.

A small, ugly pleasure welled up, matching the small, ugly voice that whispered how Sheetal had known it would wound Charumati. How she'd wanted it to.

She'd wanted Charumati to hurt the way she'd hurt Sheetal. To make her sorry.

Her bow flew into motion, the dilruba's strings and the astral melody asking the question she couldn't. *How could you leave me behind? You're my* mom!

The music was an ambush, an indictment, a plea. It smashed over Charumati like a tsunami.

Her mother scrubbed away a tear. It was such a human gesture that even though she was sitting right there, Sheetal missed her so dearly it felt like she would snap in half.

"I wanted you to have your life with your father." Charumati unhooked the lotus from behind her ear and offered it to Sheetal. "I could not, I would not cheat you of that. Even if it meant I must watch you from afar."

The starry melody rang out with her grief, raw and bare.

Holding the lotus close, Sheetal wondered who the stars turned to for wisdom. "But what about you?"

Charumati selected a blue rosebud from the trellis and stripped it of its petals, as if playing *he loves me, he loves me not*. "Sheetal, leaving you behind was the hardest thing I have ever had to do. Your father always understood we were existing on borrowed time." She tossed the petals into the air. "Yet how was I to tell you that? How could I ask you to choose?"

"What do you mean?" Sheetal asked cautiously, her palms burning, icy fear singing thin, high notes in her veins.

"I would never have left you, had I the choice. But I did not. Every star, whether of the royal houses or not, has an aspect that—" Charumati tapped Sheetal's solar plexus. "Your core. You can feel it, yes?"

The area beneath her mother's fingers flared, as though someone had ignited a silver sun there. "Yes."

"That is the part of you that illuminates the darkness. We

271

are always connected to our positions in the sky, even as we move around and talk and live." Charumati broke the contact between them and gripped the pallu of her sari. "One cannot stay away from it as long as I did. I began to break."

Dad had said something like that, Sheetal recalled. Her anger sputtered. "But—but—you never even came back to check on me!"

Charumati's discomfort distorted the starsong. "I was a fool," she said. "Your foi persuaded me you would never be able to blend in among the mortals if I constantly pestered you with my presence."

Radhikafoi was the one who'd kept them apart? Sheetal clutched at her moonlight lotus, her fingernails carving crescents into its petals the same way her mother's words hacked at her heart. "Gods! Why is she always interfering in *everything*? Can't she just leave me alone?"

"She is no villain." Charumati held up a hand to stave off Sheetal's objections. "She wished to protect you, as did I. I do not fault her for that."

"Yeah, well, I do," Sheetal said. She was never going to forgive Radhikafoi. Never. "I could have had you all those years instead of . . ."

She trailed off. There were no words to explain what it had felt like, being abandoned. Unwanted. Alone, with no one to guide her.

Charumati lowered her head. "I will never stop regretting having left you. Never. It was the greatest mistake of my life."

Sheetal's eyes blurred with tears. She hadn't known how hungry she'd been to hear that. "It wasn't okay. You messed up, Mom, and maybe it'll never be okay."

Her mother went still. "Do you mean that?"

"No! I don't know. I thought I was fine with it, but—I'm not. I mean, you say you're not ashamed of me, but you left me." Sheetal poked her ragged cuticle, shame warming her. "I . . . I needed you to be my mom."

The distance between them was as vast as a galaxy and as microscopic as a photon. How could mere words possibly cross it?

"Ah." Charumati toyed with a stray wisp of gleaming hair. "What if I could be there for you now?"

Sheetal was sorting through too many layers of anger and betrayal to answer, and underneath them all huddled a trembling thing she wouldn't expose to anyone, let alone the person who'd hurt her.

She mulled over her mother's words. It wasn't a cure. It definitely wasn't going to fix everything.

But maybe, said that trembling thing, that part that had never stopped missing her mother, it could be a start.

Charumati grasped Sheetal's hands, the lotus a lantern between them. "I cannot make up for the past, yet perhaps I can assure our future." She waited until Sheetal nodded. "You will return home with the blood. I am certain of this. But let us speak of a moment beyond that."

Sheetal frowned. "Huh?"

"Your nani intends to close the gates between the worlds once more. She would see no more interaction between stars and mortals. Worse, she has many convinced she is right."

"Wait, she doesn't want to see me anymore? I thought she wanted me here."

"The inverse, my daughter," Charumati said, releasing her. "She would keep you here for good."

Considering Sheetal had already assumed as much, having her guess confirmed had no right to sting as much as it did. She buried her nose in the moonlight lotus's silky petals.

"We have all seen the harm that mortals wreak on one another. Her younger sister, my masi, was assaulted by one. Yet I believe I have conceived—"

"Back up a second. Her sister?" No wonder Nani had refused to discuss her.

"Ojasvini, yes." Even Charumati's dismay was delicate. "That vile man imprisoned my poor masi and bled her for profit."

Dev's vision washed back over Sheetal, every gruesome detail. It couldn't be a coincidence. "The first star hunter. I saw it."

How achingly sad—Ojasvini's fate had been so awful that almost no one spoke of her anymore, not even the history books. To only live on in that grisly memory . . .

Charumati tilted her head, and her hair flung silver starlight over the dark grass. "Did you?"

Sheetal stared out at the star-glittered water. Everything she thought she knew had turned in on itself like a kaleidoscope, the

274

pieces tumbling over one another until they formed an entirely new picture. She'd had a great-aunt. Dev's and Jeet's forebear had known and tortured that great-aunt. What were the odds?

Astronomical, she was sure—a pun Dad would appreciate. And yet here they all were, the sidereal song swelling and shimmering around them like stardust. As briefly as she could, she explained how she'd witnessed the memory.

"Ah." Charumati nodded, unfazed. "Bridging hearts. It is a revealing act, an intimate one." Her way-too-perceptive look made Sheetal want to gag. Not even the moonlight lotuses could ease the nausea.

She punched the loose soil down with her fists. "Ugh, can we get back to your masi, please?"

"Nani rescued her sister, but Ojasvini was never the same. In the end, she left the court, and Nani's grief warped into hatred of the mortals who would permit such violence." Her mother's smile was anything but happy. "So you see how my breaking the taboo against interaction with mortals might not have sat so well with her."

Sheetal had to admit she would probably want to close the gates after that, too.

Not that she was going to let Nani do it now. "So what happened to that guy? Please tell me he didn't just ride off into the sunset."

A peal of laughter like a bell escaped Charumati. "Hardly. Your nani, shall we say, meted out justice—with the same blade he had used on Ojasvini."

*Mind. Blown.* Nani was a badass. Sheetal was kind of freaked out and impressed at the same time.

Charumati waved her hand, bangles tinkling. "About a century ago, House Revati convinced House Dhanishta to reopen the gates separating our worlds on the grounds that keeping the realms apart was doing more harm than good. But it was all to spite Nani. Just as it has now selected Jeet as its champion. Nani is determined to overturn House Dhanishta's judgment."

"So how do we stop her?"

"As I was saying, I have conceived a plan." Charumati stretched out a long leg until her toes dipped into the water. "Our power of inspiration is strong. Combined, our houses could put an end to mortal self-destruction.

"Tell me, dikri, what have you dreamed for your world? What would you change?" Her words were a soft breeze from far away, but her notes in the starry song rang out solid, even resolute.

What would Sheetal change? So many things. An end to war, for starters. And hunger. And . . .

"I met some of the women your foi works with." Pain rippled through Charumati's voice. "I saw the scars, both of the body and of the spirit, from the abuse they endured. Imagine if the men and women who inflicted that abuse carried this light in their hearts. Imagine if the entire mortal world did. Imagine if everyone lived from their highest potential, and all people were safe and kind to one another. Nani would have no reason to close the gates to that world."

Chills ran down Sheetal's spine. "That would be like magic."

"Bingo." Charumati laughed. "Your father taught me that word on one of our first dates. If only all mortals were as sweet and considerate as he."

A world full of people like Dad. Sheetal could picture it perfectly, down to the smallest detail. Wasn't that the world society should be striving toward? Peace and harmony? Compassion and kindness? Generosity and equal distribution of resources?

"But we can't *make* them be like that," she argued. Could they? "What about free will?"

"If you witnessed a rabid animal attacking a child, would you not intervene?" Charumati spread her palms, and bands of starlight swirled from them to the rosebuds on the trellis. They bloomed in response, petals unfurling like prayers. "They behave this way because they know no better. If they woke from their sleep, they would not."

Of course Sheetal would intervene. "You're talking about enlightenment."

Charumati leaned close and kissed Sheetal's temple. Her quiet urgency flowed between them. "Yes. And above all, you, my daughter, would be safe. Free to move at will and in full sight between the realms. Since you were born, I have dreamed of nothing else."

To have Dad and Mom both, Earth and Svargalok. To never need to hide again. It sounded too good to be true.

But what if it wasn't?

Sheetal dipped her own feet into the cool water and listened to the shifting tones of the sidereal song, its sparkle in her veins in that moment like the ceaseless serenity of the cosmic dance. "How would this plan of yours work, if you need the whole court for it? It's not like Nani and Nana would just sit back and say, 'Okay, go ahead and railroad us. We're cool with it.'"

"In practical terms?" Charumati closed her eyes, and the starsong *opened* to Sheetal like a movie. As part of the ruling nakshatra, her mother would seek out the younger generations, the ones who remained curious, like Kaushal and Beena, even Padmini. She would select scouts from each of the nakshatras, speak to them of her own time on Earth, and remind them that stars were meant to walk unobstructed among mortals, inspiring them to greatness.

Those scouts would move from mortal nation to mortal nation, using their stardust, their silver flame, to awaken humans in positions of power and those around them. Those leaders would then begin to make changes that actually served the greater good.

After that, Charumati would lead her delegation back to Svargalok, where she would demonstrate the results of her plan and recruit the rest of the court to help enlighten the masses. Left without a good rationale for keeping the worlds separate, Nani and Nana would have no choice but to succumb.

And the mortal realm would unfold like a moonlight lotus, baring the jewel at its center.

Sheetal fell back, dazed. It sounded like a dream come true, but more than that, she could feel her mother's conviction, her love, her need to gift Sheetal a world where she would be safe.

She wanted that, too.

"That, dikri," her mother said drolly, "is the power of a star's inspiration. To bring even my daughter to her knees."

She picked up Sheetal's bow and handed it to her. "For now, from the top. An instrument is nothing without its player, and we still have a competition to win."

"Okay, boss," Sheetal said, laughing.

Charumati responded with a single note as pure as wind kissing a crystal chime.

# 22

Wiped out but glowing, Sheetal slipped in the back entrance to the common room and made a beeline for the snack table. She crammed her mouth with nuts and sweets. Some training—no matter how much she ate, she burned right through it.

Charumati had run her through the song five more times, stopping every few seconds to critique her posture, her timing, even her emotion. "More melancholy, perhaps, and less desire to claw the cosmos to ribbons."

Sheetal had sung until her throat ached. She'd strummed the dilruba until the bow grew slick with sweat.

Despite all that, she couldn't shake the image of Ojasvini—her great-aunt—locked in the star hunter's cage. Or the image of his wicked knife slicing into her skin. She couldn't stop thinking of Nani showing up to bring her missing baby sister home and finding *that*.

Would it really be so bad to fill mortal hearts with light and make the world a better place? Didn't humanity deserve that?

Didn't Sheetal?

Doubt bloomed somewhere in the depths of her own heart, but she ignored it. It wasn't like people were making good choices the way things were, or they wouldn't be dealing with poverty and climate change and the threat of nuclear war.

Anyway, this was about *her* life. Her chance to have what she always should have had. Her family—all of it.

A valet stood at the crystal fountain this time. Sheetal made sure to smile as he handed her a cup of the skyberry cordial. He glanced away.

*Um, okay,* she thought, gulping down the drink.

Hands gripped her shoulders, making her spin around. Her drink splattered onto her sari. "What—?"

"Where have you been?" Minal almost shouted. "They think you stole Priyanka's marionettes!"

Padmini started dabbing at the cerulean stain. Sheetal just frowned. "I didn't steal anything."

"Well, *I* know that. Let's get out of here." Minal nodded to the exit, but a commotion in the middle of the room stopped her.

"Too late," Padmini whispered.

The other champions and their attendants had barged in, led by Priyanka, her spiky hair wild and her slitted eyes promising murder. "There she is!" When her escorts tried to shush her, she shrugged them off and stuck her face in Sheetal's. "Give. Them. *Back*."

Minal and Padmini moved to flank Sheetal on either side. "Leave her alone," Minal warned.

Sheetal touched her arm. "It's okay. I've got this." The cordial coated her stomach, quieting her nerves. She turned back to Priyanka. "If you have something to say to me, come over here and say it. I don't bite."

Priyanka bore down on Sheetal until they were almost nose to nose. The ruby in her nostril glinted, a slowly fusing dwarf star. "You really thought we wouldn't figure out it was you?"

"Are you sure someone took your puppets?" Sheetal asked, sipping her drink. "I mean, you *were* whacking things all night; maybe you broke them?"

"Excuse me, Ms. I'm a Star and Shouldn't Even Be Here, but some of us have to practice."

"Look, I'm sorry your puppets are missing, but I didn't take them. Why do you think I did?"

Priyanka grimaced. "Witnesses saw you leaving my room."

Luckily for Priyanka, Sheetal couldn't shoot her flame from her eyes. "That's a lie. I *never* went into your room. Ask Minal."

"Can you be certain? Were you with her every second?" Sachin asked, and of course Minal couldn't say yes. Sheetal glared at him, really wishing she had built-in starry lasers.

Jeet slunk up next to Priyanka. Dark shadows circled his eyes. He ran a hand through his mop of curly hair. "I gave you the benefit of the doubt," he said, agitated, silver light zigzagging over him. It happened so fast, Sheetal almost missed it.

She exchanged a startled glance with Minal. What in the world?

Before she could say anything, Jeet resumed his tirade. "When everyone said it was a cheat for you to be here, I stood up for you. I said it wasn't your fault who your parents are. But now you're going around sabotaging people and trying to charm your way into my house?"

Even Leela seemed disturbed. Leela, the only other champion to be kind to Sheetal.

"Bhai, she didn't do it." Dev, who'd come up behind Jeet, pulled on his arm, trying to get his attention. "She's not like that." But Jeet didn't even look at him.

"Charm my way into your house?" Sheetal echoed.

One of Jeet's attendants held up a Ziploc with a few crumbs.

She laughed; she couldn't help it. "You think because I felt bad for Urjit and gave him a snack, I'm trying to, what, turn him against you?" It was the stupidest thing she'd ever heard. "What's *wrong* with all of you?"

"Sheetal," Minal murmured. "Don't let them get to you."

"I'm sure you didn't," Priyanka said loudly. "Just like you didn't steal my marionettes."

"Jeet, Priyanka, both of you just chill," Dev said. "You're way overreacting."

Sheetal mustered a calm she definitely didn't feel. Her head still hurt like someone had run it through a food processor, and this was only making it worse. "Look, for the last time, I didn't steal your stupid puppets, and it's not like I chose to be here."

"Really, Sheetal," Sachin jumped in, "I thought we were all friends here." He kept glancing at Jeet, then Priyanka, and back at Sheetal, like he couldn't get enough of the drama.

She wanted to sock him. Her hands were only too happy to play along if she would just let them, so she kept her gaze on Priyanka instead. "I don't have time for this. You all seem to think I'm out to take you down or whatever, but I don't even know how any of this works, okay? Lay off already."

Crap. Her core had kindled, and silver flame was sparking in her palms. She curled her hands into fists, but that wouldn't control it for long.

Both Minal and Padmini watched in mute trepidation. They'd seen her hands, too. So had all the stars silently watching. Great, another thing for everyone to gossip about.

Sheetal broke out in yet another layer of sweat. This was ridiculous. She hadn't even done anything.

"How about we all just calm down, maybe have a drink?" Dev suggested. He nudged Jeet, who'd bent over. "Hey, man, you okay? You're burning up."

Jeet grunted. "Not feeling so hot."

Sachin rushed to his side. "Let's get you back to your room," he said. Dev nodded, looking back once at Sheetal before helping Jeet upright. His dark eyes were sad as they traced her face.

Sheetal's heart snagged on that look, so she didn't notice Priyanka inching closer until Priyanka purposely bumped into her, knocking her against Padmini. "You better get my marionettes back to me while you still can, cheater."

Smirks. Taunting. That nasty feeling of being on the outside and defenseless. Had Sheetal blundered back into high school?

She flared, her radiance blinding. Everyone flinched, even the other stars, and somebody yelped. It might have been Sachin; she couldn't tell for sure. "I didn't take your stupid marionettes!"

Even Priyanka stepped back, eyes wide, before she glared again. "Cheater," she repeated. "What are you even doing here?"

Sheetal wrapped her arms around herself, trying to stop the pinpricks of electricity crackling through her body. It felt like the flame at her core had hardened into lightning and was electrocuting her from the inside out.

She'd just made Priyanka's point for her. *Way to go, Sheetal.*

Minal took hold of her wrist, breaking the current. Sheetal exhaled in relief. Thank the gods for Minal.

"That was rough," Minal said, hurrying her out the back exit. "How're you holding up?"

Sheetal wanted to tell her about Charumati, about her plan to stop Nani, about Rati's offer. About how Dev had ignored her last night. The words got tangled in one another and clogged her throat. "Everything's happening too fast," she choked out. "I need to see my dad."

Minal nodded and took her arm. "I'm coming with you. I'll wait outside, but— Did you even sleep? You look exhausted."

"Not really," Sheetal admitted.

"I thought so." Minal grimly pulled her along. "Sheetu, you

can't do this. If you don't take care of yourself, of course you're not going to be able to control your light. Promise me you'll sleep tonight."

Sheetal groped for an answer. How could she explain about the cosmic dance? Minal couldn't understand. No one could.

A wave of homesickness washed over her. All she wanted was to sit with Dad again, even if the closest she could come was through a mirror, and remind herself of why she was doing any of this.

"I'll try," she agreed finally, because what else was there to say?

The Hall of Mirrors was blessedly empty, silent but for the silvery chimes of the starsong. Sheetal knelt before a flower-shaped looking glass and watched Dad's gray-brown face among the briar patch of tubes, watched the rise and fall of his shallow breathing. Her own heartbeat responded, turning into a hum, a mantra of waking.

The air around the mirror glittered, and she hoped Dad could feel it.

Sheetal sang softly to her sleeping father. She told him everything about Svargalok, about her mother and Rati, about the competition, all the while wishing she could do more. Wishing she could go to him right now with the drop of blood in hand and rouse him.

Would he want her to take Rati's offer?

She prayed he'd forgive her, because she couldn't. Not now.

Sheetal didn't know when it had happened, but the fire inside her had tempered all those taunts like a sword, turning them into steel. Minal had been right; she needed to show everyone what she could do. She needed to show herself.

No, she did know. The cosmic dance had woken something in her she didn't want to deny anymore. She was half human, sure, but she was also half a star.

*Tomorrow,* she promised. *Tomorrow, I'll be home to save you.* And then, because the shame of delaying sat like a boulder in her stomach, she added aloud, "I love you, Daddy."

She checked her schedule to see what was next. Another practice session. Good. She needed all the preparation she could get. Only hours left before her birthday.

"Hello, mortal girl," someone called from the doorway.

Sheetal glanced up to see Rati. Why hadn't Minal stopped her from coming in? Her reflections swarmed the mirrors as she entered the chamber, an elegant star maiden clad in a blue-and-silver sari so vibrant it glowed to match the hair piled high on her head. "You should have taken my offer."

"Considering you still haven't given me a concrete reason to trust you, let's call that a hard no." Sheetal tried to push past, but Rati blocked the way.

"You may not believe it, but I have no wish to embroil you in something for which you share no blame." She spoke with kindness, almost enough to make Sheetal believe she meant it. "Perhaps you would hear me out?"

Sheetal sighed and folded her arms. "How do you keep finding me, anyway? It's like you're stalking me."

"If you persist in carelessly blasting your emotions to the entire court, can I truly be held responsible for responding?" Rati smiled and curled one of the starlight tendrils framing her face around her finger. "You may wish to consider more restraint in the future; you never know who might be listening."

Cursing herself, Sheetal located her feelings in the starsong and yanked them loose. She made a special effort to find her embarrassment at Rati's reprimand—how many times was she going to forget to shield herself?—and tear it out by the roots. "Look, I'm not leaving. This is my competition to win."

"Take comfort, girl; no one has time for the trifling struggles of Charumati's daughter."

"So why do *you*?"

Rati reclined on a nearby divan, looking for all the cosmos as if she expected to be fed grapes and fanned. "It is my belief," she said, enunciating each syllable, "that you lack the information you need to be able to determine your own actions. I wish to correct that oversight."

Sheetal fiddled with her braid. The tip felt smooth, not ragged. When Padmini had dressed her earlier, she must have worked some kind of cosmetic magic to hide the split ends. "Can you at least hurry it up? I have things to do."

"For most of our lives, your mother and I were inseparable. We knew each other's hearts as only the truest of friends can."

"So what happened?"

Rati took a moment to answer. "One of our most favored activities was watching you mortals. We would visit the Hall of Mirrors as often as we could, and together, we made secret plans to descend to your world after reaching majority."

"Right . . ."

"Over time, we both found mortals we wished to meet, and so we selected a date and discussed how we would slip past the guards. Though the gate was open, no one could leave without their respective Esteemed Matriarch's and Patriarch's consent. My parents agreed, yet we knew Charumati's never would, so we had to proceed with stealth.

"The fateful day came, and Charumati and I approached the guards. I was to divert them while Charumati sneaked off, and then I would follow." Rati's chuckle lacked any humor. "All plans shine bright in theory, but the execution is often muddier than anticipated. I did not lie well enough, it seemed, for the guards detained me. Your mother, however, ran past them and escaped."

Reluctant compassion stirred in Sheetal as she listened. She and Minal would have done the same thing, but Minal would never have left her behind. "That sucks, but shouldn't you be over it by now?"

"Foolish girl!" Rati rebuked her. "If it had ended there, yes. It did not. I had never seen your grandmother so riled. She could not punish Charumati, so she punished me, shaming me before my house, claiming I had corrupted her precious daughter and persuaded her to break the taboo of consorting with mortals." Silvery flame limned her form, but the astral melody only tinkled and chimed.

"Even that I might have borne. Yet when your mother did not return, I was stripped of my rank as princess. Your grandmother pressed for it, and my parents knew of no other way to mollify her wrath. After all, I *had* sought to break the taboo."

So that was why Rati didn't wear a circlet. And now she had to watch Charumati remain princess of her nakshatra.

That was awful. In her place, Sheetal would probably want to make everyone pay, too.

But she wasn't in Rati's place, and she couldn't afford to get involved. "I'm really sorry to hear that," she said, "but as you yourself pointed out, it's not my fault. So maybe leave me out of this petty revenge scheme?"

Rati's expression went dark as the night sky without any stars. "Hear me well. I gave you the opportunity to leave. You chose not to take it, and now any culpability for what happens next lies with you. Do not be surprised if it is not to your taste, puppet thief."

In a single motion, she stood and sashayed from the chamber.

By the time Sheetal made it to the hallway, Rati was gone. Instead, she found Minal and Padmini, with squares of plain black fabric over their laps and spools of colored floss neatly stacked on the low table before them.

"I'm pretty sure Rati just threatened me," Sheetal told

them, breathless. She recounted the conversation as fast as she could.

"Oh, Sheetu, I'm sorry," Minal said. "I got distracted. I didn't even notice her."

*Well,* thought Sheetal, a little miffed, *if you hadn't disappeared yesterday at the library, you would've known to be wary of her.*

But that wasn't fair. Minal wasn't her bodyguard.

Padmini began packing up the cache of supplies. "I am glad you did not accept her offer. Their enmity is old, and we need you here with us."

Feeling contrite, Sheetal changed the subject. "What are you two doing, anyway?"

Minal held out a needle threaded with blue floss. "Padmini's teaching me how to embroider! You know how much I love making things."

Sheetal, who also knew how much Minal avoided anything that even slightly resembled sewing, raised her eyebrows.

"Did you know Padmini designs all the fabrics for your nakshatra?" Minal gushed. "She spun this floss out of night winds."

"Very cool," Sheetal agreed. "So what're you making?"

"We are working up to a peacock feather," Padmini explained.

Sheetal stared suspiciously at the tangled lumps of floss on Minal's square. They looked nothing like the feather on Padmini's. "Right," she fibbed. "I totally see it."

Padmini winked, letting her fingers graze Minal's under the guise of smoothing out her fabric square. "Everyone must start somewhere. I am certain your next attempt will show great improvement."

"Oh, for sure," Minal said, though she looked sheepishly at her mess of lumps. "Why stop at one feather? We can do a whole peacock next time."

"It is good to have dreams, or so your mortal television claims," Padmini teased. She bopped Minal on the nose, then got up and excused herself. "Sheetal, do not forget your next session is a rehearsal period."

The second she was gone, Sheetal nudged Minal with her shoulder. "A palace full of amazing things to explore, and you thought, 'I'll just take up embroidery, a thing I hate with the passion of a thousand suns, today.'"

"Hey," Minal protested, "I have to keep myself busy some-how."

"Please. I saw that wink."

"I don't know what you're talking about." Minal ran a finger over her mutilated feather, all studied innocence. "I'm just gathering intel for you."

"Such a noble sacrifice you're making on my part. I'm sure it doesn't hurt that she's beautiful."

"Is she?" Minal's eyes brimmed with mischief. "I hadn't noticed. Funny that you think so, though."

Sheetal screwed up her face in disbelief. "Out with it. What's going on with you?"

"Okay, fine." Minal danced in her chair. "We've been

talking every chance we get. She's so pretty and smart and nice and loves fashion. I've been showing her some of my designs on my phone." She slowed just enough to take a breath. "She's a really good sister, too. I think there's this part of her that wants to be this secret rebel—you'd never guess from the way she follows the rules—but she has to look out for her brother, so she hides it."

Sheetal laughed. She'd never seen Minal like this. "I knew you had it bad, but . . ."

"I know, I know, but Sheetu, she took me to this orchard under the stars!" Minal's voice grew dreamy. "It was all glowy, and we sat under a tree and ate blue mangoes."

"And?"

"There might have been some kissing. . . ." Minal craned her neck to stare up at the heavens. "I really like her. Like, a lot. And she likes me, too."

Minal almost sparkled, she was so happy. It was another reason Sheetal had to stay and see things through. "She'd be stupid not to."

And if she was being honest, her heart pointed out, she had a third reason, too: she really wanted Dev to hear her sing.

She'd kept that private for so long. The thought that she didn't have to anymore, that he would actually hear what she could do, that it was his turn to be enchanted while her voice soared and dipped as it cast a starry spell, sent bubbles through her blood. The thought of his eyes on her, awed, was like a balloon rising inside her, getting lighter and lighter. Filling her with a rush of giddiness.

Except then the balloon popped. It was too late, like everything. They were pretty much broken up, and anyway, what if the only reason he had ever cared about her voice—about her—was because he knew she was part star?

She couldn't let herself brood about that anymore. It hurt too much.

"I don't know what to do about Rati, but I can prove I didn't take those puppets. We have to find who did. They've got to be in someone's room, right?" she asked. "I mean, unless a star hid them, but let's pretend that's not an option for now."

She really hoped it wasn't—any of the delegates from the convocation had enough reason to do it, and she'd never know.

"And it's not like I was just wasting time learning how to sew feathers." A grin spread across Minal's face, making her blue eye shadow shimmer. "Padmini might have let slip that she knows where the spare keys to all the champions' rooms are. . . ."

"Excellent." Sheetal steepled her fingers and cackled like a supervillain. Hadn't Minal said Padmini secretly wanted to rebel? "So I just have to convince her to get them for us."

Minal waggled her perfectly plucked eyebrows. "I always wanted to be a spy."

23

Just like Sheetal had arranged, Padmini came to get her two seconds after Minal and she had sat down in the dining hall. Padmini didn't have to pretend to be irritated; she'd barely agreed to the scheme to begin with. "Do not tell me you forgot your fitting with the tailors? They were kind enough to make time for you, and yet you keep them waiting. Come!"

Sheetal made an aggravated noise that wasn't exactly fake, either. After three hours of vocal and dilruba practice that left every part of her body aching and another half hour persuading a skittish Padmini to help, she could have gobbled up every plate the servers were bringing out now. So to smell the bouquet of aromas—the rich, savory spices; the promise of creamy, flavorful lentils and fried puri; the delicate scent of nine-vegetable biryani studded with cashews and sultanas—and have to leave it all behind? Her stomach cramped in mutiny.

Sachin and Priyanka snickered with Sachin's companion, obviously loving their front-row seats to the Sheetal-getting-scolded show. Jeet, however, still looked out of it, and Leela and her companion politely disregarded the whole spectacle.

Dev wasn't anywhere in sight, and Sheetal couldn't be more grateful.

"But we didn't get to eat yet—" Minal whined, laying it on a little thick.

"There is no time," Padmini cut in. "Let us go."

In case any stars were tuning in to the sidereal song, Sheetal played up her exasperation. She let a few nerves ring out, too. Let them think she was intimidated. "Ugh, *fine.*"

She glanced back at the feast set out before the other champions, then followed Padmini to the exit.

"Remember," Padmini said, "we are only going there to be seen. Answer their questions, but avoid being drawn into deep conversation." She held herself tensely, and Sheetal wondered if she might still back out. "When I return from the storage room with the keys, follow my lead."

The next few minutes were a blur as Padmini rushed them through the ornamented halls. At first, Sheetal avoided meeting the eyes of the stars they passed. What if she gave herself away? Or worse, what if she already had?

But Padmini took full advantage of being on display, waxing lyrical about potential style concepts and the availability of specialty silks until no one could possibly mistake where they were going. She was much better at subterfuge than Sheetal would've guessed, and she even seemed to be enjoying it.

They reached the tailors' atelier. It was like the fabric stall at the Night Market, but on a much grander scale and fully in the stars' trichromatic palette. Saris hung from ceiling racks like Persian carpets, gleaming and glittering; silver looms whirred in midweave, strung with ropes of cloud and moonbeam; tables sat laden with scrolls displaying various patterns and design sketches. An open closet overflowed with loops of silver, blue, and black embroidery floss. Stars of all genders bustled about, nattering as they went.

This was where Padmini worked? Sheetal wanted to climb right into the bins and bury her face in the fairy-tale fabrics. Next to her, Minal looked like she might explode with glee.

Padmini led them right into a conversation about the stars' lives, the people they knew, their worries about being able to finish all the outfits for Nani and her family in time for the ball tomorrow, their excitement for the competition. She casually mentioned how well Sheetal had been honing her abilities and assured the others their preparations were proceeding right on schedule.

It felt cozy, the sidereal song reflecting the warm, comfortable atmosphere, and even though this whole visit was just a ruse, Sheetal couldn't help feeling regretful for the parallel universe where this would have been her life.

"While we are on the subject of schedules, I do need to hunt out those textiles I spoke of." Padmini slipped away, leaving Sheetal and Minal to it.

Some of the tailors were wary and kept their distance, but others, like Beena from the library, twinkled with anticipation. "I cannot believe we have such an opportunity! Oh, Sheetal, you will shine like the princess you are at the ball."

"Sure!" said Sheetal, confused. What was Beena doing here?

But she set that aside and imagined Dev seeing her all dressed up, let her delight at sorting through the clothes for the ball pervade the astral melody. An alibi should be thorough, right?

Oops. She cringed. She'd let some of how she felt about Dev seep through, too. No need to be *that* thorough.

Next to her, Minal asked questions about the different fabrics and fielded queries about her makeup, so soon Beena and her friends surrounded her.

And Sheetal was on the outside again. She felt a pang of envy. How was Minal always so *good* at this stuff?

Padmini finally reappeared, swaying under the weight of a mountain of tidily folded fabrics. "I am certain many of these will be to your liking."

*The keys.* Sheetal relaxed slightly. *She got them.* "I'm sure, too."

"Here, let me help you with those." Ignoring her protests, Minal plucked half the hoard right from Padmini's arms.

"We should go look at them right now," Sheetal suggested.

She prayed it didn't sound as artificial to everyone else as it did to her ears. "I can't wait!"

But the tailors only wished them a good night as they left the atelier. Minal and Padmini bantered about fashion as they hurried back to the champions' quarters. Sheetal made sure to smile and nod every so often, like she wasn't terrified someone would figure out what they were really up to. Or worse, walk in on them doing it.

Once they arrived, Padmini urged Sheetal and Minal into their room. "I cannot be seen with you after this," she reminded them. Her gaze darted back and forth before she dropped her stack of fabric on the dresser and produced a ring of keys. "If you get caught, it would put my brother at risk, and I have worked too hard to secure a place in our house."

"Trust me, the last thing I want is for Kaushal to get hurt," Sheetal said, and she meant it completely. The idea that someone would single him out for having once been a half-star like her made her sick.

Minal piled the rest of the fabric on a chair. "We won't get caught. But if we do, we'll take the blame for everything. Please?"

Padmini hesitated, as if she might still take the keys and run. "Only because I remember how it was for my brother when he came to live among us. The Esteemed Matriarch and Patriarch have been good to us. I must repay that as I can." Her long silver waves glittered and sparkled as she uncurled her fingers from the ring and held it out.

Even from where she stood, Sheetal could tell each one was embossed with the symbol of its corresponding nakshatra, just like the doors to the champions' dorm rooms.

Instead of taking the key ring, Minal folded her hand over Padmini's. Murmuring words Sheetal couldn't hear, she flashed a flirtatious smile.

Padmini ducked her head, though not before Sheetal saw her grin. She tenderly brushed aside a lock of Minal's hair and kissed her cheek. "This was fun," she whispered. "But please be careful."

*Just gathering intel, huh?* Sheetal had never seen Minal with hearts in her eyes like this. It was kind of adorable.

As Padmini sidled past on her way out, she added quietly, so only Sheetal could hear, "Be mindful of your emotions."

Sheetal stared after her. *Great.* Had she been careless enough that someone besides Padmini had noticed?

All business again, Minal divided up the keys. "Let's split up and meet back in our room."

Sheetal chose the ones for Houses Magha and Revati. "Knock first, and keep it to five minutes, tops. Ready?"

It hit her then, what they were about to do—break into other people's rooms and go through their stuff. She quailed. Dad would never, ever approve of this. Honestly, neither did she.

But someone was trying to get her thrown out of the competition, and this was the only way to find out what had happened with Priyanka's marionettes. How did they even know she hadn't made the whole thing up?

At Minal's nod, Sheetal headed into the hallway and knocked on Priyanka's door. Her heart slammed in her chest. What if she drew too much attention and a star came to investigate—what if Priyanka walked in . . . ?

Oh, no—had she let that leach into the starsong, too?

Nana hadn't told her how much more work it was to keep her feelings tamped down and out of sight when she was under stress. Stress like breaking and entering.

No one answered her knock, and no footsteps sounded either inside the room or out in the corridor. Palms prickling, Sheetal turned the key in the lock.

The door swung open to reveal a room like hers, down to the cloud mattresses, except clothes had been strewn all over the floor, along with dishes and cups, and someone had pushed the desk to the center of the room and buried it in tools: a hammer, a pair of needle-nose pliers, miniature bottles of paint, wires, and paintbrushes. In the corner by the bed, Sheetal spied a partially open hard black carrying case, like for instruments, but this one's red lining held two puppet-shaped gaps.

Among the mess of wadded-up tissues on the dresser sat a framed photo of an old man with a mustache making a Kathputli puppet dance. That had to be Priyanka's grandfather. Sympathy Sheetal didn't want to feel spilled over her. Why did it have to be like this? *She* didn't even want the prize!

Padmini's warning sounded in her ears, and Sheetal hurried to cull her reaction from the astral melody. That was all she needed: pity for Priyanka, of all people, giving her away.

Half expecting a starry hand to land on her shoulder at any second, she checked the bathroom, under the beds, and between the sheets. Even Priyanka's roller suitcase. No puppets.

*At least*, she thought, relieved, *Priyanka wasn't lying.* She peeked into the hallway to make sure no one was coming, then a second time, before hurrying back out and locking the door behind her.

Minal had just come out of Leela's room. *Nothing*, she mouthed.

Sheetal shot her a thumbs-up and knocked on Jeet's door. No answer here, either. After inspecting the hallway in both directions, twice, she inserted the key into the lock.

Then came the sound she'd been dreading: voices in the distance. *Oh, crap.*

As she ripped the key back out, the door opened, and she fell into the room, sprawling painfully over somebody's foot.

She rolled onto her back to see Dev crouching down next to her, and his expression was anything but friendly in the light of the dangling star lanterns. The familiar lock of hair tumbled into his dark eyes, and she found herself wishing she could tuck it behind his ear. Wishing she could reach up and cradle his cheek.

"What are you doing here?" he demanded, his face nearing hers.

She met his question with a challenge of her own. "Why weren't you at dinner?"

"So you broke in?" Dev shook his head. "You're something else."

"Oh, so you think that's worse than someone trying to frame me for theft?" Sheetal wanted to shake him. To kiss him.

He reached out a hand, almost brushing her face, and her lips tingled in anticipation of his touch. But then he ran it through his hair instead. "What do you want me to say, Sheetal?"

She couldn't let him see how lonely, how stupid she felt, so she scrambled to stand and put some space between them.

What did she want him to say? That he missed her. That he wanted to kiss her, too.

"You tell me," Sheetal said finally. She appraised the room. Two backpacks, a duffel bag, and a suitcase sat arranged in the corner, though half-folded clothes spilled from the duffel bag. She could guess whose it was. Neat piles of books, pens, notebooks, and even a tablet with an attached keyboard covered the intricate ebony desk. Nothing suspicious in sight.

She scooted around the beds and reached for a silver cabinet handle. "Where are the puppets?"

"Stop that!" Dev said, pulling her away. His hands were warm on her arms, and despite herself, she shivered. "Why are you trying to ruin things between us?" It was almost a plea.

"Me?" Sheetal cried, outrage kindling the fire at her core. Silver radiance flared through the room. She didn't care anymore about keeping her voice down. "Why don't you ask everyone else why *they're* ruining things?"

The door banged open again, and two people appeared in the doorway. "Get *down!*" Dev hissed.

303

Sheetal instinctively threw herself to the floor by the second bed. *Crap. Crap, crap, crap!* Grabbing the edge of the coverlet, she tugged it down and over herself to hide the glow until she could will it away.

Luckily, Jeet was too wrapped up in his guest to notice. "Thanks for listening. I really appreciate it."

"Thank *you* for helping look for my marionettes," Priyanka said, her voice pitched low. "That was really sweet."

Then Sheetal heard footsteps as they came into the room, followed by soft smacking sounds. She drew back in disgust. Unfortunately, that made the blanket slide off her face, giving her a perfect view of the action.

"So what did you think?" The note of hope in Jeet's voice made him sound younger. He held a black Moleskine notebook. "That story was my first ever pro sale. I wanted it to be a raw look at the exploitation of the working class and the sickness of corporate greed. It's, like, the monster that lurks in the shadows, you know?"

If only Sheetal could pull the blanket over her eardrums.

"Oh, totally!" Priyanka said. "Those themes in it really resonated with me. I felt slapped—but in a good way." She laughed, all sultry, and tilted her wineglass so the ice-pale liquid sloshed as she leaned into him. "Besides, that bottle of wine you found didn't hurt, either."

From where he stood by the wall, Dev coughed a very fake, *I'm here, too* cough. "Uh, what are you doing?"

"We went for a walk," Jeet slurred, obviously having had a glass or two of his own already. "But where were you? You never came to dinner."

"Yeah, I—" Dev frowned and stepped closer to him. "Wait, are you *drunk*? The competition's tomorrow!"

"It's just frostberry wine. This stuff doesn't last." Twisting slightly so Priyanka and Dev couldn't see, Jeet tipped a tiny vial over his wineglass. Turning back, he gulped down the drink. "Anyway, you can celebrate with us now. Look, Priyanka, my cousin-brother's here!"

"I'm not really in the mood," Dev said, his neck and shoulders stiff, and Sheetal realized he was deliberately not looking in her direction. "How about we just call it a night?"

Jeet ruffled Dev's hair. "Relax, man. It's my job to play big brother, not yours."

"It's called letting off steam," Priyanka said, clinking her glass against Jeet's. "We'll still be ready to compete tomorrow, all bright-eyed and bushy-tailed."

Dev's jaw worked, but he said nothing.

"Look," Jeet said, "I know you liked her, but girls come and go. You can do better, trust me." He tapped Dev a little too hard on the shoulder.

Sheetal narrowed her eyes. Like Jeet was any catch, with that charming personality.

"Is that what you think this is?" Dev asked. "That I'm upset about Sheetal? Bhai, I'm trying to look out for *you*."

305

"I don't need you to," Jeet said. "I just need you to back off."

Priyanka twined a finger through his curls. "So where's that book you were going to show me?"

Dev's fed-up look told Sheetal he'd seen more than enough. "Party if you want, but I need to sleep," he said flatly.

"Fine, we'll go somewhere else. Lighten up, little brother." Jeet swapped his empty wineglass for a book on the desk, using that as cover while he deposited the vial he'd palmed into a drawer. Then he put his arm around Priyanka. Together they staggered into the bathroom.

But not before Sheetal glimpsed the contents of the vial— shimmering silver liquid.

She'd seen something like that before, in Dev's memory. Star's blood.

Jeet's starry cast made sense now. So did the dark bags under his eyes. The hollows in his cheeks.

*He's drinking it.*

What had the library book said? Something about heightening inspiration?

Mortals. Her mother was right; they couldn't help themselves. Even the good ones got pulverized under the heels of the rest.

The bathroom door clicked closed. Sheetal and Dev were alone again, the air around them weighted down with the burden of everything they now knew.

Sheetal hauled herself to her feet and made straight for the drawer before Dev could stop her. Her fingers closed around the vial, and she gave it to him. "Dev," she whispered, so Jeet and Priyanka couldn't hear, "he's—he's drinking this."

He stared at the vial, its silver light staining his skin, as if he could make it disappear.

"I need to take that," Sheetal said as gently as she could. "I have to show my mom and my grandma."

"No." Dev pocketed the vial. He wouldn't look at her.

She sighed. "See, this is why I hate secrets. They make you think people are different from how they really are. You think you can trust them."

Dev wasn't listening. "You should go. I need to talk to my cousin." His words clumped together like the breath had been knocked out of him, and from his bewildered expression, Sheetal could tell he was barely keeping it together.

Her heart hurt. Who knew better than she did what that felt like?

She took his hand. "I'm sorry," she murmured. "I'm just . . . sorry."

"Oh, yeah?" He observed their joined fingers. "Then why did you come here?" His laugh was pained. "Congrats. Now Jeet can get kicked out instead of you. So can you just go?"

Trying not to sob, Sheetal left.

## 24

The morning of Sheetal's seventeenth birthday began like any other morning in Svargalok—fresh, scenic, sparkling. She watched it happen from the balcony in her room, the star-scattered darkness gradually submitting to the golden grandeur of Lord Surya as his chariot, drawn by seven white horses, rolled past. The brilliant blue sky that came after him was rich enough to eat for breakfast, and she scowled at it.

Some birthday. Today was the day she had to save Dad's life.

If she hadn't burned him, she'd be waking up right now, and he'd be in the kitchen, carefully assembling a stack of mixed-berry waffles drenched in maple syrup and vanilla whipped cream. There'd be a new biography, maybe movie tickets or a bookstore gift card, plans for a day trip somewhere, a new outfit of chaniya choli or salwar kameez from Radhikafoi and Deepakfua, and of course, a hug paired with the old one-liner about how soon she'd be taller than Dad if she kept having birthdays.

And Minal would drop by with a silly plastic tiara, glittery balloons, and five or six beautifully wrapped presents she'd set aside over the course of the year. A couple would be gag gifts, but at least one would be a thing she'd made herself, a clay unicorn figurine or a bracelet or a batch of rose-raspberry truffles.

Sheetal let her hair fall over her face like a curtain. Not only was she missing all that, but today would have been her first birthday with a boyfriend. She struggled to keep her chin from quivering.

She hadn't told Minal about the vial of star's blood because she knew what Minal would say. It was the same thing Sheetal would say in her place—that she had to turn Jeet in right now.

Maybe it made her weak, but she couldn't do that to Dev, not when she'd seen the reverence in his eyes, heard the devotion in his voice, whenever he'd mentioned Jeet. Not without giving them a chance to talk first.

The despair in his face last night, the break in his words when he'd asked her to leave, ate at her. What if she'd lost him for good?

*Get over yourself,* she ordered. *You get to have a freaking ball for your birthday!*

She didn't know why seventeen was so special by star standards, or why that made her an adult, but she'd take it. Maybe when she got home, she could tell Radhikafoi to quit bossing her around.

The sun blazed higher in the sky as if mocking her. Okay,

fine. Not even magic could accomplish that.

Sheetal got up and reached for her journal in its silk bag, wanting to sink into the entries she'd read more times than she could count. Charumati's stories, of the naga maiden, of the various heroes and heroines who had declared their goals and then set off after them. Wanting them to fortify her with their reminder that she could do this.

As she fumbled with the strings, the bag slipped out of her grasp and disappeared under the bed. So, birthday or not, it was going to be that kind of morning. She knelt to retrieve the journal, and her fingers bumped against something hard.

Her stomach took a nosedive. *You've got to be kidding.*

"Happy birthday, Sheetu!" Minal called, hurrying to her side. "I'm sorry I couldn't grab your gifts before we left. I'll make it up to you when we get back."

Sheetal pointed under the bed, where two small wooden heads could be seen. "The missing marionettes? Not so missing anymore."

Minal bent to look. She swore a very expressive string of curses.

"Happy birthday to me." Fury like Sheetal had never felt, not even when Radhikafoi admitted to hiding Charumati's letter, boiled up in her. She retrieved the marionettes and stood, her flame crackling until the room blazed like a quasar.

Minal threw a hand over her eyes. "Can you dial that back a little?"

"Sorry." Sheetal picked up a hair clip on the dresser and put it back, jitters coursing through her as she toned down her light.

Still blinking, Minal took the puppets from her. "They look okay, at least."

"They were basically out in the open. Someone wanted them to be found. And me to get blamed. Who hates me that much?"

"I think it's more who sees you as a threat," Minal said. "Definitely not Leela. Sachin or Jeet?" Sheetal shook her head. "Priyanka? No, too obvious."

"One of them must have access to a key, too, or at least to a very helpful star who doesn't mind bending some rules. Like Rati. I mean, she *did* tell me I wasn't going to like what happened."

"But who did she—"

Someone rapped at the door. Sheetal nearly burst out of her skin at the sound. Minal shoved the marionettes back under the bed as far as they'd go.

"Lady Sheetal?" Padmini called.

*Okay, that's not so bad*, Sheetal thought. Padmini could help them figure out how to deal with this. "Come in."

But it was Beena who sailed into the room with a cache of cosmetics and clothes. "Oh, this is so exhilarating!" She practically skipped over to the vanity, where she hurried to unload her burden. "I could scarcely contain myself for anticipation. Such an honor to be chosen to attend to you as your lady-in-waiting on this of all days, Lady Sheetal, and you as well, companion Minal!"

Sheetal fought not to let her annoyance show. It wasn't like Beena knew she was in the way.

Padmini trailed in, her subdued demeanor a total contrast to Beena, who was busy hunting through drawers and exclaiming over the objects she dug out.

Elation warmed Minal's face like a candle. "Hi."

Padmini, though, kept her gaze down. Her strain in the astral melody was concerned, even frightened, before she veiled it. "I have requested Beena take over my duties today, as I am needed elsewhere."

Still beaming, Minal tried to catch her eye. "You do remember it's Sheetal's birthday, right? Her natal day, you called it?"

But Padmini only muttered something incomprehensible. Minal bit her lip, her happiness dimming. Sheetal couldn't decide whether to hug her or yell at Padmini.

"Your hair is quite lustrous today, Lady Sheetal," Beena noted. "A true star's mane."

"You can thank Padmini for that," Sheetal said, grateful for the opening. She smiled at Padmini, who stepped in front of her. "So what's this magic hair cream, and where do I sign up? It felt like I didn't even have any split ends yesterday."

Padmini spoke coldly. "I did nothing."

Fear knocked at the back of Sheetal's skull. "But that's not possible." She separated out a shimmering tress and curved it around her hand so the ends showed. They were as smooth and level as if she'd just had a routine touch-up. "You didn't trim it when I wasn't looking or something, did you?"

"How should I have done that?" Padmini gripped Sheetal's chin in one hand and angled it right, then left, examining her face while never meeting her eyes. "Beena, she will not need much in the way of cosmetics, either."

"Why not?" Sheetal asked. She felt for the bulbous Rudolph's nose of a zit Padmini had covered up for the past two days.

It was gone. So were the smaller bumps around her chin.

"If that is all, I will leave you in Beena's capable care," Padmini announced, turning to leave.

"Wait! Can you give us a second alone, Beena?" Minal asked.

"Certainly," Beena said. She'd been sorting through a box of bangles, and now she took it out onto the balcony.

"Padmini?" Minal moved toward her. Padmini frowned at the floor.

All Minal's confidence must have flown out the door with Beena and the box, because she turned desperate eyes on Sheetal and mouthed, *Do something!*

Well, Sheetal figured, they had nothing to lose at this point. So she dropped the bombshell. "Someone hid Priyanka's puppets under my bed. I just found them."

"That certainly is a terrible thing to hear," Padmini said stiffly.

"What's with the freeze-out?" Sheetal asked sharply, fed up with her ice queen act. "Last night, you were giving us keys, and today you don't know our names?"

Padmini finally looked her way. Her lush mouth was set, her otherworldly eyes impenetrable. "That was not the only thing to happen last night." Indignity burned acidic in her words. "The Esteemed Patriarch approached me with the kindly reminder that all eyes are upon us. My obligation is to our house first and foremost, and I must take care not to fraternize too closely with any one mortal."

Sheetal heard the implication: *Or else.* Oh, no. Had Nana really threatened Kaushal?

"I don't understand," Minal said. "I left the keys where you told me. Did someone else find them?"

"No, it's your brother, isn't it?" The words came out louder than Sheetal had meant. "Is he okay?"

Padmini made an irritated sound. "No, Lady Sheetal, he is not. Seeing you, listening to you, has roused his mortal memories." Her voice feathered off into a whisper. "I had believed him to be past all that."

Alarm bells went off in Sheetal's brain. "Past what?"

Padmini held herself rigidly, as if she would break otherwise. "Kaushal is speaking of permanently returning to the mortal realm."

What else could possibly go wrong? "I didn't— He's just confused."

"That may be," Padmini allowed. "Yet I cannot risk it. Should anyone learn of his daydreaming . . ."

"Padmini," Minal pleaded, reaching for her, "you can't think we'd ever let him do that. We'll stay away from him after, I swear." Her eyes glistened and her voice wobbled as Padmini pulled away, a chilly elegance in each step. "Please just help us get the marionettes back into Priyanka's room."

"I know we're asking a lot," Sheetal added, "but please just help us this one last time." She kept talking, as if that would make a difference. "I'm shocked no one's come barging in to 'prove' they're here."

"I am sorry, Lady Sheetal, but my brother is too dear to me." Padmini opened the door. "I cannot endanger his fate for anyone. I will not."

Then she was gone.

25

Sheetal stood outside the Hall of Mirrors, praying this was the right decision. She only had a few minutes while Minal distracted Beena with questions about their outfits for tonight.

Her stomach churned. If Padmini found out what Sheetal was up to, she'd never forgive either of them, any more than Sheetal would forgive someone putting Minal in danger.

Why did Nani and Nana have to make things like this? There was nothing wrong with being half human.

She consoled herself with the thought that she was working toward a future where Nani couldn't blackmail half-stars anymore, because that stupid stigma just wouldn't exist. Annihilated as part of her mother's grand plans.

Before the convocation, Nani had said something about contacting Nana through the astral melody. Sheetal searched for Kaushal's thread in the tapestry and gave it a good tug. Not uprooting it, like when she removed her own emotions, but just catching his attention. Hopefully that would work, and if not, well, at least it would give her a moment to check on Dad.

She floundered through the process two more times, then entered the hall to wait.

All the mirrors reflected a girl with soft, shimmering, flashing silver hair that fell to her waist, with unblemished brown skin so smooth it looked airbrushed, as if someone had taken a palette knife to it as she slept and smoothed away all the pores. Wait—had her eyes become larger? Yep, and they'd turned brown-silver, glimmering with the suggestion of a pewter flame.

Padmini had been right; this face didn't need any extra enhancements.

Sheetal glanced down. Her ragged fingernails had grown into perfect ovals, and even the scab on her right thumb was nearly gone.

Something nettled her—the suspicion she'd tried to bury ever since the starsong first beckoned at Radhikafoi's party. Ever since the dye had leached from her hair. Something huge, something that flooded her with horror and relief at the same time.

She was stellifying, catasterizing, just like the harp sisters had predicted.

For once, her mind was empty.

She stared at herself, at this stranger she'd become, until she couldn't take it.

*Dad,* she thought, wishing she could reach out with her arms, not just her heart. *Dad.*

The mirror closest to her erased her image, replacing it with the now horribly familiar one of Dad comatose in the ICU bed. A nurse checked his vitals and recorded the results before leaving him all alone. But it was the most beautiful birthday gift Sheetal could've asked for.

*Dad,* she said to him, inhaling the imaginary aroma of homemade waffles, listening to the whispers of the biographies he'd given her, dreaming of past museum dates. *I don't know what to do. This isn't fair, and you're not here, and even if I can save you, what if nothing's ever the same again?*

The hardest question hissed in the tingling of her hands, in the flame burning around her. *What if I can't go back to you?*

She could hear his heart's steady rhythm, and while it offered no answers, she clung to the sound, pressing her hand to the glass as if she could press right through to him.

The sidereal song shifted then, and Sheetal knew before she turned that her mother stood there, along with Kaushal. She pulled her hand back.

Well, she couldn't be totally star yet—not if she still left smudged, oily fingerprints behind. Somehow that only made everything even worse.

"I'm changing, aren't I." She whirled on her mother. "You knew, and you didn't say anything. That's why you wanted me here for my birthday."

Only then did she realize she was shivering, like the

warning signal before a volcano erupted. "You knew, and *you didn't tell me!*"

Charumati and Kaushal watched her, saying nothing. She felt their pity in the starsong, saw it in their unearthly eyes. The eyes she now shared.

"That's why the competition is today, isn't it? Before I turn full star, so you can still exploit me." More tremors coursed through her, tremors the whole cosmos should be feeling.

How had the palace not fallen apart? How were the mirrors still whole instead of a billion jagged shards?

Charumati put her arms around Sheetal and began stroking the top of her head. "Dikri, would you have come if you had known?"

"No, of course not," Sheetal blurted. The contact was so soothing she couldn't help but soften. "I mean, I guess I would have had to at some point, right? Isn't that why you said you had to leave?"

"Yes," Charumati said simply. "We belong in the sky. Even our bodies know it."

Kaushal spoke for the first time. "My father was a member of this house, and he strayed with a mortal woman. She soon wasted away of grief, and I wound up in an orphanage. I had no option to disguise my hair but to shave it off, and I set one too many things aflame." He laughed, grim. "Before long I was on the streets, alone and starving."

"Until my mother found you," Charumati put in. She loosened her embrace, but Sheetal didn't move away.

319

"I had no wish to go. I blamed my father for abandoning me. But the Esteemed Matriarch offered me a much better life, and a sister, so in time I agreed." Kaushal touched his necklace. "Once I got here, I transformed within days. Sheetal, it is nothing to fear. It would have happened in any case."

"They threw you out of the orphanage?" Sheetal imagined little Kaushal, all ribs and skin, fighting bigger kids for scraps and getting beaten up in the process, and she wanted to reach back through time and rescue him.

Charumati spoke fiercely, her flickering eyes like living jewels. "See? If we raised humanity to its highest potential, no one would behave like this. No one would be harming you or anyone else, my daughter."

"Mortals do not understand," Kaushal said. "They walk around blindfolded, thinking only of themselves. Some understand compassion, but they are few and far between."

Sheetal begged to differ. Dad was a great example of compassion, always reminding her to think of the other person's point of view. Minal had stood by Sheetal through everything. Even Radhikafoi cared in her way, or she wouldn't have made it her life's work to help domestic violence survivors.

But then there were Bijal and Vaibhav from school. Oncologist Auntie and her gang. Dev's ancestor, the star hunter. All the people who'd made Charumati feel like she had to hide. Kaushal wasn't wrong, not really.

Sheetal stepped out of her mother's hug. "Why do you want

to go back to Earth, then? Is it because you miss the stuff you left behind?"

Kaushal and Charumati traded puzzled glances. "I assume you spoke with my sister," Kaushal said.

"It's not that great," Sheetal went on, pretending not to hear him. "I should know." The words tasted weird in her mouth. Some of it wasn't great, that was for sure, but other parts were awesome. Forests, amusement parks, Dad, to start with.

"Then why does the thought of the transformation trouble you so, my daughter?" Charumati asked archly.

"I admit to harboring a certain amount of fascination with mortal advancements." Kaushal gazed into a mirror, and Marine Drive in Mumbai appeared, curving around a sparkly blue sea. Cars zipped along its breadth. "There were no sports cars in my time! But it is not that. Your mother has shared her plan with me, and I think she is right. There is no reason the mortal world must struggle like this."

"When you take your circlet tonight, beti," Charumati said, "you will join our house, and we will work together to enlighten humanity and show Nani and Nana there is no cause to close the gates." She smiled. "But first, you must get through the competition."

*Back up a sec.* This was too much for Sheetal to deal with right now. "So I'm going to become a full star no matter what?"

There it was, out in the open. Even if everything inside her was spinning around and around like a carousel. Even if it felt like the ultimate betrayal.

"Yes," said Charumati. "Every child of star and mortal parents does by the time they come of majority." She took Sheetal's tingling hands in hers. "That is why I did not bring you with me; I wanted you to enjoy your mortal life with your papa as long as possible."

Kaushal glowed, making all the mirrors shine with silver radiance. "But now we can walk together among the mortals and heal their world!"

*Save Dad,* Sheetal told herself, reining in her threads of panic before they could be heard in the astral melody. What she needed to do to make that happen hadn't changed. She could figure out the rest later.

Kaushal's innumerable reflections beamed with fervor. "I know others will join us. Your mother's plan is a wise—"

"Like my mom said," Sheetal interrupted, "let's get through the competition before we start recruiting people. And for me to do that, I need your help." She explained the situation with the marionettes, carefully leaving out the bit about Padmini's disapproval. "We just need them to get back into Priyanka's room without anyone seeing. Only if you want to, of course."

Kaushal was already nodding. "Whatever help House Pushya and its champion need, I will give."

Sheetal wasn't so sure that was a good thing.

Advisors, ladies-in-waiting, and various other attendants all tore in and out of Nani's and Nana's study, dodging the wait-staff who replenished the breakfast dishes every few minutes. Sheetal, trying not to flip out every time she remembered what was happening to her, ate and ate and ate her feelings. At least now she knew why her stomach had turned into a black hole.

"Oh, beti," Nani rhapsodized between discussions about centerpieces and lighting, "such a ball we have prepared for your natal day and ascension into the court! I have waited seventeen years for this."

She sounded so truly happy that, for a minute, Sheetal just gave in and sank into a daydream, one as comforting as a warm bubble bath. In it, she'd grown up here without the game-playing or the assumptions, just with magic and knowing where she belonged. Now, on the cusp of her ascension to the court, she stood by her mother and grandmother, their three voices and hearts joined in harmony rather than discord, as they poured jar after jar over the balcony railing until stardust illuminated everyone on Earth with silvery light, motivating them to create beauty and art and innovation.

A shiver ran through her. She hated to admit it, but that image was starting to feel more natural than the one of her going back to high school and then to college to study astronomy and folklore.

What did she need to study astronomy for, the astral melody, the cosmic dance, the flame at her core all whispered, when she could *be* it?

Nani clapped for attention, reminding Sheetal where she actually was, and ordered everyone but the family to leave. She nodded at Charumati, who directed Sheetal through her warm-up exercises. By now, even the lip trill didn't make her want to cringe.

Which was good, because the rest of her was about to spill out of her skin in a mess of—in a mess of something. She didn't know what, but nerves crackled through her like exposed wires, and they wouldn't let her sit still.

She was seventeen today, and she was turning into a star. The astral melody pealed through her, as much a part of her as her own blood. All she wanted to do was set it free.

Nana interceded at the point when Sheetal began to sing. "Save your voice, dikri," he said. "You will need it soon enough."

Nani beamed, scattering silver light across the ebony table. Even the white streaks in her immaculate bun shone with it. "That reminds me; we must talk of the ceremony itself." Sheetal nodded. "You will be expected to present yourself with grace when your name is called. To stand and take your place at the platform, where Padmini will inspire you."

"Perhaps, jaan, she would like to choose which attendant inspires her," Nana suggested.

Nani acknowledged him with a nod. "To stand and take your place at the platform, where either Padmini or Beena, as appointed by you, will inspire you. We have arranged for an instrument to be brought out, but it will not be revealed until the necessary moment."

"To build the suspense. I get it." Sheetal might not have performed in public before, but she definitely understood the value of a good flourish.

Like the way Dev played to the audience when he was onstage.

Nana grew stern. "And to protect you. We know of the attempt to incriminate you for the loss of the marionettes, beti, and have warded your room against unauthorized entry."

"Wait, you do?" Sheetal should have expected that. Of course they would have their spies. "Do you know who it was?"

"Do not trouble yourself further with this matter, beti. We will take care of it." His voice warmed. "I do wish you felt you could have come to us. We are your family, and it is our responsibility to look out for you."

Sheetal considered that. She wanted to probe more, but if they knew who the perpetrator was, they might also know Kaushal had smuggled the puppets back to Priyanka's room. Or at least that he was involved somehow. And she wasn't about to remind them of that.

She caught her tongue between her teeth. *Please let them not know that part of it.*

"Thank you," she said finally. "I appreciate that."

"Such a wretched act reeks of the perpetrator's insecurity, a belief that their skill alone cannot be enough." Nani spoke with confidence, a majestic matriarch blessing the newest child of her line. "You, however, have nothing to fear."

"Nothing at all," Charumati chimed in. "Once you have

been inspired, you will have an hour to prepare and perform your song. Do not rush; that hour will more than suffice." Like Nani had done a couple of days ago, she cupped her hands around a single silver flame. "Trust this, the spark within you."

Nana refilled Sheetal's cup with blue mango juice as Nani sighed. "My hope was that you would be able to perform first," she said, "that you might make the freshest impression and then rest while others bore the burden of strained nerves. But it is not to be."

*In spite of your best threats and bribes, you mean.* Sheetal could imagine what Nani had tried. It was a shame none of it had worked; getting her turn over with and relaxing sounded fabulous.

"Unfair as it may seem," said Nana, an amused gleam in his eye, "ours is not the only house to wish that for its champion." He sipped his cordial. "In order to prevent underhanded maneuvering and jockeying for position, the Esteemed Matriarch and Patriarch of House Dhanishta will draw names from a silver bowl."

Nani huffed. "The most important thing to bear in mind is that whatever the other champions might produce, it is immaterial to you. You are a daughter of a great nakshatra, and music flows in your veins."

"And soon," Charumati said, touching her starry diadem, "you will receive your circlet. I cannot wait. So long we have waited to share everything with you."

The sidereal melody resonated with her family's pride and affection, ornaments and silver bells abounding. The glimpse of Nani's soft smile, so unlike her, loosened the knots in Sheetal's belly and made her feel a little shy. A little happy, even.

Underneath her ambition, Nani *did* care. And Sheetal wanted her to.

"It is a blessing for us all," Nana agreed, placing his hand over hers. "Welcome home."

# 26

Nani and Charumati ran Sheetal through another two hours' worth of training and last-minute advice before Nana finally sent her off to relax.

T-minus three hours and counting until she had to get it together and save Dad. Sheetal's pulse sent fire shooting through her veins, and it was all she could do to veil her anxiety.

"Go now and seek the company of those your own age," Nana urged, opening the door to the corridor. "There is time yet before you must be dressed for the ball."

The ball. Her birthday ball. Sheetal had almost forgotten about it in worrying about everything else.

With an indulgent smile, Nani shooed Sheetal out of the study. "Oh, look, Meena is here! Perhaps you two can retire to the common room for refreshments."

"I believe you mean Minal," Charumati corrected. She made an irked face behind Nani's back.

Sheetal wasn't sure "Meena" was much of an improvement on "that one you brought," but she just couldn't add another plate to the ones she was already desperately juggling. She would become a full star by tonight. Her mom and her grandmother each had plans for her that she still didn't know what to do with. And before any of that, she had to win a celestial competition in front of the entire starry court with her singing and playing. Oh, and one of her rivals was her ex's cousin-brother.

"Ah, yes, Minal," Nani agreed, just before the door closed behind Sheetal. She stepped into the hallway, where Minal waited, having overheard the last bit of their conversation.

Being Minal, she looked unruffled, even amused. "So? How'd breakfast go?"

"It was fine." Sheetal didn't want to get into the whole *hey, I'm not really human anymore* thing right then. She knew she'd have to soon, but for now, she needed a chance to catch her breath. To enjoy the wonders of this palace she'd barely even gotten to see, never mind experience. "Can we go for a walk?"

Minal grinned. "Whatever you want, birthday girl. Consider 'Meena' at your service." She slipped into the faux-subservient tone she'd used with the guards outside the palace gates. "Might I accompany you on a survey of your domain, my lady?"

"Why, certainly," Sheetal said in the snottiest voice she could muster, offering her arm. "My apologies about Nani. The older generations are so set in their ways." Minal just laughed.

Arms linked, the two of them strolled through the palace,

from the library to the common room to the night-flower gardens to the theater where other heavenly beings performed at the stars' invitation.

Pushing everything else from her head, from her heart, Sheetal ate up the portraits, the statuary, the inlay work and carved pillars, the lavish textiles and patterned floors, the ceilings that opened onto the firmament where the cosmic dance spun in eternity. It felt like magic, like a fairy tale come to life.

How weird—all of this was hers. Well, shared with the other stars in the court, but still. Hers.

Part of Sheetal had always known this waited for her. She wasn't going to stay, not with Dad waiting on Earth, but knowing she *could* left her heart as light and fluffy as a rosewater cupcake.

This was why she hadn't taken Rati's offer. Why she wouldn't.

Minal didn't talk about Padmini, and Sheetal didn't talk about Dev or Jeet or Charumati. Not that they had any time to—everywhere they went, stars stopped them to say hello and wish Sheetal luck. Some belonged to her nakshatra, and others didn't, but all of them glowed enthusiastically in greeting. Over and over again, Sheetal heard variations of, "Minal has told me what a fine songstress you are, how clever and spirited! I look forward to cheering you on."

In the common room, a few excited stars even tried to pull Sheetal and Minal into their game of cards and shells. Minal politely declined. "I wish we could, but Sheetal needs to rest before tonight."

"Another time!" the stars insisted before letting them go.

"People like you here," Minal said, smug, once they were alone again. "I made sure of it."

Guilt gnawed at Sheetal's chest. All that time she'd been wallowing in self-pity, whining about how her best friend fit in here better than she did, Minal had been doing PR on her behalf.

That ugly shade of envy green didn't suit anybody, least of all her. She would do better, she swore, and filled Minal in on the conversation with Kaushal and Charumati.

"I always knew you'd end up here," Minal said finally, when they were back in the champions' quarters. She parked herself beneath the sconce next to their door. Its miniature starbursts glowed with diminutive silver flames.

"You did?" Sheetal had been prepared for pretty much any other reaction.

"Sure. I mean, look at you." Minal pointed, and Sheetal instinctively peered down at herself. "I heard what Padmini said. She didn't touch your hair. Or do your makeup. But she didn't need to. I'm not stupid, Sheetu. I know you're changing."

While Sheetal tried to figure out what to say, Minal added, "Like I said, I always knew. I just hoped I'd get to come along for the ride."

"You weren't supposed to get hurt by anyone, though!" It made sense why Padmini had backed off, but Sheetal still kind of wanted to shake her.

Minal's mouth flattened into a line. "Just a stupid crush. Don't worry about it."

Except Minal hadn't liked anyone that much for a long time, if ever. Sheetal picked her words carefully. "Okay, but what about Kaushal—"

"It's your birthday. Let's talk about *you*," Minal interrupted. "Just because you're turning into a star doesn't mean you can forget about me, you hear me?"

"As if I could." The very idea made Sheetal laugh. It didn't matter how long she lived; that was never happening.

"Good. How do you feel about the whole star thing, anyway?"

Sheetal reached for the silver crystal doorknob. "Can we talk about that *inside*? I mean, you were the one who said I need to rest."

"Nope." Minal pressed herself back against the wall. "I live here now. By this beautiful light fixture. We can't bear to be parted."

"Riiiight. Maybe *you're* the one who needs a nap—"

Loud voices sounded nearby, muffled but angry. It took Sheetal a second to pinpoint the source—Dev's and Jeet's room. She shot a nervous glance Minal's way.

The door flew open, and Jeet blustered into the corridor. "Just stay out of it!" Dev rushed out behind him, calling his name.

It was the most absurd thought to have, but Sheetal couldn't help noticing how good Dev looked in dark blue. Like he belonged there against the silver-starred walls.

Minal squirmed. "Uh, Dev, this isn't what we—"

Jeet's snarl made Sheetal take a step back. She took another one when his skin flashed bright as mercury. This time there was no doubt about it: the light was no trick of her eye, no reflection. It was him. Glowing.

"You're all the same, just messing with us." His voice was as dark as a dead star. "I *deserve* to be here. I worked hard. I did everything she asked. And now I have to give up my turn? Like hell I will."

Dev laid a hand on his shoulder. "Jeet, man, calm down—"

Jeet shrugged it off. "Don't touch me!" He closed in on Sheetal. "You think your family likes you? Maybe you should ask your grandmother what she *really* thinks of half-stars."

"That's enough," Dev said, stepping between them. "If you're mad at Rati, fine, but you need to stop."

"You know what? Why don't you just stay out here if you know so much." Jeet slunk back into their room and slammed the door so hard the wall rattled.

Minal stared after him. "That was intense."

Sheetal wanted to agree, but it felt like Jeet had sucked all the air out of the hallway.

"That's one word for it," Dev said. Their gazes found each other, and a shock of recognition passed between them, soft and still as starlight. "Listen, can I talk to you? Just you?"

Before she could open her mouth, Minal had pushed her toward him. "Yes, you can talk to her. Just her," Minal said, smiling victoriously as she patted the sconce. "Now you know why I couldn't leave my friend here."

"I guess that's a yes?" Sheetal said, glaring. They would

have to have a chat later about letting people decide for themselves if they wanted to talk to ex-boyfriends.

Dev took her in like he was seeing her for the first time, really noticing her, and she saw her flame mirrored in his dark eyes. "Good."

Suddenly she couldn't remember why she was mad at Minal. Or at him.

"Happy birthday, Sheetu!" Minal sang out before disappearing inside their room.

Sheetal was worried about Jeet, worried about Charumati, worried about Dad and the competition and the drop of blood. But in that moment, with her heart swelling at that soulful look, all those things receded into the background like shadows before the sun.

She crossed her arms tight. The thing was, a single glance, no matter how many shivers it sent through her, couldn't make up for the fact that he'd only tried to get close to her so he could help Jeet. "You arranged this?" she asked coolly.

He nodded, biting his lip.

"Because you want to talk?"

"Yeah," he said softly.

There was a universe of possibility in that one word. It would be so easy to just grab him and pull him to her. Her heart screamed at her to do exactly that. To tell him none of it mattered.

But it did. Sheetal turned away and started walking. "Come on, then."

Dev loped up beside her a couple of seconds later, and they wandered along the marble hallway until Sheetal found a vacant sitting room with a velvet love seat.

Ironic. A couch would have been better, but this would have to do.

She sat down next to Dev, way too aware of just how near he was. Her eyes wouldn't stop tracing the defined line of his cheekbones, the flicker of his long lashes, the way his strong nose dipped at the tip. Her body wouldn't stop urging her to close the distance between them already.

Her breath came in flutters. "So talk," she managed to say.

Dev gazed straight ahead. "I'm sorry you had to see that. I really am."

"Me, too."

"Rati's been on his case from the start, but when I found out he was drinking that blood . . ." Dev shook his head. "What is happening? How is that a sentence I just said?"

Sheetal pressed her lips together so she wouldn't interrupt. Or, as a treacherous part of her suggested, try to kiss him.

He sighed. "I thought if he won this, it would be good for him. He'd see he had something special, too. We always looked out for each other. And now . . ." Dev shook his head again, and a lock of hair fell over his eye. "Just—how does he not know how *stupid* that is?"

Sheetal nodded. She didn't trust herself to speak.

"Look, I'm sorry I let him convince me to get to know you." He broke off. "No. I'm glad about that. I am sorry I didn't tell

335

you that I knew what you are. And I'm really sorry about last night." He finally turned to face Sheetal, and the despair she saw there rocked her. "I'm not sorry, though, that I met you. I just—I just wish it could have been without all this."

She tried to imagine Minal so desperate she'd willingly drink someone's blood to get what she wanted, while Sheetal herself could do nothing but watch it happen. It made her furious. It made her understand Dev's position more than she wanted to admit.

A rift appeared in her meticulously honed icy resistance, and even though she knew she shouldn't, she laid her hand on his.

Dev gripped it like a lifeline, lacing their fingers together. "Don't listen to what he said, okay?" he pleaded. "I swear he wasn't like this before. If only I could get him to quit." His voice wavered. "And—and what if that's it? What if he can't come back from this?"

A lump burned in her throat. That was the question for all of them.

"Gods, I wish Rati had never found him. I know she gave him that blood."

Rati. Dev didn't know about her offer. Sheetal quickly brought him up to speed. "The worst part is, I don't think she actually cares about House Revati winning. Rati just wants to see my nakshatra go down."

He whistled. "This place is a trip."

For a few minutes, no one said anything.

Dev tentatively twined a strand of her shimmering hair around his finger. The flutters migrated to Sheetal's stomach, a whisper of light green luna moths, and her heart matched them wingbeat for wingbeat. "When Jeet told me about you," he said, "you weren't real. He was. It had always been him and me, you know? It was easy to say sure, I'd see if there was anything to tell him."

Even now, it stung to hear him admit it. She had to make herself keep listening.

"Then I actually met you, and there was no way I was going to wreck that." He uncurled the strand of hair. "I told him I changed my mind."

"But you let me inspire you," she reminded him, shaky. There it was, the doubt loitering like a thundercloud between them. The biggest reason she'd fled his house that day.

Dev tweaked her nose. "Star girl, the whole reason I wanted to start writing songs again was so I could write them for you." His smile was amused and embarrassed at the same time. "I mean, yeah, it was great to be composing again. I thought I was blocked for good. But I don't care about that—not enough to mess this up."

"Not even the teensiest bit? I don't believe you."

"You got me. I liked being inspired. I really, really liked it." Awe spread over his face, illuminating his eyes. "It was this rush of being able to make *anything*."

*Anything.*

Sheetal dropped his hand and willed herself to disappear

337

into the floor's intricate patterns. Of course he liked it. Who wouldn't?

Dev tipped her chin back up. "But after seeing Jeet, I don't ever want that again."

She focused on her breathing, which had gotten shallow and tight. "You don't?"

"No." This time his smile was sure. "I just want you."

The last of the rime in her chest dissolved. *I just want you, too.* Still she waited. "Why not, though?"

Dev's expression turned thoughtful. "It's funny; everyone thinks you make art to get rich and famous and have your legacy, but is that really such a good thing?"

"Well, everyone wants to be seen, don't they?" The sidereal song rang out around her, all chimes and bell tones, reminding her just how seen she was here.

"But all the time? And it's not like they know you. They're making up who they think you are. Celebrity worship."

Sheetal shrugged. She hadn't had a chance to think about it, but if she won the competition, her name would be on every mortal's lips for the rest of history. Did she want that?

Did anyone, really?

"Nobody should have a prize this huge, but if it has to be someone here, I'd go with Priyanka. At least she could do some good with it," Dev said.

"Priyanka? After how she treated me? Yeah, right."

"Well, she's here by herself, and you've got an entire family backing you, not to mention your best friend. Jeet's got me—or at least, he did." Dev sounded rueful. "Imagine how you'd feel if you were all alone. You might say some stupid stuff, too."

Sheetal finally believed him. He didn't want this.

Gentle as a whisper, she reached up to tuck the stray lock behind his ear. He shuddered as her knuckles brushed his skin. "You don't have to be so logical all the time," she teased.

Savoring the solid feel of him, she relaxed against his side. Dev, however, held her delicately, like she might flee if he even wiggled a toe.

After a minute had gone by, he spoke. "Hey."

"Hey."

"Where does a pixie sleep in the enchanted forest?"

"No." Sheetal groaned. "Oh, no. Don't do it."

Dev grinned grotesquely, wide and openmouthed like a clown. "On her Sealy queen mattress, of course!"

Treating him to her best withering glare, she let light rise out of her skin. "Are you *trying* to get rid of me?"

He laughed. "Never."

She pressed her ear against his chest, listening to his heart. She would have to get going soon, of course, but for now, this was the only music she cared about.

"So I hear it's your birthday," Dev said. "What if I told you I have a present for you?"

Sheetal leaned back to look at him. Gods, he was beautiful, with that lopsided grin and that little dimple next to it. "I would get super excited but then really sad when I figured out you don't have anything with you."

"How do you know? Kurtas have pockets."

She held out her hands. "Show me, then."

"The pockets or the present?"

She didn't bother to dignify that with a reply.

Dev smiled, then glanced away. He wiped his palms on his kurta.

*He's nervous!* She clamped down on her bottom lip to keep from smiling herself.

Then he opened his mouth, and she forgot the competition, Dad, everything.

The song was new, but she recognized the story it told: a human king, Pururavas, fell in love with Urvashi, an apsara from the heavenly realm, and then had to let her go.

But the way Dev sang it, there was no difference between the characters and the people who sat here now. Just an unquenchable yearning for a beauty, a love, that could never be satisfied again. Everything would be duller, more monotonous, for the rest of the poor king's days, while the apsara would continue on and on like the immortal she was.

*My heart was a desert*
*You moved through like rain*
*Even the soil had to smile*
*It sprouted a garden*
*I wrote your name in roses*

340

*My heart was a desert*
*You moved through like rain*
*But all clouds drift away*
*You left me to my drought*
*Now only my tears water the earth*


For a moment, it was Sheetal flying away from Dev forever, Sheetal returning to her true abode in the heavenly realm.

The song trailed off, officially leaving her a mess of half-melted goo. "That was for *me*?"

Dev was clearly trying not to laugh. "Well, yeah, unless there's another star girl with a birthday today."

"That was— I don't even— Wow." She didn't know whether to finish melting first or just pounce.

He rubbed the back of his neck. "You liked it? I mean, that's not my usual thing, but I know how you much love those old myths. . . ."

"Are you kidding?" Sheetal threw herself at him. How did he always smell so good? "I *loved* it! Best birthday present ever." She kissed her way from his cheek to his ear. "I'd better hope none of the other champions are that good, or I'm in big trouble."

*Okay,* she told herself, *enough talking.* And she kissed his jaw.

Dev's voice had gone down an octave. "Nah. It'll never happen." His eyes darkened even more as he pulled her onto his lap and brought his mouth to hers. "Happy birthday, star girl."

## 27

A throng of ladies-in-waiting, led by Beena, fell upon Sheetal like a murder of keen-eyed crows, making her nerves feel like someone had sandpapered them. Her room had never been so crowded or so busy, and she couldn't escape. Under Nani's direction, the attendants bathed her, oiled her skin, and brushed out her locks.

Poor Minal only had one lady-in-waiting attending to her—Padmini, who must not have been able to give up attendant duty completely. They were the only two silent people in all the room, their smiles brittle.

Meanwhile, Nani hovered over Sheetal, directing the others to drape here, pin there. Too bad she couldn't command away Sheetal's nerves about the competition.

Tomorrow. Tonight she would compete, and tomorrow she would have the drop of blood and go home to heal Dad.

Tomorrow everything would be better. She just had to keep telling herself that.

She reached for her scab, picking at it, almost ripping it off. Oh, gods, she'd never performed before anyone except her parents and Minal. Never, ever. Now she had to go in front of the entire starry court and be judged? How could these two days of training ever be enough?

And where was Charumati? Her mother should be there with her.

Following Nani's instructions, the ladies-in-waiting swathed Sheetal in a confection of sheer black speckled with little diamonds and bordered with silver ribbon. She recognized it from the night she'd arrived; her mother had worn this same fabric. "This is shadowsilk," Nani explained, "a textile reserved exclusively for the royal houses. You will be a dream when you play your instrument tonight."

"Great," said Sheetal. There was a fine line between excitement and panic. So far, she was still on the right side of it.

But she might go up onstage, in front of everybody, and blow the whole thing. Just fall flat on her face.

Her grandmother produced an enameled jewel box crammed with silver and platinum necklaces, earrings, armbands, bracelets, rings, and toe rings, most studded with diamonds, sapphires, or black onyx. "Our family's treasury," she pronounced, "and today I will pass your first precious heirloom down to you."

343

She touched Sheetal's forehead in blessing and selected a platinum meenakari choker with all three stones and matching jhumka earrings. "This was my favorite set when I was your age, and now it is yours."

It was like wearing the night sky, if the sky were gems and sparkle and all the incandescent promise of the myriad constellations. Sheetal didn't know what to say. "Wow," she got out at last, "thank you so much, Nani!"

Nani brushed it off. "What is there to thank anyone for? You are a child of our house. Who else would wear these?" But her mouth turned up in a pleased half smile.

The wash of affection that rolled over Sheetal calmed her fears. She returned Nani's smile.

Nani stepped away to confer with Padmini as the two sorted through the rest of the jewelry. Minal hurried over, looking incredible in black-and-silver chaniya choli with a filmy blue dupatta. "Those are stunning," she whispered. "But where's your mom?"

"I wish I knew," Sheetal whispered back.

Then they had to stop talking as a new crop of ladies-in-waiting surrounded them in a whirl of cosmetic tools and creams and cases. "Such beauties!" one exclaimed. "What an honor it is, to be chosen by the Esteemed Matriarch to help prepare you for such a momentous evening."

Another dabbed the contents of a small silver pot on Sheetal's skin with a brush. "A touch of this pearl powder here, some brightening shell there, and your natural luster will claim the room."

At least Sheetal hadn't totally finished turning into a star. That was something.

She pulled back from the brush's itchy bristles, earning a mild reproach, while Minal compared various jars. "What's in these?"

Charumati appeared in the doorway, a serene expression on her face and a cobalt glass box in her hands. "Pardon my tardiness. It took me longer than I wished to lure these friends to me."

A knot in Sheetal's chest gave way to relief. Her mom had already missed so many important occasions, the thought of her not being here for this one chafed.

"There you are." Nani's nostrils flared. "I already presented Sheetal with her first meenakari set."

"My apologies, Mother. I would like to have seen that." Charumati unlatched her box, and crystalline butterflies fluttered into the room, their wings clear and multifaceted as diamonds. Padmini coaxed them toward Sheetal with soft movements, guiding them until they roosted among the jewels in Sheetal's hair. Their tiny feet tickled.

"Where did these come from?" she asked, overcome.

"The conservatory. There is plenty yet to show you in our palace." Charumati wound wristlets of black jasmine blossoms around Sheetal's forearms, and their silver vines spiraled over her skin. Inhaling their seductive perfume, Sheetal shivered.

"You are truly one of us," Charumati said, her eyes misting over. "Seventeen. The age of majority."

The astral melody lilted through the air, through Sheetal's blood, laden with so much emotion: wonder, delight, and even a glimpse of worry before it vanished. *One of us.*

This should have been a beautiful moment, something out of a story. Long-lost daughter reunited with her family and honored with a ball. But she couldn't relax. She was already changing; what if she didn't want to go home after that?

What if she couldn't?

Beena led her over to a huge mirror whose black frame was carved with intricate images of the various nakshatras. "You are a princess!"

It was true. Starlight limned Sheetal like an aura, and if there had been any doubt as to her heritage before, there wasn't any now. The slender silver chain across her hairline, the dangling tika, the necklace and chandelier earrings, and the diamond nose ring, not to mention her butterfly-strewn sparkling hair in its low bun, all caught and reflected her illumination, transforming her features into those of Nani's heir apparent.

"My daughter," breathed Charumati, her hand at her mouth. "My beautiful daughter."

Minal clapped wildly. "You're gorgeous, Sheetu!"

Seeing her reflection in the full-length gilt-edged mirror now, made radiant by the attendants and ravishing by sartorial magic, Sheetal had to agree. Nani stood on one side of her, Charumati on the other. Three generations of star women, all aglow with sorcery and strength. Like they had fallen out of a fairy tale. Like Sheetal was still in it.

The flame at her core kindled, sending warmth and musical notes flowing through her veins. Her lips parted, her throat brimming over with words ready to splash out as song. *Soon.*

"Desi Cinderella, off to the ball," Minal cracked. She took a picture with her phone. "But no glass chappals for you. If one broke, how bad that would slice up your foot?"

Sheetal loved the way the shadowsilk traced her curves and the sweep of luminescence around her form. She could light up the heavens. She could inspire the birth of stories.

Beena nudged her. "Good! You are permitted to take pleasure in this," she scolded. "We designed you an ensemble fit for royalty, after all."

"Indeed, dikri." Charumati straightened Sheetal's tika.

Sheetal couldn't help but laugh. "Okay, fine."

She'd worry about the contest later. It *was* her birthday, after all, and no one had ever thrown a huge, no-holds-barred bash in her honor before. Definitely not Radhikafoi, who kept things small when it came to Sheetal.

"The ball will be splendid," Nani said, dismissing the ladies-in-waiting. "We will dine and dance together in the central court."

Sheetal glanced at her reflection one more time. The silver-tressed, brown-skinned girl before her stared back, powerful. Soft and sturdy as spider silk. Mistress of herself. A hint of starry fire smoldered in her eyes like a signal.

"I think," Sheetal said, exchanging a smile with that girl in the mirror, "it's time to go enjoy my party."

Blue lights turned everything in the court proper into a fever dream, from the crystal chandelier to the gem lanterns to the multitude of guests, all in peacock and cobalt and lapis. Some wore saris that fell in perfect pleats, others sherwanis and kurtas just as crisp and delicately embroidered, and still others something entirely unfamiliar and fine, their ebony and mercury fabrics stained azure. Candles in mosaic glasses sat sprinkled here and there, burning with flames silver as starlight.

The ball was everything Sheetal could have imagined, the picture of sidereal splendor. Silver shone everywhere, from the twenty-seven sets of paired thrones on the sickle-shaped dais to the diamond flecks floating in the air like stardust. But she hadn't anticipated the glittering garden full of night-blooming flowers—jasmine, lilacs, lanternlike bleeding hearts, and moonlight lotuses, the same flower her mother had left for her. The blooms served as a dance floor, springing right back up after being stepped on.

Nani and her team had really done a fabulous job. Sheetal almost didn't recognize the place where she'd had her first rehearsal.

From the dais, Nani and Nana beamed out at the court. "On behalf of the House of Pushya, welcome to the natal day celebration of Sheetal, House Pushya's own champion. Please eat, dance, rejoice!"

Sheetal didn't miss that Nana hadn't mentioned her heritage or majority, sidestepping the thorny question of her eligibility as a champion. She opened herself to the astral melody to gauge the reaction.

Curiosity and gladness encased her in a silver spiral. Like Minal had said, not everyone was against her. That was nice to know. Anyone else was smart enough to keep their feelings veiled.

"Your light," Charumati murmured, and Sheetal sent her pewter flame out over her skin. The butterflies in her hair, which had been so still she'd forgotten their presence, twitched. *Moths to the flame.* She should remember that one to throw at Dev later. It was only fair.

The guests applauded and called out congratulations. Sheetal soaked it all in like a sponge. For once, she didn't have to hide. It felt awesome to be seen. Not just that, but to be celebrated. It made her forget for a second that this wouldn't last past tonight.

"Go," said Nana with a smile. "Enjoy yourself, child."

As Sheetal wandered away, she counted apsaras with their golden crowns, yakshas in leaf tunics, nagas' scaly and muscular coils undulating—all dancing and feasting. For once, she was probably the least weird person in attendance.

Gandharvas played on the stage where the fifty-four Esteemed would normally sit, their music wild and swift. It reminded Sheetal of garbas back on Earth, only this song was also tinged with melancholy. A glimpse into mystical worlds

349

like this one. She wanted to drown in it.

And there was still so much more to see, so much more to taste.

Tables of food lined one wall, more than Sheetal could imagine an army being able to finish, delicacies like what she had seen at the Night Market: candied moonlight lotus petals, little silver frostberry pastries dusted with cardamom and saffron, chunks of crystallized reverie rolled with slivered pistachios.

Bonbons dipped in peacock blue and silver fondant surrounded a large, tiered teal cake, the entire thing spangled with silver swirls and blue-and-green jewels molded to look like feathers. A spun-sugar peacock perched on the top layer fanned its tail open and closed, candy eyes blinking, and called for rain: "Meh-aao, meh-aao!"

This cake, this music, this celebration was all for her. All for her! Sheetal wanted to preserve it in a snow globe, something she could shake and press to her face as the sprinkle of lights within drifted down.

She bit into one of the bonbons. Silky floral cream spilled onto her tongue, and for a moment she was borne away on the backs of enormous swans flying through the sky, each formed of shifting cumulus clouds. For a moment, she *was* the swan, bold and free.

Then she was back in the hall, among the blue lights and whirling guests. She'd somehow moved farther down the tables and now stood before a row of crystal carafes filled with glittering frostberry wine and a golden liquid that had to be amrit, the heavenly nectar. Everything she could want to try, everything she could want to help her forget her troubles.

"Permit me to pour you a drink," a voice offered. Sheetal glanced up to see a dakini, her scarlet skin purpling in the lights. Even here, she was bare of breast, her neck garlanded with a string of skulls. The dakini bore a cup aloft, and her smile was a spear. "Consider it a gesture of goodwill from your fellow champion Sachin."

Sheetal knew a little about dakinis; like apsaras, they were sky dancers, but unlike apsaras, they were also warriors who ferociously guarded the path of enlightenment. Though some were known for their compassion, this one's scorching gaze only held a challenge. "I'm all right, thanks."

"How is it a celebration if the guest of honor is not drinking to her induction?" the dakini asked.

Sheetal could smell the amrit, Lord Indra's beverage of choice. It sang to her with the strength of the stellar music, waking hidden longings. Of course she wanted to try it, to taste it on her tongue, to lick the traces off her lips.

But not tonight, and definitely not if Sachin had sent it.

She searched the room until she found him with Jeet and Priyanka. Jeet said something, and Sachin shrugged and looked away.

A few feet from them, Minal and Padmini were both chatting animatedly with people Sheetal didn't recognize, though even the most oblivious bystander couldn't miss the fleeting glances they threw each other every five seconds. It hurt to watch.

"Excuse me," Sheetal said, and headed in their direction. But before she reached them, Beena waylaid her, insisting she dance. When she looked back, the crowd had swallowed Minal. Sheetal let herself be led onto the dance floor, spinning and twirling, a pinpoint in a massive constellation of extraordinary creatures. It was like swimming inside a star sapphire.

On the stage, the gandharvas played long, mesmeric beats that grew faster and faster; and on the floor, two large circles formed, one facing the other. Sheetal took her place in the inner circle, linking hands on one side with a pari. The pari's wings floated out behind her, patterned with the same stained-glass veining as a damselfly's. In the wash of blues, Sheetal couldn't tell what colors they might be, though they twinkled in the lights floating through the room.

She glanced up to see Leela and Kirti beaming at her from the outer circle, easily keeping pace with the dance. "Are you ready for the competition?" Leela called. "I can't wait to hear you sing."

"Thanks! I can't wait to see your painting," Sheetal called back, but the thrumming of the tabla absorbed her reply.

Besides, the dancers were carrying Leela away now, their circle moving to Sheetal's left while the other circle moved to her right. She caught another glimpse of Priyanka and Jeet before a gaggle of apsaras moved into the center of the inner circle and began to spin, each movement of their hands and feet like a flower opening.

*This is what it would have been like if I had been here all along,* Sheetal marveled. Eating things straight out of a catalog of dreams. Living always in the sidereal song. Never knowing the pain of waking to a bloated belly and cramps that made you want to rip your own guts out. Never worrying about things like taxes and drunk drivers and pipes freezing in the middle of a subzero New Jersey winter.

Never learning Mom could leave, and Dad could almost die.

It was all too large to take in, too brilliant and strange. It made her want to cry at the same time it made her want to sing. She never wanted it to end. Tomorrow she would return to Dad, to find a way to live on Earth even as a star, but tonight, she danced.

She twirled, clapping to the beat and leaning backward and forward. The apsaras made beautiful things of their bodies, shaping their fingers into lotuses, each motion of their hips telling a story. Sheetal could never hope to compete with them, and she didn't want to. She just wanted to look at them, her serpentine and starry and spellbinding kin, and drink in the feeling of family.

The pari's wings fluttered open and closed, and no one seemed to mind how much space they took up, making people bump into one another. On Sheetal's other side, Beena danced with a lissome energy, way more agile than Sheetal had ever been.

Charumati approached, her starry diadem set atop silver

locks bound up into a loose pile of ringlets and her jewelry gleaming from her ears, neck, wrists, and fingers. She smiled, gorgeous as a crystal halo adorning the fullness of a late autumn moon, and reached out with one delicate hand.

The starry melody wandered from Sheetal's heart up to her throat, from her core to her fingertips. She released the pari's hand and took her mother's.

In answer, the pari slipped away, leaving a gap for Charumati to fill. They rejoined the shimmering blue dance, which had become even faster, more feral.

Sheetal had no clue whether they danced for a few minutes or hours and hours. Each beat of her pulse ricocheted in her chest in time with the gandharvas' tabla. When her grandparents entered the dance, the knowledge of their presence resounded through her. Her core flared brighter, hotter. She whirled, she shimmied, she clapped and swayed.

Suddenly Kaushal spun her around, and she laughed, letting everything but the music and the movement fade away.

"You are surprisingly adequate at this," he yelled. Feeling entirely human again, Sheetal stuck out her tongue. "What? It was a compliment!"

Behind him, Sheetal spotted Padmini stalking toward them. Her light dimmed and flickered in alarm.

Kaushal turned to see what Sheetal was looking at. "Hide me!"

Then Padmini was on them. She grabbed Kaushal by the

shoulders and wrenched him out of the circle. "I told you to stay in our apartments!"

"Perhaps I had other plans," Kaushal countered, twisting away.

Padmini pressed a hand to her mouth. Her eyes glimmered wetly. "I know he helped you. How could you ask that of him?"

"I'm sorry," Sheetal began. "I didn't want—"

"And then to flaunt him out in the open like this!"

"It was *my* choice," Kaushal snapped. "I believe in Charumati's cause."

Padmini started to respond, but then, through the shifting storm of blues, Sheetal saw Jeet approaching the table with his entourage—including Dev.

Her whole body lit up, inside and out, and her grin strained her cheeks. Dev grinned back, a private smile that warmed her down to her toes.

Rati helped herself to a frostberry tart. "Have you decided?" she inquired casually, as if they were discussing whether to rejoin the dancing.

"I told you, I'm not doing it," Jeet said, looking at Sheetal. He grabbed a piece of cake. "Cool party. Must be handy to have family here to clean up your messes and show you off before sticking you in a contest you have no right to be in. What's that like? Seriously, I want to know."

"Dude, would you give it a rest?" Dev cut in. "You're being an ass."

Jeet stiffened. "Nice. After everything, this is what I get from you?"

"I don't even know who you are anymore. Can't you just go back to the way you were?"

"This *is* who I am." Jeet's voice could have turned an entire lake to ice. "Someone who wants to win. I thought you wanted that, too."

Rati handed the remains of her tart to a nearby attendant. "Indeed. Then let us get on with the matter at hand." She studied Kaushal. "Here is as good a stage as any, and this one can tell us all about Eshana's love of half-star brats."

"Leave him out of this," Padmini cried, blocking Kaushal from Rati's view.

"Okay," said Sheetal, "someone tell me what's going on. Why do you keep talking about my grandma?"

That was all it took; the spell was spoiled, the enchanted ball an iridescent soap bubble that had burst. Now the suspicions she'd held at bay orbited her like vultures: Nani closing the gates. Nani throwing her a ball to celebrate her majority, her transformation. Rati goading her to confront Nani.

"Yes," Rati crowed, "who wishes to tell Sheetal about her dear Esteemed Matriarch and her sister, Ojasvini?"

Though her gorge rose, Sheetal tried hard to sound bored. "What about her? She used to live here. So what?"

Rati's smile widened until it was toxic, a viper's bite. "So what, indeed?"

Other stars had stopped dancing and were staring now.

356

Including Nani and Nana. Minal and Charumati rushed up, Charumati's face locked in a struggle between dread and near-smugness. "Rati," she cautioned, "do you really wish to do this?"

"That is quite enough," Nani said, her back straight and her head held high.

"What? Do I speak untrue?" Rati asked, all wide-eyed innocence.

"Go," Nana murmured to Nani. "It is almost time for the competition as it is."

Jeet moved closer to Sheetal. "You know, some of us really need this break. Ever think about that?" His contemptuous laugh couldn't quite mask the bleak tone of his question. For a second, under the sallow skin and shadowed eyes, Sheetal glimpsed the vulnerable, hopeful boy Dev had known.

She even felt sorry for him.

Until he said, "You're sitting here and sneering at my family, but you probably should have bothered to research your own history better."

Sheetal dug into her cuticle, taking comfort in the old pain. A drop of blood appeared. It was still red.

"Come, Sheetal," Nani said, softly but decisively. "You as well, Rati. You wish to speak? We will speak."

Charumati placed a hand on the small of Sheetal's back and nudged her forward. Trembling, Sheetal followed Nani out of the court.

357

## 28

Sheetal gouged her fingernails into her palms as she waited for Nani to say something. Across from her, Rati somehow dominated the familiar sitting room, making it impossible to look anywhere else.

"We are so proud of you, dikri," Nani said. "You are a credit to our nakshatra and our family." She didn't smile, but silver light limned her skin. "I have prepared a droplet of blood for you to take to your father. It will be yours tonight."

"As will your circlet," Charumati added, "when we crown you after the competition."

"Uh, thank you," Sheetal said, "but what—what . . ." How was she supposed to just come out and ask her grandmother point-blank what she'd been hiding?

"What, beti?" Nani asked pleasantly.

"Tell her, Eshana," Rati hissed. "Or I will."

Nani turned sparking eyes on her. "You. Too long you have

been a thorn in my side. You truly believe we do not know you have fed your champion your own blood, in flagrant defiance of the bylaws?"

The air in the room went cold as frost, or at least Sheetal did.

Wait. *Nani* knew? She felt like she'd been chucked out the palace window into the endless night, and no matter how hard she scrabbled, there was nothing to hold on to.

Rati's haughty smile stayed fixed in place, but a muscle in her cheek twitched. "What an odd accusation," she bit out. "Simply because you do not wish to be revealed as the self-serving hypocrite you are."

"It is easy to call names. It is harder to believe that perhaps not everyone in your nakshatra is as loyal to you as you might wish," Nani said. "And Rati, how careless, how arrogant you have been, feeding him so much so swiftly. You would have done better to be gradual in your dosing."

"You can prove nothing." Rati preened.

Nani, though, just laughed. "A simple inspection of the mortal's blood, and we will have all the proof we need."

Rati tossed her head, making the jewels in her hair flash. "You still cannot prove it was my doing, if indeed it ever even happened. Anyone might give a hapless mortal blood."

Especially one as desperate as Jeet. Sheetal saw Dev's despairing face, felt his inconsolable heart, all over again. How could Rati do that to anyone?

"And stealing the marionettes to frame our champion?"

The condescension in Nani's question could have shamed a statue. "You truly believed that would work?"

Now Sheetal just saw red, the scarlet of her human blood. Why had Rati even bothered to offer that bargain if she was just going to frame her anyway?

"Again, you can prove nothing." Rati yawned. "Are we through chasing daydreams, or can we get to the point? Tell the truth, stand down from the competition, and I will spare you."

"Ah, but you were not my only friend in your house," Charumati said coolly, "or the only one to find in me a sympathetic ear. We have all the witnesses to your blood feeding we need; it would seem some in the Revati nakshatra fear the consequences of your embittered scheming."

If Rati realized she'd been cornered, she hid it really well, only letting her skepticism show. Sheetal had to give her props for that; in Rati's place, she'd be a puddle on the floor by now. "If you expect me to grovel, I am afraid you will be grievously disappointed."

"Be that as it may," Charumati continued, calm as if surrounded by a pond full of moonlight lotuses, "I will never permit you to harm my daughter in your desire to settle old scores."

"It looks as though we find ourselves at a stalemate," Nani said. "Should you attempt to expose us, be assured we will return the favor. That is, if your rash dosing of the mortal does not expose you in the meantime. Others, if they have not yet noticed his malaise, may still."

Rati gripped the edge of the table, and both the table and

the starsong vibrated with her wrath. "You truly believe you can do whatever you want, do you not? Step on whomever you wish to achieve your draconian aims?"

"Rati—" Charumati began.

"You are both monstrous. I rue the day I called you friend." Rati collected herself with a visible effort. "Whatever you think of me, at least have the courtesy to remove your false champion from the running. You have taken everything else."

"Perhaps you should see to your own champion? The competition will begin shortly," Nani suggested, her voice mild.

"No?" Rati's gaze sharpened, and her mouth became like the curve of a scimitar. "Well, then. I will tell her—and the court—myself. May the best house win."

Her eyes shining with tears, Charumati took Rati's hand. "Do not do this, old friend. I never meant for you to struggle so after I left, and I will always regret not returning sooner for you. That was my mistake."

"Yes, it was," Rati snapped, shoving her away. "You abandoned me without a single glance backward!"

As she glided to the door, she locked stares with Sheetal, and instead of the derision Sheetal would've expected, all she saw was pity. "No portion of this is on your conscience, and yet you must live with the consequences."

Then Rati was gone.

Sheetal worked to gather herself. Wow. That was a lot. She focused on the most immediate thing. "Nani, if you knew about Jeet, how could you just let her get away with it?"

Nani regarded her uncomprehendingly. "What would you have me do, beti? He is not our responsibility. House Revati should have acted as better stewards."

"But don't you *care* about him? Can't we do something?"

"It is revolting, it is unkind, and it will likely end badly for the mortal, but do not trouble yourself with him," Nani said. "Blood or no blood, he cannot match the song in your heart. And once House Revati's challenge to our authority has failed, Rati will have no option but to back down."

She sounded like Charumati, spinning her plan for awakening mortals. "Mom," Sheetal protested, "you can't just ignore this."

"Your nani is right," Charumati said, though her expression was troubled. "We may not interfere. The best thing we can do right now is attend to the competition."

Sheetal couldn't believe her ears. Jeet was a person. How didn't they get that?

How were these the same shimmering beings from the cosmic dance? The ones who knew their link to the rest of the universe and everything in it?

*Maybe you should ask your grandmother what she* really *thinks of half-stars.*

The words raced out of her at light speed. "You can't hurt Kaushal just because he used to be a half-star like me."

"Oh, beti, I would not waste our precious preparation time on the past—"

"*No.*" The syllable echoed in the confines of the room. "Tell me. I need to know he'll be safe."

"I have no intention of seeing him otherwise." Nani frowned. "Rati seeks to stir up trouble wherever she goes. You must not listen to one such as that." She rose. "It is time for your blessing."

"But what happened to Ojasvini? What's the truth Rati kept talking about?"

Nani lifted her chin. "It is in the past, and that is all you need to know."

"Nani!" Sheetal all but screamed. "I'm about to go out there and win a competition for our house. The least you can do is answer me. Why isn't she here?"

The furrow in Nani's forehead deepened. "Not. Now." Pinching her nose, she closed her eyes.

"Let it be," Charumati whispered. "We will discuss it all later. I promise."

Everything Sheetal had been holding back, all her anger and disappointment and anguish, collided like a flint against the steel of the starsong. Sparks caught and spread, igniting years' worth of loneliness and shame, until she combusted, her heart a raging conflagration of fury.

She'd had it with being pushed around like a chess piece, with almost everybody in her life deciding what was right, what she should know and what she should do.

The silver luminosity of the stars streamed through her,

lighting up all the shadowed places and demanding she direct it outward.

*No. Not yet.*

Keeping it in check, keeping herself veiled in the astral melody, was the hardest thing she'd ever done, but she did it.

She had to save Dad first.

The door to the suite opened, and a string of bells chimed. A mix of pride and affection relaxed Nani's elegant visage. Padmini, Beena, and Minal all stood in a line, each holding a silver bell. Behind them, though, Nana had three. "Come," he said. "It is time." He handed Nani and Charumati the extra bells.

"Already?" Nerves writhed to life in Sheetal's belly, joining the anger boiling there.

Padmini and Beena rang their bells, pressed their palms together before their faces, and stepped aside.

"May you burn bold in the deepest night," Nani said, ringing her bell, and knelt to touch Sheetal's feet.

"May you burn bold in the deepest night," Nana said, ringing his bell, and repeated the gesture.

"May you burn bold, my daughter, whatever meets you," Charumati said, ringing her bell, and kissed Sheetal's forehead.

Minal rang her bell, then hugged Sheetal. "Showtime. Knock 'em dead."

Nani collected the bells and, swift as rays of light from the sun, strung them on a garland, which Nana then hung over the door. "Victory to our champion! Victory to our daughter!"

As mad as she was, Sheetal still felt their love like the crystalline butterflies that even now opened and closed their wings in her hair.

She drew on that, collecting her disappointment, her compassion, her hope and immolating them all in the fire of her fury. "Let's do this."

## 29

Unseen bansuris played, their lilting call summoning the court to attention.

As one, the various members of the twenty-seven houses rose to receive their rulers, their arms lifted in greeting as if casting a spell. A sea of many stars, cresting through the grand court. Not a trace of the blue lighting remained, and the buffet, too, had been cleared away, as if Sheetal's brief celebration had never been. Even the garden was gone.

The fifty-two Esteemed Matriarchs and Patriarchs who hadn't attended the ball now swept onto the sickle-shaped stage, clad in black finery threaded through with silver and iridescent blue that flashed like a jewel beetle's wings in flight. Each of them wore a circlet of stars reminiscent of Charumati's and Nani's, reminiscent of the one Sheetal would receive just hours from now.

So these were the leaders of the twenty-seven nakshatras,

she thought, as she stood before their stage. They were magnificent. They were frightening.

She tried not to feel uneasy, tried not to notice her grandparents among them, and failed miserably.

"Be seated," the matriarch of House Dhanishta commanded, and the audience sat. The other Esteemed followed, claiming their places in the semicircle of thrones looking down on a large oval pool, which definitely hadn't been there before.

"Good. Let us begin," the ancient patriarch of House Dhanishta said. "Competing houses, lead your champions and their companions to the viewing pool. Escorts, you may follow."

Sheetal stared up at him. Here was the star who would soon relinquish his throne to become a supernova and ultimately a black hole.

She accompanied Minal and Charumati to the viewing pool. On one side, across from the semicircle of the Esteemed, five tents containing black-and-silver tables and blue upholstered chairs had been lined up in a row, with the respective nakshatra's banner hanging over each tent. A platform stood before them, waiting for the champions. On the other side was the judges' long table, unoccupied.

"The judges are already in their places," Charumati explained. "Simply hidden."

The whole thing felt like a faux-medieval feast. Sheetal worried a loose thread on her sari. Normally, she would be in the audience, not getting ready to be skewered as the entertainment.

There was still time to run away. . . .

*No*, she told herself, holding Dad's face in her mind. No, there wasn't.

The champions, companions, and attendants of the other competing houses took their seats. Leela and Kirti rested quietly between Leela's patrons, hands folded in their laps, while in contrast, clouds of nervous energy wafted from Priyanka's and Sachin's sections. The two of them glared at each other, and Jürgen's lips pinched in disapproval. They all wore candy colors—pumpkin orange, berry pink, and emerald green—that only made Sheetal even more uncomfortably aware just how much she looked like a star in her own clothes.

The looks Priyanka and Sachin directed her way burned with scorn, as if they knew what she was thinking and couldn't agree more. Sheetal averted her gaze. Good thing Priyanka didn't know she'd seen her in Jeet's room.

Meanwhile, Jeet, in a gray kurta that made his sallow skin look even sicklier, exchanged heated whispers with Rati.

The schadenfreude Sheetal felt at that probably made her a bad person. Oh, well. She *was* sorry for Jeet, but she also kind of hoped they were fighting, too.

Dev, who was sitting as far from Rati and his cousin as he could, caught her eye and held it. Like a star, he wore black and silver, and like a star, he enthralled. Her stomach took a dive, stage fright and anticipation all tangled up in a ball. Oh, gods, he was going to hear her sing. Oh, gods!

What if she choked like during rehearsal?

She remembered again how he'd said he wished he could make Jeet quit. She wished that, too. She wished she could make them all quit.

The Esteemed Matriarch of the Dhanishta nakshatra smiled, a munificent turn of her mouth framed by deep wrinkles. "You may proceed." The supporting Esteemed Matriarchs and Patriarchs then raised their arms, awash in starlight.

The viewing pool began to glimmer. A picture appeared within its illuminated depths before being projected into the air. It depicted the platform that had been set up near the pool and all the champions gathered around, like some kind of futuristic hologram.

The Esteemed Patriarch lifted a hand, dispersing the enchantment cloaking the long table and revealing the panel of judges.

As the Patriarch of House Dhanishta named them, each one rose: five stars from nakshatras not in the competition and one middle-aged human man who described himself as an art history professor. "Wow me," he said. "Technique and craft have their place, but what I really want is emotion. Move me. Make me *feel*."

Nana had told Sheetal the mortal judge would be ensorcelled to believe this night was just a detailed dream, but his vote remained vital. She shivered. What if her talent wasn't enough?

These last few days hadn't wholly felt real. There had been so many preparations, so many distractions keeping her occupied. But now the truth assailed her: The competition really was happening. She really had to win it—on a measly two days' training—to save Dad's life.

Suddenly it was like she was standing by his bed again, smelling the air of the ICU, hearing the feeble beat of his pulse. *Dad. Oh, Dad.*

The ruling Esteemed Matriarch clapped loudly, and the court hushed. "A reminder: Each champion will be allowed one hour to complete their work. During that time, they must not be disturbed for any reason. You are welcome to show your support, but do so silently."

"And now," announced the ruling Esteemed Patriarch, "for the main event!" He reached into the silver bowl on the stand between his throne and that of the Esteemed Matriarch and plucked out a black slip of paper.

Sheetal held her breath. Please let it be her. She was going to die of nerves.

"Please welcome our first champion, Priyanka Chauhan of House Magha. She will perform a puppet show using marionettes she crafted herself."

At the platform, Priyanka held out her arms and cracked her knuckles. She shot Sachin another lethal glance over her shoulder. Sheetal frowned. What was going on there?

One of Priyanka's attendants set down a painted wooden stage that came up to her waist. As before, the viewing pool projected a magnified version of the scene into the air. Another star from her coterie stood before her, fingers uncurling.

Light vaulted from that star's hands into Priyanka, rendering her brilliant. Her eyes glowed like moonlit lakes, and with a theatrical flourish, she opened the red velvet curtains, then knelt behind the stage so only her puppets could be seen. There were two, a princess and her shape-shifting tiger consort. Somehow Priyanka had rigged the puppet so that with a simple flick of her wrist, the consort's long tunic flipped up to bare the tiger beneath and actually became the animal's striped skin.

Sheetal hadn't really done more than glance at the marionettes when they were in her room, but now it was obvious why Priyanka had panicked after they'd gone missing. They were unsettlingly sophisticated, able to convey degrees of emotion and mood with the subtlest movements, and Priyanka's control over them made Sheetal's breath catch. Her chaotic thoughts—it would be her turn soon, oh, gods, it would be her turn soon, what if she couldn't do it, *what if she couldn't do it what would she do oh gods*—slowed as she found herself sucked into the world Priyanka and her puppets created.

The princess, a fierce lady who carried her kingdom in her knapsack to safeguard it from a sinister sorcerer, roamed the land with her consort in search of injustice. Each day, the pair would rescue a village or do away with a ruthless employer or just make certain everyone had enough to eat.

They encountered thieves, immoral landlords, even cruel schoolmasters, and vanquished them all. But the biggest threat to the kingdom, the greedy sorcerer, still lurked just out of sight.

"Funny," growled the tiger. "They say the pen is mightier than the sword, but when it comes to getting things done, there's a lot to be said for a sharp blade and a good set of claws."

The princess hefted her sword. "You have to address people in the language they speak."

At the end of each day, the duo set down the kingdom, unfolding it like a board game, to enjoy a repast with the royal family, ramble through the rose gardens, and sleep soundly in their silken palace bed.

When the tiger fell victim to the sorcerer's poison, obliging the princess to trade her kingdom to the sorcerer in exchange for a healing spell, the court wept. When she later tricked him into returning the kingdom, the court cheered. When the now-hale tiger slashed the sorcerer into gory strips, at last liberating the kingdom from his tyranny, the court roared.

Using nothing but dialogue and well-timed gestures, Priyanka had compelled the entire starry court to care about the fates of a pair of inanimate wooden puppets. The whole audience gave her a standing ovation.

While her attendant removed the stage, Priyanka and her puppets took deep bows. A proud smile wreathed her face. She would be hard to beat, and she knew it.

"That was amazing," Minal whispered.

"Yeah." Sheetal had to compete with *that*?

As the judges scribbled notes in the ten-minute break, she glanced at Jeet. He'd affected an apathetic expression, and even Dev was glowering at him.

She looked over to catch her mother eyeing Rati. Rati inclined her head and stared back.

The break ended, and the Esteemed Matriarch selected the next name. "Please welcome our second champion, Leela Swaminathan of House Krittika. She will paint the loss of innocence."

One attendant set up her watercolor palette, canvas, and brushes on the platform, while the other inspired her, the act as simple and unpretentious as Leela herself. Stardust ringed her like a corona, and Leela seated herself at her easel and chanted a short mantra to Sarasvati Devi, goddess of speech and knowledge and patroness of the arts.

Then, her back to the audience, she began to paint.

The stars were enraptured, drinking in every brushstroke. Even Minal watched with fascination. To Sheetal, however, it was torture, even with the time-lapse magic that allowed each artist to complete a new work within their allotted hour. All she could think of was her own performance and the drop of blood Nani had waiting, and of the post-competition coronation with her starry circlet, when she would become a full star.

What . . . what if she was already too much of a star to be inspired?

If she failed, if she lost, would Nani, the same person who had instituted an absolute separation of stars and mortals, still help Dad? What would keep her from closing the gates the second Sheetal left?

Apparently Sheetal was still human enough to break into a

sweat, because she flushed all over. Had she been stupid not to accept Rati's bargain?

She wanted to grab Minal and Dev and beg them to think of something, to point out the all-important detail she'd overlooked. Instead, she had to sit and wait as Leela deliberated and swept the canvas with her brush just so.

After what felt like a week and simultaneously no time at all, Leela stepped back and evaluated her painting. With a nod, she set her brush down.

When she moved aside, revealing the canvas to the audience, Sheetal felt sliced in half.

There, somehow far more than mere red and black and brown paint, was pain, was rage. There was the anguish of having trusted and been betrayed time and again until the world was nothing more than a nightmare carousel. There on the canvas was a feral woman with disheveled, filthy hair and disillusioned demon's eyes but also a calloused, bloody heart that refused not to beat. Not, deep inside where it counted, to hope.

It was so gorgeous, so hideous, that Sheetal almost sobbed.

*There*, she wanted to tell her mother and her grandmother and Beena and Rati and the entire starry court. *You want to understand humans? That is what makes us—and art—what we are. That choice to keep getting back up and trying again in the face of suffering and injustice and despair.*

Would she lose that when she became a full star?

"It is certainly passionate and interesting in its execution," Charumati whispered, "yet it puts me in mind of your foi's

374

clients, the misery that brought them to her door. Rather than exalt these emotions, would it not be better to heal their cause altogether?"

"If only," Minal said sadly.

Sheetal squinted at her mother. She wanted to see her, really see her, the way artists saw values and shapes and not what their minds told them they should be seeing. She squinted, and she saw brown skin, curves and long hair, and someone whose veins ran with the silvery essence of the stars.

What she didn't see was a mortal. They might resemble ridiculously beautiful human beings, but Sheetal had forgotten how alien the stars really were. The human part of her heart twinged, but before she could figure out why, the Esteemed Patriarch selected another slip of paper.

"Please welcome our third champion, Sachin Khanna of House Ashvini," called the Esteemed Patriarch, holding up his paper. "He will be sculpting in his chosen medium of reclaimed metal objects."

Maybe Sheetal could go fourth, at least?

Sachin, forehead damp, rose from his seat. His attendant offered him a towel, which he used to blot away the perspiration. For someone an entire house of stars had chosen, he didn't seem very confident.

Priyanka, who had been furiously muttering with her attendants, yelled, "I don't care! I'm saying it." She jerked free of their restraining hands and leaped to her feet. "Excuse me, Esteemed Matriarch and Patriarch, but this man stole my marionettes!"

Sachin let out a squeak.

*So that's Rati's patsy.* Had she intimidated Sachin into the sabotage? Or had he just been that desperate?

The ruling Esteemed Matriarch and Patriarch considered Priyanka. "Then how were you able to perform?" the Esteemed Patriarch asked. "Were those not your marionettes?"

Priyanka frowned. "Yes, but—"

"Do you have proof of this theft?"

Priyanka ignored the laughter and murmurs from the audience. "I don't know who brought my marionettes back, but it wasn't him. You can't let him compete." She pointed to Jeet. "Ask Jeet; he's the one who caught him stealing again."

Jeet waved. "I found him sneaking off with my notebook. I told him if he didn't confess to Priyanka and give the puppets back, I'd turn him in."

"And he never did," Priyanka said.

Jeet smiled. "So I'm turning him in."

"Mortal Sachin Khanna," the Esteemed Matriarch inquired, "is all that true?"

Sachin froze, then protested, "This—this isn't right. I was going to put them back." Jürgen approached but stopped just short of touching him.

"So you admit having taken them?"

Sachin slumped forward. "Yes."

Jürgen gaped as if Sachin had grown a second nose. "You did what?"

Leela rose and called out, "I have reason to believe he may have put sand in my paint tubes. I didn't say anything because I couldn't prove it, but someone did it."

Jürgen shook his head slowly, like he was trying to wake from a terrible dream. Sachin grabbed his arm. "I didn't know if I could give you the house! I thought you'd leave me."

More exclamations from the crowd, and stars in Sachin's own nakshatra were staring at the floor. Anger and confusion warred for dominance on his face as he laid into Jeet. "The puppets were already gone when I went to get them. You know that. What was I supposed to do?"

Sheetal almost felt bad for him, except he'd brought this on himself. If Kaushal hadn't interceded, she might have gotten kicked out.

"Come on," Jeet said lazily. "You didn't really think we'd just let that go. You tried to sabotage us." Sheetal imagined the silver blood crawling beneath his skin and gagged.

"No!" said Sachin. "You said *she*—"

The Esteemed Matriarch pointed to the platform. "Please reserve all theatrics for the actual performance. You may begin your turn while we contemplate this situation."

As they spread out an array of tools, Jürgen whispered something to Sachin that caused his chin to drop to his chest. Then Jürgen trudged back to their tent. At this point, Sheetal wasn't sure he would care if Sachin won.

The star who'd accompanied them from House Ashvini's

tent hastened to inspire Sachin, then withdrew. Alone at his table, Sachin donned protective goggles and gloves. Then he carved. He welded. He soldered. Drills whined, and sparks flew. A fresh patina of sweat beaded on his forehead, but he didn't stop working to wipe it off.

After an hour or five years—Sheetal couldn't have said which—Sachin set down his tools to reveal a marble-and-metal sculpture of a white man in a top hat from Victorian times facing an Indian warrior bearing a golden mace. Sheetal could tell at a glance how good it was, how much raw feeling and narrative it communicated. It deserved a ton of applause and more.

But like the rest of the audience, she was really just waiting for the Esteemed Matriarch and Patriarch to reach their decision.

Finally the Esteemed Matriarch spoke. "The issue of the theft is disappointing, certainly, yet you did attempt in good faith to return the marionettes. That was a wise self-corrective measure, and one we endorse."

Sachin, who'd been stooped over his table, sat up now, and he beamed at his companion. Sheetal's breath came faster. They were going to pardon him, she knew it.

"However, the string of thefts and attempted sabotage concern us far less than the motivation behind them: You do not appear to trust your own ability to stand against other artists. Weakness of character does not become you, nor does it become the house for which you serve as symbol," the Esteemed Patriarch declared. "Therefore, you are dismissed."

Shock rumbled through House Ashvini. For his part, Sachin said nothing, his eyes glassy. He didn't respond when Jürgen turned his back or even when his escorts led him away.

# 30

The court buzzed as a cluster of stars from the disgruntled Ashvini nakshatra rushed the stage and started arguing with the ruling Esteemed Matriarch and Patriarch.

The rest of the stars had risen from their seats and were discussing the decision in various tones of giddiness and anger, like they intended to lap up every bit of the tension. Sheetal remembered the apsara saying nothing exciting had happened here in a long time.

So disgusting, like they were all ghouls. No matter what Sachin had done, he had just lost everything.

The Esteemed Matriarch clapped for silence, cutting the chatter short. "Please welcome our fourth champion, Jeet Merai of House Revati," she announced. "He will be composing and presenting a short tale."

"Here we go," Minal muttered, and Sheetal glanced up to watch Rati ascend the platform next to Jeet, the pleats of her sheer sari accentuating her graceful, statuesque frame. Contempt simmered in her gaze.

Sheetal went numb. She'd gotten so enmeshed in her own fears, she'd forgotten about Rati.

The entire court was listening, including the stars of the Dhanishta nakshatra. And no wonder; in the projection from the viewing pool, Rati's antics were full of cinematic flair.

Rati smiled, unabashedly exulting in the attention. "It is true House Revati's champion will tell the court a story it cannot possibly resist. Is that not so, Jeet?"

Jeet bristled but nodded.

What was she up to? Sheetal looked over at Dev. A muscle twitched in his jaw. Maybe they should rush the stage, too.

"You may take your seat," said the ruling Esteemed Patriarch, "and begin."

*No*, Sheetal wanted to shout. *No taking seats! Don't begin!* She didn't dare look at Nani. Charumati reached for her hand.

Rati didn't wait. She injected Jeet with so much stardust he blazed like a comet. His eyes flared like fluorescent bulbs, and his fingers and curly hair turned to torches. Sheetal was sure he'd pass out, if the jolt of inspiration didn't burn him up altogether.

But the light vanished just as rapidly as it had come, and he swaggered to the front of the platform, letting the curious crowd get a good look at him. Finally, he smiled a wide, ironic smile, parked himself at the table with the scroll and ink pot set out for him, and began to write.

It was a good thing Charumati was holding her hand, because Sheetal wouldn't have been able to keep from ripping her cuticles to shreds. In his tent, Dev fidgeted and probably wished he had something to tear up, too.

Minutes passed. Normally Sheetal couldn't think of anything more boring than staring at someone scratch ink onto paper, but right now, she prayed to any of the gods who might be listening that it would never end, that whatever Jeet was writing, it wouldn't be good.

Padmini offered both her mother and her glasses of blue mango juice, and Sheetal gulped hers down. She was so thirsty. So hot and so thirsty.

Would he ever finish? *Please don't let him finish.*

After what seemed like hours, Jeet set down the quill and stood. He cleared his throat and began to read aloud.

"One day, long ago but not so long that the world was round instead of flat, a man went out to watch the sky through the new telescope his older brother had given him. He saw a planet that winked in and out and wondered what it was. Had he discovered something no one else had?

"It seemed what the man had been watching was a planet, but the more he watched, the more she started to look like a human woman, dainty and soft, long of hair and arm, and short of temper. The brothers fought for the telescope, giving up weeks of sleep just to stare at her. All they talked about was how they would capture her and have their own traveling show."

*Gross,* Sheetal thought. Next to her, Minal rolled her eyes.

"The planet could feel their attention on her atmosphere like ants crawling over human skin, until she couldn't think of anything else. Her soil dried out and cracked, and she suffered earthquakes and avalanches and eruptions like pustules."

After all the hype, that was the best Jeet could do? Sheetal couldn't believe it. *That* was the kind of writing that won grants? How about some actual characterization and description?

The audience, too, shifted restlessly. No one spoke, and the astral melody was silent, but Sheetal didn't need that to tell her when someone was bored.

"The breaking point finally came," Jeet intoned, his words climbing dramatically, "the way breaking points do, when she jumped out of the sky and landed on the ground with a thump. Her feet left big holes in the ground that would turn into ponds after the first rain. That night, though, was a clear one, so clear that the brothers were forced to watch as the planet came closer and closer. 'Ogle me, will you?' the planet huffed, but the brothers were so busy staring, imagining the fortune they would make by taking their discovery on the road, that they completely failed to see her giant hands reaching—"

Sheetal glanced at Rati. Her grand champion, the one meant to take down the Pushya nakshatra, sucked at writing! She must be so humiliated.

From where she sat in House Revati's tent, Rati watched Jeet through hooded eyes. When he looked back, her eyes flashed, and stardust leaped from her fingers so fast Sheetal nearly missed it. But Jeet didn't.

He broke off midsentence and blinked a few times. His lip curled, and he gave a minute shake of his head. To anyone else, it probably looked like he'd lost his place.

Dev chewed on a fingernail as he watched his cousin. Whatever he'd said to Jeet, he definitely still cared. Sheetal wished so hard she could spare him whatever was coming.

Rati only waited, shackling Jeet with her daggerlike stare. Sheetal saw the moment when he caved, his eyes closing, his head bowing slightly.

When Jeet started again, it was in a completely different tone of voice, one much lighter. "I will spin you a tale so rare it is unknown to most of this court—its true ending concealed to date. You may consider it a secret history of the star hunters."

Minal gripped Sheetal's arm hard enough to bruise. She barely noticed the pain. Rati had warned them. *I will tell the court myself.*

Only she was making Jeet her microphone.

Nana and Nani descended from the stage and onto the platform in a flood of silver light. "Be still, boy," Nani commanded, while Nana bore down on Jeet. "We have no time for your misguided attempts at horseplay."

Sheetal sneaked another glance at Dev. He sat frozen.

Jeet kept reciting as if Nani hadn't spoken, projecting his voice until it carried to the farthest corners of the chamber. "Upon learning the mortal man Chandrakant had willingly bled her sister, Ojasvini, stealing her lifeblood daily until she nearly perished, the Esteemed Matriarch of House Pushya,

384

Eshana, journeyed to the mortal world in search of retribution. There she sought out Chandrakant and ended his life with the same knife he had used on Ojasvini. . . ."

Sheetal tasted acid at the back of her throat. All around and through her, the starsong trembled with indignation and support for Nani's actions. How dare that mortal treat a star so cruelly?

If Rati had expected the court to condemn Nani for that, she couldn't have been more off.

Smug and relieved both, Sheetal peeked at Rati to see how she was taking being so wrong.

The smirk on Rati's face might as well have been a bucket of ice water, the way Sheetal froze. The story wasn't over yet, after all, and from the cunning way Rati watched Jeet, whatever he was about to say would be beyond horrible.

*Stop*, Sheetal silently begged Jeet. *Just stop.*

". . . but not before she cast away the child Ojasvini had borne him. Her own daughter Charumati's cousin."

The starsong exploded into a thousand screams.

Child? Sheetal reeled. There had been a child?

"That is more than enough," said Nana. "You are wasting the judges' time."

"Ah, but my champion is permitted the entirety of his turn," Rati called from her tent. "And I for one would hear the rest of his story."

The Esteemed Matriarch of House Dhanishta nodded. "She is correct. Continue, mortal Jeet Merai, if you would."

Nani's mouth puckered in anger, but there was nothing she could do.

"Though she might have brought him here," Jeet narrated with a little too much fanfare, "instead Eshana abandoned the poor babe, her sister's offspring, to a mortal family, leaving them no guidance.

"Traumatized by her ordeal, Ojasvini made no protest as her sister ripped the infant from her arms. In shock, she accompanied Eshana to the gates of Svargalok. But as Eshana moved to enter the palace, Ojasvini's clouded eyes cleared. 'I will not forsake my child,' she said. 'I must go back for him.'

"'But you cannot bring him here,' Eshana replied. 'Not when that man nearly bled you dry!'

"'The court has always accepted all our children, mortal blood or no, and raised them into full stars,' Ojasvini said. 'It is our duty to do so. Moreover, he is my son, and I love him as I once loved his father.'

"Eshana knew this to be so, yet she could not abide the thought of that mortal's child living among the stars. 'You must not do this. I will not permit you.'

"Ojasvini grew sorrowful. 'You would punish my son for the sins of his father? Well, I will not. Tell me where he is.'

"Eshana refused. 'I have placed him with a mortal family. That is all you need to know.'

"Ojasvini implored her, even throwing herself at Eshana's feet, but Eshana would not yield. Finally Ojasvini turned away to descend once more. 'No matter how long it takes, I will find him,' she swore.

"Eshana's overweening pride outweighed her compassion, and though she knew stars could not survive for long in the mortal realm, she let her sister go. She was certain Ojasvini would soon come to her senses and resume her life among the stellar court."

Listening, Sheetal grew sicker and sicker. Would Nani have abandoned her, too?

She spun one of her bangles around and around. Worse, would Nani lock the gates behind her as soon as the competition was over?

"Time passed, yet Ojasvini did not return. Eshana initially attributed it to obstinacy. Then more time passed, and even her hard heart could not withstand her sister's absence. Eshana began to rue her own rashness and slipped away to the mortal realm to find Ojasvini—and the babe she realized she should never have given away.

"But there was nothing to be found. Eshana had waited too long. By the time Ojasvini had located her son, his flame had escaped him and razed the house where he dwelled, taking his foster family and him with it. Though the firmament soon tore at her tattered heart, mandating she return, Ojasvini spurned its many calls. She would not leave without her son, and so, she slowly extinguished."

Nani drooped all at once, no longer a fearsome matriarch

but a sorrowing old woman. Her thread in the starsong frayed just enough to betray her grief before she regained control and raised her head high.

"In her wrath, Eshana petitioned for the gates between the realms to be closed, ending all contact between the starry court and mortals," Jeet finished.

His vague expression solidified into confusion as he looked down at the audience, then went hollow with horror as Rati came up beside him. "You made me do that!" he rasped, clutching his throat like she'd choked him with a spell. Maybe she had. "I didn't even finish reading my story."

"Patience," Rati said, not bothering to glance at him.

"Your turn is complete," the ruling Esteemed Patriarch said. "Please vacate the platform."

"What? No!" Jeet looked like he was about to detonate. Silver light swam under his skin, and his hands shook. "Tell him, Rati! Tell him I'm not done."

Rati ignored him. "I told you the best house would win."

Nani simply raised her eyebrows. "Do go on, both of you. I am certain everyone here can appreciate a good show." To the watching Esteemed, she added, "Surely all of you see how ruthlessly Rati has manipulated her house's champion, going so far as to feed him her blood. You cannot believe any words she puts into his mouth. She is using this hallowed tradition to further her own agenda."

The court shimmered with the stars' sheen, their hair and

skin resplendent. All Sheetal could think, her mouth parched, was that Nani was going to get away with it.

Then Charumati rose and crossed the platform until she stood by her parents and Rati. "Jeet speaks true. Now I will offer the coda to his tale."

Sheetal almost fell out of her chair.

Rati glowed like she'd just won the cosmic lottery.

Nana bent to whisper something, but Charumati shrugged him off. "When my mother returned from the mortal realm," she said to the court, "only Nana even knew what she had done. Together, they concluded that though heinous in nature, her crime had not been unwarranted, and justice would best be served by closing the door on what had surely been an error born of passion. In return, she agreed to atone."

She positioned herself opposite Nani. "Yet you did not. You became convinced that separation was the only way to heal the rift created between our peoples, and you have done everything in your power to make it permanent."

"Was I then wrong?" asked Nani. She motioned to Jeet. "Is this mortal man then not after our blood?"

Jeet crossed his arms and glared at all of them. The tremors running through his body grew stronger as Dev took him aside.

"And these others—do they not seek us only for the glory we might provide them?"

Charumati's eyes flared with silver flame, and her body blazed, limned in starlight. "You speak of selfish agendas.

389

Yet you would use my daughter to serve your own. Even now, instead of viewing this moment as an opportunity to heal old wounds, you plan again to sever us from humanity altogether. My *husband* is mortal. My *daughter*, who stands before you and bears your blood in her veins, is half mortal. And still you would dismiss them as readily, as thoughtlessly, as specks of dirt swept off the floor."

"What nonsense you speak!" Nani pressed her lips into a line.

"It is far from nonsense," Rati said. "You care not who you hurt when they stand in the way of furthering your aims."

The starry melody jangled, sending Sheetal's already-fried nerves sparking. If she only knew what to say.

"Enough," boomed Nana. He, too, shone like a torch. "Charumati, you are spoiling your own daughter's competition."

"If you cared about my daughter," Charumati retorted, "you would not have coerced me to return here while she was still a child. You, Father, how *you* charmed and nagged, alleging I was harming us all by remaining below. *You* assured me it was for the best."

A tiny door closed inside Sheetal. He had? Was *anyone* on her side?

In contrast to the smoldering room, Nani's fire was controlled, scarcely evident in her face. But Sheetal could sense how she seethed. "Did we prevent you from bringing her along? *You* chose to leave her behind."

"So you could turn her against the father who had nothing but love for her? So you could shame her for her heritage until she burned it away in self-loathing?" Charumati laughed, soft but disparaging. "I made many impulsive choices, yet even I knew not to do that."

Nani sighed noisily, permitting the entire hall to hear her vexation. "And what, exactly, do you think to accomplish by throwing this public tantrum, my child?"

"Mother," said Charumati, "the time for secrets is past. Humanity is suffering, and it is up to us to heal it."

"Is that so," Nani said dryly.

What was her mother *doing*? She'd told Sheetal she wanted to have enough supporters behind her before putting her plan into gear. Confronting Nani in public like this was only going to make her dig her heels in even deeper.

"It would appear there has been some turmoil in the House of Pushya," said the Esteemed Patriarch of House Dhanishta, a sardonic cast to his mouth. "Perhaps you should consider withdrawing from the competition and tending to your internal affairs elsewhere? We do have a competition to complete."

Nani joined her palms before her face. "My deepest apologies, House Dhanishta. We will not disturb the proceedings again."

Did Nani even realize she was in the wrong? Had *anything* Charumati said hit home?

Just as Sheetal had opened her heart to Dev's, she now opened it to this woman's. Her grandmother's.

And then she heard it, a small but singular strain of notes in the starsong: guilt.

Nani felt guilty. The fulfillment she'd taken in her momentary act of vengeance had rotted into regret and self-recrimination. Sheetal only glimpsed it for a second, but that was all she needed. Nani had built an entire worldview to justify a mistake she had made long ago.

Not caring if it got her kicked out of the competition, Sheetal stalked to her grandmother's side. "Nani, did you really hate that guy so much that you'd rather throw away your sister's child than raise him to be yours?"

"He nearly murdered Ojasvini." Nani stood proud and tall. "If I had not found her when I did, he would have."

"But the baby would have grown into one of us. He didn't need to know his father."

Nani shook her head. "Not with that taint in his blood."

"'Taint'?" The word stung Sheetal's lips, her heart, like a toxin. "Do you think *I'm* tainted?"

"Of course not. You are mine."

*Mine.* "You think I'm just going to forget all about Dad if you keep me up here long enough, don't you?"

Nani's voice was compassionate yet resolute. "Naturally you will not forget him, Sheetal. But he will age and pass on, and you will remain. Do you not feel the changes occurring in you even as we speak? You will never be truly content among mortals. Your heart belongs with us, as do you."

"So it's okay to trap me here?" Sheetal bit out. "To ban anyone from giving me blood to help him, so I have to stay and win this competition for you? What kind of love is that?"

That at least must have rattled Nani, because she stepped backward.

Charumati gave Sheetal a significant look. "You see?" she asked. "Look how the ripples of one malignant mortal's actions have corrupted our court. You should never be made to choose. You deserve to move freely between the realms, as we all once did."

The air and astral melody both juddered under the weight of disgusted protest. Sheetal heard the term "mortal lover" scornfully tossed around more than once. The invisible arrows impaled her, one after another, leaving her smarting. How many of these people, her people, agreed with Nani's stance?

But hesitant tendrils of curiosity were sprouting, too, Urjit's among them. Sheetal found his strain in the sidereal song and felt her shoulders drop. At least she'd gotten through to him.

"Did you know that upon my return to the court, I beseeched Rati's parents to reinstate her title? They rebuffed me. They find her too embittered, too acrimonious." Charumati dabbed at her eyes. "We cannot remain like this. Let us look forward, to redeeming humanity and preventing future suffering."

Kaushal materialized at her side as if he'd just been waiting for the chance. "I will help. In fact, I volunteer to resume my life among the mortals as part of the delegation to wake them."

Padmini's wail carried through the crowd. She raced to the platform, pursued by Minal. "No!"

"No," Minal agreed. "I promised I wouldn't let anything happen to you. This counts as anything."

"Patience, Kaushal," Charumati chided gently. She addressed the audience. "The truth, which so many of us wish not to acknowledge, is this: We cannot cut ourselves off from mortals. We thrive by coexisting with them. It is our duty to see them thrive and improve as well." She pointed to Jeet. "It is our duty to inspire them to be better."

"Let us inspire him right now!" Kaushal suggested. "It will mean more if we can demonstrate our plan."

Dev frowned, dubious. "I'd say that didn't really work out the first time."

Sheetal remembered his plea for Jeet to turn back into the person he had been. "Dev," she whispered, knowing it was a risk, "what if we could fix Jeet? Make him better? Would you want me to try?"

Jeet laughed cynically. "You think *you* know what better is?"

Even when they'd fought, Dev had never looked at her like this, like she was her own evil twin. "You mean, mess with him like Rati did? Hard pass, thanks."

"No, I mean, enlighten him. Inspire him to be better."

"How is that any different?" Dev challenged. "No, seriously. Would you decide one day you needed to fix me, too?"

The air went out of Sheetal. She'd forgotten her mother meant all the imperfect mortals on Earth, which of course meant every single person in existence, good or not.

If they inspired all mortals' choices, no one would ever make a mistake or have a moment of doubt. That sounded beautiful, but . . .

She forced herself to picture inspiring Dev like that. He'd never burn her cookies or be shy writing her a song. He'd always do everything right.

He wouldn't be Dev.

Even Minal was staring at Sheetal like she didn't recognize her. "Listen to yourself! Three days here, and you're talking about mind control?"

Put like that, the whole thing sounded so unbelievably ridiculous. So self-important.

Sheetal's heart cracked. No. Absolutely not. It *wasn't* any different from Rati's games. Charumati had made it sound noble, but it was only a different version of pulling strings. They'd be turning mortals into puppets, and unlike Priyanka, Sheetal didn't want to be anybody's puppeteer. She didn't even know how to keep her own strings from tangling up.

Minal's glare was as scary as Radhikafoi's during one of her rants. "You can't *enlighten* us, Sheetu. That's not how it works."

Dev ran a hand over his face. "How can you even ask that?"

Mortified, Sheetal stared at her glowing palms, then at her mother. Really saw her, the star who had come to Earth for adventure. Worry and love shone in those eyes bright as gemstones. Sheetal knew Charumati loved her, just like she knew her mother wanted her to be safe.

And because of that, she'd let herself get swept up in her mother's grand plans, never stopping to check in with the people they were supposed to help. Like what Minal, what Dev, what Dad wanted didn't count. Like she'd already written off her own mortal heritage.

Kaushal hadn't had anyone to love him on Earth. And Charumati might love Dad, but she'd never really belonged down there.

Sheetal, though, did. She knew what the people who lived there were worth.

"No," she said. "I'm sorry." She looked at her mother. "Mom, they're right. Would you 'redeem' Dad, too?"

Charumati's serene expression turned stricken.

"I mean, you'd have to, right?"

Her mother gazed at something only she could see. "I . . ."

"He's not perfect. He's done things wrong. He's hurt people. Like you said, everybody does." Sheetal appealed to Kaushal. "We can't take people's mistakes away from them."

Any more than anyone could take hers. People had to grow on their own, make their own decisions, good and bad. It was those mistakes and the choice or refusal to learn from them that gave life—and art—their texture, their meaning. It had to be a choice.

And if being a full star meant she might forget that, well, she had to find another way.

Before her mother could protest, Sheetal addressed the Esteemed Matriarch and Patriarch of House Dhanishta. "I'm ready to perform."

# 31

Sheetal and Minal stood on the platform by the viewing pool, where a turbaned man set a dilruba made of black crystal and gleaming silver strings before them and stepped aside. Nani had definitely delivered. Just the sight of it made Sheetal's fingers itch with longing, made the flame at her core spring up, burning away every other thought, every fear. It was an instrument fit for a goddess, one who would use her music to show the stars what it felt to be human, to open their eyes at last. . . .

A goddess! Sheetal rubbed her sweat-slick palms together. She was just a girl, and way too much was riding on her performance. What if her fingers slipped? What if a string snapped?

What if she forgot how to play? Would the stars laugh? Mock her?

Worse, would her own family even listen to her after that?

"Try it," Minal murmured. "Just to see."

Sheetal nodded.

Even before she tested the strings, she knew they'd be in tune.

The sound rang in her ears, rich and high, and above all, impossibly pure. Nectar for the ears, night made music. There were no flaws in these strings. They were formed of light.

All her fears of failing melted away. Only the lure of the music existed—and Sheetal.

She couldn't *wait* to play.

When she tapped into it, the starsong thrummed with anticipation. Everyone knew whatever happened tonight would change everything.

Outside their tent, Dev and Jeet were arguing. Jeet scowled. "Shut up, bhai. You're a shitty cousin, you know that?"

Dev recoiled. He opened his mouth, paused, and opened his mouth again. "Maybe I am, but I can't do this anymore. I'm sorry, man."

"So it's like that. Picking a girl over me." Jeet's face was as cold as the void between the stars. "Some brother you turned out to be."

Sheetal could see the hurt poisoning Dev like venom. She knew it wasn't her fault, but watching him crumple broke her heart.

"We have discussed this," Nani said, coming up behind her. "That mortal boy and his ilk are irrelevant. Focus instead on your future and your life here."

Sheetal almost laughed. Had Nani heard a word she'd said? No wonder Padmini wanted to keep Kaushal out of sight. And Charumati wasn't going to just give up, either.

Saying no wasn't enough. Grand speeches wouldn't do it. The stars needed her to remind them humanity was worth something, but she couldn't do that as their champion. What would that accomplish except prove what they already believed, that stars were superior?

There had to be something else she could do. She didn't have long before her birthday would be over and her transformation complete.

Her transformation. That was it.

The solution had been right in front of her. It was drastic. She didn't know if she could pull it off.

Sheetal felt a pang of regret. Was she really about to give up her opportunity to be seen?

Yes. Yes, she was.

"And now, welcome our fifth and final champion, Sheetal Mistry of House Pushya," proclaimed House Dhanishta's Esteemed Patriarch. Jeet was still fuming, but his attendants finally said something to quiet him down.

"Come, Sheetal," Charumati said, touching her forehead in blessing. "It is your turn to shine."

Everything had a cost; it just depended on what you were willing to pay.

Her pulse sprinting at top speed, Sheetal sat down on the

cushion behind her dilruba. She brushed her damp palms on her sari. Did full stars have this problem, or was she just lucky that way?

Until now, she hadn't really accepted she was transforming. Somehow she'd still believed she could stay right where she was, precariously balanced between mortal and star.

What did it matter if someone asked you to choose between hands and wings when wings weren't real? But now they were, and she had to deal with it.

"Minal," she asked as casually as she could, "can you help me with this string?"

Minal, who'd never bothered with music since their earsplitting unit on the recorder in fifth grade, dropped down next to her. "What's going on?"

"Tell Padmini to bring me my circlet," Sheetal whispered. "When she comes to inspire me."

"What?"

"Tell her to bring me the circlet." Sheetal might not need the circlet for her scheme, but it would make a great symbol.

Minal nodded and left.

Her belly slackening in relief, Sheetal arranged the neck of her dilruba against her shoulder.

That simple contact sent the music flooding through her. It longed to live, to be expressed, to float from heart to heart.

She could have dissolved into it. She could, even now, just give in. But she didn't; a few wisps of humanity remained within her, and she clung to them like a rope.

The court of stars watched her, expectant. Waiting for her to wow them; waiting for her to colossally wreck it all.

She shut her eyes, imagining being inspired. In her mind, music danced from her onto the strings, notes ringing out in a metallic glossolalia like a human's voice.

Story. She was nothing but the words of a story, one tale weaving imperceptibly into the next. She was the loom that wove the tapestry. She was the tapestry that joined all things.

Her insides had been hollowed out, leaving only melody and harmony, scales and song. A remote part of her mind observed that the entire hall had hushed, all whispers silenced, but that observation had no meaning.

Sheetal let her fingers shimmy along the strings, cajoling the instrument to surrender its secrets. It was a love song, a paean to the dreams she had once sung in a backyard full of green grass and white daisies.

The music blazed inside her, demanding release. Now she understood why Nani and Charumati had chosen her as their champion, why they'd planned this moment for when she stood in the space between worlds. The stars gave voice to the sidereal melody, but only Sheetal could actually reach past that and create her own song.

*This is what you were born for, star daughter,* the starsong told her. *Songcraft.*

The song was right.

Giving this moment up was going to be the hardest thing she'd ever done.

"Stop!" Charumati cried.

Sheetal opened her eyes, her core alight, to see the court gawking at her mother. It was happening. She had just enough time to think, *I'm going to be sick,* before Padmini appeared before her, box in hand.

She could feel Minal, Dev, Padmini, and even Beena eyeing her with concern, and she shut them all out. It was the only way she'd be able to do this.

Before Padmini could ask what was going on, Sheetal wrested the box from her hands and prized out the starry circlet. Her mother and Nani were both running toward her, but they couldn't reach her before she jammed the circlet onto her head.

And then, finally, finally, finally, she set her fire free.

Instantly her fingers stung as if brushed by invisible nettles. Ice stabbed through her, a knife of cold dousing her inner flame, before it flared again, filling her.

Then she relaxed backward into the song, into the cosmic dance that linked all beings, celestial and earthbound, through all time and space.

The room grew silver with starshine. Sheetal's temples throbbed in time with her galloping heart.

She sank her teeth into her tongue, taking solace in the pain. First this flame, ignored and suppressed for so long, had burned Dad. Then she'd thought maybe she could use it to fix everyone else. But it had always been waiting to transform her.

A voice came from far off, high with alarm: "Sheetal, dikri, what did you do?"

She was warm, so very warm. Her brain pounded with heat. The song rushed in and around her, discordant, raucous. It hurt so much. But she stayed with it, studying the individual strands, teasing out their meaning.

"Oh, no," someone else said. Minal.

Sheetal's blood swirled, afire. Her skin burned so horribly, she wanted to scratch her face off just to stop the pain.

There was anger in the song, wrath and disdain and undisguised hatred. It felt like lava, guzzling everything in its path before it cooled to stone. Its flood of fury and malice nearly washed her away.

This was old, old anger, woven into the very fabric of the starry court, and Sheetal couldn't blame anyone for feeling it. She'd never be able to undo what Dev's ancestor had done.

But not everyone wanted revenge. Not everyone thought the old taboo needed to be carried down through generations. She could hear Padmini and Kaushal, full of affection and protective worry.

Sheetal concentrated on that, tuning everything else out. She was sure it would cleave her in two: the call of the constellation, her family in the nakshatra, her blood that even now twisted into a new shade, a new substance.

Every star joined hands in the cosmic dance, encircling her. The mortal part of her submitted easily, folding into the part that was star and shining silver and hot enough to melt anything that resisted it.

Her cells shifted from flesh to light while her core burned

as if it would consume her whole. Her sense of time expanded from the brief leaf dance from branch to ground of a human girl to the vast spectrum of days known to a star.

Out of nowhere, Dad appeared in her mind—his laugh, his wit, his love. Memories floated by: their first astronomy lesson, when he'd taught her about quasars and neutron stars and joked about the level of radiation she was putting out. His proud expression whenever they discussed the biographies he'd given her. The moment when she'd seen him lying in the ICU bed, harmed by her hand. *No.* She wouldn't give Dad up. Not now, not ever.

*Wait,* Sheetal screamed. *I don't want this! I was wrong.*

Terror ate black holes in her as she tried to get away. But there was nowhere to go, and so she sang. She sang and sang, her voice tearing free and dissolving into starlight. She sang her love, her defiance. She sang for herself. It was a song no one else could hear, a song of flame, of transformation.

Continuing to sing, she ripped open the scab on her thumb, and a drop of still-human blood appeared.

As she thrashed and tumbled through the cosmos within herself, she pinned her attention to that red bead. *This is who I am.* She drove it like a stake deep into the soil of her heart and secured it with her love for Dad, Radhikafoi and her family, Minal, and Dev. Whatever else happened to her, that part would always bloom.

"Sheetal!" Nani's voice lashed through the night. "Stop this."

But it was too late. Sheetal's radiance flooded the universe as she took her place in the Pushya nakshatra.

When she opened her eyes, she stood by the viewing pool, and she knew right away that everything was different. The way it gleamed brighter, felt more ethereal . . . the way she now realized the starsong she thought she'd heard so distinctly before had been muffled, scratchy, like a video call with bad reception. Now it rang out in unadulterated perfection, each note a miracle.

The whispers and murmurs intensified until they hissed around her like vipers.

Sheetal saw understanding dawn in her grandmother's silver-brown eyes.

"Beti," said Nani, a volcano of grief and fury bubbling just beneath her outer layer of calm. "You cannot do this."

Sheetal should probably feel triumphant. Instead, she just felt sad and exhausted. And she still wasn't done.

Minal gave her a searching look. "Are you okay? That was . . ."

Sheetal obliged her with a strained smile, then faced the hundreds of pairs of disbelieving eyes. Blood fizzing bright in her veins, she could only pray she'd done the right thing.

"Yes, I am," she told Minal. "Yes, I can," she told Nani. "You swore as long as our nakshatra won, I could have the blood. You didn't say *who* had to win for us."

Charumati laughed with sheer delight.

Forgetting the rest of the court, forgetting its whispers,

Sheetal turned to the boy who had come such a long way to support his cousin—but also to support her. The thing she was about to ask was so huge, she wouldn't blame him if he said no. "Sing for me?"

To his credit, Dev sounded more skeptical than anything. "You want *me* to compete."

"Yep. As my champion."

Next to them, Jeet snorted. "Pitting my cousin-brother against me? That's your plan?"

Sheetal jerked. She'd forgotten he was even there.

Dev glanced at Sheetal, his dark brown eyes even softer in her new vision, then at Jeet. His mouth tightened. "Okay. I'll do it."

Something sharp glittered in Jeet's grip. "I don't think so. You're not going to screw me over like this."

"Whoa, bhai, what are you doing?" Dev dove for him. "Have you lost it *completely*?"

"Stay out of this," Jeet snapped, jumping aside. "You betrayed me. Both of you."

Minal grabbed for the knife, but he shoved her away.

"What?" he taunted Sheetal, his blade glinting. "Don't tell me you thought Dev would save you."

And in the dark tradition of his ancestor, he cut her.

## 32

Sheetal stared at her bleeding stomach, at the silver liquid gushing from the wound. Seconds later, the agony hit, a sharp shriek, just as Dev pinned Jeet's arms behind him, aided by guards who had come rushing in through the wings.

Jeet's eyes were fixed on the blood. The rancor was gone from them, displaced by desperate need. "Just give me a drop," he wheedled. "I can still win!"

Padmini, Charumati, and Nani all surrounded Sheetal. "Oh, dikri," said Charumati, bending to examine the wound. "Oh, my daughter. I never wanted this."

"Nor did I," said Nani. Through the starsong, which was now woven around her like a net, Sheetal could feel Nani gathering healing magic.

Jeet broke free of Dev's hold. He lunged, and Sheetal cried out, but he wasn't even looking at her. At least, not at her face.

In the next instant, he was kneeling before her, swiping at the blood that had collected like mercury at her feet.

"Jeet!" Dev pleaded, his whole broken heart in that one name.

Before anyone could stop him, Jeet licked his finger.

Sheetal's heart swelled with revulsion and pity. No one should be drinking star's blood. Ever. And Jeet had been tricked into it. She had to help him.

Gritting her teeth against the pain, she grabbed his arm, the one that had held the blade, and hoisted him to his feet. Then she ignited.

She flared; she smoldered; she *burned*. Her silver radiance ratcheted higher and hotter, higher and hotter, until she blazed like Nani, as dazzling and fiery as a supernova. Dev lurched backward, and Minal hid her face against Padmini's shoulder. Charumati and Nana clasped hands, while Nani observed with a hawkish scrutiny.

Sheetal's near-unbearable brilliance bleached the room of everything else. White, blinding, but the opposite of a snowbank. Pure light, pure heat.

The flame sprang from her into Jeet, but this time, unlike with Dad, she was in control. She conducted it like a song: the pitch, the tempo, the scale. Jeet paled with that peculiar silvery cast as she scorched the stolen stellar blood right out of him.

He moaned. Sheetal knew he felt every second of the flame, felt it searing through his bones and into his marrow in search of every last droplet, and she didn't care. Let him suffer a little. It was only fair.

The pilfered blood rose around him in a halo of smoke and sparks, so bright no one watching could possibly miss it. The court erupted in shouts until Sheetal could hardly make out her own thoughts. For the first time ever, she felt whole.

She also felt like she was going to faint as her wound started spurting blood again.

"There," she cried, dropping Jeet's sleeve. He fell to the floor, panting. "See what happened to this mortal because of all these power games?"

With a detached expression like he'd removed himself from what was happening, Dev held out the vial he'd taken from Jeet's drawer, and the viewing pool magnified it a million times. "Like this."

"Don't forget, Rati gave him that blood," Sheetal called so the entire court could hear. "He didn't exactly have to twist her arm, either."

The sidereal melody grew deep and ugly, hungry bass notes where there should have been a clear treble. It raged around them, an inward assault. The ruling Esteemed Matriarch and Patriarch looked furious.

Rati, though, only seemed amused, a sly smile slipping over her face. She vanished into the audience, probably to leave the court while she still could. Well, she'd gotten what she wanted—seeing House Pushya publicly disgraced.

Both Charumati and Nani approached Sheetal then. She instinctively stepped back.

"Be still, child," Nani said. "We are trying to heal you."

"Child?" Sheetal laughed. "I thought I was an adult now?"

She felt more than saw Charumati steady her as Nani grasped her hand. "Hold fast, beti."

Sheetal half-heartedly leaned back into her mother's arms. But seconds later, she clutched at Charumati, writhing as Nani inundated her with heat, with radiation, with power.

When Nani let go, the wound was gone, the skin perfect.

Sheetal felt amazing, like she could soar through the universe and never stop. Or kiss Dev for hours. Or eat all the things she'd missed on the banquet tables at the ball.

While Charumati held the bloody knife by its hilt and incinerated it, Nani advanced on Jeet.

"What is the meaning of this?" Her barely checked wrath made Sheetal's look like cooling cinders in comparison. "You intrude into my court and harm my family? Did you truly believe you would succeed?"

Sheetal glanced from Nani to Jeet, and her fury trickled out of her as swiftly as it had come, leaving only sorrow. Pain bridged the gaps between them. And how very fast unchecked pain could fester, one terrible choice turning into a chain of terrible choices through the centuries, each feeding the next. "You really hate me, don't you?" she asked him.

"You took my chance from me," Jeet said hoarsely. "What do *you* think?"

She turned to Nani and Charumati. "Honestly? I think it's time we all stop holding grudges."

Her grandmother, however, loomed over the still-pinioned Jeet.

Her words were antagonistic, full of barbs. "This mortal boy will be made a black hole and loosed into the night sky. It will be his fate to spend eternity fruitlessly swilling all things into himself, always thirsting for the light that can never warm him."

The crowd hummed with shock. Even Nana looked perturbed. But he merely said, "As you will, my wife."

Sheetal exhaled irritably. There Nani went again, taking over. "No."

The crowd whirled in its seats.

"I get it," she said, glowing with all the fire she could call up. "I do. He did a horrible, horrible thing, and I kind of want to cut him back. But we can't do this anymore."

Charumati touched her arm. "He hurt you, my daughter."

"And that's why I'm the one who gets to decide what happens to him."

Sheetal knelt before Jeet, who flinched. He might have done some seriously awful stuff, but he was far from the only one, and it wasn't like he'd gotten to this point alone. She wouldn't let Nani ignore the stars' own culpability and pin everything on him.

This was Sheetal's story, and a fairy-tale crime deserved a fairy-tale punishment. "Don't worry, I'm not going to lay a finger on you. I don't have to, not when the stars will turn

411

their faces from you. And you know what that means? No more inspiration. You wanted to be remembered for all time? Too bad. Feel free to toil away in obscurity, though."

He blanched.

"And," Nani vowed, not to be outdone, "though it is traditional to do so, *your* memory will not be cleansed. You will recall every moment of this. I will see to that myself."

Sheetal wanted to argue—that was way too harsh; none of the other contestants would ever remember they'd been here, and wasn't losing inspiration enough of a blow?—but Nani's merciless manner made it clear that if Sheetal pushed any further, Nani would just override her completely. At least this way, Jeet got to live.

So even though she ached to think of what it would do to Dev, Sheetal let it pass.

"Oh," she went on, "and if you try to pick up a knife to hurt anyone ever again, it'll rebound and cut you. Probably better to steer clear of knives altogether."

She didn't actually have that power, of course, but it wasn't like Jeet knew any better.

"You can't do this," he spat. "I'm under House Revati's protection."

Sheetal swept her arm to encompass the court. "Do you see House Revati up here with you? No? Then I guess they're not protecting you anymore."

"You're a poseur," he informed her. "You only got this far by luck, and that'll never hold out."

Sheetal let the words spray over her like sea foam. The wave might sting, but in the end, the foam would dissolve. "You can still fix things with Dev. Just, you know, do better than this."

Jeet's gaze hardened as he met his cousin's devastated face. He stared, cold as a midwinter night, then turned away.

The ruling Esteemed Matriarch, who had been observing from the stage, nodded in acknowledgment. "A fine solution. Remove the mortal," she told the guards. "It is time for the judges' deliberation." She glanced quizzically at Sheetal. "I trust you understand that, having relinquished your mortality, you are now disqualified from acting as champion?"

"I do, but hang on." Sheetal inhaled down to her diaphragm, siphoning strength from the sidereal song as it enveloped her in its notes. "We're not done yet."

Nani and Charumati had been right about one thing. This was her blood, her birthright. This was her.

She stood tall and addressed the court. "I, Sheetal Mistry, of the Pushya nakshatra, name mortal Dev Merai as my champion. He will be singing an original composition for you today."

That would have to be eloquent enough.

The audience exclaimed, sending currents of delight and dismay through the starsong, mixed with relish at the unexpected scandal. Jeet screwed his eyes shut before the guards dragged him away.

"This is ridiculous," said Nani. "You have hardly reached majority!" Sheetal heard voices in the audience that agreed, that supported Nani and her stance on separating the realms.

"Well?" asked the Esteemed Patriarch of House Dhanishta. "We will honor this declaration, but do not expect us to wait."

"*I* refuse to honor this declaration," Nani said.

"Stand down, Eshana," warned the ruling Esteemed Patriarch. "We will hear Sheetal's champion. I must confess, I am intrigued."

"So you were saying, dikri?" Charumati asked, her mouth twitching like she was suppressing a smile. Nani's look, on the other hand, threatened to burn the entire court to ashes.

*For Dad,* Sheetal thought. *And for me.*

If she didn't stand up now, she'd always be trailing after people who thought they knew better than she did about all things, whether it was Radhikafoi or Nani or even her mother. Cowering in their shadows instead of shining her own light.

"Do it, Sheetu," Minal whispered. "Whatever you're going to do."

Dev watched her with trust in his eyes. "Ready when you are, star girl," he whispered.

Sheetal reached deep inside herself for the feeling that had come with overturning the jar of stardust, the feeling of inspiring another person, as well as the memory of actually being inspired. Her heart flashed to life, illuminated as it pumped the starry song through her veins. Her palms and the soles of her feet prickled.

Would this work? Her core sputtered with doubt. Maybe Nani was right, and she *was* too young.

No. She'd earned this.

While her flame bathed her body in a wash of power to rival Lord Surya himself, Sheetal threw her inspiration at Dev as hard as she could.

The energy passed into Dev and disappeared. But instead of feeling depleted, Sheetal felt even more alive.

*Yes.*

For a second, Dev looked like he'd been shocked. Then he smiled.

And then he began to sing.

The last line of the song floated through the room, so bright and mournful and resonant that for a long moment, no one moved.

Sheetal's heart was done for. Dev had basically ripped it out of her chest and ground it to pulp. That song, that *confession*, had to have been the best thing he had ever done, his masterpiece, drawing on everything he'd gone through over the past week and making the choice to hide nothing and instead offer it all up as a gift: from the day he met her to nearly losing her to where they stood now, every word wrapped in love.

And *she* had inspired that.

She shivered. The lyrics, the utter power of his voice, reverberated even now through the court, imprinting themselves on the most resistant of House Pushya's detractors.

But what would the judges say? They could be biased or just plain have bad taste.

And the other nakshatras, the ones the starry judges

belonged to, had no reason to love House Pushya.

Dev's final notes, rife with sorrow, with hope, faded until only a hush remained. Glancing around, Sheetal glimpsed tears sparkling on more faces than she could count. At least she wasn't the only one crying.

Charumati and Nana looked troubled, but Nani sat with a stone face. The astral melody betrayed nothing of her actual state of mind as Dev stumbled down the platform and headed toward House Pushya's tent.

*Oh, Nani. Come on. I know that moved you. I know it.*

Looking dazed, Dev took the extra seat Beena had placed next to Sheetal's. "How was it?" he whispered, his beautiful eyes lit from within.

"You . . ." She shook her head. "I can't."

The judges had retreated behind their curtain of invisibility to deliberate. Sheetal started gnawing on her cuticle before catching herself. So becoming a full star hadn't changed everything.

If they didn't win, she reminded herself, she'd done her best. They both had. She found Dev's hand with her own, not minding at all when he squeezed back too hard.

A few minutes later, the judges reemerged, led by the mortal man. "We have reached our decision."

Hanging on to Dev's hand, Sheetal tuned everything out but the judge's words. "Each performance was a piece of art," he droned. "I wasn't even sure we'd be able to pick a winner. All of you should be proud."

416

*Ugh,* she thought, *get on with it.*

"But alas, a choice had to be made, and I'm glad as can be to announce the winner of this competition: Dev Merai, with his song from the heart!"

Applause thundered through the court, laced with shouts of gratification and grumbles of disappointment. Sheetal could have screamed. He'd done it, he'd done it, *he'd done it*! He'd won!

Dev looked flabbergasted. In front of everyone, he pulled Sheetal out of her seat and spun her around. "I don't believe it!"

"I do." Grinning, Sheetal returned the spin. Minal grabbed her in a bear hug, while Padmini and Beena formed an impromptu dancing circle around them. A few of the younger stars from House Pushya, including Kaushal, rushed down from the stands and joined in.

The former ruling matriarch gave one sharp clap, silencing the court. "Many congratulations to House Pushya on its victory this day. House Pushya will succeed House Dhanishta as next to rule over our court."

Even Nani had to be happy about that.

Along with the rest of her house and her friends, Sheetal cheered. Her skin exuded silver flame, her hair shimmered and flashed, and her mind whirled. There was so much to do, so much to think through. First, of course, she had to get home and save Dad. Nothing was going to stop her from doing that. And now, she realized, her breath catching, she didn't even need anyone else's blood to do it.

Nani wouldn't close the gates, then. If she tried, she'd be trapping Sheetal on Earth, leaving her to burn out like Ojasvini had.

"And now," declared the former ruling patriarch, "it is time to present the winner with his well-deserved prize. Mortal Dev Merai, please approach the dais."

Only too late, far too late, her stomach falling ten stories, did Sheetal remember the prize for winning the competition had to go to someone. The prize Dev had never wanted.

And from the horrified look on Dev's face, he did, too.

Nani and Nana held a whole conversation in a glance, and when Sheetal checked the starsong, they'd bricked their feelings away behind a harmonious front. Whatever Nani thought about her plans being usurped and her secret revealed, she would never dream of letting it travel outside their immediate family. Let rumors spread as rumors would; she wouldn't bother to address them.

No, she would take her revenge in subtler ways. Sheetal's euphoria curdled like expired milk.

"How fortunate our desires align." Nani moved toward Dev like a panther coiled to spring. "Certainly the Pushya nakshatra can do no less than honor our champion and his victory by presenting him with his award."

"I don't need any award," he said hastily. "Give it to Priyanka. Or better yet, keep it. I was just filling in. Like a substitute teacher. No one rewards substitute teachers."

418

"No," said Nani, silky as a snake's hiss, "I insist. You won the competition, and we would be remiss as hosts to deny you that."

"Mom?" Sheetal tried.

Her mother merely gave her a frail smile. "The Esteemed Matriarch is correct. It is stated in the bylaws: the prize must be awarded to the winner."

Nani's next words came as a whisper only those closest to her could hear. "Make no mistake; the mortal boy will get what he has earned—eternal renown. What you, my dikri, have helped him earn."

"Nani, please," Sheetal begged. "Please don't do this to him."

Nani only laughed. When she spoke, her voice was as imperious as Sheetal had ever heard it. "You are young, Sheetal. So very young. You do not yet know what you do not know. If you must purge this youthful rebellion from your system and wander the mortal world for now, I can wait. Heal your papa. Enjoy your time with him. I have had many eons in which to learn patience."

Nana and she linked arms with a shell-shocked Dev. "But do not forget that what is a lifetime to a mortal is but a blink of an eye to a star, and as you mature, you will find battles are not won in a single day."

Then they escorted him to the stage to receive his prize.

Charumati settled in beside Sheetal. "Seizing power is one

thing, and holding it is quite another," she said. "It is like trying to grasp water or sand; eventually it spills through the cracks and into the hands of those keen to catch it."

Her starry diadem sitting heavy on her head, Sheetal wondered if now might be a good time to find out just how long she could stay sober on frostberry wine.

# PART THREE

*Be humble, for you are made of earth.*
*Be noble, for you are made of stars.*

—UNKNOWN

*M*y mother's speech was both bright and dark, twinkling in and out of reach. She wore diamonds in her hair like war wounds. I saw the flame that burned within her, hungry and silhouetted with the shapes of secrets.

I saw how those shapes separated my mother from her mother, how they forged gulfs and filled them with poisonous waters. I saw how those same waters threatened to submerge us all.

I lay back in the grass and spread my arms, digging my fingers into the soil to remember myself. Then I took to the skies and burned to transform. But still my heart, with its human memories rooted deep inside, remained mine to rule.

And in keeping it so, in guarding it well, I learned how to make that flame my own.

—FROM SHEETAL'S JOURNAL

## 33

Charumati and Radhikafoi stood at either side of the hospital bed, watching Sheetal. Only the occasional beeping of the machines broke the silence as Dad slept on. It was all up to her now.

Sheetal lowered the collar of his hospital gown, then reached for the sterilized safety pin in her pocket.

She could already feel the difference, and she hadn't even stabbed herself yet.

Her blood hadn't been enough before, but she'd quested for Dad's sake, competed for him, even sacrificed for him, and along the way, she'd made it enough.

She pricked the meat of her thumb and gasped at the rush of pain. A drop of blood appeared, pure silver without a single spot of scarlet.

Sheetal let the drop fall. It landed on Dad's chest, flooding the sterile room with silver starlight that diffused over his skin.

And Dad flared bright, beautiful, with a star's flame. Sheetal's core mirrored him, singing a story of healing. For an instant, the glow was so potent, she couldn't see anything else.

Behind her, Radhikafoi cried out. "What happened? Is he all right?"

The radiance dimmed.

Two heartbeats passed, then three.

Alarms blared as Dad sat up, his face ten years younger. He looked healthy and strong enough to run a marathon. Best of all, he looked like Dad again. "What did I miss?"

Sheetal hugged him hard, and he returned it just as firmly. He felt so real, so human, with all the sweat and troubles and joys that mortality brought with it. Her throat dammed up as she listened to his pulse, counting the beats and assuring herself it wasn't fading before letting go.

Radhikafoi instantly grabbed his hand and pressed it to her heart. "You did it, beta," she said. "You really did it."

Then Dad caught sight of Charumati, whose eyes were wide with wonder and wet with tears. A spectrum of emotions played out in his expression, from incredulity to sadness to hope, as she tugged off the scarf tied over her head. Her hair tumbled down, sparkling and shimmering like the starshine it was. "My Gautam, my jeevansaathi," she murmured, her words like song. "You waited for me."

"And I'd do it again," he said. "You haven't aged a day, my Charu jaan, not like me."

She laughed, and Sheetal wondered how even a single human had ever heard it and taken her for anything but magic. "Nonsense, you are just as dashing as the day we met. Perhaps more so."

Both Sheetal and Radhikafoi reluctantly stepped aside as Charumati glided toward the head of the bed. "We have much to talk about, my love," she said, soft as a secret. Dad nodded and took her delicate hands in his own.

Sheetal followed Radhikafoi out and shut the door behind them.

"I'm proud of you, beta," her auntie said abruptly. "I should have told you about the letter sooner."

"Uh, thanks." Sheetal felt all shy and embarrassed. They didn't talk like this. Not ever. It was awkward, but nice, too.

"Don't think this means you're not still enrolled in the PSAT course. I arranged for you to make up the days you missed." There was something strange about the way Radhikafoi was staring at her, almost like she expected Sheetal to argue and storm off.

Like she was worried Sheetal didn't need her anymore.

The class sounded even less appealing after three days surrounded by the stars. But sometimes love came in the weirdest packages. Sheetal hid her smile. "I wouldn't dream of it."

"Oh. Well, good." Radhikafoi rummaged in her enormous purse until she found a candy bar, then thrust it at Sheetal. "Here, have a snack. You'll need your energy to help me keep them out so your mummy and papa can talk."

Sure enough, an army of doctors and nurses was descending on Dad's room. Sheetal nodded at Radhikafoi, then chomped down on the candy bar and steeled herself to guard the door.

Tomorrow there would be chores to do and biographies to read, fathers to make dinner with, aunties to surprise with celestial golden sofas. For now, though, Sheetal was back in the Night Market with Minal, who'd wasted no time claiming her magical shopping spree. So far, she'd found a dress made of wildflowers and a tablecloth that whipped up complicated pastries on command.

Sheetal sang a single note, high and clear. In response, Padmini appeared, bearing a silver-stringed black crystal harp.

Vanita and Amrita rushed to pet the harp and test its strings. When they knocked on the body, the crystal rang out with the sound of wind on a frosty evening. "Yesssssss," hissed Vanita, her long curtain of white hair stark against the golden green of her eyes. "You have learned to hear with your dead mortal ears."

"Play a song with us, one of laughter and starry tears," added Amrita, her teeth flashing, her black hair blending in with the harp. She pushed a chair toward Sheetal.

*Darkness in light; light in darkness.*

Sheetal sat down on the chair and rested the crystal harp against her thigh. She glanced up at the sky, where her family twinkled among so many other stars, all watching her. All singing, all lending her their magic. Padmini smiled at her, twinkling, too, and nestled closer to Minal.

Sheetal's fingers pranced and pirouetted over the strings, and her voice poured forth, telling the story of the girl who, though technically full star, was still half mortal at heart and would have it no other way. The harp sisters joined in, their notes weaving together with hers in a web that, for the span of a song, fell over the entire Market and held it captive.

When they drew to a close, the spice trader nodded. "Like the heavens themselves were singing." Others murmured their assent.

"Star girl!" called a familiar voice. Every hair on Sheetal's arms and the back of her neck stood as straight as the guards at the gates to Svargalok.

He'd heard her sing at last.

Her whole body tensed. He couldn't have hated it, but what if he did? Or what if it just didn't live up to what he'd expected?

Dev sauntered out of the shadows, one hand tucked behind his back. She couldn't tell from his face what he thought. "There was a long line."

"Ooh," called Amrita. "A tall, dark, mysterious stranger!"

Vanita offered a lascivious wink. "Just in time to save you from danger?"

"Nah, I can save myself just fine," Sheetal tossed back. Hoping she sounded casual, she tapped her foot and asked Dev, "So did you find me non-horror-movie ice cream or not?"

Dev revealed a dripping version of one of the foot-high

cones Sheetal had seen on her first visit to the Night Market. "Starry macaron sundae sounded harmless enough. Not to mention appropriate."

He offered her the cone with its tower of swirling silver-blue-and-purple scoops.

She took a giant lick. Why wasn't he saying anything about the song?

The harp sisters watched with glee. "Tell us this story! In all its glory!" they sang.

Dev nodded at them. "Nice to meet you, uh . . ."

"Amrita and Vanita," Sheetal said around a mouthful of the richest, most satisfying ice cream she'd ever had. It tasted like wonder mixed with wine, if wine were the night sky distilled into a thick syrup.

"So?" asked Minal. "Did you hear her sing?" Next to her, Padmini covered her laugh with her hand.

Sheetal glared. "Minu! Come on."

"Well, did you? We're all dying to know."

Dev's face went soft as he looked at Sheetal. "I've never heard anything like that. It's like . . . you're a star. That's the only word for it. Like listening to the sky."

She smiled. She was pretty sure it was the dorkiest smile ever.

"Awwww, he likes it!" Minal heckled, and the moment was broken. "So sweet."

"Thanks again for the ice cream," Sheetal hurried to say before anyone else could chime in. "It's really good."

"The guy at the booth recognized me and said I didn't have to pay." Dev didn't sound pleased about that. Ever since they'd gotten home, the recordings online of him singing had gone viral, and it showed no sign of stopping. Talent agents were calling and e-mailing, fans were flooding his inboxes on social media, and people on the street were calling out to him for autographs.

He'd even tried putting up a garbage song to scare people away—deliberately off, hoarse, and scratchy, with terrible lyrics. It didn't matter; they only clamored for more.

Sheetal winced in sympathy. Dev was going to be seen whether he wanted to be or not. And as his girlfriend, so would she. Maybe the secret of the stars would be out again before long, no matter what Nani had to say about it.

At least then she wouldn't have to wear this stupid wig. Even here in the Night Market, she hadn't found anything to disguise her hair.

"I'm really sorry," she said for what seemed the billionth time.

Dev didn't answer. She couldn't blame him if he was still mad. At least he hadn't dumped her.

Padmini broke the silence. "So all of you are familiar with Orion's Belt?"

Sheetal nodded. "Yeah, why?"

"It is a waist of space." Sheetal stared at her. Padmini grinned. "When Dev was teaching me mortal names for our

430

constellations, he insisted I learn this particular jest and use it to aggravate everyone I encounter."

Minal groaned. "Oh, gods, it's like a virus. Soon the whole universe will be infected by all these puns. Thanks a million, Dev."

Dev sneaked a lick of Sheetal's ice cream. "You bet."

Sheetal elbowed him. "Get your own."

"Maybe later." He held out a hand. "Can we take a walk?"

Sheetal gestured toward Minal and Padmini, who were too busy gazing at each other to notice. "I think we could walk to the North Pole and back, probably."

She took another bite of ice cream, but there was no way she was finishing this behemoth without dying of sugar shock. She gave the cone to Vanita. "It's all yours."

Then she laced her fingers with Dev's, and they strolled along one of the curving paths between the stalls.

"So," Dev asked lightly, "how are you doing with everything?"

"About like you are," Sheetal admitted. "I mean, I'm so glad my dad's okay, and he seems really happy to see my mom. But what's going to happen now? Will I age super slowly? What if Nani's so mad, she'll never listen to me?"

It wasn't enough to have won the competition for her nakshatra; Sheetal couldn't pretend she didn't belong up there anymore. But she couldn't throw away everything down here, either.

And that meant splitting her life between two worlds.

She didn't add that if she did age slowly, Dev would get older way before she did, but he didn't need her to.

"We'll figure it out," he said. "Keep checking the Night Market, keep looking in old books. Maybe there's a spell or something. You can't be the first star who wanted to stay here and live out her mortal life. Besides, your nani needs you. She'll come around."

Sheetal hoped so. Nani had made it clear she wouldn't give up without a fight, and Sheetal was still upset about having been treated like a pawn, but she did want to be part of her starry family—and *that* meant finding ways to work things out.

Besides, someone had to be there to help Kaushal remind the stars why humanity mattered.

As for Charumati, she actually seemed proud of Sheetal. *Like mother, like daughter, I guess?*

"Don't force me to make the obligatory wish-upon-a-star joke," Dev threatened.

Sheetal burst out laughing. "Okay, okay! Just no more puns for at least the next twenty-four hours, all right?"

"No promises," he said. "Anyway, Minal's right, and I hope you'll sing with me. I mean, ice cream taller than you are should be worth at least one duet, right?"

Sheetal nodded. "I will. Any word from Jeet?" Jeet had been ignoring all Dev's text messages, calls, and e-mails. When their family tried to intervene, Jeet had warned them to

432

mind their own business or he'd cut them out, too.

It wasn't fair that the other contestants didn't remember anything about the starry court or the competition, but both Dev and Jeet always would. At least Priyanka had apologized for doubting Sheetal before they'd left the starry court. For her part, Sheetal had promised to do what she could to help Priyanka's family.

Not that Priyanka even knew who she was now.

Dev's smile crumbled. "I don't want to talk about it."

"I'm so sorry," Sheetal said again, knowing how useless it was even as she said it.

"It was my decision, too," he reminded her.

They stopped in front of a stall illuminated by glowing jasmine blossoms. The proprietor stared, as though trying to place Dev. Sheetal quickly cupped his face in her hands and kissed him hard, kissed him like he was the air and water and earth to her fire, letting her lips say everything her words couldn't.

When they pulled apart, she whispered, "What are we going to do about the inspiration thing? I can't inspire you. Not after all that."

"I've been thinking." Dev ran a thumb over the back of her hand. "You know how your dad never got inspired by your mom after that first time? Well, I asked her about it, and she said you can control it."

Sheetal wanted so much to believe that. She thought back

to Dev's dream, to the pitiable people who had physically fallen apart as they forgot anything outside their work and their muses. Who had burned away from too much inspiration.

But Dad had never been like that. The only flame in him was the torch he kept burning for his wife. He nurtured her memory and grieved her absence, and he still lived.

It hurt to accept, but maybe he'd never wanted more from his career. Maybe all he'd ever wanted was to spend his days studying the sky and dreaming of the stars. "Go on."

Dev hummed a few bars of his birthday song. "You didn't notice I wrote that one without your help?"

Sheetal didn't even try to hide her doubt. "How do you know that, though?"

"There's nothing like a star's inspiration. It's this stupid, impossible high that you just ride to the end of. There's no struggle. Nothing standing in your way. That's what makes it so addictive." He gave her a bashful grin. "Let's just say writing that song was, uh, not like that."

"Okay, so? How do I not inspire you on purpose, then?"

"Whenever you're down here and feel like doing it, just inspire someone else instead. Energy needs to flow, right, so instead of fighting it, redirect it! The world's full of blocked people."

She considered that. "Sounds simple enough. Like something my dad would say."

"It was actually your dad's idea," Dev said, reaching up to

play with her wig. "He told your mom to try it, and it worked."

Sheetal tore off the wig and stuffed it into her bag. After all, she didn't need it here in the Night Market. "I should've guessed."

Dev smiled his answer against her mouth, and he tasted better than even the ice cream. Sweet, warm, and full of sunshine. Her own light flared, brilliant against her closed lids.

Harp strings began to trill, saturating the air with shimmering ornaments. "That is quite enough of your face-to-face!"

"Such thoughtless knavery in this, *our* place!"

Sheetal took the hint and let go of Dev, though not without rolling her eyes. "I think we're being summoned."

"Shall we sing again?" asked Vanita when they got back. Judging by the smudge near her mouth, she'd happily polished off what was left of the ice cream cone.

"Perhaps one about your mother?" asked Amrita, smacking her lips. Sheetal didn't want to know what *she'd* been eating.

She looked from Dev to Minal, who was cracking up, to Padmini, who'd been staring at the heavens, and smiled. Tomorrow they would deliver sofas and make dinner with fathers, deal with irate cousins and grandmothers and unexpected singing careers, and figure out how to navigate life between magical and mundane worlds.

Right now, however, she had friends who saw her—the real her—and a shining crystal harp. "Well, I do know a few more stories. . . ."

435

# Acknowledgments

They say it takes a village to raise a child or publish a book, and I'm here to say that's one hundred percent accurate. Heartfelt thanks go out to:

First readers Amy Bai, Casey Blair, Roshani Chokshi, Rosamund Hodge, Jessica Kormos, Justine Larbalestier, Claire Legrand, Anna-Marie McLemore, Caitlyn Paxson, and Jennifer Walkup, who read what amounted to a seed striving to sprout and offered some much-needed Miracle-Gro.

Nova Ren Suma and the summer 2015 Djerassi workshop. Nova, your praise and notes spurred me to go much deeper.

Vinod Mishra, for telling me about the nakshatras. Danielle Friedman and Kunal Thakrar, for helping clarify what an intensive care unit is like and what could have landed Sheetal's dad there.

Vashti Bandy, B. A. Barnett, Victoria Sandbrook Flynn, Annaka Kalton, Jocelyn Koehler, Claire Legrand, Jennifer Mace, Anna-Marie McLemore, and Renee Melton, for your invaluable insights and encouragement through the years of revising and rewriting. I'm so happy to call you friends and read your work, too!

Patrice Caldwell, a true advocate of diverse voices. You did so much to help me get here, and I'll always be grateful.

J. Koyanagi, for the love, heart talks, and clear sight.

Cindy Pon, for insisting my day would come and being one of my dearest friends and favorite writers. Karuna Riazi, for never once doubting, reading so many snippets, and always reminding me we both can and must make our magic. Sukanya Venkatraghavan, for the talks, love, and Kali earrings. Mikey Vuoncino, for your unwavering belief in me and the stories I have to tell, plus the suggestion for why Sheetal's dad won the Nobel Prize. The Sisterhood of the Moon, for tons of folklore and glitter along the way. You're the best supporters this dreamer could ask for.

Cheerleader readers Jessica B. Cooper, Jennifer Crow, and Grace Nuth, for reading and squealing about how awesome the book was long and loudly enough to get me past the precarious spots when I was ready to throw it all in the trash.

Diana DeVault, you blessing with rainbow hair, you. I would have given up long before now if you hadn't been there with your love, steadfast enthusiasm, and excellent hugs!

Lindsey Márton O'Brien, for your love and faith and for my sparkling jewel of a website, and Asma Kazi, for plucking the Night Market right out of my imagination to form the backdrop of that website.

Terri Windling, for nurturing such an inclusive mythic arts community in a time when I didn't see stories like this one anywhere and for believing my voice a necessary part of it.

Holly Black, Plot Whisperer Extraordinaire. A glass of frostberry wine and a front-seat ticket to the celestial art competition for you. If I ever do find those sentient cloud barrettes, they're all yours.

Laini Taylor, for your beautiful "Stars" Laini's Lady quotation and for inspiring me with your own enchanting tales and love of whimsy.

Neil Gaiman and Charles Vess, for your splendid illustrated novel *Stardust*, which first inspired *Star Daughter* ("I know, I'll write a story about a girl whose mother is a star in a Hindu constellation!").

The We Need Diverse Books organization, for awarding me an inaugural Walter Dean Myers Grant while I was revising an early draft of this book, and the late Walter Dean Myers himself, a champion of inclusion and real representation in media. We all deserve to have our stories told—in our own voices.

Super agent Beth Phelan, for your no-nonsense editorial eye, your business savvy, and your kindness—and to the entire Gallt & Zacker agency for caring so well for its clients. Here's to many more books together!

My brilliant editor Stephanie Stein, who got my vision and guided me with liberal amounts of stardust, wisdom, and support to make it real. This book is what it is because of you. You deserve an entire table of astral sweets and a trip to the Night Market, World's Best Editor.

Charlie Bowater, for your cover art that leaves me gasping at its impossible beauty. You brought Sheetal to life in a way I never even dared dream of. And that moonlight lotus!

Corina Lupp, for your incredible cover design that makes me swoon every time I see it. (That title treatment! That fili-gree detail! It's all so gorgeous!)

Louisa Currigan, Kadeen Griffiths, Jessica Berg, Vanessa Nuttry, Michael D'Angelo, Shannon Cox, Deanna Hoak, Mary Ann Seagren, and all the other delightful people with and at HarperCollins for everything you've poured into making this book a magical object people can hold in their hands. What an amazing team! Thank you, thank you, thank you.

My beloved husband, Ed, who wouldn't stop bugging me to finish this book whenever I felt like quitting. And look what happened; I sold it. Maybe I should listen to you more, huh?

My teacher Shankara, who sits with me in Truth. Thank you, thank you, thank you.

And finally, Devi, who always pushes me to bloom. May we all seek to be light in the world, through art and compassion. ॐ

# DON'T MISS THE NEXT
# **MAGICAL READ**
# FROM SHVETA THAKRAR

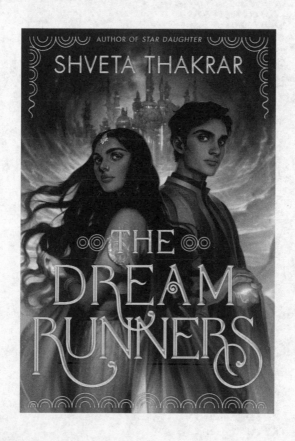

## KEEP READING FOR
## A SNEAK PEEK!

Wind whooshed past the rolled-down windows and sprayed Tanvi's bangs back into wings as she floored the gas pedal. The old Honda Civic's engine growled in response, underscoring the music blasting from her phone, and the tires gobbled up the curving highway mile by mile. On her left, the mountain glinted in the afternoon light like someone had painted it with honey. "Never gonna stop, never gonna stop, never, never, never gonna stop," Tanvi belted out, her voice high and breathy, and zoomed around a bend in the road.

Suddenly she stood on a bridge over a green-brown lake, the relentless sun glaring down over everything. Too hot. So hot. Tanvi was going to melt.

Wait, where was the car?

She turned to find it idling next to her at the edge of the bridge. No, not idling so much as smashed into a guardrail,

1

the front half folded into a perfect accordion. The pleats in the metal twinkled at her like a taunt.

Acidic horror ate through Tanvi, from the pit of her stomach right down to the tips of her toes. It wasn't her mom's Civic—but her stepdad's precious Maserati GranTurismo. Cherry red and flashy, the car he'd dubbed his baby, the one whose black leather interior he spent hours buffing to prevent cracks. He'd never let Tanvi sit in it, let alone drive it.

He was going to *kill* her.

Her phone rang from the mangled passenger seat, and Tanvi wrenched it free. Somehow, unlike the car, it was fine. She tilted the screen to see who was calling—

And woke to find herself gasping for air in a stranger's shadowy bedroom. A phone chirped inches away, half tangled in the actual dreamer's sheets.

Tanvi yanked back her empty hand from where it hovered over the sleeping girl's forehead, coaxing out the nightmare's substance one translucent wisp at a time, and muted the phone. She scowled down at the girl. Who slept with their ringer on?

The scowl turned to a shudder. Though her dream had been interrupted, the girl's dismay still pulsed, slimy and wet, in Tanvi's chest. It made her small. Terrified. Weak.

She hated this part of harvesting—having to inhabit the dream and become the dreamer. Knowing their innermost thoughts. Wanting what they did. Feeling what they felt, even when it was as banal as this.

2

Desperate to shove the dream residue away, Tanvi pulled the cork from the waiting amethyst dreamstone vial a little too hard. It came loose with an audible *pop*.

She swore under her breath, bracing herself to be caught, but the girl only shifted and mumbled.

In the meantime, led by Tanvi's will, the smokelike wisps she'd reaped floated over to the vial. Now she physically motioned them inside. As if the girl knew her dream had been lured elsewhere, she twisted again, craning her neck at an awkward angle. But as long as she didn't wake up, Tanvi couldn't care less if the girl sleep-somersaulted onto the floor.

The instant the final wisp entered the vial, Tanvi jammed the cork back in. Just like that, the glut of emotion dissolved. Tanvi was herself and only herself. Her head clear, she examined the vial. She'd definitely captured the nightmare—the purple dreamstone flickered with a faint inner fire—but it had cut off right as things had gotten interesting.

"Come *on*," she muttered into the gloom. She'd made the trek to this upscale apartment complex, staking her night's take on the people who lived here. She'd let her inner sense tell her, with its bright and dark spots, who dreamed and how deeply. And all she'd gained for her efforts was the sludge at the bottom of the barrel?

At least this one had some meat to it; the scraps she'd harvested from the girl's neighbors weren't worth the vials Tanvi had stored them in—running out of toilet bowl cleaner

3

and studying for an exam that got canceled. Junk-drawer dreams.

A last bit of residual fear quivered through her. *What if Venkat doesn't want them?*

Dreams were Tanvi's bread and butter, or in naga terms, her roti and ghee. Without engaging ones, she had no boon. No boon meant no bracelet. She'd have to keep hunting if she wanted to bulk up her skimpy harvest.

Shaking off the fear, she stowed the vial next to the other dreamstones in the pouch at her waist and pulled the drawstring shut.

The bedroom and the hallway past it were silent. Sometimes pets detected her presence and would meow or bark until their owners woke up. Nobody was home to check on this girl, it seemed. Good.

Not bothering to glance back, Tanvi tiptoed to the window, sucked on a lozenge that made her as boneless as liquid, and stole out into the night.

☾

A haze of exhaust shrouded the early autumn sky over Philadelphia. It seared Tanvi's lungs as she slunk through the city streets, determined to fill her two vacant dreamstones.

In the distance, the Ben Franklin Bridge arced over the river, glittering like the sea goddess's giant tiara it had been in a vision she'd harvested a few months ago.

Now *that* had been a boon-worthy dream.

Even though it was late, a buffet of potential dreamers drifted around her, from the wealthy people in Rittenhouse Square leaving swanky restaurants to the buskers and tourists on South Street to the office workers heading home from bar crawls in Center City. If only she could follow them all and reap every one of their dreams.

Glass crunched under her shoes, a pair of ballet flats Asha had given her to help her blend in on Prithvi. Tanvi vaguely registered that she'd stepped in the shards from a smashed bottle. She kicked them into a nearby drain.

The smart thing would be to call it a night. She had three dreams, even if two of them were boring.

But Venkat might not want them, and Tanvi knew she could do better than the meager wares she'd pulled in so far. Besides, it wasn't like she'd be back in Philadelphia anytime soon.

Dream runners circulated around the mortal world, never staying in any one place. That meant they could harvest from the full spectrum of dream flavors without the risk of being recognized. Recently Tanvi had gone to Beijing, Aix-en-Provence, Rio de Janeiro, and a tiny hilltop town in Mongolia where the sheep outnumbered the people—and often starred in their nocturnal rambles. Even there, she'd found the best wares, so how could she accept anything less tonight?

All she had to do was hurry.

Her mouth growing dry with excitement, she quickened her pace. What sorts of dreamers would get her closest to her bracelet?

Something collided with her, all muscle and hard bone. "Watch it!" a voice scolded, as near as a breath—way too near.

Tanvi's stomach clenched. Dream runners weren't supposed to let themselves be noticed, never mind getting so caught up in possibilities that they bumped into people. She might as well have been daydreaming.

"Sorry," she muttered, avoiding the boy's eyes, and brushed past him. The faster she got away, the faster he would forget her.

She hurried toward a crosswalk, her breath coiled, snakelike, in her lungs. Fifteen seconds passed, then thirty. But the boy didn't follow, and Tanvi could exhale again.

That had been careless of her. Foolish.

Her whole body still tensed for discovery, Tanvi peeked over her shoulder. No sign of the boy. The traffic light changed. Using the crowd around her as her shield, she stepped into the crosswalk.

"Wait up!" someone else shouted.

Tanvi kept walking. What potential dreamers said to one another outside their dreams wasn't any of her business.

"Hey! Didn't you hear me, Nitya?" the voice asked from beside her. "I saw that guy slam into you. He didn't even apologize."

Another step, and Tanvi made it to the other side of the street. So did the speaker, a Hmong girl with a shiny bob. No one Tanvi had ever seen before. But the girl was clearly talking to her.

Her insides swirled. *Two* people had noticed her? She had to get out of here—now.

"You look kind of out of it. Are you sure he didn't hurt you?"

Tanvi stared past the girl, gauging the best direction to run.

"Um." The girl gave a nervous laugh and changed the subject. "God, Mr. Collins is a *sadist*. Two pop quizzes in a row, like chem's the only class we have?"

"You're confused," Tanvi informed her. "I'm not whoever you think I am."

"But—" the girl began. Tanvi took off before she could hear the rest.

*It's okay*, she told herself, even as her stomach churned harder. So she'd been spotted. The boy would never remember, and the girl had mistaken Tanvi for someone else. She'd just have to be much more careful from here on out.

But the tight feeling wouldn't leave her chest. She kept checking behind her as if someone might be there.

Tanvi had never been afraid before, had never worried about anything but earning the boon that would get her bracelet. She didn't like it.

Stupid dream residue. It made you feel, and that was the last thing any dream runner would want. Stupid dreamer and her stupid phone.

Tanvi clutched her pouch close. Soon she would be home, and soon she could buy her bracelet. Nothing else counted.

The thought of the bracelet soothed her, with its dangling charms and glittering gold. *Soon.*

7

But first, she had a job to do.

Tanvi ducked into a side street in Queen Village to finish her harvest. She inhaled deeply and felt around for dreamers.

Her mind lit up like a radar screen. Almost everyone on the street was dreaming, and like a bonus, two of the row houses blazed with especially promising options. If she hustled, maybe she could nab both.

She slipped inside the first house and followed the beacon to the couch. The man she was looking for lay before his blaring TV, drunk enough to have blacked out. Perfect. Without much effort, Tanvi harvested his vision about a ship that sailed through sweet meringue oceans to a land of salted caramel almond bark trees. Sweet and quirky, with the flavor and texture of candy.

One down, one to go, and the boon was hers.

The second house had a pineapple knocker. Annoyed, Tanvi filtered it out. Details were only relevant if they had to do with her harvest. Every runner knew that. She homed in on the source of the dream instead, a teen boy located on the third floor.

Tanvi crept inside and up the stairs, her awareness pinned on the dream above her. As she reached the second floor, a woman padded out of a bathroom, yawning. Tanvi pressed herself back against the wall, a lozenge at her lips, while she waited for the woman to pass.

Then, fueled by adrenaline, she raced up the last flight of stairs and toward the boy's bed. After swapping the lozenge for a dreamstone, she dove right into his dream—the boy and his

8

friend had broken into an abandoned mansion at twilight to film their documentary. It was scary and silly both, with giant spiders that attacked before turning into plush toys.

The boy didn't move while she was harvesting except to grunt when she corked the vial.

There. Tanvi had done it—and had two awesome dreams to show for it, dreams Venkat would be begging to buy. She coasted back down to street level.

No one burst out of the night to misidentify her as she raced toward the river. No one talked to her at all.

That, Tanvi thought, was more like it.

☾

At Penn's Landing, Tanvi leaned out over the railing and studied the murky water. The Delaware River wasn't something she wanted to dive into at any time, but it was almost dawn. She'd stayed out too long as it was.

Tanvi fingered her pendant, a writhing black-and-gold serpent, and tapped it between its sparkling emerald eyes. The river below immediately rose up, forming a sapphire doorway with shimmering arches. She leaped through it and landed on a sloping liquid platform that funneled her downward. The watery walls surrounding her merged back into the water as she descended.

When she reached the bottom, no other runner was reporting to the guards flanking the cramped side entrance to the palace. Tanvi shivered. She'd never been this late before.

A younger naga beckoned her forward. Keeping her head lowered, she gripped her necklace.

"Name?" the guard barked, his voice oddly loud and grating.

Any other night, he would have faded into the background. Now, though, she could feel his smirk boring into her. He didn't expect a reaction, and she didn't give him one. Still, her hand trembled as she flashed her pendant at him.

"Tanvi," she said, without inflection.

"Cutting it close, are we, Tanvi? I doubt Nayan would like that."

The mention of Nayan made her lapse sting all over again: if she'd been paying attention, that boy wouldn't have run into her. That girl with the bob wouldn't have seen her. Tanvi had already forgotten the girl's face. Too bad she couldn't erase their conversation so easily.

She'd been reckless. There was no denying it.

Her muscles stiffened with something new and awful. It took her a few seconds to name the feeling.

*Panic.*

*Never again*, she vowed, praying the guard couldn't tell.

The guard waved her through without another word, unlike some of his colleagues, who inevitably demanded to see the wares. They couldn't afford what Nayan and Venkat charged for a dream, so they tried to steal brief glimpses of what lay within the jewels the runners brought back with them.

Tanvi stalked through the hidden passage to the dream

10

runners' isolated quarters and then her own door. A jerk of the knob, and she rushed into the room. She wouldn't be able to sleep until she'd reassured herself that *it* was still there, exactly as she'd left it.

With the same fluttering in her belly she always got, Tanvi went straight to the closet.

The wooden shelves sat empty except for a lone gold-lidded enamel box. Her panic ebbing, she undid the lid. The lush pink velvet setting greeted her, ready for the bracelet she would soon earn with her boon.

Tanvi drew in a relieved breath. An image of her bracelet appeared in her thoughts, its golden links and charms untarnished and glossy like naga scales. She would never wear it, of course, never risk losing or scratching her treasure. It would be enough to spend endless hours here in this closet, gazing at the bracelet's perfect beauty.

The ghost of Tanvi's extinguished heart twinged in satisfaction. She couldn't understand why humans wanted anything else. The promise of her bracelet was all *she* needed.

For the chance to win it, she would gladly harvest dreams. Even if that meant going into the humans' world and dealing with their messy, irrational behavior.

Like that girl. Anger flared in Tanvi again, galling but remote. She would never endanger her bracelet like that again. Not ever.

*Next time*, thought Tanvi, a promise to her bracelet as much as to herself. *Next time I'll get it right.*

Alone in Nayan's appraisal vault, Venkat prodded the lackluster dream fragment again, as if that would somehow make the panel in the wall across from him slide to the right to reveal Jai. But the runner who'd sold him the fragment a week ago was nowhere to be seen.

A mix of annoyance and concern spread through him. This was the third time Jai had been late in a fortnight. Venkat's stable of runners all knew how important keeping these dawn appointments was. Every other morning, in the privacy of the vault, they brought him the dreams they'd harvested, the best of which were packed with drama and emotion, and Venkat paid them accordingly. He'd often thought it would be easier if his runners could walk around in public, but then their identities would be known, and anyone could try to poach them.

Still no Jai. Venkat's concern grew. Could he be—?

*No.* Venkat peered through the lone window, which was

translucent as a topaz lover's tear on this side but opaque golden wall on the other. In contrast to the cramped vault, the vast palace archives beyond buzzed with people: messengers sent by King Vasuki and Queen Naga Yakshi, wealthy patrons impatient to purchase dreams, merchants looking to horn in on the dream trade, would-be suitors and admirers, and scholars combing the stacks for novel ways to strengthen the nagas' defenses against their ancient enemy, the garudas.

Lord Nayan, a notorious firebrand in his youth, now presided over the archives as their curator and court historian. Nephew to the ferocious, exceedingly poisonous Nagaraja Takshaka, he also held a seat on the royal war council. And he was the only dream broker in all Nagalok.

So of course everyone wanted to get close to him.

That was where Venkat came in. As Nayan's apprentice, he served as gatekeeper, redirecting and deterring, leaving Nayan free to address his larger duties.

It was a job, Venkat thought, he couldn't do while waiting here. He didn't want to give up on Jai, but the archives beckoned.

"So?" a familiar voice demanded, making him jump. "How much?"

He wheeled around to find Jai slouched against the panel in the wall, his impassive, shadow-ringed stare fixed on the fragment in Venkat's hand. He looked like he hadn't slept or eaten since his last visit, and his crumpled kurta wore him instead of the other way around.

Relieved that he'd shown up at all, Venkat said, gently, "I paid you for this last time."

Jai scoffed. "Not that one." He thrust an orange dreamstone vial at Venkat. "This one."

A new harvest? Curious, Venkat accepted the carnelian vial. Maybe things weren't as bad as he'd suspected.

He slid the cork out with ease, and the escaping wisps formed a scene in the air, the prelude to a feature film only he could see. Unlike his customers, who fell into them, Venkat observed harvested dreams from the outside.

The dreamer had illustrated her soul mate on a canvas, skillfully rendered in oil pastels. But once she set it on her altar, a spell to summon him to her, the pigment peeled off in ribbons until it lay on the floor.

When at last she found him in real life, he didn't recognize her. Tears dripped down her cheeks, and she threw herself at his feet, desperate to convince him they belonged together. Her raw, naked anguish made Venkat cringe in sympathy, even as he estimated its value. Dreams like this, ripe with undisguised pining and need, were a naga favorite. Jai had chosen well.

The sequence hiccuped a few times before going dark, a decaying reel with bits eaten away. Sorrow bloomed in Venkat's chest. So things *were* that bad. Jai had plainly lost control of the wisps mid-harvest, and some of them had evaporated into the ether.

When the choppy nightmare resumed, the dreamer huddled, devastated, in a patch of unripe strawberries while her soul mate tucked a blue flax flower behind the ear of a laughing woman in a pretty sundress. Venkat guessed the man must have rebuffed the dreamer for this woman, but he'd never know for certain, not with the middle section missing.

Dodging Jai's dull gaze, Venkat steered the remnants of the dream back into the twinkling dreamstone and set it down. "Show me what else you have."

Jai's frown lent some feeling to his face. "This is it."

Fighting to hide his dread, Venkat crossed his arms. "You only harvested one dream?"

What survived of the dream was good quality, its level of immersion deep and its quotient of heartbreak high. But in two nights of harvesting, all Jai had managed was a single half-reaped dream. Venkat wasn't sure Jai had even caught the holes, and that only made him sadder.

He considered quietly buying it anyway, but the damage was too extensive.

Venkat knew better than to care about his runners this much. But while his kin were gone, at least he had Nayan. His runners had no one. He'd promised himself that no matter how long it took, no matter how many times his experiments failed, he'd come up with something to help them.

Jai pushed the carnelian vial at Venkat again and held out his empty palm. Venkat knew he was itching to get his hands on his particular obsession, a tricycle. Jai was way too old to ride one, not that he cared. The dream runners wanted what they wanted.

Venkat imagined telling Jai that getting the tricycle wouldn't grant him any lasting happiness. "I'm sorry," he said instead. "Bring me something else, all right?"

If only Jai would argue. If only he'd do something to prove Venkat wrong.

There was no reason to expect that, not after the initiation had done its work, but Venkat couldn't help scrutinizing him. *Something. Anything. Please.*

Jai closed his fist around the rejected vial, snuffing out that wish along with the soft light from the ruined dream. "One boon," he said flatly. He darted back through the panel, presumably toward his room in the runners' quarters.

Swallowing a sigh, Venkat opened his logbook to the day's acquisitions and drew a blank line after Jai's name. At any rate, he thought, running his finger down the page, Indu and Srinivas had both delivered excellent wares earlier.

All dream runners burned out eventually. Venkat knew that, he'd always known that, and yet his heart still hurt. He was failing them, like he'd failed his family back on Prithvi.

He pressed his forehead down on the page. If only he could disappear into the workshop and focus on his trials.

But the line by the desk wasn't going to get any shorter. Venkat groaned, picturing ants swarming over him like he was a juicy ball of rose syrup—drenched rasgulla dropped on a sidewalk. There'd be nothing left of him if he wasn't careful.

Donning a noncommittal smile like well-oiled armor, Venkat left the vault through his own panel.